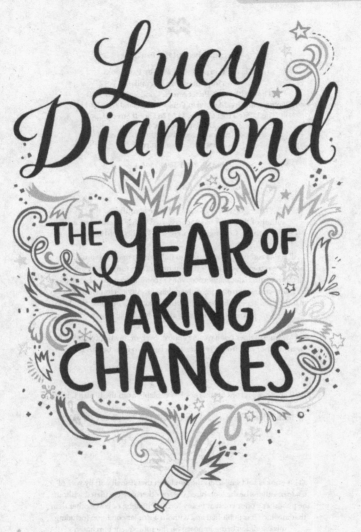

Lucy Diamond

THE YEAR OF TAKING CHANCES

PAN BOOKS

First published 2015 by Pan Books

This edition published 2016 by Pan Books
an imprint of Pan Macmillan
The Smithson, 6 Briset Street, London EC1M 5NR
EU representative: Macmillan Publishers Ireland Ltd, 1st Floor,
The Liffey Trust Centre, 117-126 Sheriff Street, Upper
Dublin 1, D01 YC43
Associated companies throughout the world
www.panmacmillan.com

ISBN 978-1-5098-1565-4

9

A CIP catalogue record for this book is available from the British Library.

Printed and bound by CPI Group (UK) Ltd, Croydon, CR0 4YY

Visit **www.panmacmillan.com** to read more about all our books
and to buy them. You will also find features, author interviews and
news of any author events, and you can sign up for e-newsletters
so that you're always first to hear about our new releases.

The Year of Taking Chances

LUCY DIAMOND lives in Bath with her husband
and their three children. When she isn't slaving
away on a new book (ahem) you can find her on
Twitter @LDiamondAuthor or on Facebook at
www.facebook.com/LucyDiamondAuthor.

In memory of Linda Brown,
the lovely lady next door, who taught me to
sew many years ago.

Acknowledgements

Thanks, as always, to the dream team at Pan Macmillan – Caroline Hogg, Natasha Harding, Jodie Mullish, Becky Plunkett, Anna Bond, Jeremy Trevathan, Wayne Brookes and Eloise Wood. Please tell me your collective New Year's resolution is to keep being awesome.

A million thank-yous to Lizzy Kremer at David Higham for all your hard work, phone calls and genius ideas. As well as being a completely brilliant agent, you are a seriously lovely person too. #TeamKremer all the way!

Thank you to Rebekah, dressmaker extraordinaire at Love Design Room in Bath, who answered all my stupid questions with great patience. Any mistakes are my own.

Thanks to all my lovely readers, especially those who chat to me on my Facebook page and, of course, Lucy's Diamonds – now there's a cool group of women, if ever I saw one!

Finally, an extra-special sparkly thanks to my wonderful family – Martin, Hannah, Tom and Holly – who are the best cheerleaders an author could wish for, even when I'm sunk in the depths of I-can't-write despair. (My New Year's resolution is to stop being such a drama queen about it all!) Thank you for so much laughter and loveliness. I don't need a fortune-cookie to tell me that you four are definitely my 'Happy ever after'.

Prologue

There should be some kind of warning given the day your life changes for ever. A tingle in the air, a whisper on the breeze, a gentle celestial nudge urging you to treasure what you've got before it's too late. But for Gemma, the morning began with deceptive familiarity: the sound of Spencer crashing around in the bathroom next door, the shower being turned up to its most torrential setting, then his voice belting out an enthusiastic if tuneless rendition of 'My Girl'.

Gemma pulled the pillow over her head to block out the noise. Five more minutes, she promised herself. Five more minutes, snuggled beneath the warm duvet and then she'd force herself up and into action.

Sleep stole over her like a soft blanket, though, and she drifted back into a dream, not noticing when her husband placed a steaming cup of tea on the bedside table nearby, nor when he yelled a cheerful goodbye ten minutes later.

If she'd known then what would unfold in the space of a single morning, she'd have run after him, thrown her arms tight around his body and refused to let him leave the house. *Not today,* she'd have said. *You're going nowhere, Spencer Bailey.*

But she didn't know. She had no idea. And so the day began.

Chapter One

Three weeks earlier

It was New Year's Eve: night of a thousand parties, of champagne corks bouncing off ceilings, bright fireworks cracking open the sky, and the finest frocks ever to grace a dance-floor. Across the nation, Christmas had been discarded like old tinsel and reindeer antlers in readiness for one last alcohol-fuelled, throw-caution-to-the-wind knees-up before the austerity of do-gooding January dawned, cold and forbidding. In bars and clubs and village halls throughout the land, they were ready: umpteen bottles of fizz corked and chilling, clingfilmed buffets laid out on linen-clothed trestle tables, cutlery and glasses polished to a soft gleam. In the bathrooms and bedrooms of all the towns and cities, they were ready: glittery make-up applied, hair primped and sprayed, the hiss of the iron as it smoothed down fabric creases, and the worst of the Christmas excesses glossed over by control pants and many a muttered New Year dieting resolution.

Down in the small Suffolk village of Larkmead, however, Gemma Bailey was one burned canapé away from a total meltdown. How was it, she wondered crossly, that their original plans for 'just a small gathering' with a few friends, some experimental cocktails and a bowl of posh crisps had metamorphosed into an everyone-welcome house party, which would totally turn the new neighbours against them? Daft question. It was down to Spencer, of course, her gregarious husband, who'd seen fit to invite all his football mates and their other halves to the party, as well as some of the lads from work. He'd even asked some woman last seen when they were teenagers, who was back in Larkmead after the death of her mum, for heaven's sake. ('I felt sorry for her!' he'd protested when Gemma gave him a long-suffering look. 'What was I supposed to do?' 'Oh, I don't know, pat her arm and say "Sorry for your loss", like a normal person?' she'd replied, rolling her eyes.)

As if that wasn't enough of a random guest-list, a fortnight ago, at the primary-school Christmas quiz, he'd proceeded to get completely smashed, commandeered the microphone from the quiz-master – the deputy head teacher, no less! – and invited basically the entire hall of parents along, too. Gemma had opened her mouth to protest, but only the faintest whimper came out. It was too late anyway. Everyone was already saying they'd love to come, they were all *dying* to see what she'd done with the new place. The new place, by the way, that still had woodchip wallpaper and manky carpets in every room, strange-smelling drains and the most horribly pink bathroom suite known to mankind. Gemma had not been planning any kind of open house until at least the summer, thank you very much, especially not to some of the competitive mums in Darcey's class who had houses like museums and could sniff out bad hoovering and dusty surfaces in approximately ten seconds.

(She still felt a flush of shame when she thought about the time her son Will had brought one particular friend home for tea, aged about seven. Jack Barrington – that was it – a tufty-haired little boy with a piping treble back then, although, these days, he was almost six foot with acne and a newly deep voice. Jack's mum had come to pick him up and, as she thanked Gemma at the front door, Jack said, 'Will's house is *really* messy, Mum!' in a voice hushed with shock. 'And we had *chips* for tea!' It was a bit like that in Larkmead: competitive mothering. Gemma had long since given up trying to win any accolades in the field.)

'You don't mind, do you?' Spencer had asked, as they staggered home in the wintry moonlight after the Christmas quiz ended. 'Might as well make it a proper New Year party, don't you think?'

'I'm not sure the house is ready for a party,' Gemma had replied, her mind flashing from one horror zone to another: the faded, dusty curtains the previous owners had left behind, the mouldy patch of wall in the kitchen, the spidery downstairs loo with the blown light bulb that she still hadn't got round to replacing. They'd only been in their house six weeks, after all, and hadn't even unpacked all of the boxes, let alone performed any DIY miracles.

'Yeah – exactly! So it doesn't matter if it gets trashed, right?' He elbowed her. 'We don't have to worry about people spilling wine on the carpets – we'll be ripping them all out soon anyway. And it's such a great house for a party.'

He had a point. It was a great house, full stop; or rather it would be, once they'd done it up. They'd completely overstretched themselves, buying the gorgeous old stone farmhouse on the expensive side of Larkmead village, but it would be worth it one day. There were four big bedrooms, a lovely long garden and a garage to house the sleek black Mazda that Gemma swore Spencer loved more than her. Bags of potential, the estate agent had said. Bags of charm.

It was also going to take bags of energy and hard labour to turn it into their dream home, especially as they didn't have any funds left to pay painters and decorators. But that was fine, they agreed: this was their forever home, the only one they'd ever need. There was no rush. Well, there hadn't been anyway, until Spencer invited half the village round on the biggest night of the year.

Still, she was getting there. The kitchen and living room were now pretty much spotless, as was the downstairs loo.

She'd laid out a buffet table, hiding her rather unappetizing-looking home-made canapés at the back, and decanting plastic tubs of Waitrose dips into her nicest blue-glazed bowls. There was also a large quiche from the deli, a ton of cheeses left over from Christmas, and half a brandy-drenched Christmas cake, which had you seeing double after three mouthfuls. That would have to do. (And if the competitive school mums wanted to raise their eyebrows at her half-arsed catering, then let them. She didn't care. Well, only a little bit.)

Spencer, meanwhile, had taken the children over to his parents' house, where they'd be spending the night. They were only ten minutes down the road, but he was taking a suspiciously long time to return. No doubt his dad, Terry, had uncapped the whisky and they were both setting the world to rights in front of the fire. He could be hours yet.

Sighing a little, she polished all the champagne and wine glasses with a clean tea-towel and lined them up on the work-top, wishing she could fizz into more of a party mood. There was something about New Year's Eve that always brought her up a little short – that taking-stock moment when life seemed to hinge between two planes, past and future, and you were forced to examine exactly where you were. Recently she'd had the uneasy feeling that the years were slipping by, each faster than the last, and she wasn't doing enough with her life. Sure, she was a wife to Spencer and a mum to Will and Darcey, and she was grateful for all of that. But in what other way was she leaving any kind of imprint on the world? Sometimes she felt she could vanish tomorrow and nobody would even notice.

'What does your mum do?' Gemma had heard Nicolette Valentine ask Darcey a few weeks ago as they went upstairs to Darcey's bedroom. Nicolette was new to Larkmead, and had a semi-famous actor mum and a dad who'd recently got a job as a registrar at the local hospital.

'Oh, not much,' Darcey replied. 'She's just a mum.'

She's just a mum. Like that was nothing. Darcey had even sounded embarrassed to say the words, as if fully aware of Gemma's failings.

She had tortured herself ever since that she was not a good role-model. All of her other friends with children were back at work now, with part-time jobs that required smart clothes and make-up, pursed lips as they checked their smartphones in the playground. And what was she? A chubby housewife, who did the laundry and the shopping and made sure everyone got to school and work on time, with the occasional dressmaking job on the side. *She's just a mum. Not much.*

Sometimes in her darkest hour she wondered if Spencer thought that of her, too.

'Come on, Gems,' she muttered aloud, trying to shake off her gloom. Once she had her new dress on, she'd feel better, she reminded herself. She'd made it at the start of the month and had been dying to wear it ever since: a midnight-blue velour off-the-shoulder beauty that cinched her in at the waist and fell into a flattering tulip-shaped skirt. With a few well-placed darts, the dress accentuated her hourglass figure, making her bust and bum appear voluptuous and curvy rather than plain old fat. There were even a few black sequins twinkling here and there. Hopefully a bit of sparkle on the outside would make her feel sparkly on the inside, too.

(She had wrestled a few demons in the past over her size, it had to be said. In her early twenties she had become kind of obsessed with calorie-counting, slimming right down to the size of a twig for a while. Had she been happy, though, denying herself carbs and puddings for the sake of squeezing into skimpy dresses? No, she had not. She'd hated the weak, hollow emptiness that gnawed inside her when she had starved herself. Thankfully all that nonsense had been nipped in the bud long ago. No New Year's crash diets in *this* house, thank you very much.)

The doorbell rang just then, making her jump. Ah, that would be Spencer — forgotten his keys, she bet. Her spirits lifted at once: knowing Spence, he'd pour her a cocktail, rig up the glitterball and tease her for worrying about something as ridiculous as canapés, and all of a sudden she'd feel a million times better.

She opened the door, but saw an unfamiliar woman standing there, rather than her husband. A thirty-something woman with coppery hair tied back in a messy ponytail, a pale freckled face and a blue Puffa jacket. She didn't look like an evangelical Jehovah's Witness on a mission to convert the world to Jesus, but you never could tell.

'Hi,' Gemma said. 'Can I help you?'

'Hi, yes, sorry to bother you,' the woman said. 'I'm meant to be staying in the cottage next door, but the guy I'm renting it from — Bernie Sykes? — isn't answering his phone, and I've no way of getting in. I don't suppose you know how I can get hold of him, do you?'

'Ah. Right.' The previous owners of their home had warned her about this. The pretty cream-painted cottage next door was rented out as a holiday let by Bernie, the larger-than-life landlord of the village pub. Unfortunately Bernie was usually too busy holding court in his bar to remember to answer his phone, or even notice it was ringing, let alone pay attention to his bookings diary. 'Don't worry, I've got a spare key. Come in a sec while I find it.'

The woman stepped into the hallway as Gemma returned to the kitchen and fished out the key from its hiding place in the old red teapot on her dresser. 'Here,' she said, holding it out. 'Knowing Bernie, he'll have had a few drinks already and his phone's probably lost down the back of the sofa. You can always find him in the pub, though — The Partridge, at the end of the road and left. He's the landlord: loud, whiskery, slight resemblance to a walrus. You can't miss him.'

'Thanks so much,' the woman said, and opened the front door again. 'Cheers.'

'No problem,' Gemma said. 'And happy New Year, by the way. Looks a lovely cottage. Perfect for a romantic getaway.'

The woman's mouth twisted. 'It's just me staying, actually,' she said. 'Thanks again. Happy New Year to you, too.'

Oh. That was strange. Gemma watched her go, unable to imagine what it would be like to spend New Year's Eve alone. *There*, she told herself sternly. It could be worse, see? You could be all on your own next door, rather than here with a house full of guests and gallons of booze. It certainly put a few crap canapés into perspective.

An hour later Gemma was multitasking rather impressively by running a creamy, scented bath while drinking a very welcome glass of cold Pinot Grigio. It was slipping down a treat after all her hard work.

'Gems? Where are you?' she heard Spencer shout as the front door banged behind him.

'Up here, stark naked and awaiting your pleasure, sire,' she yelled back, even though she was still in her old jeans, hair scraped back in a scrunchie, with an unattractive onion aroma lingering on her fingers. 'Come and get me!' She swished her hand through the water, making the bubbles froth. That should get him pelting him up the stairs, she thought. Spencer took the slightest raising of an eyebrow as an invitation that she was desperate for his bod.

She and Spencer had been together for fifteen years now.

They had met one sunny Saturday when she'd gone to visit her dad in Stowmarket and accidentally crashed into Spencer's van. Whatever he might say, Gemma was sticking to her guns: the prang was totally his fault. If he hadn't distracted her by walking along the street with no shirt on, his chest tanned and muscular, his sloe-dark eyes so soulful and his black curly hair so gorgeously tousled, there was no way her foot would have slipped on the accelerator. As it was, she'd been halfway through a parallel-parking attempt, and had reversed into the vehicle behind her with a horribly loud bang.

'Oi!' he'd cried, breaking into a jog. 'That's my van, that is. Look what you've done!'

Pink in the cheeks, Gemma clambered out of her car, mortified at what had just happened. She was also kind of breathless at being so close to this handsome stranger, even if he was in a blistering rage. 'I am so sorry,' she gulped. 'Shit, this isn't even my car — it's my flatmate's. She's going to kill me.'

His eyes softened, perhaps because she was wearing a turquoise minidress with a huge zip that went all the way down the front. She had been small and slinky back then, a size eight and two stone lighter than she was now. With her long conker-coloured hair, heart-shaped face and large brown eyes, she was the kind of person that you couldn't stay mad with for long. 'Don't worry,' he said gruffly after a moment, inspecting the mercifully intact bumper. 'No harm done. Are you all right?'

Her insides went swimmy as his gaze fastened on her, and her pulse quickened. *I am now*, she thought.

Gemma was living in London at the time, working as a designer for Pop, a cheap-and-cheerful fashion range, but it took just three months before she and Spencer were happily shacked up in a rented red-brick terraced house in Larkmead, the small Suffolk village where he'd grown up. A year later they were married and then, just as she was starting to tire of the London commute (as much as two hours, door-to-door, on a bad day) she fell pregnant with Will and took an early maternity leave. Sometimes she wondered how her life would have turned out if Spencer hadn't been in Stowmarket that day, or if she'd chosen a different place to park. Funny how everything could change course so dramatically in one fateful moment.

'Hell-o!' he called now, bursting into the bathroom. 'Hey,' he added, seeing her still in her full scruffbag get-up. 'I was promised nudity and sex. Where's my nudity and sex?'

She laughed at the indignant look on his face, then her breath caught in her throat as he pulled his shirt over his head and approached her with a wanton gleam in his eye. She might have let herself go over the years, but he certainly hadn't. He was as beefy and muscular as he'd ever been.

'Now then, Mrs Bailey,' he said, sliding his arms around her and tugging at her top. 'Let me help you take off these clothes . . .'

Chapter Two

On the other side of Larkmead, past the village green where the summer cricket matches were held, and over the curving brick bridge that crossed the mill-stream, the houses were a mix of narrow Victorian terraces and smaller cottages, some with their original thatched roofs. Up on Butler Row, two streets back from the greengrocer's and post office, was White Gables Cottage, the house where Caitlin Fraser had grown up, and where she'd come back to in recent weeks, after her life had fallen in like a toppled house of cards.

Slumped on the sofa now, she was sorely tempted to blow out the whole New Year thing and go to bed early with a hot-water bottle and a pint of wine. *Don't be such a wet lettuce!* she heard her mum exclaim in her head. *Go to bed early when it's Hogmanay? I don't think so, lassie.*

Caitlin rolled her eyes at herself. Jane Fraser had become more Scottish than ever, now that she was dead and existed only in Caitlin's memories and imagination. Mind you, her mum had always loved New Year, making a whole raft of resolutions every year, only for them to peter out and be forgotten before it was February. 'It's like a promise to yourself to do better this year,' she'd explained to Caitlin, the first time she'd let her stay up till midnight and see in the New Year. 'So, for instance, I've made a promise that I'll help Maud Simmonds with her allotment, whereas your daddy's promised to stop smoking those stinking cigarettes. Haven't you, Steve?'

'What? Er . . . yes,' her dad said, although he didn't look quite as zealous as Jane did at the prospect.

A promise to yourself to do better this year. Put like that, it sounded pretty good, Caitlin thought, remembering how she and her mum had sat in their nighties and dressing gowns on this very same sofa together, cheering as they watched the fireworks exploding over the Houses of Parliament on telly, while her dad snored like a hippo in the armchair. If she leaned back and shut her eyes, she could almost imagine she was there, slipping back twenty-five years in a single heartbeat.

Almost. Except that her dad had died when she was twenty and wouldn't be snoring in his favourite armchair again, and her mum wasn't there this year either, to cheer at the fireworks and splash them another tot of whisky each.

Caitlin's eyes fell upon the Sympathy cards gathering dust on the mantelpiece (she must take them down soon; they depressed her every time she looked at them); the family photographs that had an added texture of poignancy, now that the curly-haired lady smiling in a sundress was dead and gone; and the small urn of ashes still waiting to be scattered. It had been over a month since the funeral, but Caitlin was stuck in a half-lit limbo of grief and hadn't yet been able to say that final goodbye.

'She wouldn't want you moping about,' Gwen, the old lady next door, had said, whenever she popped round on her way to her book group or sewing bee. (It was kind of dispiriting when a pensioner was more outgoing socially than you, to be honest.)

'Let me know if you want me to tidy up the garden for you,' Jim over the road had offered when she bumped into him in the street. 'I used to do some of the digging for Jane, when she needed a hand.' Even Spencer Bailey, whom she hadn't seen since they were at school together, had accosted her outside the village shop one Sunday morning, saying he was sorry to hear about Jane, and then rhapsodising that she'd made the best cakes he'd ever tasted. He'd done her extension, he explained, when Caitlin looked puzzled. He was a builder now, still in Larkmead, married with a couple of kids, he went on. (She remembered he'd always had that easy-going, friendly charm, even when everyone else was an awkward teenager.) 'Hey,' he said, just as she was about to make an excuse and end the conversation, 'if you're still here at New Year, we're having a party, by the way. Come along, if you want.'

She had smiled politely, thanking him and saying she wasn't sure of her plans yet, but then Gwen had knocked on the door that afternoon with a hopeful look in her eyes and asked if Caitlin would accompany her to see a swing-band up at Radnor Hall for New Year. 'Jane was going to come with me, you see, so I thought you might like her ticket. Could be fun!'

Could be *fun*? Could be a wake-up call that her social life was in danger of expiring, more like. She had never been more glad to reply, quite truthfully, that she'd been invited to a party – sorry, Gwen. 'Thanks, though,' she added, as her neighbour's face fell. *Christ*, she thought to herself, closing the front door afterwards. Things had got pretty bad when someone seriously thought you might want to go to some geriatric swing-band evening because you had nothing better to do. On New Year's Eve!

Still, she realized soberly, it was only by chance that she *did* have something better on offer. If ever anyone needed a resolution to sort their life out, it was definitely her.

Half an hour later Caitlin was leaning in towards the long gilt-edged mirror to inspect herself. Even now it felt weird to be getting ready in her mum's bedroom, as if she'd be ticked off any minute for snooping around. The light was best in there, though, plus there was that enormous mirror – the kind that only a glamorous woman with a love of dressing up could hang on her wall. Caitlin was not this type of woman, but Jane Fraser had always loved an excuse to 'put a face on' and doll up for a night out. She must have racked up hours standing right here, painting her eyelids and lips, sweeping blusher onto those high cheekbones and dithering over which of her many pairs of high heels to wear.

Even at the end of her life, when she'd been too weak to feed herself, dozing in and out of consciousness, Jane had begged Caitlin to put some mascara on her and brush her hair. Imagine that! Mascara and hair-brushing wouldn't get a look-in on Caitlin's deathbed, that was for sure. Coffee, perhaps. A last bag of chips, with lashings of salt and vinegar. Maybe a bloody big whisky to finish her off.

The irony was that her mum had been as fit as a fiddle almost until the end. Lean and rangy, she had shimmied through Zumba in the village hall every Thursday evening apparently, and was always out gardening or cycling around the village on her old upright bicycle. Then, one Tuesday in October, she'd gone to the doctor complaining of stomach pains. The doctor told her it was probably gallstones and prescribed painkillers, but the next day Jane was vomiting and feverish, and ended up being rushed into hospital with acute pancreatitis.

'I'll be fine,' she told Caitlin on the phone that night when she broke the news. 'Lot of fuss about nothing. I should be home in a few days, don't worry.'

'Are you sure? I'll come and see you at the weekend. Or sooner, if you want?'

'What, and miss work? Your boss would love me for that, wouldn't he? Don't be daft, I'll be home before you know it.'

Only it didn't quite turn out like that. Jane never went home again. The doctors tried keyhole surgery to remove the dead tissue in her pancreas, but an infection occurred, which spread into her blood. Then a nurse telephoned Caitlin from the cottage hospital and said in that very British sort of way, 'She's extremely poorly. You might want to be here.' Caitlin had left Cambridge that evening with a bag of clothes and a frightened heart, kissing Flynn goodbye with the promise that she'd be back as soon as she could. But three days later, despite everyone's best attempts, Jane's major organs failed, and then she was dead. The whole thing, from stomach pains to death, had taken less than six weeks.

Tears swelled in Caitlin's eyes as she remembered those nightmarish hours at her mother's bedside, holding her hand, praying under her breath, trying to bargain with a god she didn't even believe in. That was how desperate she felt. That was how frightened. But none of the antibiotics, drugs or prayers had had any effect.

Jane was rambling at the end. 'I'm sorry, hen,' she said a few times, gripping Caitlin's hand. 'I should have told you. I never knew how to say it.'

'Told me what? What do you mean?'

'We thought it was the right thing to do,' Jane said,

shutting her eyes. Then her words became indistinct and mumbling, however close Caitlin leaned in to hear.

'Don't worry, Mum. Whatever it was, it's fine.'

Then Jane's eyes shut and her face fell slack. *BEEEEEEEP* went the monitor, and it was all over.

Caitlin took a long, shuddering breath at the memory and raked a hand through her hair. This wasn't getting her ready. She would be late, if she didn't hurry up. Taking a deep breath, she peered into the mirror again and her reflection stared back warily. Eyeshadow, mascara, lipstick: done. It would take a scaffolder to prop up her eye-bags, and even Leonardo da Vinci would struggle to brighten her sallow skin, but she'd tried her best. She'd unearthed a clean pair of jeans and had Febrezed a sparkly top that had been at the bottom of her suitcase for six weeks. Hell, she'd even pushed the boat out and blow-dried her shoulder-length dark hair. She actually looked halfway presentable.

You look a picture, lovey, her mum said in her head. *A proper picture. Now go out there and knock 'em dead!*

'Don't get carried away, Mum,' Caitlin muttered with a small smile.

An unwanted memory flashed into her mind. This time last year she'd been getting ready for a night out in Cambridge with Flynn: dinner in town, then on to a house party off Mill Road. She'd worn a scarlet dress and dangly earrings, her skin shimmering from the fancy scented body lotion she'd rubbed in. As New Year struck, they found each other on the dance-floor and kissed, really kissed, like two people who were madly in love. They *had* been two people who were madly in love back then, she reminded herself grimly.

She sank onto her mum's soft double bed, its floral duvet cover still in place, and wondered miserably what Flynn was doing tonight. The last time they'd spoken – several weeks ago now – he'd been curt with her, verging on aggressive, his sympathy and patience long since evaporated. He wanted her to 'snap out of it', to 'pull herself together', like it was that easy, like she could just click her fingers and return to normality. Was she coming back or not?

Not, she told him. *No way.*

She got up from the bed abruptly, not wanting to give in to despondency. 'Come on, Eeyore,' she said to herself. 'You can do it.'

Grabbing a bottle of red wine, she pulled on her boots and coat and was out of the front door before she could change her mind.

Chapter Three

It had seemed a good idea to Saffron at the time: a quiet getaway, all on her own. She could escape from Max, escape from work, her parents, London . . . everything, basically. She would leave it all behind and enjoy a few days of rural bliss in a Suffolk village, while she worked out what on earth she was going to do.

Baker's Cottage had looked delightful online, the perfect place to enjoy some peace and solitude. With its thatched roof and double frontage painted the colour of vanilla ice-cream, it was like something from a children's storybook — a warm, welcoming place, she imagined, with home-baked muffins cooling on a tray and the softest, most blissfully enveloping beds. The photo on the website had obviously been taken in the summer and showed a front garden full of colour: tall lupins and delphiniums, bright cornflowers and scarlet poppies, and — yes — sprays of white roses climbing around the door. She could practically smell their fragrance as she spontaneously clicked her mouse and made the booking.

Several hours later an email pinged in from the owner, one Mr Sykes:

I'll leave the key under the mat. Full instructions for everything else in a folder inside. Have a splendid New Year!
Yrs, Bernie

After living in London for seventeen years, the thought of leaving a door key anywhere other than safely in a handbag close to your body felt completely alien. How charming, she thought. How heart-warmingly trusting!

Ha. More fool her. She should have known such slapdash arrangements could only mean trouble.

It was dark when she arrived and she had to drive around Larkmead several times before eventually spotting the sign reading 'Pear Tree Lane', half-covered in shrubbery. There was no proper street lighting, so she crawled along the road, headlights blazing, peering blindly at the shadowy houses on either side. Then, once she'd finally found the cottage itself, she lifted the mat to find a complete absence of keys. Off to a great start.

Two fruitless phone messages later, she was grateful for the helpful neighbour who produced a spare key. But, once inside, it took only seconds before the cold water of disappointment poured all over her. In reality the cottage was a lot less delightful than she'd anticipated: damp, cold and clammy, as if no living human had set foot inside for weeks on end. Her nose wrinkled at the mildewy smell as she poked her head first into the small ('cosy') beige living room with its old stone hearth, then the even smaller ('compact') galley kitchen with a couple of desiccated pot plants by the sink and a dripping tap. Upstairs were two chilly bedrooms with moth-eaten velvet curtains, and a very turquoise bathroom.

It was a far cry from the boutique hotels she occasionally stayed in for work purposes, she thought regretfully. No sign of a monsoon shower or luxury bedding under *this* roof. Still, she'd made her bed, now she had to lie on it, as her mum would say. With or without the expensive Egyptian-cotton sheets.

Once she'd dumped her case upstairs and unpacked her provisions in the fridge, she located the folder Bernie had mentioned and worked out how to turn the heating on. The boiler obediently rumbled into life, the radiators began valiantly belting out heat and she found her spirits lifting a little as she made herself a cup of tea and sank into the squidgy cord sofa. Maybe this would be okay after all. She had warmth, she had solitude, her phone was off and her out-of-office email reply was on. She didn't have to do a single thing now for three whole days except relax, go for long walks in the countryside, read books and sleep. Oh yes. And maybe make a few big decisions about what, exactly, she was going to do about Max, and the terrible discovery she'd made on Christmas Eve. But not now. That could wait.

Saffron's temporary peace and tranquillity didn't last long. Not even the night. She was just settling down in front of the telly that evening with an enormous box of chocolates when the lights went out. The TV screen turned blank. From the kitchen she heard the fridge making a depressed-sounding groan, as if to say *Here we go again, fellas,* as the place was plunged into unearthly darkness.

'Bollocks,' she muttered, patting around for her phone and switching it on, so as to give her some kind of light, however feeble. It was spooky just how thickly, blackly dark it was, out here in the sticks.

Six new emails buzzed in as her phone came to life, then a succession of beeps, indicating new voicemails, too. Ignoring them all, she pulled up Mr Sykes's phone number and rang him again, without holding out much hope of a reply.

'Bernie here, leave me a message and I'll get back to you,' she heard eventually and groaned. Was there any point leaving another message? When – if ever – would he 'get back' to her? It was New Year's Eve after all, and he was running a pub. From his hands-off approach so far regarding the cottage, she could easily be waiting until January. Bloody hell. She was just going to have to track him down in person and get this sorted properly.

Saffron was pretty sure she'd seen The Partridge as she drove into the village earlier: a white-painted timber-framed building with large, lit windows looming on a corner of the main street. It wasn't far. And it was either that or falter around blindly, trying to find the fuse-box herself in almost total darkness. She had visions of her limp body flung back by a jagged bolt of electricity and lying dead in Baker's Cottage as the New Year rang in. If Bernie Sykes was as slack at checking over his property as he was at answering his phone, she could be mouldering here for weeks.

It was raining as she began walking along the road, a spiteful, needly sort of shower, horribly cold. She pulled up her collar and walked faster. Luckily she was used to solving problems. Working in PR with all sorts of divas and egomaniacs, you had to think quickly and get results, however dramatic a hissy fit you were faced with. She'd track down Bernie and drag him out to the cottage, in a head-lock if need be, so he could sort everything out. In half an hour this would already feel like a distant memory and she'd be back on the sofa, lights blazing through the cottage once more. With a bit of luck, her only dilemma then would be whether to have a hazelnut praline or a dark-chocolate truffle first.

Bernie Sykes was a booming ruddy-cheeked giant of a man in his fifties, or thereabouts, with rumpled hair and an un-ironed shirt. He was leaning over the bar pumps when Saffron walked into the pub, addressing a couple of men with gusto; no mean feat when you were wearing a lopsided purple paper crown.

She stood at the bar, rain dripping from her hair, waiting for him to finish so that she could catch his attention.

'And then I said to her, "Well, bloody hell, this is not some kind of *circus*, you know, dear, you can't behave like *that* in here . . . "'

Saffron could feel her nose turning pink as the heat from the pub warmed her face. She coughed discreetly, hoping he would notice her before January began.

'And she said – you'll never guess what *she* said . . . '

On second thoughts, this sounded like one of those shaggy-dog stories with no ending. 'Mr Sykes?' Saffron said.

Bernie and his two friends both turned and looked at her. 'That's me,' said Bernie, his face suddenly falling. 'Oh dear. Not from the *Gazette*, are you? Or the council again? I've said everything I intend to about the horse incident, and it's all getting rather tiresome, to be honest.'

'I'm Saffron Flint. I'm renting Baker's Cottage from you?'

Bernie's face cleared and he thrust out a large pink hand. 'So you are! Greetings, Miss Flint. I trust everything is to your satisfaction?'

'Well, no, actually,' she said. 'I had to borrow a key from the lady next door – Gemma? – before I could actually get into the property, and now the electrics have gone.'

'Oh, Bernie,' said one of the men at the bar mock-sorrowfully. One of his front teeth was missing, Saffron noticed, as he wagged a finger at the landlord. 'Not good.'

'Standards, Bern,' said the other man, making a tsk-ing sound. 'Standards are *falling*.'

'I'm so sorry,' Bernie said. 'That sounds an absolutely dreadful way to begin your visit. Can I pour you a drink, by way of apology? I've got some very good malt whisky, which is just the ticket on a night like this. Or I've a rather tasty Chilean red, if you're more of a wine-drinker.'

'No, thanks,' Saffron replied. 'I'd just like you to come and put the electricity on, please. I'd do it myself, only I don't have a clue where the fuse-box is and it's very dark.'

'Of course, of course,' Bernie said. '*Absolument*.' He peered around the busy pub. 'Tell you what, I'll find my son. He'll sort the whole thing out for you – very competent lad, much more use than his idiot father. Where's Harry gone?'

The man with the missing tooth scratched his beard. 'Harry? Off to Spencer's tonight, isn't he?'

'Course he is. Bother.' Bernie frowned thoughtfully, then brightened. 'Wait, that's right next door to you, Miss Flint – perfect. Go back and knock at The Granary – the big farmhouse alongside the cottage – and ask for Harry, tell him his dad sent you and you need him to sort the electrics. He won't mind popping round for two minutes to fix things.'

Saffron hesitated, feeling awkward at the prospect of

bothering her neighbour again, let alone hauling out one of her guests on New Year's Eve. 'Unless you could maybe nip down and have a look yourself?' she suggested weakly.

He shook his head. 'Sorry, love. On my busiest night of the year? I'm needed here.'

As if to prove his point, a group of rowdy women burst into the pub in fancy dress. The cowgirl twirled a lasso around her head, nearly knocking off the wall a large photo of Bernie holding an enormous fish. The naughty nurse screeched in delight and slapped the cowgirl's fringed bottom. The fairy started running around the pub in her pink kitten-heels, flinging silver glitter over everyone.

'Here comes trouble,' said missing-tooth man with a gappy smirk.

'It's the Village People,' sniggered his mate, as the last woman, dressed as a Native American, complete with towering feathered headdress and war-paint, entered, announcing 'HOW!' to the room in a loud voice.

Bernie looked thrilled and dropped into a bow. 'Ladies, good evening,' he cried. 'How splendid you all look tonight. Can I tempt you with some rather delicious Lambrini? A cocktailette?'

The women thronged at the bar, all orange faces, cleavage and hairspray, demanding Bernie's attention in shrill voices. Saffron knew when she was beaten. 'Okay,' she muttered and slipped back into the night.

*

It was only when she was ringing the doorbell of The Granary that she wished she'd had the foresight to ask Bernie to phone his son in advance, give him some kind of warning that she was about to descend for the second time that evening. She wished, too, that she'd thought to bring an umbrella with her to Suffolk, as she was now thoroughly drenched after walking to and from the pub, her long hair plastered unbecomingly around her face and her feet soggy where water had seeped into her old boots. Uggh. This was not how she'd envisaged her peaceful getaway turning out.

She heard footsteps coming towards the front door and then it was pulled open, golden light spilling out into the darkness.

Standing there was the woman she'd spoken to earlier, now dressed in the most gorgeous dark-blue party frock, with her hair piled on her head. 'My God,' she cried, her mouth dropping open at the sight of the soaked, bedraggled creature on her doorstep. 'Are you all right? What's happened?'

'I'm so sorry to bother you again,' Saffron said, her teeth chattering with cold. 'My electrics have gone, and Mr Sykes – Bernie – said his son Harry was here and that he might be able to help.'

'Course he will. But come in for a minute, you look half-frozen. Honestly, Bernie – I could cheerfully strangle that man sometimes. No clue whatsoever, has he? Can I get you a drink? I'm Gemma, by the way.'

Saffron could hear music and laughter from further inside the house and felt like an intruder. Bloody Bernie Sykes and his brilliant ideas! 'No thanks,' she said, twisting her fingers. She wished now she'd tried to find the fuse-box herself, dealt with the problem in the first place. 'I'm Saffron – and I'm really embarrassed about turning up here in the middle of your party. Should I come back later?'

Gemma looked appalled at the suggestion. 'Don't be daft. I can't let you go and sit there in the dark,' she cried. 'Look, why don't you join us? It *is* New Year, after all. Nobody should be on their own on New Year's Eve! Besides,' she added, dimples flashing in her round cheeks, 'the more people we have here, the harder it'll be to see all the peeling wallpaper and damp patches. You'd be doing me a favour, really.'

A dark-haired man had appeared now, handsome and rather rakish, with a mop of unruly curls. 'Everything all right, Gems?' he asked, putting a proprietorial hand on the small of her back.

'This is Saffron, she's staying next door,' Gemma explained. 'Bernie's sent her round for Harry, because the electrics have gone in the cottage.'

'Oh, don't worry, we can sort that for you,' the man said. 'Half the local building trade here tonight, love. We won't even charge you.'

Gemma elbowed him. 'I was just saying Saffron should

join us for a drink.' Then she checked herself, turning back to Saffron. 'Unless you're in a rush, of course?'

Saffron thought quickly. Much as she had looked forward to some peace and quiet on her own, the thought of being with a group of other people for at least part of the evening in this warm, bright house was kind of appealing. Although she would feel pretty self-conscious venturing in like this . . .

Gemma seemed to read her mind. 'Leave your coat on the radiator to dry,' she said, 'and follow me. I got a new hair-dryer for Christmas and it'll sort your hair out in seconds, I swear. Come on!'

Chapter Four

By the time it was eleven o'clock Gemma had drunk enough margaritas and Prosecco to be pleasantly squiffy and was enjoying herself enormously. People were dancing, led by Spencer's gorgeous gay cousin Jonny, who was moving up to Newcastle in a week's time and seemed to be treating this party as his last chance to buff up some signature moves. The canapés had been devoured – even the ropiest-looking ones – and nobody had been rushed to A&E with food poisoning (yet). Several of Spencer's football mates had turned up in drag, for some unexplained reason (Gemma had been secretly thrilled to see how twittery and giggly even the snootiest school mums went at the sight of all those muscled, hairy legs in fishnet stockings) and almost everyone had been lovely about the house, apart from Sarah Russell, who had said, several times now, 'God, it's going to need a *lot* of work, isn't it? You *are* brave!' in such an annoyingly patronizing way that Gemma had been tempted to strangle her with the fairy lights. Still. Up yours, Sarah Russell. Everyone else was making it a brilliant night.

Spencer had been right: this *was* a great house for a party. The rooms were generously sized with high ceilings and, despite the large number of guests, it still felt spacious rather than cramped. Besides, having a rafter-shaking party definitely christened a place. A house wasn't a home until you'd shaken your thang under a glitterball to 'Like a Virgin' on your very own living-room dance-floor, after all. Wasn't that what the property experts always said?

Weaving her way unsteadily into the kitchen, Gemma headed for the cocktail shaker and the sticky collection of bottles lined up on the work surface. 'Cocktails!' she announced. 'Who's up for another?'

A woman with dark hair and a long, pale face, who was standing looking rather awkward on her own, raised a hand. 'Twisted my arm,' she said shyly.

'Cool,' Gemma said, swaying on her heels. 'What do you reckon: vodka, raspberries, Cointreau . . . ' She began sloshing in ingredients with reckless abandon. 'What else?'

The dark-haired woman looked alarmed. 'Oh God, I don't know. I'm not very sophisticated when it comes to things like that.'

Gemma snorted. 'I'm the least sophist—' she stumbled over the word; too many syllables for this time of night, damn it, 'sophisticated person in the world. As you'll realize when you drink this.' She added some crushed ice and edible gold glitter — well, it *was* New Year — and shook up the mixture. As she did so, she noticed that Saffron, the woman from next door, now with dry hair, borrowed make-up and a squirt of Gemma's Chanel No. 5, was currently trapped in a corner with Spud Morton, the most boring potato-headed man of Larkmead. Was that an actual *raisin* stuck in his beard? Catching her eye, Saffron made a *Help!* face, and Gemma hurried to the rescue.

'Spud! There you are!' A wicked idea popped up in her mind. 'Hey, Sarah Russell was looking for you. Said something about having a big, smoochy New Year's kiss she wanted to give you . . .'

He left immediately, the raisin trembling with the momentum as he hurried away. *Ha, Sarah Russell, that's what you get for dissing my house,* Gemma thought with a grin.

'Thanks,' Saffron said.

'No worries. Sorry you got lumbered with him — pickled-onion breath and all. Now, let me pour you a glass of this gorgeous little concoction.' She took the lid off the cocktail shaker and filled three Martini glasses with the dark-red liquid, admiring the shimmering effect from the glitter. 'Yum! Knock yourself out with *that*, ladies. Not literally, mind.'

The dark-haired woman took a long slug of hers and smacked her lips, but Saffron shook her head. 'Um . . . I don't drink,' she said apologetically. 'Thanks, though. And thanks for letting me gatecrash your party as well, by the way.'

'Me, too,' the dark-haired woman started saying, just as a group of basque-wearing footballers burst into the room, chanting a song about beer. One was wearing long turquoise feathers in his hair for some reason, and the dark-haired woman – who *was* she anyway? Gemma wondered – shrank back self-consciously.

Despite being three sheets to the wind – four sheets, now she'd just necked that delicious cocktail – Gemma couldn't help noticing there was something fragile about the dark-haired woman. She was all long, gangly limbs and held herself at uncomfortable-looking angles, as if she'd never quite grown into her height. Gemma leaned closer as the lingerie-clad footballers cut a noisy path past them and out the back door for a smoke. 'I'm Gemma, by the way. I don't think we've met.'

'Caitlin,' said the woman. Her fingernails were nibbled down and she had a gaunt look about her. 'Oh. You're married to Spencer, right?'

'That's me.' *Caitlin*, Gemma thought, her brain feeling misty. Caitlin? The girlfriend of one of the football crowd, maybe? No. One of the mums from school? Definitely not. Then she remembered Spencer coming back from the news-agent's the other Sunday looking shifty, before confessing that he'd invited to their party yet another person Gemma didn't know. Ah, got it. She was the one whose mum had died, whom Spencer knew from primary school or something. No wonder she looked a bit shell-shocked.

'Well, bottoms up!' she said cheerfully, sharing the dregs of the cocktail between the two of them. 'Glad you're both here. Have you got anything amazing lined up for the New Year? Any life-changing resolutions or adventures? Tell me you're not going on mad diets or . . . I don't know, competing in triathlons or something sickeningly worthy and impressive.'

'As if,' Saffron said, stuffing the last wedge of quiche into her mouth. 'I can't think of anything more soul-destroying than cottage cheese and celery sticks. In January? As if. Bring on the pies and chips.'

Caitlin smiled. 'Maybe we should resolve to eat *more*,' she said. 'Make some anti-resolutions. I might take up smoking,' she went on. 'Pipes, perhaps. Or cigars.'

Gemma giggled. 'Yeah, I might try to do less exercise. If I try really hard, I might not do the London Marathon this year.'

'Oh, I'm going to try not to do that, too,' Saffron said. 'And I'm definitely not going to do a single press-up or star jump, either.'

'Just say no,' Caitlin put in, draining her glass. 'But just say yes to more cocktails. What else have you got?'

Gemma grinned, pleased that Caitlin seemed to be warming up. Ah, the magic of cocktails. She quickly invented another, this time chucking in apricot brandy, gin, orange

Lucy Diamond

juice, ice and some mint leaves. 'Oh my Lord, that's absolutely rank,' she said, tasting a mouthful. 'Sorry, Caitlin. I think my career as a mixologist is over.'

'Don't worry, my career at Cambridge Graphics is also over,' Caitlin said, raising her glass tipsily. 'Made redundant two months ago.'

Ouch. There was such pain in her eyes, Gemma wanted to hug her. She wished she'd made her a better cocktail at least. She grabbed the Christmas cake and cut Caitlin a slice instead, as the next best thing. It was probably every bit as alcoholic, besides. 'Have that,' she said, 'with my condolences.'

'I kind of wish *my* career at Phoenix-sodding-PR was over,' Saffron added. 'I would love to stick two fingers up at my boss and walk out.' She pulled a face. 'We're a right bunch, aren't we?'

'Balls to it, ladies,' said Gemma, biting into a mini-sausage roll, 'let's go into business together. What shall we do? Cake-testers? Chocolate . . . um . . . eaters?'

'Holiday reviewers,' Saffron suggested.

'Oh yes,' Caitlin agreed. 'We could go round checking out all the hotels and beaches, testing the pools and spa facilities . . . '

'I could definitely manage that,' Gemma said. '*Or*,' she added, as a brilliant new idea came to her, 'we could form a girl band. I'm always up for a bit of karaoke.'

'Good one,' Saffron laughed. 'I reckon I know all the dance

moves to "Single Ladies". I knew that would come in handy one day.'

'Fame and fortune guaranteed,' Gemma said with a grin. Then she leapt up suddenly, her memory jogged. 'Oh! I forgot the fortune-cookies!'

She lurched over to the cupboard above the fridge, pulling down the box and ripping open the packaging. 'Here,' she said, proffering the contents and taking one herself. 'Let's see what the magic fortune-cookies predict for this year. World domination, a stadium tour for our band, or at least a bit of respect from stroppy children, please!'

Snapping it in half, she unfolded the paper strip inside and read the message inside. 'Oh,' she said. '"For success today, look first to yourself."' She rolled her eyes. 'I'm not sure about that.' *She's just a mum*, Darcey said again in her head, and Gemma looked away. Exactly. She *was* just a mum. What kind of success would she ever achieve, except perhaps a clean house and the children handing in their homework on time? 'What did you two get?' she asked.

'"Do not trust hapless pub landlords renting out mouldy cottages . . ." No, not really.' Saffron squinted at her paper. '"Have courage! Mistakes can become adventures." Oh God,' she groaned. 'Who comes up with this tosh?'

'I like to think it's an incredibly wise, wrinkled old Chinese man sitting on a golden throne,' Gemma said. 'But I reckon it's probably a soulless computer program. How about you, Caitlin?'

Caitlin looked uncertain. '"Your destiny is within your own grasp,"' she read. '"Take a chance!"' She pulled a face. 'I was hoping for "Tall, dark stranger" or "Lottery win", or even "Don't worry, someone else will sort your destiny out for you – take the year off."'

'Bloody rubbish.' Gemma took another cookie. 'I think we must have picked the wrong ones last time, ladies. Try again.' She snapped a second cookie in half and pulled out the fortune. 'This is more like it. "Follow your bliss and the universe will open doors where there were once only walls."'

'Follow your bliss, eh? Sounds like a romantic weekend away with your hubster,' said Saffron.

'Or that chocolate-testing job. I'm not sure which I'd rather.' Gemma took another glug of the horrible cocktail and gagged. 'Ugh. Well, that's not blissful, anyway.' She tossed the fortune-paper over her shoulder. 'I was hoping for a more exciting prediction. Something extraordinary, not just another same-old humdrum year.' She glanced up at the ceiling comically. 'If that's all right with you, dear kind Universe – thank you.'

The others smiled. 'I'd like a new man for the new year, if we're putting in requests,' Caitlin said. She rolled her hand into a megaphone and spoke through it, addressing the same corner of the ceiling as Gemma had. 'Did you catch that, Universe? New man for Caitlin Fraser, please, preferably with a hot bod and no frigging issues.' She winked. 'Then I'll take a bit of action.'

Harry Sykes chose that moment to burst through the kitchen door, wearing somebody's pink Stetson. 'Did somebody call?' he asked.

The three women collapsed in laughter. 'That was fast,' Saffron gurgled. 'Good work, Universe.'

'Harry, you knobhead,' Gemma said affectionately. 'Nobody called you. And what's *that* on your head?'

He took it off and bowed low. Harry was Spencer's best mate – charming, funny and blond, with quite the most complicated love-life in Larkmead. 'Just thought I heard . . . ' Then his eyes fastened on Caitlin and he broke off. 'No way,' he said. 'Tell me it isn't.'

Caitlin flushed, looking awkward. 'It isn't,' she replied deadpan.

'It is, though, isn't it? It's only Caitlin Fraser, last seen with goth make-up and a leather jacket.' He tapped the side of his head. 'Never forget a face.'

'Um . . . ' Caitlin looked lost for words.

Gemma helped her out. 'This is Harry. Harry Sykes?'

'Oh God! From school.' Caitlin turned even pinker. 'Hi.'

Harry perched on the worktop, dangling the Stetson between his legs. 'So tell me, Caitlin Fraser. Where have you been hiding for the last fourteen years?'

Caitlin opened her mouth to reply just as Jade Perry, Harry's girlfriend, marched into the room on the sort of towering stilettos that would give Gemma a broken ankle within seconds. 'There you are! Come on,' she said, grabbing his hand so hard he almost toppled off his perch. The silver sequins on her tight little dress flashed and twinkled under the strip-lighting as she pulled him away. 'The countdown's about to begin.'

You could tell Caitlin felt foolish as Harry allowed himself to be dragged from the room, with an apologetic flourish of the Stetson, but then they heard the noise levels rise from the living room. 'Ten! Nine! Eight!'

'Come on,' Saffron said, jumping to her feet.

Gemma realized she'd absent-mindedly broken open a third cookie, and read the message – 'Poverty is no disgrace' – before dropping it in alarm. No poverty, thanks. Not when they had the scarily big new mortgage hanging over their heads.

'Seven! Six! Five!' They ran out of the room together, all of them trying to think of the perfect resolution.

This year I'll do something amazing or brave or exciting, Gemma vowed. *And Darcey will never think of me as 'just a mum' again. Oh, and I'll definitely take my make-up off EVERY night too. I promise!*

Talk to Max, get fit, get promoted, Saffron thought in a rush, *stop eating crisps all the time, look after my skin better, sort out a proper haircut, stop biting my nails.*

I promise I'll make you proud of me, Mum, thought Caitlin with a pang of emotion. *I'll put last year behind me and move on.*

They'd reached the living room and for a moment Gemma

couldn't see Spencer anywhere. 'Four! Three! Two!' Then his eyes caught hers across the heaving throng and she felt a hot surge of love.

'One! HAPPY NEW YEAR!' everyone chanted, and Gemma jostled her way through to him just in time.

'Happy New Year, wife,' he said into her ear, his arms tight around her. The room around them was a whirl of hugging and kissing and exclamations; people were singing 'Auld Lang Syne' at the tops of their voices.

'Happy New Year, you,' Gemma said, kissing him passionately.

'It's going to be a good one,' he told her.

'The best,' she agreed.

Full of bubbly and fortune-cookies, surrounded by loved ones and in her own soon-to-be-amazing home, Gemma felt rich with happiness. The New Year was here at last. She could hardly wait to get started.

Chapter Five

As midnight struck on New Year's Eve, the potato-headed man with the health-hazard beard turned his attentions to Caitlin and stuck his tongue down her throat, almost asphyxiating her with his rancid breath. Uggh. Ngggaarggh. Time for another emergency resolution: *I promise I won't ever let that Spud-head near me again,* she vowed, escaping his clutches as a rowdy chorus of 'Auld Lang Syne' started up. She glanced around for Harry, half-hoping for an excuse to get into a clinch with him instead, but he seemed to be having an argument with the woman in the silver dress, which culminated with her stamping right through the crown of the Stetson with her stilettos.

It was probably just as well. Harry had been the hottest boy in the sixth form, as well as a serial heart-breaker. She could do without any more grief in that area of her life, especially when she still had the loose threads of her last relationship to tie up. *Sort out Flynn,* she thought, as yet more resolutions occurred to her. *Clear out Mum's cottage and sell it.*

Decide what to do with the rest of my life. Have some fun. There, that would do.

Then Spencer grabbed her hands and pulled her into the circle. 'For Auld Lang Syne, my dear, for Auld Lang Syne!' they sang.

This year would be different, she promised herself. This year she'd do better.

Two weeks later, January had settled in with a grim vengeance and nothing much seemed to have changed. Storms were battering the country. The streets were full of wheezing joggers skirting around the dead Christmas trees abandoned on the pavements, while the shops were already packed with Valentine's displays and Creme Eggs. Meanwhile, Flynn was being a prick – *quelle surprise.*

Caitlin read the latest text that had arrived from him, her lip curling in annoyance, and typed one furiously in return:

Yes, all right, keep your hair on! I'll pick everything up on Wednesday. Can you bear to have my possessions contaminating your space for another 48 hours? They won't kill you. More's the pity. Caitlin

She read over her words, her finger poised on the Send

button. Should she? Dare she? No. Better not. Delete, delete, delete. She thought for a moment and then typed again:

Fine. I'll pick everything up on Wed. C.

That was better. Cool, calm and civilized – not that he deserved it, mind. She pressed Send, feeling as if her heart was calcifying. The brave optimism she'd felt at New Year shrivelled away as she remembered what he'd done, how shabbily he'd treated her. The sooner she closed that door of her life and walked away, the better.

Three days later she sat in her old blue Clio, hands on the steering wheel, motionless in the driveway. *Come on, Cait. Removals ninja – get in, get out, get it over and done with. Now start the engine and go.*

All she had to do was drive to the flat – Flynn's flat, as she needed to start thinking of it – and load up the rest of her belongings. By the end of the day she'd have washed her hands of him forever. As a man who was verging on OCD when it came to hygiene and cleanliness, he would probably approve of that metaphor.

Right. Key in the ignition. Let's do this.

The last time she'd seen him was when he came to the cottage after her mum died, a nervous look in his eyes as he put his arm around her while she cried. 'Jess doesn't mean anything,' he'd mumbled. Yeah. Course she didn't, Flynn.

Come on. Start the engine and get the heater going — it's Baltic in here. And look, you've steamed up the windscreen now, all this sitting still and breathing. Crank up the de-mister and let's hit the road. Go!

Gritting her teeth, she turned the key in the ignition . . . then let out a moan of frustration as the engine made a feeble croaking sound and fell silent.

'No,' she muttered, smacking the steering wheel and trying again. *Whirr-whirr-clunk.* Oh, *knickers*, she thought. Of all the days for the car to give up on her, today was not a good one.

Popping open the bonnet, she strode round to inspect the car's inner workings, her breath steaming in the wintry air. 'Right,' she said, in as can-do a voice as she could manage. 'Let's see, then. So . . . '

She stared at the jumble of cables and mechanics, hoping something obvious would leap out at her. Nothing did. Wires were still connected to . . . things. There was plenty of water in the container. Oil. How did you check the oil? 'Oh, for fuck's sake,' she snapped, hating herself for not knowing. It was all very well being a can-do independent twenty-first-century woman, but sometimes she just wished her dad was still around to take care of stuff like this. *Budge over, Cait*, she imagined him saying. *Make yourself useful and get us a cuppa, eh?* He'd been a good dad, mending punctures on her bike, never losing his patience when he taught her to drive, fixing the heater in her student flat when she first left home. Loving her and telling her she was beautiful, hugging her and saying, husky-voiced, how proud he was of her when she passed all her nursing exams. Then he'd gone and ruined it all by dying stupidly early, of a massive, unexpected stroke.

Maybe she should just hire a van for the day, she thought, slamming the bonnet shut in defeat. Flynn would go nuts if she didn't turn up as arranged, after all his impatient texts. He was a bit of a control freak; he hated it when things didn't go to plan. He was the sort of person who wouldn't think twice about sending food back in a restaurant if it wasn't exactly to his taste. Caitlin, meanwhile, was the sort of mug who'd silently chew down overcooked steaks or lukewarm chips because she didn't want to make a fuss.

'Everything all right?'

The voice made her jump. She turned her head to see a man leaning out of his van window, engine idling where he'd pulled over at the kerb. Harry Sykes. 'Car trouble?' he asked.

'Yeah. Won't start,' she said. She spread her hands help-lessly. 'A pretty basic failing, when it comes to going anywhere.'

He laughed, the sound carrying on the cold air. 'Want me to have a look?'

Oh, a man with a toolbox. HELLO. 'If you don't mind. Please.'

'No problem.' He parked the van and jumped down. 'Could be the battery. Did it make any kind of sound?'

Men were so keen to fix things, weren't they? Caitlin mused

as he clambered into the driver's seat and tried the key himself. *Whirr-whirr-clunk. Whirr-whirr-clunk.* See problem – must solve it. Flynn had been the same when his precious, expensive coffee-maker gave up the ghost, and had spent hours taking the wretched thing apart on the kitchen table, fiddling around with wiring and valves. If only he'd taken such care to try and fix their relationship rather than chuck it out so swiftly.

'Let's try cleaning the battery connectors,' Harry said, getting out of the car again.

'Good idea,' Caitlin said, teeth chattering. 'I checked the water,' she added helpfully, not wanting Harry to think she was a total bimbo.

She watched him work, a little frown deepening between his eyebrows as his hands made their way around the innards of her engine. Was it good old biological programming that made the sight of a man with a wrench in his grip seem so damn sexy, she wondered absently. Was it the cave-woman in her that reacted to such clichés of masculinity, that appreciated a capable man? Or was she just acting out the crush she'd had on him as a lonely sixteen-year-old, in a rather naff 'damsel in distress' episode?

Oh, shut up, Dr Freud, she scolded herself. Just be grateful that some bugger's fixing your car, all right?

' . . . fuel-injection system,' he was saying.

'What?' And now she'd been caught out not paying attention.

'I think you'll have to get a proper mechanic to look at this,' Harry repeated. 'I reckon there might be a problem with the fuel-injection system.'

'Right. Damn. But thanks.'

He shut the bonnet again and leaned against it, not seeming in any hurry to leave. 'I can give you a lift somewhere if you want, though. Where were you going?'

'Cambridge,' she said. It was about an hour's drive away, too far for a casual lift. 'Don't worry about it. Thanks for taking a look.'

'Okay,' he said, to her surprise. 'Cambridge is fine.'

'What? Oh no – honestly, you don't have to. I'm actually . . . ' She ground to a halt, not wanting to have to spell out why she was going to Cambridge, but his expectant face gave her little choice. 'I need to move my stuff out of . . . of my old flat,' she mumbled eventually. 'I couldn't possibly ask you to—'

'That's fine. Seriously. We've had to stop work on the site anyway – everyone's waiting for the plumber to finish the bathroom, and it's John the Snail, so he'll be hours yet.' His eyes twinkled and he gestured to the van. 'Besides, it's either this or helping my dad take a load of stuff to the dump. Hop in.'

Caitlin's heart gave a thump. 'Thank you.'

*

Harry's van had a noisy heater and was littered with a surprising selection of detritus in the passenger footwell: a stray child's trainer, an empty apple-juice carton and a cat-patterned hairband. There were also a number of stickers plastered across the dashboard. *I ♥ One Direction,* announced one. *I Know, Right?* said another. Oh God, he has kids, she thought, with a flat feeling of disappointment. Of course he had. A man as charming and good-looking as Harry had probably sired a whole brood since they'd parted ways after sixth form. No doubt there was a coterie of ex-wives lurking gimlet-eyed in his past as well.

'I didn't have you down as a One Direction fan,' she said lightly, clicking in her seatbelt.

He laughed. 'Yeah, big fan. Love a bit of moshing at a One-D gig with the teenyboppers.' He started the engine and winked at her. 'Oh, no, wait, I'm getting muddled up with my niece. I take her to gymnastics lessons every Friday afternoon, and that seat has become an extension of her bedroom.' He removed a red school sweatshirt from where it had been stuffed down the side of the handbrake and hurled it into the back. 'The hairband's mine, though, obviously. If you could avoid treading on that, I'd be grateful.'

She smiled. 'Have you got kids yourself, Harry?'

His eyes were on the road and she couldn't see his expression. 'No. You?'

'No.'

'Any aggressive, tattooed husbands I should know about, who'll be lying in wait for us in Cambridge, cracking their knuckles and giving me menacing looks?'

She snorted. 'No. You're quite safe.'

He glanced over at her as he slowed at a roundabout. 'Any ex-husbands at all? Go on, let's hear it. My Glorious Life, by Caitlin Fraser. Tell me the lot.'

'No ex-husbands.' What the hell, she thought. They wouldn't be in Cambridge for ages. 'I worked as a nurse for a while, then . . . '

'Excellent. Love nurses.'

She rolled her eyes. Was there a man on earth who didn't? 'Lived in Norwich for a while with Serious Boyfriend number one, who was this mega-brain computer boffin.'

'Hmm. I don't like the sound of him.'

'He was all right.' Jeremy Langley, geeky and earnest, but so talented that he'd been lured by big money and glory in Silicon Valley. 'I think he loved computer programming more than he loved me, though.'

'The bastard. What happened next?'

'Then I gave up nursing. I'd only gone into it because of my parents anyway. Mum was a midwife, Dad was a hospital manager. But then I had this sort of epiphany—'

'A what? Is that like a seizure?'

'No! I had a change of heart – and I don't mean a heart transplant either, before you ask. I just decided life was too short to spend it giving bedbaths and fending off piss-heads in A&E on a Saturday night.'

'Ah, the rebellion moment. Good for you. So what did you do next? No, don't tell me . . . Bareback-rider in a rodeo.'

She laughed. 'Not quite,' she said. 'I went back to college and took up graphic design. Got a job building websites, and never looked back.'

'Excellent. Carry on. Ah – let me guess. You were reunited with the computer programmer and made beautiful websites together. Whispered passionate lines of code into each other's ears.'

'No!' She spluttered at the thought. 'Maybe I should have done, though. He's probably a kazillionaire by now, working for some faceless tech-corporation in Seattle.'

'Gutted. You slipped up there, Fraser. Want me to drive you to the airport instead?'

'Cambridge will do, thanks,' she said. 'And it's your turn now, by the way. Fill me in on Harry Sykes: The Glory Years. The juicier, the better.'

The journey flew by as they caught up on each other's lives. He told her about working in Auckland for six months as a painter and decorator, nearly marrying a Kiwi woman in a whirlwind romance, his parents' divorce, nearly marrying

Shelley Bridges who'd been at school with them, training to be an electrician, nearly marrying a much older woman who'd seduced him while he was rewiring her house, moving out of Larkmead, moving back to Larkmead, nearly marrying a crazy French woman, and how his New Year's ambition was to stop nearly marrying people.

'That sounds a wise move,' Caitlin said.

'It's got me into a lot of trouble,' Harry said ruefully. 'My romantic proposing habit.' He slapped the steering wheel. 'No, this year will be different. Completely different. I have a new strategy, see. The Ten-Date Rule.'

'Enlighten me. How does that work then?'

He glanced sidelong at her, to see if she was taking the mick out of him, but she kept a straight face. 'It was my sister's idea really,' he confessed. 'I've been a bit . . . impulsive in the past and things have got kind of complicated.'

'No. Really?' This time there was no getting away from the fact that she was teasing.

'Hard to believe, I know. So Sam, my sister, laid the law down, told me to try the Ten-Date Rule this year and stay out of trouble. She reckons if you go on ten dates before you sleep with a partner – or propose to them – the relationship stands a better chance.'

'I see. And how's it going so far?'

'Well, it isn't, to be honest. I've only just split up with Jade and she's still giving me earache. But we shall see.' He waggled his eyebrows and pulled a comic face, and Caitlin felt a twist of envy for whoever Harry fell for next. He really was gorgeous, like a naughtier version of Daniel Craig – the same strong face and wide mouth, with eyes that seemed to see right into you. Phew! Was it her, or was it getting hot in here?

'Left at this junction,' she said hurriedly, glad of a reason to stop thinking about how good-looking he was. Calm down, she ordered herself. And don't flatter yourself that this is anything other than a lift – a favour – okay?

They drove along in silence for a few minutes, Caitlin remembering the last time she'd been down this road. It was the morning her mum died, when her eyes were gritty with lack of sleep, her bones aching from being crunched in the bedside chair, her heart raw and broken. The first rays of morning light were painting the sky with golden strokes; people everywhere would be yawning and stretching, and stumbling towards coffee, with no idea that a terrible, momentous thing had just happened to her. All Caitlin had wanted was to feel Flynn's strong arms around her, the comfort of love.

'You okay?' Harry asked.

Caitlin stared, unseeing, through the window for a moment, images from that morning falling into her mind like jewels in a kaleidoscope. The unfamiliar car in her parking space. The voices in the flat, laughter pausing abruptly as she walked in. The smell of toast and bacon, the radio playing a cheerful song, her friend Jess's bare feet up in Flynn's lap as they sat at the table in dressing gowns. *Her* dressing gown.

'Yeah, sure,' she said dully. 'It's right here, then right again just after the church.'

Flynn's flat was part of a modern block on Cromwell Road – soulless and kind of boxy, Caitlin had always thought privately, but when he had asked her to move in with him, back in the first flush of romance, she'd been so happy and excited that its square rooms and lack of outdoor space didn't bother her at all. After living in her mum's cottage recently, with the charms of its generous garden and beamed ceilings, she was struck anew by how chilly and impersonal this place seemed.

'Well, this is it,' she said, pushing open the front door. Tension knotted inside her with every echoing step along the tiled hall floor. She had lived here for two and a half years, but it had never really felt like home, she realized. Even walking in now put her on edge. She was holding her breath, half-expecting Flynn to appear and say something caustic. Sometimes it was only when you had moved away that you noticed how unhappy you'd become.

'Very smart,' Harry said politely, his eyes sliding around, as Caitlin sorted through the pile of post on the hall unit.

Flynn being Flynn, he had boxed up every last bit of her stuff and stacked it all neatly in one corner of the spare room, just waiting for her to remove it. There were spaces like missing teeth on the shelves where her books had been, and the mantelpiece looked boringly empty without her photos and ornaments. Caitlin also noticed a smart slate-grey woman's coat hanging up in the hall that definitely wasn't hers, and a new red toothbrush in the bathroom. He and Jess hadn't wasted much time then.

'Christ, who's that?' Harry asked, gesturing at the large canvas on the living-room wall. It was a black-and-white photo of Flynn's sleeping face on the pillow; a gift from a former girlfriend apparently. Caitlin had always secretly loathed it.

'That was my ex. Flynn.' A handsome devil, with his beautiful long, dark lashes and high, sculpted cheekbones. But, seriously, what sort of narcissistic prick hung a ginormous canvas of themselves in their own frigging living room?

She could tell Harry was thinking the same thing, but was too well-mannered to say so out loud. 'What happened with you guys then?' he asked, as they huffed and puffed down the communal stairs, clutching the boxes of her belongings.

'Oh . . . just didn't work out.' She didn't feel like giving Harry the lowdown. He unlocked the van and pushed in his box, then took hers from her and shoved it in alongside.

'Want me to kill him for you?'

She laughed. 'Don't tempt me,' she said.

Embarrassingly, it took a mere fifteen minutes to load up her stuff in the back of Harry's van. You'd have thought a person would have more to show for themselves after thirty-two years on the planet – some decent pieces of furniture, evidence of being a proper grown-up. Nope. Not Caitlin.

'Well, that was easy,' Harry commented, as they crammed in the last two boxes. 'Shall we head back?'

'I'll just have a last check around,' Caitlin said. 'Won't be long.'

Up in the flat again she walked slowly through the quiet rooms one final time, touching the walls with her fingertips. It was all so pristine, she thought, noting the obsessive way he'd lined up the mugs in the kitchen cupboard and alphabetized the spice jars in the rack. In the bathroom the towels were folded perfectly, as if it was a spa or a hotel room. She thought of her mum's cosy cottage with its higgledy-piggledy order, the mismatched crockery, the gaudy fridge magnets from Cornwall and Tenby, the jumble of family photos everywhere. That was a proper home, not this. No wonder she'd never been able to relax here.

She gazed into the bathroom mirror and saw echoes of herself there: too thin, too anxious, putting on make-up to cover her acne scars, plucking out her first white hairs before he noticed them. Trying to be something she wasn't, for him. She found herself fantasizing about scrawling a lipsticked message on his mirror before she left. UP YOURS! maybe, or SCREW YOU!

No, that was childish. She mustn't. He'd go berserk.

'Are you ready to go?' called Harry, who'd reappeared in the hallway.

'Just coming,' she replied, without moving. Her mouth twisted as the urge grew stronger to make a last bit of mischief before leaving for good. Should she? Dare she? She probably shouldn't.

Last few checks: nothing hanging on the back of the bathroom door, all toiletries removed from the shower. Ah – the bathroom cabinet, she hadn't thought to look in there. She opened the mirrored door and her eyes went straight to the packet of condoms inside. Ribbed for extra pleasure, according to the box. Oh. Back in the day, they hadn't used condoms; she'd gone on the pill because he said he didn't like the rubbery smell. Obviously he'd got over that particular problem pretty swiftly, though.

She opened the box; not many left inside. Tosser, she thought, flinging the last few messily over the floor in a burst of hatred. Then she pushed his folded towels out of place and rearranged his toiletries, knowing he'd notice. She ran into the kitchen and muddled up the spices, putting the Cardamom Pod jar where the Turmeric should go, swapping Ginger for Cumin, Fenugreek Seeds for Chilli Flakes.

Harry was in the living room, perched on the arm of the sofa. ('You're not meant to sit on the arm, you'll spoil the shape,' Flynn always fussed whenever Caitlin had forgotten and did the same thing.) 'All done?' he asked, and then, as Caitlin walked straight past him, taking the lid off her traffic-stopping red lipstick, 'What are you do—? Caitlin! Bloody hell!'

'What do you think? I reckon they suit him,' Caitlin said, standing back and admiring the red heart-shaped glasses she'd drawn on the canvas picture of Flynn's face. Adrenalin thumped through her. Flynn would go mental when he saw what she'd done. Absolutely mental.

And serve him bloody well right, she thought, smirking at Harry, who was roaring with shocked laughter. 'All done,' she said. 'Let's go.'

Chapter Six

London seemed loud, grimy and foul-smelling when Saffron returned, a couple of days into the New Year. There were roadworks near her East London flat, ominous yellow police signs on the pavement describing two new stabbings and appealing for witnesses, burger wrappers bowling along the road in the wind, and a new streak of grey-white pigeon shit down her living-room window. She'd lived in London since she was twenty-one and, for the first time ever, she had to admit it was losing its appeal.

On her last full day in Suffolk she'd put on wellies and her great fat duvet of a coat and had tramped for miles on her own, the sky wide and clear, with only the far-away thrumming of a tractor and sporadic bursts of birdsong disturbing the stillness. She'd seen spiders' webs glittering with frost, a rabbit scuffling urgently into the hedgerow, a hawk hovering high above the bare brown fields, then suddenly plummeting towards unsuspecting prey. You forgot how magnificent nature could be when you were usually surrounded by concrete and traffic. Mind you, nature had played a pretty terrible trick on her recently, with that curve-ball on Christmas Eve. She'd sat on the edge of her parents' bath gripping the white plastic stick, her hands trembling in disbelief as first one blue line appeared, then a second. Oh, she thought dully. Not food poisoning after all, then.

Life hadn't felt quite real, carrying the enormous secret by herself, without being able to share it. She couldn't tell her parents – no way. They were gentle souls who pottered around in soft fleeces, nurturing seedlings, walking the dogs, making disapproving noises at the television. They lived a quiet life of comfortable routines. Telling them over the Christmas dinner that she was unexpectedly pregnant would have been like lobbing a hand-grenade into the roast-potato dish.

Her sisters? She couldn't tell them either. Eloise was going through IVF for what felt like the tenth time, poor woman. If Saffron let slip that she was accidentally up the duff and wasn't sure if she even wanted the baby, Eloise would probably lamp her one. She'd never speak to her again. And Zoe . . . Well, Zoe and she had once been close enough that they knew everything about each other, but her younger sister was in Western Australia now, after a crazy love-whirlwind with a gorgeous surfie-chick called Alexa had turned into something more serious, and geography had forced the sisters apart. Oh, they Skyped and emailed and did their best, but Skype and emails didn't come close to a proper heart-to-heart with a glass of wine somewhere intimate. Not that she was drinking wine now, of course. (God, she was desperate for wine. Desperate like she'd never been desperate. Was it possible that one of your pregnancy cravings could be a chilled glass of Sauvignon blanc? Or a slim, tall glass of sharp, bubbling champagne? It had been the first dry New Year since she was fifteen. It had practically killed her to say 'I don't drink' at Gemma's party.)

As for Max . . . No, she hadn't told him the big news, either. How could she? He was only meant to be a bit of fun, after all – one of those no-strings flings where your heart remained intact, even if your knickers didn't. Besides, he had baggage by the cartload: a shrewish ex-wife, Jenna, who always seemed to be bollocking him down the phone, plus two teen-age children of his own. The last thing he'd want from Saffron was an awkward 'I've got something to tell you' con-versation. She could already imagine the way his animated face would sag; how the light would vanish from his eyes in an instant. *You're what? Are you kidding?*

God, it was complicated. What was she going to do?

Being away in Suffolk had been like putting on a sticking plaster, temporarily covering her worries from sight. Walks and fresh air, and even an excellent party in the house next door, with an actual conga around the living room after mid-night. (She must send flowers to that lovely Gemma. It had been way better fun than sitting in and watching the London fireworks all on her own.)

Now she was back in the real world, though: in the cramped and rather grotty East London flat she'd rented since her marriage went tits-up two years ago and she'd been left out of pocket. Her suitcase was yet to be unpacked, there was a mountain of laundry to tackle, and her somewhat pathetic needle-shedding Christmas tree needed to be dragged outside for the recycling lorry, before it turned completely bald. With the holiday over and work looming tomorrow, January was already looking grey and joyless.

She was lying on the sofa, crunching through a bag of salt-and-vinegar Hula Hoops, when her phone started ringing. *Max*, she saw on the screen and let it go to voicemail, hating her own cowardice. In the next moment she remembered her own midnight vow at New Year – *Talk to Max* – and felt a stab of guilt. Resolutions were cobblers anyway. And she *was* going to talk to Max. She was! Just not now. Not this minute.

She and Max had met at the glitzy launch of Faster, a new sportswear brand, in a Covent Garden hotel. He was Faster's Account Manager, while she worked for the PR agency co-ordinating the evening. She liked him even before she'd laid eyes on him – his emails were charming and witty, and his deep voice on the phone always made him sound as if he was on the brink of laughter. Then she'd met him in person and her whole body reacted. Whoa. He had a rangy, athletic physique, salt-and-pepper hair, and a way of looking at you with those melty brown eyes as if you were the only other person in the world. They bonded over their willingness to try ridiculous-sounding cocktails, and before long she could hardly look at him without wanting to grab his shirt and kiss him. Emboldened by lust and all those cocktails, she pressed her business card into his hand at the end of the night. 'Let's do this again,' she said daringly.

'Let's,' he agreed.

Two days later a package arrived at her desk and out fell a turquoise hoodie with the Faster logo stamped on it in pink lettering. 'He's sent you a *fleece*?' asked her colleague Kate in withering tones. 'Who said romance was dead?'

Saffron read the note. 'He's booked us in for a snowboarding lesson,' she said, her heart giving a little flip. 'Said the hoodie might come in handy.'

Kate raised an eyebrow. 'Okay, I take it back,' she said. 'That's kind of smooth. And a snowboarding lesson is a damn sight more interesting than a night down the pub, that's for sure.'

The snowboarding lesson was hilarious, as was their second date, kayaking along the Thames. For their third date, Saffron offered to cook Max dinner at her place, but they hadn't eaten so much as a mouthful before they were pulling each other's clothes off and tumbling onto the sofa together. ('I like him,' she told Kate the next morning. She had tingles just thinking about him, the way his skin felt against hers. 'I actually really like this one.') Then it was December and the whirl of tinsel-spangled Christmas parties swept them both up, and they'd only managed to see each other a couple more times amidst the mayhem. And now she was pregnant.

Her hands crept around to her belly and rested there gently. Yesterday he'd texted her details of a great beach for kite-surfing that he'd found near Southend, if she fancied it. *Maybe we could make a weekend of it?* She was starting to think Max might be undergoing something of a midlife crisis, with all these adrenalin dates he kept suggesting, but hell, she was game for anything. Kite-surfing sounded a laugh, even if it was January and freezing cold. He'd probably look sexy in a wetsuit, too . . .

But then she had remembered the two blue lines on the stick, and wondered if pregnant women were still meant to do things like kite-surfing, and the next minute she was engulfed in doubt. What was she going to *do*? Did she even *want* a baby? How would she manage in this poxy one-bedroom Walthamstow flat? It was a hopeless idea. Impossible.

All the decisions that lay ahead made her feel queasy. Or was that the hormones? Whichever, there was no escaping the fact that she would have to start sorting her life out soon, pinning down a few certainties like markers on a map. *This way. Then this way. And don't look back.*

❖

Being pregnant was like having the volume whacked up on all your senses, Saffron thought the next day as she went back to work. Noises around her — roadworks, traffic, other people's voices — seemed amplified to irritating, headache-inducing levels. Smells assaulted her with a new, horrific violence: perfume and aftershave on the Tube, sickly vanilla scents pumped out from the doughnut shop, diesel fumes and cigarette smoke — disgusting, all of them. Flavours tasted weirdly different, too, all of a sudden. Coffee, for instance, her own personal rocket-fuel, now repulsed her with its bitterness, her mouth shrivelling and crimping in disgust whenever she tried to drink it. How had she ever been able to stomach the stuff?

Once in the office (ravenous already — how would she survive the morning without constant snacking?), Saffron opened her emails to an avalanche of 'Dry January' and 'Wonder Diet' spam. Oh, the irony.

'Saffron! There you are!' came a plummy voice. 'I was starting to think you were avoiding my calls.'

Charlotte Hargreaves was the director of Phoenix PR; a large, commanding woman with big hair and stentorian tones, whose entire existence revolved around the agency and her role at its epicentre. She was also the sort of boss who had no qualms about taking all the credit for any success achieved by the agency, whether she'd had a hand in it or not. Saffron had often fantasized about marching out dramatically — 'I quit!' — and setting up her own rival agency, which would win awards and make Charlotte look a complete amateur. The sooner she plucked up the courage, the better.

Yeah, but hello? What about the baby? Maternity leave? Think about it! snapped a voice in her head.

Oh, yeah. The baby. She'd overlooked that tincy-wincy factor.

'Happy New Year,' she said, putting on her dazzling PR executive smile as Charlotte approached.

'What? Oh. Yes. Anyway, I don't know if you've seen the email yet, but the Yummy Mummy baby-food account is now yours. They want a full PR strategy plus visuals by mid-month, so I said that would be fine. I trust you'll be able to manage it?'

Saffron blinked, trying to process this deluge of information. 'Um . . . yes?' she said tentatively, then frowned. 'I thought Kate was handling the Yummy Mummy thing?' *Kate* would be a good person to talk to about the baby, she realized just then, but when she glanced around she noticed that Kate's desk was empty, and the photos of her flame-haired, gap-toothed kids had vanished.

'We had to let her go,' Charlotte said briskly. 'Too much time off for school consultations and doctors, and whatnot.'

What? Was this some kind of joke? Saffron's insides clenched with the injustice. Admittedly Kate had been in and out of hospital with her accident-prone younger son, who seemed to be on a quest to break every bone in his body, but she'd always managed to get her work done on time – and consistently good it had been, too. 'Oh,' she said faintly after a moment, fury for her friend mingling with fear at the thought of Charlotte finding out she was pregnant. Just like Kate, she'd be pushed out of the agency in a heartbeat. *We had to let her go. Too much time off for midwife consultations and childbirth, and whatnot.*

'So you've got the brief and the contact details. Joseph's handling the artwork, so you two can liaise on progress. I'll leave it in your capable hands.'

As soon as Charlotte had marched back to her office, Saffron furtively fired off an email to her friend:

From: Saffron@PhoenixPR
To: KateMcKay@jetmail
Subject: WTF?!

Hi Kate
Just heard the news – so gutted for you. What happened? Are you okay?
S x

Then her phone rang. 'Phoenix PR?'

'Hey, Saff, it's Max. Happy New Year!'

She swallowed. 'Hi, Max, same to you.' *I'm carrying your baby, by the way, Max. Whoops! Contraception-fail!* 'Um . . . ' She pulled herself together. *Act normal.* 'Good Christmas?'

'Great, thanks. The usual complicated children-passing, but we muddled through. How about you?'

Children-passing? She wrinkled her nose. He made them sound as if they were an inconvenience to be managed. If she had his baby, would he speak about it in such careless terms? He'd better bloody not. 'Er, yeah, good,' she replied after a moment. 'Quiet, really. My parents and one of my sisters, and her husband. Five go mad in Essex, you know.'

He laughed. He had a nice laugh, Max – a proper, genuine one. You heard a whole orchestra of fake versions in PR. 'Excellent.' He paused. 'Listen, I've been trying to get hold of you all week,' he said. 'Are we all right?'

We. He thought there was a 'we'. Well, there was, but it included an extra person these days. 'Um . . . ' she said, not sure how to respond. 'Yes, sorry – I saw you'd tried ringing. I was away for New Year, didn't have much of a signal.'

That was all true at least.

'Okay.' He sounded hesitant now. 'So . . . do you want to do something soon? Did you get that kite-surfing link I sent? I thought it might be a laugh.'

She bit her lip. Oh Max. It would have been a laugh a fortnight ago. They would have had a blast. If it wasn't for those two wretched blue lines, she'd be floating up like a bunch of shiny helium balloons right now, delighted that he wanted to 'make a weekend of it', already googling gorgeous boutique places to stay. 'I . . . ' she said awkwardly. *Help.* 'I'm pretty busy actually,' she blurted out. 'I've just been given this new account, you see, so my diary's hideous for the next few weeks.'

Also true. Her diary was crazy! Although she did actually have two free weekends this month, either of which she'd have happily spent with him, sleek in wetsuits, laughing and shrieking on a kite-surf in the North Sea. But how could she? How could she carry on without telling him? This way was for the best, really. It was.

'Oh,' he said, and the laughter fell away from his voice. Now he sounded more clipped, as if he was speaking to a colleague he didn't know very well. 'I see.'

You don't, she thought miserably. *You have no idea.* She fiddled with two linked paper clips, twisting the wires round and round, trying and failing to think of something to say.

'Well, in that case, I'll leave the ball in your court,' he said, brisk and businesslike after a short silence. 'You've got my number, so . . . Yeah.'

'Okay,' she said, dying a little inside. One sharp end of a paper clip scraped her skin and she winced. *Sorry,* she felt like blurting out. *Sorry! If you knew, Max, you'd understand why I'm doing this. You'd agree that I was doing the right thing!*

'See you then, Saffron,' he said.

'See you then, Max,' she echoed, replacing the phone. Well, that hadn't gone very well. She wished she could rewind the last few minutes, let him down more gently. Actually, scrub that: she'd rewind even further, given half a chance, right back to the start of December. Then she'd make sure the condoms were to hand every single time, before it was too late. Before this situation ever had the chance to unfold.

But it had unfolded, of course, and she'd clumsily made a mess of that last conversation. And now he'd be across town, staring at his phone and wondering how he could have got it so wrong about Saffron Flint. *What's up with* her? he'd be thinking, perplexed. *I thought I was onto something. I thought we liked each other!*

She imagined one of his colleagues glancing across the office and noticing Max's handsome features creased with a frown. *You okay there, Max?*

Women, Max would say, shaking his head, still confused. Maybe he'd start to feel exasperated, rolling his eyes in a long-suffering manner. *Women!*

He was better off without her. He was. And now here came Charlotte, and she needed to stop fiddling with paper clips and look busy.

'Saffron? Time for a quick word? I've been going through the accounts, and I've got another one that's right up your street . . .'

Chapter Seven

January was a great time for new starts, Gemma always thought. You could draw a veil over the excesses of Christmas and start with a nice clean slate and a lovely long list of good intentions. Oh, she would be a saint this year, she really would. She'd be kind and patient, her house would be transformed, she'd do tons of voluntary work and be everyone's best friend, not to mention the most devoted and wondrous wife, mother and daughter that ever lived.

She hadn't got very far with her plans for a new job yet, though. It had been so long since she'd worked anywhere, other than her own kitchen and ironing board, that she couldn't help feeling apprehensive at the prospect. After an extended maternity leave with Will, she'd gone back to work at Pop, the fashion label, but it hadn't been easy. Returning as a part-timer, she found herself falling down the hierarchy and shunted sideways, away from the really funky front-page-of-the-catalogue end of the brand, into the less-glamorous ranges: swimwear for a while, and then knitwear, neither of which she felt particularly passionate about. Plus Will took a while to settle into nursery, and then came down with bronchiolitis the first winter and was quite poorly; and then, whenever she did actually make it into the office, she'd often find herself unable to think of anything but his sad little *You're-leaving-me?* face as she'd said goodbye.

Even though she loved working with clothes, she could never quite lose the breathless pain of being away from her child, the tension she felt whenever the train juddered to a halt halfway home and she started to panic that she'd be late to pick him up. Mercifully Spencer had realized just how anxious the juggling act was making her and stepped in, telling her he was happy for her to stay at home and look after the children if that was what she wanted. Her boss was understanding and said she'd keep Gemma on file as a freelance, but the work had dried up pretty quickly. So that was that.

Gemma hadn't really minded back then, especially as her daughter Darcey came along soon afterwards and she threw all her energies into making both children happy. But now that Darcey was nine and Will thirteen, motherhood no longer had the same manic urgency of the early years. The children showered and dressed themselves, they could make their own breakfast, they could work half the household gadgets a million times better than she could . . . they needed her less, basically. And she was starting to feel — well, not *redundant* exactly, she thought, tossing some Playmobil people and a naked, pouting Barbie into a cardboard box, but maybe a little bit worthless. And just the tiniest bit bored, if that didn't make her sound too ungrateful. *She's just a mum*, she heard Darcey say again in that dismissive voice and felt herself cringe.

It was all right for Spencer, with his job on the building site. He had a whole other world outside the home – a world of bacon sarnies and banter, nipping to the bookies in his lunch hour and to the pub on his way home. He'd come back covered in plaster dust and a muck sweat, glowing with the satisfaction of a hard day's work. Meanwhile, what had she done? Ambled round the supermarket and sorted piles of laundry, maybe had a coffee with some of the other mums. It didn't feel enough any more.

Her mobile rang just then. She was in the playroom, cross-legged on the floor, surrounded by half-clothed Sylvanian Family creatures who appeared to be having some kind of woodland orgy (maybe that was just her dirty mind), the dressing-up box from which a single Buzz Lightyear leg dangled (Will hadn't worn that costume since he was four years old!), board games and jigsaws, unfinished craft projects and half-built Lego spaceships. Ripe for an overhaul, she thought distractedly, reaching to answer her phone. She should have ditched half of it when they moved, but now was her chance. She could turn this room into a proper teenage den, with beanbags and maybe a little TV . . .

'Hello?' she said, imagining a pinball machine in one corner, a dartboard perhaps. No, not a dartboard. Too dangerous. Could they squeeze a pool table in here? Spencer would love that.

'Gem? It's Harry. Listen, there's been an accident. Are you sitting down?'

The virtual pool table vanished into the ether. 'An accident? What's happened?'

There was a sob in Harry's voice. A *sob*? 'It's Spencer. He . . . Someone fucked up with the scaffolding, Gem. He's fallen. It's pretty bad.'

All of a sudden it was hard to breathe. Her body froze rigid with the horror; her mind raced with terrible images of her husband plummeting through the sky. 'Is he dead?' she croaked.

'No, but he's unconscious. They've airlifted him to Addenbrooke's. I'm going to head over there now, shall I pick you up?'

Stupid thoughts pinballed into her head. She hadn't hugged him that morning. He liked to be up and out early, Spencer, and she'd still been in bed when he'd left. What if she never hugged him again?

'Gem? Shall I pick you up?'

She swallowed. Get a grip, Gemma. This was happening – her worst nightmare – and she had to deal with it. 'Yes,' she said hoarsely. 'Yes, please.'

*

The hospital was about an hour's drive usually, but it felt as if entire dreadful days passed before they reached the car park in torrential rain. Harry tried to make conversation – something about seeing Caitlin, the girl from the party – but Gemma couldn't concentrate. Apparently the scaffolding had collapsed on the first storey of the building they were working on, and Spencer had plunged to the concrete below, landing in a crumpled heap, out cold.

Gemma felt sick at the thought of him lying on the ground, unmoving and unresponsive, his beautiful face empty of any expression. He was the most unashamedly *alive* person she'd ever met. Once, a few months after they'd started seeing each other, they'd been walking into a rosemary-scented pub garden one warm Sunday afternoon when he suddenly smiled at her, eyes brilliant, then put his arms in the air and shouted, 'God, I love this woman!' People had turned and smiled at his exuberance. Someone had even cheered.

Please let him have come round by now, she thought as they hurried to the Accident and Emergency centre. *Please let us get there, and for him to be sitting up in bed with a cup of tea, joking with the doctors.*

He wasn't sitting up in bed, though. He hadn't even come round. He was lying flat, strapped into a neck-and-back brace so that he couldn't move, having just returned from a CT scan. He had broken his ankle quite badly and fractured three vertebrae, the softly spoken Indian doctor told them. They weren't yet certain how his spinal cord would be affected.

Gemma burst into tears of shocked disbelief. She'd watched enough hospital-based TV shows to know that spinal injuries could be devastating. 'You mean he might not walk again?' she asked, choking on the words. Oh my goodness. Spencer in a wheelchair, his legs useless? Football-mad Spencer never running or kicking a ball for the rest of his life?

'We can't rule anything out yet, I'm afraid,' the doctor said gently. She put a hand on Gemma's arm, and Gemma stared at her polished red nails in a daze. 'We're going to do an MRI scan, which should give us a clearer indication of any damage. The good news is that we can't see any bleeding on the brain, although we won't be able to make a full assessment of his head injury until Mr Bailey comes round.'

Head injury. Bleeding on the brain. That terrifying-looking brace clamping him in position. The possibility of him being paralysed, an invalid for the rest of his life. Gemma's head swam with one terrible thought after another. He'd never walk Darcey up the aisle, if she got married. He wouldn't be able to work. He'd no longer be able to throw himself into swimming pools on holiday, drenching them all deliberately with one of his 'bombs'. He'd never dance with her again . . .

She passed a hand through her hair, trying to breathe naturally. 'I need to sort someone out to pick up the kids,' she said, imagining the scared looks on their faces when they saw their strong, capable daddy broken like this. Dear God, she couldn't bear it. 'I need to . . . ' She swayed on her feet, suddenly dizzy, and Harry clutched her just in time.

'You okay? Are you feeling faint? Sit down, Gem,' he ordered, guiding her to a plastic chair. 'Do you want a tea or something?'

A cup of tea. Like that would make any difference. What she wanted was for Spencer to open his eyes and grin at her, to sit up and stretch his arms over his head as if he'd just woken from a nap. 'I'm fine,' she said weakly, reaching out to take Spencer's hand. His fingers felt warm in hers; if she shut her eyes, she could imagine everything was perfectly normal. Almost.

'We'll let you know more, once we've done the MRI,' the doctor said kindly. 'Ah, here's our porter now. Thanks, Mick.'

And away they wheeled him, leaving Gemma and Harry alone and staring at one another. 'Oh, Harry,' she said, burying her face in her hands. 'I'm really frightened. I'm so, so frightened. I just want him back.'

'I know,' Harry said wretchedly, staring after the porter in a daze. 'Me too.'

Cometh the hour, cometh the mums. After one single tearful call to her friend Eliza, Gemma had countless texts from other mothers from the school, offering help, sleepovers, dinners, sympathy and wine. *OMG, just heard, hon. Is he going to be ok?* they wrote. *What's the latest?*

Gemma didn't know how to reply. The words were too huge to condense into a mere text. *Oh, possibly paralysed, head injury, you know . . .* No. She stuffed her phone back in her handbag, feeling a wild sort of hysteria building. She hated herself for not hugging him that morning. She hadn't even said goodbye! She'd been wearing her tartan flannel pyjamas, the ones Spencer always groaned at and called the Passion Killers, and she'd rolled over in bed and put the pillow over her head to muffle the sound of his singing. What kind of wife did that? Why hadn't she got out of bed too and kissed him goodbye before he left?

It wasn't until later that afternoon when the rain ceased for the first time all day that Spencer finally blinked, then opened his eyes. Thank God. 'What . . . the . . . fuck . . . ?' he croaked, bewildered.

Trapped in the back-and-neck brace, his head was fixed so that he was staring up at the ceiling, and Gemma leapt to her feet, leaning over him. 'You're in hospital, sweetheart,' she said, her voice cracking on the words. 'You had a fall at work.'

His eyelids fluttered again, those sooty lashes sweeping his pale skin. 'Did I?'

'Hello, mate.' Harry stood up, too. 'We were doing the Melvilles' development, remember? The scaffolding gave way and you fell.'

'Jesus Christ,' he groaned. 'My head's killing me.'

'I'll get the doctor,' Harry said, vanishing.

Spencer was still staring at Gemma as if he had never seen her before in his life. She felt a lurch of panic. 'It's me, Gemma. Can you remember who I am?'

He shut his eyes. 'Gemma,' he repeated, slurring the syllables. 'Gemma?'

'Yes, that's me, Gemma. Your wife,' she said desperately, but he was already gone, slipping back into oblivion. 'I'm your wife, Spencer, do you remember?'

81

Chapter Eight

Maybe Caitlin had been kidding herself, but after the road trip with Harry she'd half-expected him to get in touch. Had it been a figment of her imagination that he'd flirted with her? All those questions he'd asked, the growing feeling of intimacy as they swapped confessions in the One-Direction-stickered cab of his van, the way he'd even (jokingly) offered to kill Flynn, as if he was allying himself with Team Caitlin . . . When they said goodbye and she thanked him for all his help, there was a momentary hesitation when she was convinced, for a split-second, that he was about to ask her out for a drink, or even sweep her up in his arms. Instead he just leaned in, gave her a peck on the cheek and said he'd see her around. She'd drifted back inside, her fingers rising to touch her skin where it had been grazed by his lips, wishing she'd had the nerve to grab hold of him and put her mouth to his for a proper kiss.

Perhaps she'd been plain wrong about any chemistry, deluding herself that she had felt the vibes. For all she knew,

Harry was like that with everyone; one of those charming, easy-going types who slipped through the world with ease, a Pied Piper of women, attracting jostling, flattered hordes in his wake. All those proposals and almost-marriages, remember — a woman in every port, by the sound of it.

She'd probably had a lucky escape, all things considered. He might even already be back with the woman who'd trampled his Stetson all the way to hat-heaven. Anyway, she reminded herself, lying in bed, staring up at the ceiling, it wasn't as if she was in remotely the right place to start a new relationship. Hello? Rebound klaxon!

Whatever. It was all academic, seeing as she hadn't heard a thing from him since that day, let alone glimpsed him around the village. The only evidence that they'd been to Cambridge at all was the pile of boxes she'd dumped upstairs, yet to be unpacked, and the bill Flynn had sent her to cover the cost of cleaning his precious canvas, along with a furious note, ranting about her immature act of vandalism:

You stupid bitch, you are MENTAL. Seriously, you have major problems. Do you think anyone else is going to want you? You're not even attractive. You're a fucking JOKE.

She wished she hadn't read it now, but the words were burned into her subconscious. If he thought for a minute he was getting any money off her, though, he was lost in Dreamland. Let's hope he stayed there.

She put her head under the duvet and sniffed, wrinkling her nose. Getting a bit whiffy, Cait. Personal hygiene had fallen by the wayside since she'd been back in Larkmead. There was a definite monobrow taking shape between her eyebrows, not to mention the shadowy line above her top lip. A crop of small red spots had appeared around her mouth, she had a coldsore blistering on her lower lip and there was a greasy sheen on her forehead. Her hair had completely grown out of its bob and was bushy and kicking out around the ends, while her fringe was wonky where she'd tried to cut it with some nail scissors two weeks ago. As for her legs, they positively bristled with new growth. Spring has come to the forest! Well, to her hairy calves anyway.

Her hand wandered down to her belly and squidged it. Caitlin had always been tall enough that she could eat whatever she liked and didn't have to worry about putting on weight, but that was before she spent days lying on the sofa watching endless daytime TV and stopped leaving the house. There was a definite creeping roundness to her tummy and hips, and a new tightness to her jeans. Much more of this lifestyle and she'd become a hairy, wobbling beast, half-ape, half-blob. Attractive — said nobody, ever. If she didn't pull herself together, make an effort and re-enter the human race soon, she'd end up being carted off to a freak show.

Her eyes drifted around the room, as if seeing the place for the first time. It wasn't only her that needed a spruce up and polish; the cottage did, too. There was dust on the mirror; an open suitcase containing a jumble of clothes; cold, mouldy cups of tea and coffee along the chest of drawers and a row of tights drying on the radiator, toes dangling, like the ghosts of a cancan girl troupe.

Downstairs was even worse. She knew without stirring that there was an embarrassing number of congealing, sticky Chinese takeaway boxes silting up on the draining board ('Ah, Miss Caitlin, how are you today?' the woman at Golden Dragon had taken to saying. 'Chicken chow mein and prawn sesame toast, yes?') Something in the bin smelled as if it was in its death-throes and there was a pool of strange green liquid collecting at the bottom of the fridge. If Jane was still alive, she'd have a fit at the state Caitlin had let the place get into.

She'd never even meant to stay in Larkmead this long. Once it was clear that she and Flynn were no more, she'd planned to tidy up White Gables and sell it, then move some-where completely new and start over. The weeks were passing by, though, and she'd achieved very little so far.

Sorry, Mum. I'll get it sorted. I really will. Any day now.

First, though, she'd just shut her eyes and go back to sleep. Well, why not? She was unemployed, she was single, and it was at least an hour before *This Morning* with Phil and Holly was due to begin. She rolled over, pulling the musty-smelling duvet over her head, and wriggled into a more comfortable position. You couldn't rush these things, after all.

Later on she padded downstairs, made a coffee, turned on the TV and arranged herself on the sofa, tucking her dressing gown around her bare feet to keep them warm. Her phone chose that moment to ping with a new email and she reached out a hand for it automatically. Probably just spam, or another grumpy message from Flynn, but she might as well have a look, while the ads were on.

From: Saffron@PhoenixPR
To: CaitlinF@fridaymail
Subject: Web design

Dear Caitlin,

I don't know if you remember, but we met at the New Year's Eve party in Suffolk – I was the one from the holiday cottage next door who gatecrashed!

I'm just emailing because you mentioned you were looking for web-design work, and one of my clients has asked me to source a designer who can overhaul her website. Might you be interested? The client in question is a young singer who's launching her debut album in the spring.

Give me a ring if you'd like further information. The fee we
can offer is . . .

There followed a figure so exorbitant that Caitlin had to
shut her eyes for a moment, then look again, in case she'd
imagined it. No, she hadn't.

Wowzers. Was this seriously the going rate in the music
industry? No wonder they all looked so pleased with themselves, if they could waft the dosh around with such ease. She
read the email again, feeling a prickle of interest. It had been
ages since she'd done anything creative or constructive and,
with this kind of budget, she could pull together something
really spectacular.

If she could be bothered, that was. If she could actually
get off her ever-increasing bum, turn the telly off and
knuckle down to some proper work.

She sat up a little straighter and muted the celebrity chef
who was about to make a superfood-smoothie, for all of the
January dieters. Then she grabbed her phone and dialled
before she could change her mind. What the hell. Chances
like this didn't come along every day.

'Saffron? Hi, it's Caitlin Fraser here, from Larkmead . . . .
Hi! Yes, thanks so much, I'd love to hear more about the
job . . .'

Chapter Nine

'She did what? She gave you Bunty? Oh, man. She really *does* hate you.'

Saffron nodded, feeling weary and long-suffering. 'Yep. That was my reaction, too.'

It was a Thursday evening and she was in a Dean Street bar along with hordes of sharply dressed media types and Kate, her former colleague. Saffron had suggested a drink to see how Kate was faring following her redundancy, but also, if she was honest, because she was desperate for a good old bitch about her latest client.

Bunty Halsom was a very loud forty-something journalist and minor celebrity, who dashed off endless tabloid articles, usually about what a disgrace young people were these days and why a woman's place was in the home, even though she preferred to hang out in the Groucho and wouldn't have a clue how to work a Hoover, let alone cook a meal from scratch. She'd appeared on a few reality-TV programmes in the past year where she'd both shocked and transfixed the nation, first by appearing to have a mental breakdown on *Celebrity Big Brother*, then by launching herself at a fringe politician on the ill-fated *All-Stars Nightclub* fly-on-the-wall documentary. Her subtle chat-up line – 'Bunty likes a big one' – had gone viral, appearing in hashtags and gossip columns, and emblazoned on market-stall T-shirts across the land.

Brazen, domineering and incredibly needy, Bunty had been Kate's worst nightmare of a client. But now, as of this morning, she was Saffron's.

'Oh God. Well, you have my sympathy. My complete and utter sympathy. Leaving Phoenix was awful but, even as Charlotte was ditching me, I thought "No more Bunty" and suddenly felt a whole lot better. A solid silver lining, if ever there was one.'

Saffron managed a small smile. She didn't need reminding how dreadful Bunty was. She'd worked with Kate long enough to recognize the rictus smile on her friend's face whenever Bunty called; the tired droop of her shoulders, the barely contained impatience in her voice when Bunty was being particularly difficult. 'Any advice you can offer? Coping strategies? The number of a good therapist?'

'Don't let yourself be railroaded,' Kate said. 'Stand up to her, otherwise she won't give you any respect. And lay down strict parameters – no phone calls after seven in the evening, or at weekends. Refuse point-blank if she starts trying to get you to pick up dry-cleaning and organize dinner parties for her. Be prepared to say no, and stick to your guns.' She swigged back a mouthful of beer. 'It's like dealing with a toddler, really. Or a naughty dog. You've got to show her who's boss – while maintaining the illusion that you think she's absolutely wonderful, of course.'

Saffron had no experience with dogs or toddlers. She'd grown up in a cat-loving family, and had no nieces or nephews on whom to practise being strict. Her heart sank. Charlotte, her boss, had spun this as a new opportunity for Saffron, a chance to push on up to a higher level of PR, but working for Bunty was sounding more like a punishment by the second.

Noticing her silence, Kate rummaged in her bag for a square red purse. 'You need a drink,' she announced, getting to her feet. 'A strong one. What can I get you? Let's start the Bunty-proofing with alcohol. It helps, trust me.'

Oh, a drink. That would be lovely. A bottle of beer like Kate's, misted with cold. A massive bugger-it cocktail with a paper umbrella and jaunty dangling cherries. A knockout vodka martini just to take the edge off her day. 'Um . . . a lime and soda, please,' she said, pushing the temptations forcefully from her mind.

Kate's eyes widened. Saffron was never usually one to refuse booze. 'On the wagon, eh?' she asked. 'Dry January?'

'Yeah,' Saffron said, then hesitated. 'Actually, no. I'm pregnant.'

The words were out before she could stop them and hung in the air. Kate sat back down. 'God,' she said. 'Wow. Wasn't expecting that.'

'Nor me,' said Saffron.

'Right.' They exchanged a look. 'So . . . how are you feeling? Are you okay?'

How was she feeling? Well, not exactly radiant, put it that way. Saffron was not enjoying being pregnant very much at all, in fact. The tiredness was like being beaten down by a sledgehammer. She woke up every morning and had to leap out of bed immediately in order to hang her head over the toilet and puke. As for her rampaging hormones, they seemed to have cranked up her emotions to 'lunatic' level. She'd wept the other day at the sight of an elderly Asian couple holding hands at the bus stop.

'Knackered,' she said, 'and confused. And I keep bursting into tears over the slightest thing. I cried at an Andrex advert yesterday. It's like there's no Off switch any more.'

Kate put a hand on her arm. 'Let me get you that lime and soda,' she said. 'I'll be right back. I take it you haven't told Charlotte yet, by the way?'

Saffron shook her head.

'Good,' said Kate. 'Keep it that way.'

Saffron leaned back against her uncomfortable, trendy plastic chair while Kate weaved through the crowd of designer-clad twenty-somethings en route to the bar. It was weird, releasing her big secret after weeks of secrecy. 'I'm pregnant,' she said again under her breath. She'd half-expected the sky to fall in, but the world was still turning.

'Here you are,' Kate said, putting the drinks on the table and sitting down again. 'So, what are you going to do? I can't tell from your face whether you're happy or sad, or plain old freaked out.'

'I'm still at the freaked-out stage,' Saffron confessed. 'I mean, me and Max, we were barely even a couple. I'd only been out with him a few times before this happened.'

'But you liked him, didn't you? I remember all those flirty phone calls. What does he say about this?'

'Um . . . '

Kate's forehead puckered. 'You haven't told him?'

Saffron lowered her eyes and sipped her drink. God, lime and soda really was the most boring, joyless drink in the world. 'I'm not sure how to,' she admitted eventually. 'Maybe it's kinder not to tell him anything at all. I mean, he's got two kids already, and I hardly know him. I don't want him to feel tied to me in any way, or responsible, if he's not interested.'

'Yeah, but he is responsible, technically,' Kate pointed out. 'I guess it depends on whether or not you're planning to keep the baby. Tell me to mind my own business, obviously, but . . . well. Are you?'

The biggest question of all. Answering it, when she knew that Kate had three beloved children of her own, felt like tiptoeing through a minefield. For all she knew, Kate might strongly disapprove of abortions or giving babies away to be adopted. Saffron had always vaguely disapproved herself, until she'd found herself in this predicament and realized just how many shades of grey there could be. 'I didn't have myself down for a mum,' she replied slowly. 'I've never even held a baby before, let alone looked after one myself.' She swallowed. 'Sometimes I think it would be easier just to . . . ' she waved a hand across her belly, avoiding Kate's eye, ' . . . to make it go away.' Kate nodded sympathetically and Saffron rushed on. 'I just can't imagine myself with a baby, that's all. Pushing a pram. Singing nursery rhymes. Changing nappies.' She bit her lip. 'But then again, I'm thirty-eight now. Ovaries shrivelling by the minute. This could be my last chance.'

The mood had turned sombre and Saffron was starting to wish she had left this particular can of worms unopened.

'Anyway,' she said quickly. 'How are you? What have you been up to, work-wise?'

As Kate talked about making a go of a new freelance career from her dining-room table, Saffron found herself only half-listening. Meanwhile her head teemed with anxious thoughts about money and babies and Max. Nine weeks into the pregnancy now, according to the website calculator she'd looked at that morning. The baby was the size of a grape.

Time was running out. The grape's life hung in the balance. She had to make a decision soon. *And I will*, she thought fiercely, as Kate went on about social media and agency work. *I have to. Just . . . not today.*

It was raining hard as Saffron left the bar and walked towards Oxford Circus to get the Tube home, shoulders hunched under her thin coat. Puddles swelled on broken paving slabs, rainwater gushed and swirled along the gutters, and the bus wheels sent up fountains of dirty spray.

Ugh. January, you suck.

Once at the station, she hurried down the steps towards the warmth of the Underground, longing to be home. But the concrete steps were wet and slippery and all of a sudden she lost her footing and fell in a terrifying rush, landing heavily at the bottom of the stairwell. Ow. *Ow.*

People hurried past, shoes tapping urgently. Some actually stepped right over her, as if she wasn't there. She tried to manoeuvre herself gingerly upright, but felt a sharp pain in her abdomen, followed by a pulling sensation low down. The baby. The grape.

'Are you okay, dear?' An elderly lady bent over her, reaching out a hand. 'Can I help you up?'

Tears pricked Saffron's eyes. The indignity, the pain, the shock . . . and now the kindness of a stranger. It was all too much. 'Thank you,' she said, grabbing the handrail with one hand and taking the old lady's blue-gloved hand in her other.

She heaved herself up, bruised from the hard floor. 'Thank you very much.'

'Are you all right? Anything hurt?' The lady was still holding onto her and put her other hand on Saffron's back to steady her. 'There's a nice young man over there, one of the staff. Shall I get him to help you to the train?'

That low, digging sensation was still there at the very base of her abdomen, and Saffron put a hand to it instinctively. Oh, little grape, are you all right? Her vision started to flicker in and out, as if she was going to faint. 'I think I'm going to . . .' she murmured, lolling forwards like a puppet on loose strings. 'I feel a bit dizzy.'

'Okay, duckie, let's sit you down again then. Hold on to me. Excuse me! Young man! This girl needs some assistance, please!'

Saffron was dimly aware of footsteps approaching, then strong hands clasping her sides and helping to lower her back to the ground. Everything blurred before her eyes as if she was teetering on the edge of consciousness, and she struggled to pull herself back into the situation. A man with a 'Transport for London' ID round his neck and concerned brown eyes crouched in front of her. 'Are you okay? Do you want me to get you some water?'

'I'm pregnant,' she whimpered, aware of a sickening wetness between her legs. Blood, she was sure. She must be losing the baby. Tears rolled down her cheeks as she blurted out her secret for the second time that evening. 'I'm pregnant!'

Saffron had never felt so scared in her entire life as when she was waiting in the A&E department of the hospital all alone. Her spine was tender from where she'd jarred it, landing with such a thump on the concrete; her head ached, where she must have bashed it against the wall; and worst of all, a quick visit to the loo had proved that yes, she was bleeding. The vivid splash of scarlet in her knickers felt like an accusation from her own body, as if the grape was making a stand. *Well, if you can't even be bothered to decide whether or not you want me, you can whistle, if you think I'm going to stick around.*

'Saffron Flint?'

A friendly-faced nurse with a blonde ponytail scanned the waiting area. Her eyes fell on Saffron, hauling herself up from the plastic seat with exaggerated care, and she rushed over to help. 'Easy there. Can you walk?'

'I can walk, I'm just . . . ' She couldn't quite bring herself to say the words out loud initially. 'I'm worried I'm losing my baby,' she said, a sob in her throat.

'Let's get you in here,' the nurse said, guiding her into a cubicle and pulling the curtain shut. 'Lie down on the bed, that's it, and make yourself comfortable. Is anyone with you? Can I call someone for you?'

Saffron shook her head, wishing her sister Zoe wasn't ten

thousand miles away in Perth, wishing that Max was there to hold her hand. 'I'm on my own.' It had never felt more true.

Once she'd described what had happened, the nurse asked her to pull down her trousers a little way, then produced what looked like a small microphone connected to a speaker. 'I'm just going to listen for a heartbeat,' she said, 'but don't be alarmed if we don't hear anything, as you're still early along in the pregnancy. Sometimes the heartbeat can't be detected until later on, but let's just see.'

She pressed the end of the microphone thing quite hard against Saffron's belly, just above the line of her knickers. The speaker made a crackling sound, and then a faint swishing was audible, an underwater sort of noise. No heartbeat, though. Oh God. Saffron shut her eyes, not wanting to see pity or sorrow in the nurse's eyes. She didn't think she could bear it.

The nurse moved the microphone to a different position. Again came the crackling and then the watery ssshh-shhh sound. Still no heartbeat. But then . . .

Saffron breathed in sharply as she heard it. A faint but distinct rhythmic beating, fast as a galloping horse. Ba-boom, ba-boom, ba-boom.

She opened her eyes. 'Is that the baby?' she asked, filling with a sudden, unexpected euphoria. *Little grape! You're still there!*

'Sounds like a baby to me,' the nurse said, smiling back at her. 'We'll give you an ultrasound too, just to make sure everything looks okay, and maybe get you to stay in for tonight, to keep an eye on the bleeding, and that bumped head.'

Saffron wanted to hug her with relief. The baby's heart was beating. The grape was alive! It was only then that she realized just how frightened she'd been, how desperately she'd wanted to hear that heartbeat. 'Thank you,' she managed to say, leaning back against the pillows. The galloping sound was still ringing in her ears as the nurse bustled away. 'Thank you,' she said again, this time in a whisper meant only for the grape.

The ultrasound was amazing. It took her breath away. Seeing that tiny kidney-bean-shaped body in grainy black-and-white there on a screen and watching its small, jerky movements felt like magic, some kind of miracle. That little bean was her son or daughter. Her actual baby! She and Max had created this brand-new tiny person, and there it was, growing and changing, alive. Until that moment she'd never completely believed in the notion of this creature actually existing – having a smile, a personality, freckles maybe, or long legs and a cute bottom like Max. Now look at it: a bobbing seahorse, a real tiny baby. Her baby. *Hello you*, she thought. *Hello little baby*.

Her doubts fell away in a single second. Of course she could look after this baby. She *wanted* to look after the baby. Why had she even questioned herself?

The words of her New Year fortune-cookie came back to

her suddenly: *Have courage! Mistakes can become adventures,* and she felt tears in her eyes suddenly. Maybe there was some truth in that after all.

'Would you like me to print you off a picture?' the nurse asked.

'Yes, please,' Saffron said. A picture of her baby. Yes, she would like that very much.

Then her euphoria dimmed slightly as she realized something. Something really important. If she was going to keep the baby – and she was – then she really had to tell Max now. She absolutely had to. Didn't she?

Chapter Ten

It took two whole terrifying days before Spencer's concussion subsided and he began sounding more like himself. How Gemma sobbed with thankfulness when she heard him list every player in the top half of the Premier League to the doctor, correctly answer what year it was and name the Prime Minister (then add what a doofus Spencer thought he was. Yep. Her husband was back). This adroit performance, along with the brain scans, reassured the doctors that his head injuries were superficial and that there wouldn't be any long-lasting problems. So that was the first enormous milestone passed, and one they were all heartily glad to see the back of. Then came another week on tenterhooks as he underwent operations ('Bolting him back together,' the consultant had said cheerfully) and all sorts of tests. The good news was that the doctors thought there'd be no permanent physical damage, either. 'He's been very lucky,' the consultant told her.

Lucky? thought Gemma. Well, that was one way to describe it.

Spencer needed to be in hospital for two weeks overall, lying flat on his back and drugged up with morphine and co-codamol the whole time. She, meanwhile, functioned on automatic pilot, making sure the children went to school every day with clean clothes and full stomachs, but spending the rest of the time at her husband's bedside, holding his hand and doing her best to cheer him up. Her car became a kind of decompression chamber where she'd sit and sob after visits, the only place she could really let go, apart from late at night when Will and Darcey were asleep.

Anyway. He was home now, and even if life wasn't remotely normal again, she had to stay positive. It could have been worse. Much worse. As it was, he would have to wear an ankle-cast for eight weeks and a back-brace for four months while his fractured vertebrae healed. After all that, he'd still need lots of physio before he could even think about running or playing football. No driving for six weeks. Mild stretches and gentle walks were to be encouraged, but nothing more strenuous. 'What about sex?' Spencer asked anxiously. (Of course he did. The subject was upper-most in his mind about 99 per cent of his waking hours, by Gemma's reckoning.)

'It's probably best to give it a few weeks,' the doctor had replied. 'You're due to come back and see us in a fortnight, so we can discuss that then.'

'A *fortnight*?' Spencer had never looked so gutted in the

whole time Gemma had known him. In fact he had never been so miserable, full stop.

Once back at home, Gemma had fondly imagined tender nursing scenes where she mopped her husband's brow and fed him chicken soup, and he in turn gazed lovingly back at her, overcome with gratitude. But the reality was that he spent whole days slumped on the sofa, watching mindless television or locked in battle on the Xbox, glassy-eyed and unresponsive, resisting all Gemma's efforts at conversation, unless to complain that the sturdy neoprene back-brace was uncomfortable and bringing him out in a rash. He also complained that he was too thirsty, too hot, too bored, too much in pain – everything, in short. Mindful of the doctors' advice that gentle exercise would help speed the recovery of his back, Gemma tentatively suggested going for walks when the rain cleared, a stroll to The Partridge for lunch, even a spot of gardening. He turned his nose up at everything, though, barking that he wasn't feeble-minded, he wasn't a bloody pensioner yet, he didn't want to go for a fucking *walk*.

He was bad-tempered with the children as well, told them they were too noisy and snapped at them for the slightest thing. A few evenings after he came home Gemma and Darcey were sitting at the kitchen table together, making appliqué birds to sew onto one of Darcey's T-shirts, when they heard Spencer bollocking Will about something or other. 'Why doesn't Daddy *like* us any more?' Darcey whispered, anxiety shining in her large brown eyes.

The question pierced right through Gemma's heart. 'He does like you – he *loves* you, sweetheart – he's just fed up, that's all. He'll be better soon,' she soothed helplessly.

Thirteen-year-old Will was more succinct. 'Dad's being a total prick,' he growled later that evening when she went up to say goodnight. There was a wild fury about him that Gemma hadn't seen since he was a tantrum-throwing toddler, but she could detect hurt, too.

'Don't say that about your dad,' she replied with automatic loyalty. Upsetting his daughter and calling his son a loser might not be the sort of behaviour that would win Spencer any Dad-of-the-Year awards, but she knew he was like a wounded animal, lashing out at those he loved. 'Give him a bit of time,' she said. 'He'll be back to normal soon.'

That night in bed she hooked a leg over Spencer's and rolled closer to him, hoping that some wifely love might go a little way to soothe his tortured mood. Yet for the first time ever in the history of their relationship he shuffled away, muttering that he had a terrible headache. She lay there stunned, unable to believe her ears. Usually she only had to raise an eyebrow at her husband for him to leap on her with lusty enthusiasm. Through illness, hangovers, broken nights' sleep when the children were tiny, he'd never once turned her down.

'It *will* get better, Spence,' she whispered into the darkness, feeling desperately sorry for him. 'I promise it will.'

But no answer came. And the words seemed to echo around her head, as if mocking her naivety.

Gemma felt conflicted about leaving Spencer the following Monday to go and have lunch with her dad, as was their custom, but her mother-in-law came over instead and she knew he'd be waited on hand and foot in her absence. Besides, she was dying for a big old squeeze from her dad. The two of them had always been close, but even more so after Karen, Gemma's mum, flaked out and left the family for Carlos, the Ibizan waiter she'd fallen for on holiday, back when Gemma was eight.

Left to bring up his daughter and three sons single-handedly, Barry Pepper had valiantly done everything in his capacity to fill the space of two parents. He'd mastered the vagaries of the washing machine and the never-ending filthy sports kits; he'd shepherded them all to school on time, in just about the right uniform; he'd learned to cook from scratch; bought a bouncy Labrador, Sultan ('Sultan Pepper, it's a joke – do you get it?'); and even mastered an epic roast dinner by the time the first Christmas came round. Of course Gemma missed her mum – who drifted back to the UK peri-odically with an enviable tan and new tattoos – especially when it came to embarrassing things like needing a bra and her first period, but Barry coped admirably, roping in his sister Jan whenever womanly advice was required. As for boyfriends, when Gemma started dating and bringing boys back home, having three big brothers and an over-protective father in the police force didn't half sort the wheat from the chaff.

Her dad still lived in Stowmarket, where he'd been a policeman for years until a knee injury forced him into early retirement. Now he was his own boss, working as a doubleglazing fitter, and he and Gemma had got into the very nice habit of having lunch every Monday. They would go to the pub together – always the same table in The White Horse – and eat pie and chips, her with a Coke, him with half a bitter, and catch up on the world. Gemma would do anything for her dad, and vice versa.

It wasn't until she rang the doorbell of 93 Partington Road, the house she'd grown up in, that she was struck by the feeling that something looked different. After closer consideration, she realized that the living-room windows had been cleaned – a rare enough occurrence for this to be instantly noticeable – and the small front garden had been smartened up, too, so that the dustbin was now tidily in one corner rather than blocking the path. There was also an ornamental blue pot of winter pansies beside the door.

Gemma stared at those winter pansies suspiciously. Her dad's taste in plants was for wild and rangy specimens – big bristling shrubs, sweet peas romping up a bamboo wigwam, blowsy scented red roses with velvety petals. He was not a man who would ever have voluntarily bought a pot of prissy winter pansies, let alone display it proudly outside his own home. So where had it come from?

'Gems! Hello, my love, come in,' he said, answering the door just then. Barry Pepper was tubby and balding these days, more Danny DeVito than Ryan Gosling, but had the kindest face of anyone she knew, and gave the best hugs ever. As he put his arms around her now, she felt the comforting flannel of his shirt against her and breathed in his usual soapy scent, feeling a million times better already. God, she needed this.

Then she froze. A woman with streaky blonde hair and a sage-green fleece had appeared behind Barry and was giving Gemma a toothy smile. In an instant Gemma knew how the pansies by the door had materialized.

'Hello,' said the woman eagerly. 'I've been dying to meet you. I've heard *all* about you!'

'Hi,' said Gemma, extricating herself from her dad's embrace. Her first feeling was of dismay. *Not today,* she thought, trying not to sigh. *I just wanted him to myself today.*

'Ah.' Barry looked slightly shifty. 'My two favourite girls. Gemma, this is Judy. Judy, my daughter Gemma.'

Gemma tried to catch her dad's eye. *And Judy is . . . ?* But he seemed in a hurry to find his jacket all of a sudden, and turned away to unhook it from the peg. That was when

Gemma noticed the new coat rack up on the wall, and that someone had changed the pictures around. Instead of the faded old map of Stowmarket that had hung above the hall radiator for as long as she could remember, there was now a bland print of brightly coloured anemones in a clip-frame. As for the small black-and-white wedding photo of her parents that had stood on the small wooden table forever, that had vanished too, replaced by a brass bowl holding an arrangement of pine cones. What the hell . . . ?

Judy was advancing, hand outstretched, teeth exposed in another smile. 'Lovely to meet you after all this time.'

'You too,' Gemma replied reluctantly, shaking Judy's hand in a very British sort of way. Bang went her heart-to-heart with her dad then, she thought. She'd been looking forward to the chance to unburden some of her thoughts to him, have a moan, have a cry, even. Knowing Dad, he'd have her laughing by the time they'd scraped their plates clean; he'd be taking the mickey out of her parallel parking, or doing impressions of her brother Luke's new girlfriend. She hadn't counted on having to share him with fleece-wearing Judy.

She tried to get a grip. Her dad was a grown man, he didn't need to live his life around Gemma or ask her permission for a new girlfriend. After a deep breath, she plastered on her best bright smile. 'Are we ready then, Dad? Judy, are you joining us for lunch?'

Judy's face lit up. 'I'd love to,' she said, pulling on a big red Puffa jacket and stuffing her feet into Uggs. 'What a treat!'

It wasn't as if Barry had been single the entire time since Gemma's mum had abandoned them for her new life in the sun. When Gemma and her brothers left home, they had made a concerted effort to force their dad out on the dating scene, signing him up to a dating agency and scouring lonely-hearts columns on his behalf. There had been relationships with Marjorie (two months – dreary old drip), Aisling (bawdy and fun, but not settling-down material – three months) and one very nice lady called Venetia whom they all adored, right until she vanished with a load of Barry's valuables, never to be seen again.

And now there was Judy.

'So,' Gemma said conversationally, as she and her dad waited to order at the bar. Judy was already sitting down, flicking through a newspaper someone had left behind. 'Where did you two meet then?'

He beamed. 'I did her windows for her, first few weeks of January. We got chatting and . . . that was that.' He fiddled with a Carlsberg beer mat, spinning it between finger and thumb. 'The thing was, I was sitting at home on New Year's Eve, on me tod, and . . . '

Guilt stabbed Gemma. 'I did say you were welcome at ours, Dad!'

'I know you did, love. And I was very grateful. Didn't want to get in your way, though, did I? Didn't want to cramp anybody's style.' Spin, spin went the beer mat. 'But anyway, I made a resolution this year that I needed to start again, to find a new wife.'

'A new *wife?*' Gemma spluttered on the unexpected word.

'Well, not immediately, obviously. But I do miss having someone to come home to, you know. I don't want to be on my own any more. Judy's a nice woman — we've had a few evenings out together. I like her.'

'Hello, Barry. Hello there, Gemma. What can I get you both today?' asked Kev, the pub landlord just then. He raised a bushy eyebrow. 'And is that your lady friend I see over there in the corner again?' he asked, followed by a wink at Gemma.

'It certainly is,' Barry replied, an air of pride about him as he began reeling off their order.

Gemma tried to wrest back control of her feelings. Of course she was pleased for her dad that he'd met someone and seemed happy. And of course she didn't want him to be lonely, to see out the rest of his New Year's Eves alone. All the same . . . a wife, he'd said. A *wife*. It seemed such a monumental word to use. Her dad had this habit of falling for unsuitable women — her mum being a prime example. The last thing she wanted was for him to be hurt all over again. She sighed, wondering if her brothers knew about Judy yet. Had they already met her? Mind you, they were boys; they wouldn't feel the same way she did. Sam, Luke and David would just be glad that they were off the hook when it came to making sure Dad was okay all the time.

'Thanks, Kev,' her dad said at that moment, and Gemma realized there were three drinks now waiting on the bar.

'Lovely,' she said, grabbing some cutlery and her Coke. 'Thanks, Dad.'

'You're welcome, sweetheart. I've been looking forward to you and Judy meeting each other. I know you're going to get on like a house on fire.'

Chapter Eleven

Two months after her mum's death Caitlin had finally made the first few baby-steps towards dealing with her loss. She had stopped wallowing in bed for hours on end. She had accepted some work from Saffron, the friendly woman she'd met at New Year, and was actually loving the experience. She had booked a haircut, shaved her legs, done an enormous amount of washing, including all her bedding, and thrown every last takeaway menu into the paper-recycling box. She hoped the lady from Golden Dragon wasn't missing her phone calls too much.

Even more remarkably, she had actually begun sorting through Jane's belongings, one room at a time, in order to clear the cottage and get it on the local estate agent's books. How poignant the little details of a life seemed, when that person had gone. All those unopened bags of sugar Jane would never decant into the small crackle-glazed pot, to be used, two spoonfuls at a time, in her milky coffees. All those packets of twenty-denier natural-tan tights unworn in a drawer. The bags of dusty bulbs for the garden, the neatly labelled envelopes of seeds she'd never planted. Candles never lit. Letters never replied to. All those empty spaces at the end of last year's calendar that she hadn't lived quite long enough to fill.

Jane had been a kind mum, a solid pillar of a person that you could lean against, confident she would bear your weight. When Caitlin was much younger and had argued with Nichola, her best friend in primary school, her mum had emptied out the dressing-up box and ransacked her own wardrobe, suggesting they both put on beautiful outfits and have a princesses' picnic in the garden. Adorned in one of Jane's pink silk nighties, which hung around her ankles, beads, a flowery hat and some enormous red high heels, Caitlin had never felt more loved as her mum poured them Ribena from her best china teapot and they ate cucumber sandwiches on the old tartan travelling rug, 'just like real princesses'.

Another time, when Caitlin had split up with computer programmer Jeremy, she'd come back to Larkmead for the weekend, drooping with heartbreak, and Jane had known exactly what to do: drive them both out to Aldeburgh to sit on the beach with fish and chips. 'There's nothing like the sea to blow away your troubles,' she said, putting an arm around Caitlin, as they sat together on the shingle. 'Puts everything in perspective, doesn't it?'

And every year, on June 1st, Jane had always baked a

Victoria sponge with real strawberries, and she and Steve had drunk champagne and hugged each other, then Caitlin. 'Just because,' she said with a smile, when Caitlin had first asked her why this was. 'Sometimes it's good to celebrate your family, and think about how lucky you are.'

Her mum hadn't been keen on Flynn, though, she thought now, as she filled boxes with stacks of well-thumbed Mills & Boons and all manner of gory crime novels. 'Well, he's very good-looking, I'll give him that,' she'd said the first time they met, but Caitlin knew that 'good-looking' wasn't up there with 'kind', 'funny', 'loyal' or any of the other attributes Jane had valued in Steve. *So there's a silver lining to me dying, eh, chick?* she imagined Jane saying now. *You got to find out what a nasty piece of work that Flynn was, right? Look on the bright side! You could have been stuck with him for years yet, if I hadn't gone and popped my clogs!*

'You daft cow,' Caitlin said aloud to herself at the thought. She shoved the last few books into the box and got to her feet. Enough wading through the past for one day, she decided. She'd go out to the shop, stock up on bin bags, food and wine, and try again tomorrow.

Down in Larkmead's Spar, Caitlin was just paying for her groceries when she heard the distinct sound of someone crying over the cheesy background muzak. Pocketing her change, she hesitated for a moment, then ducked back into the dingy aisles of the shop to see who it was. There, in the

Household Miscellaneous section, leaning against a shelf of washing-powder boxes, was Gemma Bailey with tears streaming down her face.

Caitlin's mouth fell open in a silent O of shock at this very public show of emotion. Gemma was the last person she'd expected to see weeping over a Persil display. She had that perfect golden life – a big house, gorgeous husband and children. What did she have to cry about?

Caitlin cleared her throat, feeling self-conscious. 'Is everything . . . Are you okay?'

Stupid question. *Oh yeah, I'm great, that's why I'm sobbing over laundry powder. Have a medal, Captain Observant.*

Gemma's shoulders heaved and she wiped her eyes with her knuckles. 'No,' she said baldly. 'Not really.'

'Can I help? Do you want a cup of tea? Mum's place is just round the corner, if you want a chat?' A cup of tea, for heaven's sake. She was so bloody British. But what else could you offer a weeping woman in the Larkmead mini-mart? Gin? Valium?

Gemma took a long, shuddering breath. 'Would you mind? I can't face going home right now.'

Caitlin tried to hide her disquiet. Couldn't face going home? What on earth . . . ? 'Sure thing,' she said. 'Of course I don't mind.'

They left the shop and began walking up the hill. It was the first week of February now and the snowdrops and crocuses were shyly unfolding their petals, welcome splashes of light against the wet ground and grey skies.

'I suppose you've heard all the gossip,' Gemma said dully.

'No,' Caitlin said, feeling stupid and apologetic for not being more in tune with the village news. *They're splitting up*, she thought with a wrench of sympathy. Oh no. They had seemed so happy at New Year! The way Spencer had looked at Gemma, his eyes soft and glistening with love, it was something Caitlin could only dream of. 'What's happened?' she added cautiously.

'Oh. Well, Spencer's been in an accident. He's a bit mangled and battered, but home now at least. The doctors say he'll be fine again eventually, but . . . ' She sighed, huffing out a cloud of breath. 'I'm struggling, that's all. We're all finding it hard to adjust. He's so unhappy – nothing I do or say seems to make a blind bit of difference.'

They'd reached White Gables now and Caitlin opened the front door, hoping the cottage didn't smell too musty. She'd been sorting through all her mum's kitchen appliances recently and some of them – the elderly ice-cream maker, for instance, and the fondue set that looked as if it had come from the Ark – didn't seem to have been touched for years.

'Speaking as someone who used to be a nurse,' she said, 'it's often the case that the loved ones suffer almost as much as the patient, after a serious accident.' Aargh, the kitchen was messier than she'd thought; the table covered with ageing crockery, piles of cookery books and a heap of photos. 'Sorry about all of this, by the way. I'm having a bit of a clear-out.'

'No worries,' Gemma said, shrugging off her grey wool coat and sitting down at the table. 'I didn't know you were a nurse.'

Caitlin filled the kettle. 'I'm not any more. I went into it, really, to please my parents, but I bailed out about five years ago and started designing websites instead. Better money, no more having to remove strange implements jammed into orifices, and no one showering you in puke on a Saturday night.'

Gemma had picked up an old family photo and suddenly her face cleared. 'Wait – your mum was *Jane?* The midwife?'

'Yes, that's right. Why, did you . . . ?'

'She delivered my babies! Both of them. Oh, Caitlin, she was such a lovely woman, I'm so sorry.'

For some reason, whenever anyone said anything nice about her mum, it seemed to sap Caitlin's energy, as if she was forced to realize all over again just what she'd lost. 'Thanks,' she said, sagging against the worktop as she made them each a coffee.

'And she saved Darcey's life, you know. My little girl. She really did. I rang her when Darcey was three days old and didn't want to feed, and she leapt into action. Phoned the hospital to say we were on our way, and drove me there herself.'

'Really?' Caitlin loved imagining her mum swooping to the

rescue like that. A capable, practical woman, with her sleeves permanently rolled up, Jane had often returned from a night-shift in tired triumph. 'A lovely wee boy this morning, eight and a half pounds, beautiful home birth,' she might say, helping herself to a slice of toast from the rack, as Caitlin and Steve ate their breakfast. Or 'A bonny baby girl for the Finches, such a head of hair on her.' Her eyes would shine with the announcement of each infant, safely brought into the world. It was amazing that she hadn't had twenty babies of her own, she loved them so.

'Really,' Gemma said. 'We spent four days in hospital, with Darcey on a drip and me fearing the worst, but she was fine eventually, thanks to Jane's quick response. She was an absolute angel when I needed help.'

An absolute angel. Everyone had loved Jane. All those mothers she'd helped, the babies she'd saved, the way she'd taken lonely old Gwen next door out to bingo and Zumba every week. It was a shame she hadn't passed on the angelic gene to her awkward, antisocial daughter.

'What happened with Spencer, then?' she asked, changing the subject. 'Sounds like you've been through a bit of a trauma.'

'Fell from a first-floor building – shoddy scaffolding gave way,' Gemma said. You could tell she'd had to recount this a number of times; her voice had become brisk and emotion-free. 'Bust his ankle and a few vertebrae, massive bang on the head. Not great, basically.' Her mouth twisted unhappily.

From what Caitlin remembered of Spencer at school, he'd been boisterous and energetic, playing on the football team, bombing around on a BMX, the sort of person who'd leap off a wall for a dare. He was the boy who, aged eight, climbed to the top of the highest tree in the school playground and got stuck. Mr Winch, the deputy head, had to scramble up there after him to bring him down; it had been the most exciting thing ever to happen at Larkmead Primary. 'Poor him,' said Caitlin. 'And poor you.'

'Thanks,' Gemma said with a wan smile. 'He'll be all right, and so will I,' she went on. 'He's just not a very easy patient to live with right now, and I'm probably the worst nurse. But it won't go on forever, right?' She tapped the photograph of Jane. 'As your mum said to me when I was screaming blue murder in the throes of childbirth, "You won't remember the pain once it's over." And she was right. Hopefully that goes for injured husbands as well.'

Caitlin smiled back. 'Undoubtedly,' she said.

'By the way,' said Gemma, perking up a little. 'I hope you don't mind me asking, but is something going on with you and Harry Sykes?'

Caitlin's heart leapt, like an over-enthusiastic Labrador. Stupid heart: stay where you are. 'No,' she said. 'There's nothing going on with me and Harry Sykes. Why?'

'He just mentioned you the other week. Said something about going to Cambridge? We were on our way to the hospital when he told me, but I wasn't really paying attention.'

Did that mean 'just mentioned' or 'just *mentioned*'? Was his tongue in or out when he said her name? Now she was thinking about Labradors again. Get a grip, you moron. 'He gave me a lift,' she said. 'Helped me move my stuff out of my ex-boyfriend's flat.'

'And?'

'And nothing. That was it. He said something about giving up proposing to women, as his New Year's resolution. He's got a new Ten-Date Rule, apparently.'

Gemma snorted. 'I'll believe that when I see it.' She drained her coffee and checked her watch, then got to her feet. 'I'd better go,' she said, winding a fluffy silver scarf around her neck and tucking it into her coat. Then she paused. 'So he didn't try it on with you, then?'

Caitlin shook her head, unable to help feeling a twinge of disappointment. Had the monobrow and moustache scared him off? She ran a finger self-consciously along her now-bleached upper lip. 'If he's the village Casanova, then maybe I had a lucky escape,' she said with a little laugh as she showed Gemma to the door, but her words lacked conviction. Whatever his reputation, Harry seemed lovely. She couldn't help hoping that their paths would cross again soon.

Chapter Twelve

Saffron was feeling the heat of having Bunty Halsom as her client. Remembering her friend Kate's advice, she'd been determined to go in hard, making it clear from the outset that she had a busy client list and wasn't about to be Bunty's new patsy. None of her tricks had worked, though. Not one. Whenever she tried keeping Bunty waiting in the agency's small reception while she finished sending out the new Yummy Mummy press release or whatever, Bunty lost patience and simply marched past the startled receptionist and through the office, braying, 'Saff! I'm here, darling, what's keeping you? You didn't forget about our meeting, did you?'

Then, when Saffron arranged a series of press interviews to herald Bunty's forthcoming appearances on *Celebrity Masterchef*, she prepped her extensively beforehand on Tyler Starr, the spiky gossip columnist known for winding up his subjects until they lost their cool. But any hopes of keeping her client on a tight rein fell by the wayside as Tyler baited her with unexpected, intrusive questions about plastic surgery, and Bunty's complexion turned increasingly brick-red with ill-disguised irritation. Before Saffron could leap in and rescue her, the interview came to an early end, with Bunty throwing a glass of water over Tyler and storming out in an indignant huff. Of course the very next day the main article in Starr's column was spiteful speculation about how much cosmetic work Bunty had had done. 'Would you pay to look like THIS?' sneered the headline above an unflattering picture of her, with mottled cheeks and at least three chins, squeezed into a too-tight dress at some party or other. ('The little bastard,' Bunty hissed savagely. 'He'll get a slap in the chops if I ever see *him* again.')

And even though Saffron thought she had spelled it out perfectly clearly – several times – that she had better things to do than run around picking up dry-cleaning or organizing pet-sitters for Teddy, Bunty's ridiculously over-indulged tea-cup Pomeranian, guess what? It didn't make a blind bit of difference. Every day there'd be a new email or answerphone message that made Saffron's fists clench in rage:

Saff, darling, be a poppet and sort me out a dress for the TV Quick Awards. Anything glittery and fabulous. Try Temperley or Stella McCartney? If you could bike a selection round to my Notting Hill flat, that would be perfect. By midday, ideally.

Saff? Saffron? You really should answer your phone more often, dear. Listen, I've had an idea – see if Mercedes want to

do some kind of promo with me. I rather fancy that sporty little number they're advertising now. See if they'll lend it me for the Masterchef launch. What a hoot it'll be, me driving up in that – the paps will love it!

Saffron, I've lost my phone. Could you get me a new iPhone? Maybe one of those blingy cases to go with it; they're rather fun, aren't they? I'll be at Minty's for supper, so do send it there.

On and on it went, a never-ending stream of vapid, shallow, self-obsessed requests. Politely at first, and then with incremental degrees of curtness, Saffron tried pointing out that none of these tasks fell within the remit of her job, but she might as well have been talking to the wall. You had to admire someone with such determination, really. Admire them, or hire an assassin to deal with them, anyway. As for her new client's self-esteem, Saffron had never met anyone with such stratospheric confidence levels. Look at Bunty, deluding herself that she and Mercedes were the perfect client match, when in reality she would be far better suited to advertising a cheap-and-cheerful Fiat. And at five foot two, with knockers that could smother a man and a bum that needed its own postcode, Bunty didn't have a chance in hell of squeezing into any designer frocks. Not that Saffron would dare burst her bubble by pointing this out.

Still, she was busy at least. While Saffron was running around trying to keep her new client happy – and herself sane, if possible – she had little time to think about the tiny being inside her, which had now apparently bloomed from the size of a grape to that of a fig, according to the pregnancy app she'd installed on her phone. For something so small, it was certainly having a big impact on her body. Her limbs ached as if her bones had turned to lengths of lead piping. Her eyelids felt so heavy she had to battle to force them open for the duration of her Tube journey home. Her diary – previously crammed with drinks, dinners and get-togethers with mates – became a blank wilderness as she made excuses and cancelled everything, due to zero energy levels.

Once home, she would eat like a horse and then topple into bed by nine-thirty. She had never slept so deeply or heavily in her life. Oh, and the pregnancy dreams were absolutely crazy! Just the other night, she had dreamed she was in an operating theatre, in labour, pushing, pushing, PUSHING . . . only for the doctor in green scrubs to pull out a Jack Russell from between her legs. 'It's a dog!' the doctor announced, deadpan. The weirdest thing was, instead of freaking out that she'd given birth to a fully grown dog, in her dream all Saffron was worried about was whether to call him Jack or Russell.

'Jack, of course,' her sister Zoe laughed, when Saffron woke the next morning and Skyped her straight away in order to tell her about it. 'That's a really cute name for a boy. Hey, have you thought about names yet?'

Saffron smiled back at her sister's tanned face on her laptop screen. It was early evening in Australia, and the height of summer there. Zoe was in a white halterneck vest-top, with a ceiling fan whirring in the background, while Saffron was still in thermal pyjamas under an Arctic-tog duvet.

'Not really,' she replied. 'I've got my twelve-week scan coming up in a few days, though. I don't know if I should find out if it's a boy or a girl. What would you do?'

'Oh, don't find out,' Zoe said at once. 'Give yourself something to announce on the big day.' She peered into the camera. 'Christ, Saff, your boobs look gargantuan in those pyjamas. Jealous!'

'I know,' Saffron said, giggling despite herself. 'I can't stop looking at them. I'm going to have to get a new bra, Double-Melon size.'

'Fruity,' said Zoe and wolf-whistled. Then her face re-arranged itself into something more serious. 'Saff – have you said anything to El, yet? Only I spoke to her the other day and she was really down. Gearing up to do another round of IVF apparently. They've taken out a loan this time; she said it was their last chance.'

Saffron sighed, Double Melons forgotten, as a wave of guilt swept over her. Poor Eloise. She and her husband Simon were so desperate for a baby. According to Mum, Eloise had even started going to church and praying for a miracle. How could Saffron bring herself to announce that oh, by the way, she was accidentally pregnant a few weeks into a new fling? Impossible. 'Not yet,' she said glumly. 'You and my friend Kate are the only ones who know so far. I'm building up to Mum and Eloise next.'

'What about the Jack Russell's dad? When are you going to mention it to him?'

'I'm building up to that, as well,' Saffron mumbled.

Ending the call a few minutes later, she dragged herself out of bed and into the small dingy bathroom. The mirror showed a new swollen silhouette to her belly that made her feel like a softly ripening fruit. Hey – and this was the second morning on the trot that she hadn't immediately sprinted out of bed in order to vomit. Might this be the blooming, radiant stage of pregnancy that she'd read about? She very much hoped so.

Her sister's question about Max had struck a chord and she turned on the shower feeling thoughtful. Zoe was right: she had to let him know, and the sooner, the better. Today in fact. Yes, today she would contact him and arrange to meet. It was only fair that she put him in the picture. If he wanted nothing to do with the baby, then so be it. She was prepared for that reaction; it was a real possibility.

But there was another possibility, too – that his face would light up in delight, that he'd take her hand and gaze into her eyes. It could happen, couldn't it? And then he'd understand why she'd been so offhand about the kite-surfing, why she'd gone quiet on him since Christmas. *Whoa,* he'd say. *I wasn't expecting that.*

Nor me, she'd reply. *I have to admit, I was kind of surprised, too.*

Those beautiful dark features of his would scrunch up as he thought. *It's unorthodox, I guess, but we could make it work, couldn't we? The two of us, parents together?*

She washed her hair, trying on the fantasy for size. Mummy, Daddy and baby, living happily ever after. It felt like cheating somehow, as if they'd be leapfrogging a whole line of traditional relationship milestones. She barely knew Max. She had no idea about his favourite film, the books he liked, whether he preferred fish and chips to a curry, if he had siblings or allergies, let alone how he'd man up in a screaming, bloody childbirth situation. As for living together, for all she knew, he was a complete lazy slob who left dirty clothes on the floor and the toilet seat up; a middle-of-the-tube tooth-paste-squeezer, who'd never cleaned an oven in his life. He'd been married before, after all. There had to be a good reason he wasn't married now.

She squirted some of her favourite banana conditioner into her palm as she pondered this, but in the next moment felt her stomach contract at the smell. Oh no. Not again.

Dripping wet and naked, she burst from the shower unit, just in time to throw up into the loo. Uggggh! And again.

Shivering and spitting and wiping her nose and mouth, she knelt there on the cold lino, her optimism faltering as she waited for the nausea to pass. Who was she trying to kid? Max was already a father – he'd been there, twice over. If he had any sense, he'd steer well clear of being saddled with a vomiting new baby-mother. And who could blame him?

From: Saffron@PhoenixPR
To: Max@Faster
Subject: Drink?

Hi Max. Hope all's well with you. I've got a client meeting in Denmark Street Thursday afternoon – would be great to see you for a drink afterwards, if you're free?
Cheers
Saffron x

Later that morning Saffron leaned back at her desk and read through her email again. That would do, she decided. She sounded perfectly normal and grown-up. *Hey, we shagged like lusty nymphs several times last year, and then I went a bit weird on you, but see how civilized and mature I can be now!*

Something like that anyway. Well, it was the best she could do, and now her phone was ringing and she had a million other things she should be getting on with.

'Hello, Phoenix PR, Saffron speaking?'

'Saffron, there you are – this is Bunty. I've just had a splendid idea about a book. Maybe a memoir, or possibly a sort of self-help thing, for women who want to be more like me . . .'

Only half-listening, she pressed 'Send' on her email and watched the screen change. *Sending . . . Sent.*

' . . . So if you could set up a few meetings with publishers for me, start the ball rolling, that would be marvellous, dear. *My Bountiful Life* – that's one possible title. Or *Halsom Is As Halsom Does* – you know, a little play on my surname. Thought that was rather witty, don't you? Saffron? Are you still there?'

Max replied an hour later with a rather businesslike email suggesting they meet at the Pillars of Hercules on Greek Street. This was a small pub she knew to be crowded and noisy – not the most conducive spot for a heart-to-heart, but she seized on the opportunity with gratitude. At least he was giving her a hearing. Now she just had to work out how to tell him.

At nearly twelve weeks pregnant, Saffron's figure had definitely changed. Half her smart pairs of trousers were now too tight around the waist, and the buttons of all her work blouses strained across her inflated chest. Jumpers and forgivingly stretchy leggings were fine at home, but this wasn't the sort of outfit she could get away with at work. Out had come her range of 'fat-day' clothes: the slightly looser, more shapeless tops in her wardrobe, teamed with the high-waisted skirts that flared over her belly, disguising the small rounded beginnings of a bump. She could just about get away with her favourite jackets, although she could no longer button any of them up properly. There was no escaping it: maternity wear loomed unpleasantly ahead on the horizon, elasticated waist-bands and all.

No shapeless clothes today, though. Not when she had to get Max onside. Instead she wore a drapey black wrap-dress in soft jersey, which gave her an impressive cleavage and made her feel confident and womanly. She'd been in flats all day at work, but changed into her favourite black kitten-heels before she left the office. Her tired legs wouldn't thank her for it, but this was all in a good cause.

Max was already ensconced at a table with a pint and the sports pages of the *Evening Standard* when she arrived at the pub. He was wearing reading glasses, she noticed; another thing she didn't know about him. Did this mean the baby might be long-sighted? A picture flashed into her head of a chubby round-faced baby with a pair of spectacles on its cute button nose, then she pushed the image away as Max looked up and saw her. *Get a grip, Saffron. Get a bloody grip!*

'Hi,' she said, approaching his table. 'I'll just grab a drink. Do you want another?'

'I'm fine with this, thanks,' he said. Obviously not planning on staying long then, she thought, nodding brightly at him and joining the crush at the bar. The place was already filling up with clusters of post-work drinkers, with loud conversations and bursts of laughter all around, mingling scents of perfume and sweaty armpits. She imagined having to bellow her news in order to be heard and cringed at the thought. Maybe this wasn't the time or place after all.

'Yes, love, what can I get you?'

A massive vodka. A strawberry daiquiri. A glass of red wine with a whisky chaser. All three, with a ginormous bag of Kettle Chips for good measure.

'A Diet Coke, please,' she said with a little sigh.

'So how's work?' Max asked, folding his newspaper as she returned to the table. He had a lovely wide smile, Max. He was wearing dark-blue jeans and a mossy green shirt she hadn't seen before, rolled up at the elbows. Seeing the dark hairs on his forearms gave Saffron a pang of longing. Those arms had held her in a clinch not so long ago, his bare skin pressed against hers. God, he was handsome.

'Good, thanks,' she said haltingly. 'How about you?'

'Yeah, pretty good, too. I thought of you the other day actually – I had to take a client out rally driving, like you do. This footballer we're trying to sign up for our new ad campaign – him, his agent and a couple of us from the office down at Silverstone. Total adrenalin-rush. Have you ever tried it?'

By happy coincidence she had, although it had been with a

previous boyfriend who sulked all the way home because Saffron had beaten him in every race. Before long she and Max were comparing notes on lap times and handbrake turns, and he was telling a funny story about the footballer's agent whose legs had gone to jelly after the 'hot lap' at the end, and who actually fell over, quite embarrassingly, at the trackside, once out of the car.

Saffron felt her body unclenching as she laughed. It was as if that strange, awful New Year phone call had never happened. And he'd actually said 'I thought of you' without pulling a sick face. This was a promising start. Now all she had to do was deliver her news.

'So,' she said when there was a pause in the conversation. Her mouth went dry. *Here we go.* Mistakes can become adventures, and all that. 'I've been meaning to get in touch because—'

'Max! I thought you might be in here. Team Faster!'

Two women and a man had appeared by the table, all talking at once with animated expressions and much gesticulating. Both women had excellent haircuts and wore bright, short dresses, big parkas and thigh-boots, while the man was shaking off an enormous black military overcoat to reveal a lurid purple-and-yellow Hawaiian shirt.

'Have you heard?' cried the first woman, who had cheekbones to die for and a mahogany bob. 'We got Mtulu. We got Muh-freaking-tulu!'

'Abe is like totally stoked, he's given us the company credit card,' added Hawaiian dude, who had a goatee and artfully tousled hair. He waved a silver Amex card above his head. 'Drinks and dinner out for Team Faster. Yeah, baby!'

'You should have been there – everyone was cheering and screaming, it was totally epic,' said the other woman, who had almond-shaped green eyes. She punched the air and beamed at Max. 'Can you believe it?'

Saffron felt as if she had become invisible in her chair, a dowdy shadow in a bulging black dress who couldn't compete with so much naked exuberance. Meanwhile Max's face had lit up. 'Fantastic,' he said, high-fiving Mr Hawaii. 'Bloody amazing!' Then he turned back to Saffron, belatedly remembering she was there. 'Mtulu's the footballer I told you about, star player for Man City. Looks like he's going to be fronting our new campaign!'

'Great,' said Saffron, trying to sound enthusiastic, but her voice was lost amidst a new round of cheers and self-congratulation.

'Let's get a bottle of something fizzy,' said Mr Hawaii. 'And what the hell: pork scratchings all round. Jonty's booking us a table somewhere fabulous for dinner; he's going to text me the details.'

'I'll give you a hand,' said Almond-Eyes, linking a skinny arm through his and tottering along beside him. 'Just in case we decide to get two bottles . . .'

That only left cheekbones woman, who sat herself on Max's lap, curling cat-like into him and kissing him full on the lips. 'Looks like we're celebrating tonight,' she said with a naughty smile, tracing a finger down Max's face.

There was a lipstick print on his mouth and Saffron stared at it stupidly for a too-long moment, her heart thudding. Oh no. Was this what she thought it was?

'Saffron, this is Mia,' Max said, shifting in his seat and looking somewhat uncomfortable. Mia still had one arm twined possessively around his neck and she turned to bestow a brilliant smile upon Saffron. *He's mine, darling,* the smile said, without any doubt. 'Mia, this is Saffron from Phoenix PR. We worked together on the launch of the Gold range, back in the autumn.'

Saffron got to her feet, feeling Mia's cool, interested gaze on her the whole time. 'I'd better go,' she said, her face turning hot. What a muppet she was. As if a gorgeous, charming bloke like Max would stay single for very long. *Mia and Max.* They even sounded good together.

She brushed an imaginary crumb from her skirt so that she didn't have to look at either of them, then pulled on her coat. It wasn't as if she'd seriously expected that she and Max would become a couple again, just because of the baby, but, you know, it might have been nice to at least have had the option . . .

'Oh,' Max said. 'Okay. Well, nice to see you.'

Mia was teasingly trying to kiss him again, even though he was speaking. Rude, thought Saffron, picking up her bag. Bloody rude. 'Bye,' she said abruptly, leaving them to it before she did anything embarrassing like cry.

She walked towards Tottenham Court Road Tube station with swift, urgent strides, ignoring how painfully her shoes pinched. So that little conversation hadn't gone exactly to plan. Why had they wasted so much time talking about rally driving and gossip, for goodness' sake? If only she hadn't wussed out for so long! A better, braver woman would have announced it the second she sat down: cards on the table, *boom*.

But now Max had a new girlfriend, the very last thing he'd want to hear was that his previous fling was accidentally pregnant. Nice and friendly though he'd been, nobody wanted a hormonal ex hanging around like a bad smell.

It was damp and foggy and a horrible hair-frizzing drizzle was falling, soft and speckling. Saffron put her head down and marched on, pulling her coat more tightly around her. Well, she'd tried to do the right thing at least, nobody could say she hadn't. The question now was whether she could face trying all over again – or whether she should cut her losses and move on, leaving Max Walters far behind in the past?

Chapter Thirteen

For the first time ever, Valentine's Day came and went with barely a mention in Gemma's house. In the past Spencer had pulled out all the romantic stops: a massive bouquet of flowers, breakfast in bed, a night away in a glamorous hotel . . . He'd once even serenaded her in a restaurant, much to her embarrassment and the other diners' hilarity. Down on one knee, the works, ending with a red rose between his teeth. Everyone had cheered. Oh, he liked his big gestures, did Spencer. Unfortunately this year the only gesture he seemed to be making was two fingers. He hadn't even bothered to get her a card.

'Valentine's? Is it?' he mumbled when she presented him with a full English and a Buck's Fizz that morning, a crimson envelope propped up against the champagne glass on the kitchen table.

Her face fell. 'Yeah,' she said quietly. 'Not to worry.'

He sat down, drowning the contents of his plate with brown sauce, and didn't look at her. When had he last shaved?

she found herself wondering, noticing the dark stubble all over his chin and throat. Three days ago? Four?

'I've booked us cinema tickets for tonight,' she said, with forced brightness. 'Dad said he'd babysit. We could even splash out a bit and go to the Thai place first, maybe? If you want.'

She bit her lip, waiting for his reply, but he was chewing an enormous mouthful of sausage.

'Spence?' she prompted after a few moments. 'It's that new thriller, the one Harry was going on about. With that guy, what's his name — matey from *Game of Thrones* — and . . . ' She was babbling. 'If you fancy it, anyway.'

Her optimism was draining away. Why wasn't he answering? Why wouldn't he even look at her? It had been weeks since they'd gone out anywhere together, other than for a hospital appointment, and she'd been hoping that an evening out might take his mind off the recent traumas and make him feel more human. She'd imagined them holding hands in the cinema, a carton of buttery popcorn between them, resting her head on his shoulder in the cab ride home. She'd even secretly made the most beautiful dress ever for tonight, a gorgeous red number that nipped in at the waist, accentuated her boobs and gave her a real wiggle when she walked. It was hidden away at the back of the wardrobe and she'd been looking forward to modelling it for him. He'd never been able to resist her in that kind of outfit.

Well, before the accident, anyway. Nowadays he barely even glanced in her direction.

He gave a grunt. 'Maybe,' he said, forking in another mouthful.

She pressed her lips together, trying to hide her disappointment. Maybe it was just as well. It wasn't like they could really afford to go out anyway.

Will slunk into the kitchen then, eyes down. Not him as well, Gemma thought, with an inward sigh. 'What do you want for breakfast, love?' she asked.

'Not hungry,' he said, grabbing his packed lunch from where she'd left it on the side. 'See you.'

'Will, wait. You need to eat *something* now. All the research shows that you learn much better if you—'

'Yeah, whatever.'

'Darling, wait, I'm talking to you. Don't walk away from me when I'm—'

The front door slammed and she flinched at his vehemence. Too late. He was angry with her, because the night before she'd told him that he was going to have to pull out of the school trip to Normandy that summer.

'What? Why?' he'd asked, his head snapping round in surprise. They were in the dining room together, Will doing some maths homework, Gemma at the sewing machine, mending his torn blazer. It was the second time this year it had ripped all the way up the back.

She took her foot off the treadle to give him her full attention. 'I'm sorry, love, it's just too expensive. We can't afford it any more.'

'But everyone's going! I've got to go. For fuck's sake, Mum!'

Her jaw dropped. She couldn't believe he'd opened that luscious red-lipped mouth and said 'For fuck's sake'. To *her*. 'Don't you dare speak to me like that!' she cried. 'Look, while Dad's off work there's less money coming in. We've all got to make sacrifices.'

He sneered at her. He actually curled his lip and sneered, her lovely doe-eyed son, the same boy who'd once spent hours gluing tissue-paper flowers to Mother's Day cards for her. 'Yeah? What sacrifices have you made then, Mum? I don't see you going short.'

Her hands shook from this unexpected attack. The sacrifices *she* had made? *Well, only my marriage it seems, sweetheart. Only my bloody sanity!* 'We are all having to miss out on things,' she said, trying to keep her voice even. 'We haven't paid off Christmas yet, and we're still waiting for the money to come in from Dad's last job.' The money she'd been chasing for weeks now, only to be fobbed off by the developers each time. Whenever she looked at their dwindling bank balance and thought about all those months ahead with Spencer off work, she felt frightened. They'd had a few phone calls from 'no-win, no-fee' lawyers, trying to persuade them to sue the scaffolding firm for ridiculous amounts of money but

Spencer had told them, in no uncertain terms, to get stuffed. 'Bloody vultures,' he glowered each time as he hung up. Meanwhile the mortgage company had agreed to give them a month's breathing space, but Gemma knew they might not be so obliging if she tried asking for any more. 'Look, I'm sorry about the French trip,' she had said gently, 'but I'm afraid there's no way round it.'

'You don't understand,' he said, kicking at the table leg. He shoved his homework book away and got up suddenly. 'You've got no idea!'

'I *have*,' she said, stung. 'Will, come on, don't be like that.'

'Oh, shut up, Mum. Just shut up!' And off he went, pushing past her out of the room.

She gulped as the door slammed. 'And you can stop wrecking this blazer, too!' she found herself yelling after him, knowing it was random, but feeling the need to wrest back some control. 'Because you're not getting a new one, you know!'

They hadn't spoken since. He'd turned away from her when she came in to say goodnight later on. And now he was refusing breakfast, to make some kind of point. Great. A hunger strike was all she needed. Well, she didn't have time for another argument; he'd be halfway down the street by now and she wasn't about to run after him in her dressing gown and slippers. 'Darcey!' she yelled up the stairs. 'Hurry up! Breakfast's getting cold!'

At some point this week she'd have to tell Darcey that they

could no longer afford her riding lessons, either, and that she would have to downsize her birthday list that currently began: 1. *Disneyland trip*. But not now. Not this morning. She didn't think she could cope with three members of her family hating her at once.

She sipped her coffee – the cheap, own-brand stuff she had started buying (they all had to make sacrifices) – and wrinkled her nose at the unpleasant bitterness. *Poverty is no disgrace*, she remembered from the New Year fortune-cookie. Maybe not, but it tasted bloody awful sometimes.

'So,' she said bracingly, trying to gee up her husband, 'about tonight then, we could—'

He put his knife and fork down and looked at her for the first time all morning. 'Gemma . . . I don't feel like it, okay? Thanks and everything, but I'd rather just stay in.'

'Fine,' she sighed, as the promise of a night out together melted away like a ghostly apparition. Despondency engulfed her. She only wanted to do something nice for him! What was so wrong with that?

He must have registered how she was feeling for once, because his expression cleared and he reached for her hand. 'Sorry I'm being such a miserable bastard,' he muttered. 'It's just getting me down, that's all. I can't snap out of it.'

Her eyes felt wet and she squeezed his fingers. 'Don't worry about it,' she said. 'It's okay.'

But it wasn't okay; it wasn't even remotely okay. When, she

wondered with a heavy heart, would life start to feel okay again?

'What the frig is that?' her dad asked suspiciously. It was the following Monday and she'd gone round as usual for lunch, only this time she'd brought lunch with her: a Tupperware pot of home-made vegetable soup for them to share.

'Soup,' she replied, ignoring the way he was staring at it with such mistrust. 'I made gallons of it. Very healthy, too – loads of veggies in there.' She tried not to think about the way Darcey had pretended to be sick into the bowl when presented with it for tea on Saturday. Will had sloped off upstairs after a few mouthfuls, claiming he wasn't hungry, and then Spencer had dialled out for a pizza anyway, which completely ruined the point of her money-saving endeavour.

'Ah,' Barry said now. He gave the pot a little shake and they both watched silently as sorry-looking cabbage shreds and lumps of carrot swam through the brown liquid.

'I just thought it would make a nice change,' Gemma said brightly. She went to the cupboard and pulled out a saucepan. 'Have you got any bread? We can have toast with it.' She was going to eat the bloody soup if it killed her, she had vowed. The fridge and freezer were full of the stuff. 'Is Judy joining us or . . . ?'

'Not today,' Barry said. 'She's at work, won't finish until three o'clock.'

'Oh,' Gemma said. 'Things all right with you two?'

'Yes, very much so. We're planning a trip to Norfolk next month. Can you believe she's never been to Holkham beach?'

Gemma was ashamed to feel a stab of jealousy. The wide golden sands of Holkham were where Dad had taken her and her brothers on many seaside holidays when they were growing up. She always thought of it as a special family place, not somewhere you'd take a new squeeze. 'Oh,' she said again. 'So you really like her then? This is a serious relationship?'

'Well,' said Barry, looking surprised at the question. 'You know, it's early days and that, but . . .'

'It's just . . .' Gemma paused. 'Well, we've been here before, haven't we? Remember how you really liked Venetia, until she did a flit with all your stuff?'

'Yes, but . . .'

'And don't forget Aisling, who tried to rip you off with that timeshare villa.'

'Judy's not like that.'

Gemma raised an eyebrow. 'I'm just saying, Dad.'

There was an awkward silence for a moment. Barry busied himself by slotting four slices of bread into the toaster, then rammed down the handle. 'So! Home cooking, eh. Is this a new hobby of yours, or . . . ?' You could almost see the question marks popping up on his eyeballs, as if he was a cartoon character.

'Just watching the pennies, while Spencer's off work,' she

said lightly. Watching the pennies, indeed. Scared of the looming abyss, more like. The developer had stopped taking her calls and she'd heard a rumour from one of Spencer's mates that the build had ground to a halt. It was a lot of money they were owed; she'd been counting on it. Spencer reckoned he'd be due some compensation if the scaffold firm was found liable for the accident, but that could be months away yet. Meanwhile the only bit of work she'd been able to dredge up so far this year was some alterations on an evening dress for Mrs Belafonte up the road. Peanuts, compared to their usual income.

'You should have said,' Barry scolded. 'You can always borrow a few quid off me.'

'Thanks, Dad.' Gemma stirred the soup, her back to him. 'I'm not sure when I'd be able to pay you back, though.'

'Have it, then. What do you need? Would fifty do you?'

She almost laughed. Fifty quid wouldn't touch the sides. It wouldn't even cover the cost of new school shoes and trainers for Darcey, who had chosen exactly the wrong time to be going through a growth spurt. 'Honestly, Dad, we'll manage,' she said. It wasn't as if he had money to throw around himself. 'Forget I mentioned it.'

'But when's he going to be back at work? This is only a temporary thing, right?'

If only, she thought glumly. How she'd love for this to be a temporary blip, a month or two of tight purse-strings before they could return to their good old spendaholic ways. The reality was far grimmer. 'He's got another six weeks at least until he can go back to work,' she replied. 'And even then, reading between the lines, he may not be able to return to building work at all.'

Well, how could he, when the doctors had warned that he wouldn't be able to bear weight on his broken ankle for some time, even when it had healed? Building was hard physical work; he'd always had the biceps and six-pack to show for it. In fact, the consultant had told Gemma that it was partly down to Spencer's general fitness that his injuries weren't even worse. But if he couldn't carry on with such a job, then what did the future hold for him – for all of them? They could be back in a rented terrace come the spring, with the rest of the village laughing at them for getting above themselves.

'I might get a job anyway,' she said quickly, before her face gave her away. 'Something will turn up, we'll be fine.'

Her words of bravado kept coming back to her all the way home, taunting her. *I'll get a job, something will turn up, we'll be fine.* Yeah, like it was that easy. Like there was a great long list of jobs just waiting to be filled by someone like her.

Meanwhile, the credit-card bills were coming in thick and fast now, each bill more heart-stopping than the last. She felt sick each time she opened one and saw the list of things they'd bought without a second thought in the run-up to Christmas.

The beautiful Victorian blue glass baubles with silver trimmings that she'd found in an antiques shop in Needham Market — twelve pounds each. She'd bought ten of them and told herself they were bargains, only to have Bessie, her brother's dog, knock two of them off low-hanging branches of the Christmas tree. So that had been money in the bin.

The juicy organic turkey she'd bought, a Norfolk bronze, had cost fifty-eight pounds, and she'd ended up dumping half of it in the food waste when they'd all had their fill of turkey meals by December 28th.

The expensive haircut she'd treated herself to, the pedicure and facial she'd spontaneously booked. Reams of gorgeous velvet and shot silk from the fabric barn, which she still hadn't got round to doing anything with.

Spencer had been equally extravagant. The silver eternity ring he'd given her for Christmas was six hundred pounds, judging from his January statement. He'd taken them all to the Harry Potter studios the weekend before Christmas as an extra treat, and splashed out a new plasma-screen TV, which he'd produced on Christmas Day for the big film, as well as the latest iPhone for himself. All this when they were meant to be tightening their belts to afford the new house! The idea of so much money sloshing around so carelessly made

Gemma feel ill now. There wouldn't be any spending sprees for a while, that was for sure.

According to the government website she'd consulted, Spencer was eligible for twenty-eight weeks' sick pay, but the amount he'd receive wasn't anywhere near enough to cover their mortgage repayments and the mounting bills. It was sink-or-swim time: time to find some kind of life-raft before they were swept under by the next big wave. And while Spencer seemed to have stopped caring about anything, including his own family, there was only Gemma left to save everyone from drowning. She had to try to keep them afloat.

When she got back from her dad's there was a florist's van parked in the road. A man in green overalls was opening the back doors as she got out of the car and she couldn't help but gaze longingly as he brought out the most enormous bouquet of red roses. *Lucky cow, whoever they were for,* she thought longingly, remembering previous years when Spencer had wooed her with flowers, and dinner, and jewellery.

Wait a minute. The man in green overalls was walking up her front path towards her. So this must mean . . .

'Mrs Bailey?' he asked, consulting the little yellow envelope attached to the bouquet.

'Yes,' she said, light-headed with sudden hope. 'That's me.'

'Then these are for you.'

He held them out, smiling, and she accepted them wordlessly, cellophane crackling as she bent over and breathed in their glorious rich, sweet scent. Oh, thank God. Red roses! He still loved her. But how much had they cost? 'Thank you,' she said faintly.

'My pleasure,' the man said, whistling as he walked back to his van.

Inside the house Spencer was in the living room, lying on the sofa, still in his dressing gown. As she walked in, he grabbed the remote control and changed the channel before she could see what he'd been watching. 'I wasn't expecting you back yet.'

'These have just arrived,' she said, placing the flowers gently on the coffee table as she leaned over to kiss him, trying not to think about how sour his skin smelled. 'Thank you, they're beautiful.'

He pulled her in so that she was lying awkwardly alongside him, her face pressed against his musty dressing gown.

'Is this all right? I don't want to squash you,' she said. They'd had so little physical contact recently that it felt odd to be in such close proximity again, and she was conscious of his injuries. She still had her coat and boots on, her handbag sliding down her shoulder.

'It's fine,' he mumbled. 'Look, I'm sorry about Valentine's Day. I know I've been a bit shit lately.'

'Oh, love.' She put a hand to his face, smoothed the skin gently with her thumb. He was sallow and pasty from all the days spent indoors, and there was a sheen of grease in his dark hair. 'It's all right. And the roses are gorgeous. They must have cost an absolute fortune.'

As soon as she mentioned money she regretted it. In the space of a heartbeat, his face became taut and impassive. 'Well, it's my money,' he said stiffly. 'I can do what I want with it.'

'Yes, but . . .'

'Can't a bloke can't buy his wife a few flowers now and then? I thought you'd be pleased.'

'I *am*. I'm delighted. I didn't mean . . .'

'It was supposed to be a nice surprise, not an excuse for you to start nagging on about money again.'

She sat up, feeling as if she was fighting a losing battle. 'It *was* a nice surprise, Spence. Stop twisting things. I just meant you'd been generous, that's all. I wasn't nagging.'

'I won't bother next time. Most women would be pleased to get red roses. Should have known you'd have something to say, though.'

There was just no arguing with Spencer when he was determined to be the victim. She got to her feet and snatched up the bouquet. 'I'll put these in a vase,' she mumbled, leaving the room before he could say anything else. All of a sudden the sweet sickly scent was giving her a migraine.

Safely in the kitchen, she dumped the roses by the sink and sank into a chair, exhausted by yet another argument. How much had he spent on them? Forty quid? Fifty? Too much, whatever it was, especially as he'd turned on her almost immediately, seizing on the chance to have a go. She didn't even want roses from him. She didn't care about extravagant, hollow gestures — they meant nothing when his mood could change from loving to attack in a single moment.

Still wearing her coat, she reached in her bag for a tissue, only then noticing the three twenty-pound notes tucked inside. Her dad must have stuffed them there back at his house when she'd nipped to the loo.

The sight of those crisp notes in her hand gave her a pang. At least somebody still cared about her, even if it was her old dad.

She pulled out her phone.

Dad! she texted him.

Just found the money in my bag. Very naughty! But thank you. And I'll pay you back. xxx

No problemo! he texted back right away.

Glad to help. What are dads for??

Chapter Fourteen

From: Saffron@PhoenixPR
To: CaitlinF@fridaymail
Subject: Baby-food website

Dear Caitlin,
Thanks so much for the work you've done on Casey James's website. She is absolutely delighted! I've another client who is launching a new range of baby food and needs a site overhaul. Would you be interested in giving us a quote for the work involved? Let me know what you think.

Hope life is good in Larkmead. I was on the Tube to work this morning, packed with hundreds of commuters, like a lorry-load of cattle, and the train stopped in a tunnel for twenty-five minutes. I found myself wishing I was back in your lovely village, and never had to commute again!

All the best
Saffron x

Caitlin was pleased by the email, not least because she'd thrown all her energy into creating the website for Casey James, Saffron's singer client. With the enormous budget afforded her, she'd gone to town with a luxurious look, rich colours and elegant styling, creating a carousel of images, a fan community area, which she had offered to moderate, and suggesting specially commissioned weekly video blogs – all of which Casey had apparently loved. She had also offered to write a monthly newsletter for Casey's fans, as well as updating the site with a regular news feed, so as to keep it looking fresh.

After a gloomy few months in Larkmead, it had been energizing to flex her creative muscles again; she'd forgotten how much she enjoyed design work. When she'd made the decision to quit nursing for a more artistic career, there were some people (i.e. her mum) who simply couldn't understand why anyone would want to leave such a worthwhile vocation, not to mention all those handsome doctors/prospective husbands. 'Do you really want to sit behind a *computer* all day?' she'd asked. 'When you could be helping people?'

The equation wasn't that simple, though. Of course it was noble to help other people, but Caitlin actually found enormous satisfaction in putting together gorgeous colours and styles, and deliberating over the perfect font and images to create something bold and expressive, something that tantalized the eye. Did that make her a bad person? Not according to her tutor at college. 'You're a natural,' he'd said to her, after her second piece of work. 'You've got it, kid.'

She was just about to reply to Saffron when there was a knock at the front door and she opened it to see Gemma and a knee-high sandy-coloured dog, which was wagging its tail very enthusiastically.

'You've got a dog!' she said stupidly, as if Gemma might not have noticed.

'Only for this morning,' Gemma replied. 'Meet Oscar: I borrowed him from Mrs Belafonte down the road. I was trying to tempt Spencer out for a walk, but . . . ' She pulled a face. 'Not happening. So I wondered if you fancied coming out with us instead?'

Oscar wagged his tail again and looked from Gemma to Caitlin, as if he could understand every word. Caitlin thought of the job she'd planned for that morning – sorting through her mum's wardrobe – and took approximately 2.3 seconds to decide. 'Why not,' she said. 'Let me dig out some wellies and I'll be right with you.'

They drove out to Priestley Wood, a couple of miles away, and tramped through the mighty beech trees together, their boots crunching on the hard ground. Gemma being Gemma, she was wearing sparkly wellies, a woolly hat with a white rose corsage stitched onto the side and a pillarbox-red coat with jet-black buttons and a huge black furry collar that she'd added herself. As usual, Caitlin felt under-dressed beside her, in a plain black wool coat and a pair of her mum's muddy khaki-coloured boots.

The woods were cool, green and peaceful, the quiet broken only by the sound of Oscar's scudding footsteps when he ran to retrieve his manky old tennis ball, and sporadic snatches of birdsong. New leaves were budding on the trees, with pale primroses peeping from between their roots, and it felt as if spring was truly around the corner.

'So how's Spencer? Apart from not wanting to go out for a walk?' Caitlin asked.

Gemma took a moment to answer. 'Well, his ankle's mending well; they're pleased with it at the fracture clinic.'

She was unusually hesitant. 'That's good,' Caitlin prompted. 'And is he starting to feel a bit more like himself now?'

Gemma sighed. 'I wish! To be honest, he's like a completely different man. If I'd met this version of Spencer six months ago, I wouldn't recognize him.'

'In what way?'

Gemma bent to make a fuss of Oscar as he came back with the slobbery tennis ball in his mouth, tail wagging. She took the ball gingerly and hurled it far into the distance, Oscar bolting after it immediately. For a moment Caitlin thought she wasn't going to answer the question, but then Gemma gave another sigh, as if it pained her to speak badly of her husband. 'He's just so bloody angry all the time,' she said. 'I know he's fed up, I know his back hurts and he has this constant mother of a headache. I know he'd rather be out and about at work, at football, down The Partridge with his mates . . . We all wish that. But sometimes he looks at me, and . . . ' She shrugged. 'I swear he hates me. And the kids. It's horrible, Caitlin. I don't know what to do.'

Caitlin thought for a moment. 'You said he banged his head, didn't he, when he fell.'

'Yeah. Quite a nasty bump. The painkillers don't seem to touch the throbbing he says he has at the front of his head. I guess that would be enough to drive anyone nuts.'

'It's just . . . Well, it could still be the concussion. That can alter your personality quite radically. Did the doctors say anything like that?'

Oscar was back again, bright-eyed with triumph as he dropped the ball at Gemma's feet and gave a short, excited bark. 'What do you mean?' Gemma asked, picking it up and throwing it once again. 'Not really. He was kind of confused for a while, but it didn't last long. I thought concussion was where you lost your memory and stuff?'

'Concussion is a brain injury, basically, and it can be really mild — say, a bad headache, that clears up quickly — but there can be complications.' Caitlin foraged mentally through all the medical textbooks she'd ever studied, and all the patients she'd treated. Minor injuries had been her thing: treating burns, bandaging sprains, cleaning festering wounds, with the occasional bit of stitching for good measure. The more serious stuff – head injuries, chest pains, breathing difficulties and major trauma cases – was always whisked straight past the likes of Caitlin to the doctors. 'I'll find out for you,' she told Gemma. 'Post-Concussion Syndrome, it's called. It's quite common after a head injury.'

'And can they treat it? How long will it go on?' Gemma turned pale. 'Will I ever get him back again?'

'Let me look into it,' Caitlin said, not wanting to dish out false reassurances before she'd checked her facts. 'Don't worry. I'm sure he'll be feeling better soon.' But even as she spoke, she wasn't certain of her own words. And judging by Gemma's face, she wasn't convinced by them, either.

Life was so fragile, Caitlin thought to herself, once she was home again and making lunch. Look at her dad, collapsing with a stroke while he mowed the lawn, the lawnmower chewing right through a bed of lupins as he toppled to the ground. Look at her mum, felled by a rogue infection that had raged through her body with deadly efficiency. Look at Spencer Bailey, the life and soul of his party on New Year's

Eve and now housebound and depressed after one false move.

Talk about sobering you up. Talk about shaking you by the scruff of the neck and reminding you that life was passing you by. Hello? Big wide world out there, calling Caitlin Fraser. Activate. Activate!

The message from her New Year fortune-cookie bubbled up in her mind with sudden clarity: *Your destiny is within your own grasp. Take a chance!*

But what should she do? she thought helplessly. What did that mean?

She glanced down at the small tin of baked beans while she waited for the electric ring on the cooker to heat up, as if seeking guidance. *Serves one sad lonely fucker*, said the label, or it might as well have done. Beans for one. Was this what her life had been reduced to these days?

Come on, stupid crap cooker, she thought, her hand hovering over the still-cool ring. Then a thought occurred to her. *Take a chance*, urged the fortune-cookie, rustling temptingly at the back of her mind. *Take a chance!*

She turned off the cooker and ate the beans cold out of the tin with a teaspoon instead, thinking hard. Should she? Dare she?

Oh, sod it, she thought. Why the hell not?

From: CaitlinF@fridaymail
To: Saffron@PhoenixPR
Subject: Baby-food website

Hi Saffron,

Thanks for your email — I'm really pleased Casey is happy with the website. I'm attaching my invoice herewith. Cheers!

I'd love some more work, yes please. I must confess, I don't know a huge amount about baby food, but I'm willing to find out. Tell me more!

Larkmead is . . .

She paused and glanced over at her open diary, where she'd scribbled an appointment just now on Thursday's square, following her phone call. *Harry, 2.30*, it said. What? It was perfectly legit. He was an electrician, after all, and her cooker needed fixing, didn't it? She typed on, feeling absurdly cheerful:

. . . full of daffodils and small children on bikes. And guess what: I'm actually following the guidance of my wise old fortune-cookie, and 'taking some action'. I'll keep you posted!

Love Caitlin x

Chapter Fifteen

A letter was the answer, Saffron decided. Her attempt at telling Max about the baby face-to-face hadn't worked, what with the whole unexpected girlfriend-on-knee development in the pub. Emailing him the news would be crass; a text even worse. The thought of all the awkward silences that could unfold within a phone call — pregnant silences, even — ruled out that possibility also.

A letter, then. She could take her time over a letter, be clear, honest and articulate. He would be able to read it in privacy and mull over his reaction before responding. A letter was the grown-up, measured way to do this, reminiscent of Jane Austen, Thomas Hardy and all the best love stories. Now she just had to write the bloody thing.

Dear Max, she began, stretched out on her sofa, still in pyjamas. It was Sunday and a milky sunlight was filtering through the grimy windows of her flat. Outside a car alarm had been going off for almost an hour and she was starting to fantasize about taking a dirty great sledgehammer to it. She chewed the

end of her pen, trying to think how best to phrase the bombshell:

> *It was lovely to see you the other night. I'm glad things are going*
> *well at work. The reason I called you in the first place was because*
> *there's something I need to tell you — something important.*

She paused and read it through again. So far, so good.

> *I wanted to tell you in person that night, but didn't have the chance,*
> *unfortunately. Congratulations on your new girlfriend, by the way.*

Ugh, no, that sounded bitchy. She crossed out the last
sentence just as her mobile started ringing. Caller: Bunty. On
a Sunday morning, for heaven's sake. Hello? Boundaries?
Sending the call to voicemail, she returned to her letter:

> *I have no idea how you will react to the news I'm about to give*
> *you — I don't know you well enough to predict whether you'll be*
> *happy, angry, freaked out or completely indifferent.*

She felt her heart constrict at the last word. Surely nobody
could be *indifferent* when told they were to be a parent, even if
it was third time around for him? Was it insulting of her even
to include the word in her list, implying that he was some
kind of robot?

Her phone started ringing again. Caller: Bunty. With a flash of irritation, she pressed the Ignore button and threw the phone to the far end of the sofa.

I completely appreciate that this will be a shock — it was to me, too. There's no easy way to say this, but, Max, I'm pregnant. It's your baby. I know you're already a dad. I know you've been there and done it, and probably thought you'd made enough of a contribution towards the continuation of the human race. But

Bunty was ringing again. Aargh! What was this woman's problem? Making a low growling in her throat, she grudgingly pressed the green button to accept the call. This had better be life-and-bloody-death, she thought. Death, preferably.

'Hello?'

'Ah, Saffron. Bunty here. I just need—'

'Bunty, it's Sunday,' Saffron said crossly, before she could stop herself.

'Yes, dear, I know, but creativity doesn't stop for a day off, does it? I've had a wonderful idea for a new thing. The Bunty Bra! So many other people have done lingerie collections, haven't they, but the problem is: no boobs. A couple of fried eggs in two scraps of lace — I mean, come on! Let's have some proper bosoms here. And who's got the best knockers this side of Channel 5? We both know it's me. So, I've been thinking.'

She drew breath and Saffron leapt in. 'Bunty. Let's talk about this tomorrow. I'm right in the middle of . . . ' she glanced around for inspiration, her gaze landing on her small, bare white feet at the end of the sofa, ' . . . a pedicure. I can't chat now. Send me an email and I'll get back to you tomorrow morning. Or maybe just talk to your agent?' Like a normal person would do? Rather than badger your long-suffering PR person, who has completely zero interest in Bunty Bras?

'She's not answering her phone.' Bunty tutted. 'Sometimes I don't know what I pay that woman for. I *made* her, you know. I made that agency what it is.'

'Bunty.'

'Okay! Pedicure, yes, got it. I'll email you. I mean, I'm happy to do matching knickers too, obviously, but I think boobs are where it's at. Bunty's Bouncers. Bunty's Baps. No, too coarse. Bunty's Bosoms . . . Anyway, you're the expert, you can spin it for me. So why don't we—'

Saffron could swear that her blood was actually starting to fizz with irritation. 'Bunty, I'm going now,' she said loudly over the top of the braying voice. 'Goodbye.'

She ended the call, feeling worn-out. Bunty was like a steamroller on steroids. No wonder she had got through so many husbands and love affairs. Those poor men, honestly.

Back to the matter in hand: the letter. But her phone was already buzzing with a text message. *Got it. Bunty's Boulder-Holders!!!!*

'Oh, go away, you madwoman,' Saffron groaned, turning her phone off before any more inane messages could appear.

Peace restored, she picked up her pen again, determined to finish this time.

It's your decision, Max. If you don't wish to be a part of this, then that's your choice, but I'm going to have the baby. This could be my last chance at motherhood — I really want to take it. I'm not asking anything of you — I realize you've moved on and are seeing someone else these days, and that's fine. But this little person will be a son or daughter to us both, so it would be great if you wanted to play an active role in their life. I'm sure we can work things out between us so that everyone is happy.

I hope you understand my feelings. Please get in touch when you've had time to think this through, so we can chat. I've got a scan booked for the seventeenth at 2.30, in Whipps Cross — I would love it if you came too?

Please let me know what you think, either way. Really hope to hear from you soon.

Love from Saffron x

There. She read it all through, changed a few words here and there, then copied it out in full, folded the paper neatly and put the letter in an envelope, ready to post the next day. Excellent. Well done, Saffron. One important thing done. Next up: something even more onerous. In exactly one and a

half hours she needed to be sitting down at her parents'
dining table in Essex for Sunday lunch, and somehow she'd
have to tell them as well.

'Darling, come in. You look well. Oh! Such a cold face. It's
been so frosty lately, hasn't it? Dad thinks we're going to get
snow next week. I've been bubble-wrapping everything in the
garden in readiness.'

'Hi, Mum.'

'Did you get here all right? The roadworks have been
terrible on the A12. We were stuck in a jam there on Thursday for – what was it, Lorraine? forty minutes? – long
enough, anyway. Dear me. Anyway, come on in. Kettle's on.'

'Thanks, Dad.'

Saffron's older sister Eloise was in the kitchen, looking as
if she had a cold, as usual – red nose, droopy face, tired eyes
– as she peeled carrots. Simon, her husband, was leafing
through the business section of the *Telegraph* at the table, but
glanced up at Saffron's entrance. 'Ah! The Londoner arrives.'

Simon was quirky and slightly odd, Saffron always thought.
He reminded her of a guinea pig, with his earnest dark eyes
and short, tufty black fur – hair, rather. He was up from his
seat now, all awkward and twitchy, as if he wasn't sure
whether to shake hands with her, kiss her cheek or attempt a
light, barely touching hug. She saved him the decision by hugging both her sister and then him – like it or not, Simon.

'Good to see you!' Eloise said. She was a financial adviser for a medium-sized chain of estate agents and terribly clever, always had been. *Oh! You're Eloise Flint's sister? Really?* teachers would say, frowningly, to Saffron as she followed two years behind at school, unable to believe that daffy, dreamy Saffron could possibly share any DNA with pin-sharp, test-acing Eloise. Simon, meanwhile, did something boffiny in computing; Saffron had heard him explain his job several times to different people over the years, but still was none the wiser. Even with a gun to her head, she'd struggle to explain what, exactly, he did during the average day at work.

'How are you?' Eloise asked now, post-hug.

Well, I'm accidentally up the duff, since you ask, El. 'Fine, thanks. Busy, you know.'

'Tell me about it. Ten-hour days I've been working recently, trying to get our audits in. My brain aches just thinking about Monday morning.'

Eloise's brain must be like an enormous, bustling factory, Saffron thought: conveyor belts spinning, sparks flying from the mechanical cogs in constant motion, numbers shuttling like synapses, lightning-fast. Oh, to have a mind so efficient, so swift, so organized.

'I saw that client of yours on *Masterchef* the other night,' Lorraine Flint said, chopping Bramley apples for a crumble. 'What's her name? The one with froggy eyes who seems drunk all the time. Booby or Barbie or something.'

'Bunty Halsom,' Saffron said without any enthusiasm.

'Oh God, are you working with *her*?' Eloise said with undisguised horror. 'She was in *The Times* yesterday, some awful piece about her and her silly little dog. I was just saying earlier what a fright she is. Wasn't I, Sime?'

'You were, and I agree. Dreadful woman.'

'You don't have to tell me that,' Saffron said, pulling a face. She sat down, leaning forward somewhat so that her jumper bagged out, disguising her rounded belly. Not that anyone seemed to have given her a second look, for they were all too busy slagging off Bunty.

'I mean, excuse my language, but she's just such a publicity *whore*. She really is. Sorry, Mum, but nobody is forcing her to go on all these programmes, are they?'

'I don't know – Saffron might be,' her dad said wryly.

'Nobody's forcing her,' Eloise repeated. 'She can't get enough of the limelight. Vile woman. What have you been doing with her, Saff?'

Saffron explained, feeling, as she always did, that her career was something of a joke to her parents and Eloise. Nobody had ever said it, but she knew they all thought running around after celebrities and journalists was a silly, pointless kind of job, compared with the much more grown-up work of finance and science. Yes, all right, Saffron felt like saying, but are your jobs anywhere near as stressful as working with Bunty effing Halsom? I very much doubt it.

Conversation moved around to the safe topic of Zoe and how much they all missed her. Then, once lunch was dished up, gravy poured, everyone around the table poised to dig in, Eloise cleared her throat and sat up a little straighter. 'I know you've all been waiting to ask,' she began, a catch in her voice, 'so I'll just come out and say it. No, the IVF didn't work this time. I'm not pregnant. So there we go.' A tear dropped onto her plate and Simon put his arm around her.

'Oh, El,' said Saffron wretchedly. 'Both of you. I'm sorry to hear that.' Her heart thumped and she found herself gripping her cutlery too tightly. There was no way she could tell them her news now, surely.

'Darling, that's so sad,' Lorraine said, her mouth quivering as she reached across the table to take Eloise's hand. 'What a blow. I know you were hopeful this time.'

Eloise sniffed. 'That's the thing. We've been hopeful every time. And every time it's the same depressing result: no. However nicely the doctors say it, it's still no.' She dabbed at her eyes. 'Well, that's it now. We can't afford it again. We're not going to be parents, and that's that.'

'If it's the money . . . '

'It's not the money, Dad, it's all the rest of it. The emotional turmoil. The desperate longing, the waiting and praying, and then the cascade of despair. We can't do it again. We're through.'

'Have you thought about adoption?' Saffron asked after a moment. 'I know it's not the same, but . . . '

'We've thought about adoption, egg-sharing, surrogacy . . . We've gone round and round the whole bloody circus.' Eloise had never looked so desolate. Everything had come easily to her, her whole life: A-grades, music exams, a husband, a great career. This was the only thing that remained resolutely beyond her control. 'I'm just so tired of it all,' she went on. 'We both are. Everywhere I look there are mums and babies. Six of the women at work will be going on maternity leave in the next few months. Six! And we'd be really good parents, I know we would, and I'd love our baby so much, but . . . ' She broke off, overcome, and the sight of her downturned mouth tore at Saffron's heart. 'But I'm forty this summer and we've got to face facts. It's probably not going to happen.'

'Sweetheart, come on.' Now it was the turn of Ewan, their dad, to reach over and pat his daughter's back, discomfort writ large in his face. Ewan could talk for Britain about stereo systems, cricket batting averages, vegetable growing and what a mess the ruddy government was making of everything, but show him a crying daughter and he was lost for words. *Pat, pat, pat.* 'Don't upset yourself now.'

'But, Dad, it's so unfair. Why can't we just have a baby like everyone else?'

'I don't know, love. I wish I did. I wish I could make this all right for you.'

'It's no more than you both deserve,' Lorraine added, her eyes pools of sorrow.

'They say, don't they, that sometimes when you stop trying for a baby and just relax, that's when it happens, when you're least expecting it,' Saffron said tentatively, aware of the irony in her words. *Speaking as an expert here, someone who's got a bun in the oven right now and definitely wasn't expecting it, I mean.*

Eloise's face twisted into tearful irritation. 'Everyone keeps *saying* that. Just relax! Stop thinking about it! But how? How am I meant to stop thinking about it? I can't think of anything else, for goodness' sake!'

Saffron looked down at her plate, feeling chastised. 'Sorry.'

Eloise sighed. 'No, I'm sorry. I didn't mean to bite your head off. I'm just . . . all over the place. Don't take any notice of me.'

Looking at her plate had been a mistake, Saffron realized in the next moment, as her eyes locked onto a large, crispy-looking roast potato and refused to move. Her stomach rumbled. Her mouth felt wet with anticipation. Sorry as she was for her weeping sister – and she *was* sorry! she could not have been sorrier! – Saffron was absolutely ravenous by now. Being pregnant meant that whenever hunger struck, she felt as if she could kill someone with her bare hands if they were standing in the way of her food. Surreptitiously she cut the roast potato in half and shoved it in her mouth, while everyone else was still absorbed with poor Eloise. Then she almost choked as she discovered just how volcanic the temperature was.

'Darling, I wish there was something we could— Oh, Saffron, are you all right?'

At her mum's prompting, everyone let go of Eloise and turned to see Saffron, purple-faced, trying to gulp down water fast enough to cool her burning mouth. 'Fine,' she spluttered. 'Absolutely fine.'

It broke the spell at least, and everyone picked up their cutlery. 'Better eat this while it's hot,' Simon said, looking somewhat relieved. He speared a sprig of broccoli and looked at it with what could only be described as fondness. 'Very mathematical vegetable, the humble broccoli, you know,' he said to nobody in particular. 'Amazing fractals.'

Eloise blew her nose. 'So with me being barren, and Zoe being gay,' she said, ignoring her husband's musings, 'I guess the continuation of the family line is down to you now, Saff.'

Oh, Christ. Couldn't they talk about broccoli and fractals a bit longer? But no, Ewan was already guffawing as if this was hilarious.

'No pressure, love! Don't pay any attention.' He swished a forkful of lamb through the puddle of mint sauce on his plate. 'Poor old Saff,' he said affectionately. 'Let her find a fella first, eh?'

Poor old Saff? What was all that about? 'Who says I want a fella anyway?' Saffron asked, smarting. Why was it that every time she was with her family she ended up feeling as if she was fourteen years old again, gauche, pimply and *this* close to storming out of the room in a strop? However hard she tried to convince them she was a grown-up now – a responsible adult with a perfectly good job and her own flat in London, thank you very much – she was reduced to feelings of inadequacy within ten minutes of being in their company. Every bloody time.

'Or a girlfriend like Zoe, of course, we don't mind. But seriously, love, Eloise is only joking, all right? Your mum and I will be fine without grandchildren, if you don't want to go there.'

'*Is* there anyone nice right now, though?' her mum asked, unable to disguise the hope radiating from her face. She might as well have been holding up crossed fingers. 'Some special chap you want us to meet? We haven't been introduced to any boyfriends for a while.'

'Not since Neal,' Eloise put in. She seemed to be cheering up all of a sudden. Nothing like a bit of sister-baiting to put her in a good mood. 'God, he was a bastard, wasn't he?'

Saffron glared at her. Neal was her maverick ex-husband, the one she'd been madly in love with right up until the moment she discovered he'd bankrupted them both after a string of disastrous business deals. She was done talking about Neal with Eloise, thank you very much.

'Only I thought Zoe was hinting at some piece of news on

the phone the other day,' Lorraine went on encouragingly, her grey eyes still fixed on Saffron. 'She asked if I'd spoken to you recently, and when we were going to see you next. It was almost as if she knew something we didn't.'

'Oooh,' Simon said cheerfully. 'Don't keep us in suspenders.'

'Yes, what is it?' Eloise asked, glugging back her glass of wine. 'Don't tell us you're having a fling with one of your "celebrity" clients?' She made little speech-marks with her fingers, to show how much she valued society's idea of fame.

'Of course I'm not!' Saffron snapped, just as her dad started whistling 'Here Comes the Bride'.

'Methinks the lady doth protest too much,' Eloise teased.

'Look, it's nothing,' Saffron said doggedly. 'Can we change the subject?'

'Sounds like something to me.'

'All right, let's leave it, I don't think Saffron wants to talk about this – whatever it is.' There was Mum, the peacemaker, as she'd always been when they were growing up and fighting over stolen nail varnish and 'borrowed' clothes.

'Pour her another drink – we'll get it out of her later,' Eloise said, laughing, and then her eye fell on Saffron's glass of orange juice and she went very still. 'You're not drinking?'

A strange look passed between the sisters and Saffron felt jittery with alarm. Oh God, Eloise had guessed. She had worked it out. *Bluff it. Blag it. Don't tell her anything. Not today.* 'Well, no, because I'm driving, aren't I?' she said, but Eloise was still giving her that measured, calculating look, and she could feel her face growing hotter by the second.

'You could have *one*, though. You can have one glass of wine,' Eloise said. Her voice was silky smooth, but her gaze was steely. 'Couldn't she, Dad?'

'Well, she could, but she doesn't have to,' Ewan said mildly, but Saffron barely heard him. The room had shrunk down to her and her sister and that look in Eloise's eyes.

'You're pregnant, aren't you? That's why you're not drinking.' Eloise's tone was brittle, her mouth a taut line.

Oh fuck. Saffron swallowed, her heart thudding in panic. *Here goes nothing.* 'Yes.'

'You're *what*?' cried Lorraine, dumbfounded.

'She's kidding us. Aren't you, Saff?' Her dad rubbed his beard – his nervous tic. 'Don't say things like that if it's not true.'

'It is true.' Saffron covered her eyes, unable to bear the expression on her sister's face for a moment longer. *How could you do this to me?* Eloise's face was saying. *You traitorous bitch. That should have been my news, not yours!*

'What? Are you serious? You're having a *baby*?' Her mum's voice rose higher with every question.

'I didn't want to tell you like this.' She forced herself to turn back to her sister. 'I'm sorry, El. I know how much you wanted—'

She reached out, but Eloise recoiled as if Saffron's touch

would contaminate her. 'Don't,' she hissed, pushing her chair back from the table and getting up. 'I can't believe you'd do this to me. I hate you. I *hate* you!'

And then she was gone from the room and they were all staring at each other in varying degrees of shock.

'I'll go after her,' Simon said awkwardly.

'A baby,' Lorraine exclaimed, goggling. 'Oh, Saffron. I can't believe this!'

'Nor can I,' said Saffron miserably. 'Nor can I, Mum.'

Chapter Sixteen

After seeing Caitlin, Gemma went straight home and googled 'concussion' and 'personality change'. She read through the symptoms: irritability, depression, anxiety, aggression, mood swings, apathy, lack of motivation . . . yep. That little bundle sounded horribly familiar. Even more troubling was the fact that Post-Concussion Syndrome, as it was known, could apparently last for weeks, months or even more than a year. A whole year of Spencer's surly moods and general bad temper made her feel frightened. Did she have the patience, the stamina, to bear it that long? Yes, he was still her husband, but he definitely wasn't the man she'd married, the man who had welled up on their wedding day, who'd made her feel like the happiest woman alive. How could you stick with someone if they were continually horrible to you? Should you put up with it, just because they'd once loved you? Other people would, she was sure. Nicer, stronger people than her would tough it out, because that was what you did when you loved someone. She felt guilty for even questioning it, as if she'd been caught out in the Wife test. Not loyal enough. You failed.

It wasn't only Spencer who was in the doldrums. Darcey had fallen out with her best friend and was in floods of tears half the time. ('The only thing that would make me feel better is a pony or a kitten,' she'd sobbed, with a hopeful sidelong glance at Gemma. No chance, love.) And Will was monosyllabic and grunting these days, a far cry from the little boy who'd followed her around the house with a book of facts not so long ago, saying things like, 'Mum, did you know, you could fit all the people in the world into Los Angeles, if they stood shoulder-to-shoulder?' 'Mum, did you know, seventy-seven per cent of men in Yemen smoke?' 'Mum, where *is* Yemen?'

No facts any more. No 'Mum, did you know's. There was nothing other than a crash as he came through the front door, then a thump as he dumped his school bag in the hall. She would delay him there with a few questions about school: did he do anything nice, how was that maths test, what were they doing in PE today, did he want a snack? You could tell he was desperate to get away and hook up on his iPod, though, his eyes sliding past her, his very stance impatient. Worse, he looked so tired all the time, so defeated, as if life in Year 8 was too much for his narrow shoulders to bear.

'Will, are you home?' she called on this particular after-noon, coming downstairs from her tiny sewing room. In an attempt to cheer up Darcey she'd pulled out some of her fabric and they'd measured up for curtains in Darcey's bedroom. They didn't have enough money to buy paint yet, but Darcey had chosen a cheerful pale-blue fabric with a red cherry print, and Gemma reckoned there might just be enough left to make a matching duvet cover and pillowcase too. While Gemma cut and hemmed, Darcey had used the leftover scraps to make tiny cushions and pillows stuffed with cotton wool for her dolls' house, and they'd had a good old chat and a laugh, particularly when Darcey got her mum to say 'Dan Gleeballs' three times as fast as she could. ('Darcey Bailey, who told you *that*?' she had spluttered, trying not to giggle.)

'Will?' Gemma called again as she reached the hall. No answer, and no school bag. So he hadn't slunk in silently then – he hadn't come in at all. And she hadn't even noticed! As well as being the worst wife in the world, she was doing a good impression of the worst mother too, right now. She checked her phone, wondering if he'd gone to a mate's house, or whether the school bus had broken down again. What if he'd texted her asking for a lift and she hadn't heard the beep? But there was nothing.

The first pricklings of alarm coursed through her. Usually he was home by four-twenty at the latest, but now it was getting on for five, and dark outside. Where was he? She'd drummed it into him that he had to keep her informed of what he was up to, that he couldn't just go off and do his own thing without telling her. He'd always been good about that in the past. Maybe he'd lost his phone. Yes, that was possible. But still . . . why hadn't he come back?

Spencer was glued to the Xbox, driving a car through a desolate apocalyptic wasteland on the plasma screen. 'You haven't heard from Will, have you?' she asked. 'He hasn't phoned to say he's going to be late or anything?'

'Mmm?'

She snatched the controller from his hand, panic making her impatient. 'Spencer! Will isn't home!'

'Oi! I was in the middle of that! Give it back!'

'Has Will phoned you?'

'Give it back, I said!'

He grabbed it roughly and she staggered, almost losing her balance. 'Spencer!' she cried. Why couldn't he see how important this was? 'I'm trying to talk to you. Have you seen Will? He isn't home.'

Spencer paused the game, and at last silence fell. 'Will? No, I haven't. I thought you were . . .'

He broke off, and Gemma filled in the gaps in her head. *I thought you were the responsible adult around here, the one who noticed things like that.*

Just then they heard a key turn in the front door. *Thank goodness.* 'Panic over,' Spencer said, rolling his eyes and getting back to his game.

Gemma ignored him and rushed to the hall as Will came in out of the darkness. 'There you are! I was starting to worry! Is everything all right?'

She had her arms out to hug him, but he pushed past her – too cool for hugs these days – and chucked his bag on the floor. He looked pale and dishevelled, his hair standing up and – not again! – the school badge on his blazer pocket hanging off at a drunken angle. 'Fine,' he muttered. 'What's for tea?'

What's for tea? That was all her family seemed to think she was good for: cooking bloody tea. 'Will,' she said firmly, 'where have you been? It's gone five o'clock, you know. It's dark!'

He pulled a face as if to say 'Duh!' and walked past her into the kitchen, where he shoved two slices of bread into the toaster. 'It's *fine*,' he said again.

'It's not fine,' she snapped, then sniffed the air. Cigarette smoke and chewing gum. Oh no. 'Have you been smoking?'

There were purple rings under his eyes, she noticed, as he took out a plate and butter, and started buttering a third piece of bread, too impatient to wait for the toast. 'Mum . . . Just leave it, will you? I'm not in the mood.'

'You're not in the mood? Well, *I'm* not in the mood to be worrying about *you*, coming back at all hours, stinking of smoke. I need some answers. What's going on?'

'Nothing! Back off, Mum. I've just walked through the door.'

'Yeah, forty minutes late, pal. What have you been doing? Were you with Jack?'

'Nah.' His eyes hooded, he turned away, fiddling to pull a tangle of earphones from his blazer pocket. Then he plugged them in, a deliberate gesture of *I don't want to talk any more* and bit into his bread and butter.

Gemma watched him, anxiety clenching in the pit of her stomach. It's me – I'm on your side, she wanted to say. You can tell me, I only want to help.

But she knew it was pointless. Like father, like son. Neither of them was letting her in right now.

'Not stew *again*. Ugh, Mum, this is like totally *rank*. I thought we were having chips?' Darcey's face was a picture of indignation as Gemma served up plates of vegetable stew and mashed potato half an hour later.

'*I* never said that. You were the one who kept talking about chips. Anyway, this was all I could find in the freezer.'

'There are chips in the freezer.' Darcey's mouth crumpled into a pout and she stabbed a fork into the orange-brown stew with a look of sheer disgust.

'Well, I'm sorry, young lady, but this is what we're having tonight.' Gemma never thought she'd be the kind of person who called her children 'young lady' and 'young man', but there you were.

'Yuck. I hate stew. Dad, can't we get pizza again?'

Don't you dare, Gemma thought, catching her husband's eye across the table. If he went and undermined her again, she'd go ballistic.

'Don't whine, Darcey,' he said curtly. 'Eat up and be grateful you've got anything at all.'

Well, that was some improvement on dialling out for a takeaway at least, Gemma supposed, but his tone had been unnecessarily sharp and now tears were glistening in Darcey's big brown eyes.

'Start with your mash,' she said in a kinder voice. 'Come on, while it's hot.'

'Can I get some new trainers on Saturday?' Will said after a few moments' silence. He was still plugged into his music player and talking extra-loudly as a result.

'I only just bought you some!' Gemma said in surprise. 'Can you turn that music off, please, while we're having dinner.'

'Yeah, but the ones you bought were cheap crap,' he said. The sneer on his face was habitual these days. 'Like, totally embarrassing, naff ones. Anyway, I've lost them.'

'You've *lost* them? Oh, for heaven's sake. Have you looked in Lost Property at school?' There was a shiftiness about him that was unconvincing. Had he even heard her? 'Will, I'm talking to you, turn that music off. Have you *really* lost them? Because I'm not buying you new ones just because you don't like the others. They were perfectly good trainers, Will.'

'What – from British Home Stores? Do you *want* everyone to take the piss out of me, or what?'

She glanced at Spencer for back-up. Was he going to let Will speak to her like that? Apparently he was.

'Don't be so rude,' she said, flushing. 'There's nothing wrong with those trainers. And I—'

'He's got a point,' Spencer put in over her, and she whirled round accusingly at him. 'What? The lad's got a point. I wouldn't want to go around in trainers from British Home Stores, either.'

'Exactly!' Will was triumphant.

'But . . .' The words shrivelled on her tongue. So much for a united front. So much for spousal solidarity! 'The thing is, Will, the trainers I bought you cost about fifty quid less than Nike ones, or whatever it is you want.'

'I'm not having my son go to school like some kind of—'

'And we don't have that extra fifty quid right now,' Gemma said loudly, ignoring Spencer's unhelpful interruption.

'Right, so I'm meant to do PE in socks, am I? Great. Thanks a lot.'

'I'm sorry, love. I wish I could give you the best trainers in the shop, but the problem is that we've got to watch the pennies.'

'Yeah, I know, you've said about ten million times. Why don't you just sell some stuff, then? Like that bike you never use. Dad's Mazda. All your—'

'It's not as simple as that,' Gemma said, exasperated, before he could list any more possessions. 'Look, Dad's owed a lot of money and, until that comes through, we need to—'

'Oh,' Spencer cut in. 'I meant to tell you.'

Gemma turned towards him, not sure she wanted to hear what he was about to say. 'What?'

'They've gone bust. Melvilles. Stu rang the other day. They've done a bunk, the site's closed down, nobody's getting paid.'

'*What?*' Gemma's heart almost stopped. 'But they can't do that! They owe you nearly ten grand – I worked it out. What are we going to do?'

He shrugged. 'There's the compensation. That should be a good whack.'

'Yes, but have you actually applied for it yet? Nobody's just going to hand it over, are they?'

'All right, all right! No need to go on at me. Don't you think I've got enough to deal with right now?'

'I'm just saying . . .'

Darcey shoved her plate away suddenly, making them jump. 'Why does everyone keep arguing all the time? Stop arguing!' Then she threw down her cutlery with a clatter and ran out of the room.

Gemma bowed her head, then tried again. 'I'm just saying,' she began, but Spencer held up a hand.

'Don't,' he said. 'Just don't.'

*

Later that evening Gemma sat at the kitchen table trying to juggle the bank statement with the latest bills that had arrived earlier, and let out a sigh. They were in trouble. Big trouble. As she totted up the amount they owed and compared it with their bank balance, she was seized by a cold grip of panic. She'd been counting on the money Spencer was owed, and without it they were seriously in debt. Push had come to shove, and now she had to bring in some readies, fast. There were no two ways about it.

Should she ask her dad if she could borrow a few thousand, just to tide them over? Spencer would go nuts if he knew she was going behind his back, but she was starting to feel desperate. Mind you, the last time she'd seen her dad, at the weekend, Judy had been there and Gemma had ended up being kind of curt with her. Well, okay, a little bit rude. Barry might not want to dip in his wallet for a daughter who couldn't bring herself to be polite to his new woman.

The calls had now dried up from the no-win, no-fee lawyers, who'd been keen for Spencer to make a personal-injury claim against the scaffolding firm, but Gemma was starting to wonder if they'd been too hasty in rejecting their offers of help. Vultures and blood-suckers, Spencer had called them, but maybe it would be worth stepping down from the moral high ground if it meant they'd get some kind of payout? She sighed. Spencer would never go along with it, she knew. The scaffolders were a small family firm and a lawsuit could well bankrupt them. Skint or not, Spencer was too principled to do such a thing.

She felt as if they'd motored along bumpily so far, but now the fuel tank was empty and they'd petered to a halt. With Spencer turning his back on responsibilities, Gemma knew that the future of their family rested in her hands alone. She would have to be brave, strong and resourceful; she needed to step up and somehow get them moving forward again. But how?

'That was a gusty sigh,' said Harry, walking into the kitchen just then. He'd come round to watch the Champions League match with Spencer and was now heading towards the fridge in search of more beers, at a guess. (Sky Sports: another expensive thing she should probably cancel. Just as soon as she plucked up the courage to break the news to Spencer.) 'Everything all right?'

She tried to smile, but it was an effort. Then she gave up. This was Harry, one of their oldest friends, after all. 'Not really,' she admitted. 'We're a bit skint, to be honest. I'm going to have to get a job to keep us going. Just wondering what I can do.'

'Ah.' He pulled out two green bottles, then narrowed his eyes and pulled out a third. Easing off the metal top, he poured the contents into a glass and handed it to her. 'What sort of thing were you thinking of?'

'I've got some sewing to be getting on with,' she said.

'Curtains for Mrs Bradley at the school. And Eva Walker's just asked me to make her three bridesmaid dresses . . . ' She spread her hands, feeling helpless. 'That's about it.'

'Okay.' Harry sat down at the table with her and picked up the red electricity bill that had arrived that morning. *This payment is now overdue.* 'And how much will you charge them for that? If you don't mind me asking.'

Gemma looked away. 'Well . . . '

'You *are* charging them, aren't you? What's your hourly rate?'

'The thing is, I know Mrs Bradley's a bit skint, too,' she said defensively. 'Her poor husband's been out of work for three months now, and their daughter's getting married in May and has gone totally Bridezilla on them, so . . . '

Harry gave her a look. 'Tell me you're not doing this for free.'

'No! I asked her to bung me twenty quid, and maybe ask Mark – that's her husband – to do some gardening for us.'

'Twenty quid and a bit of gardening?' He looked appalled. 'And how long's it going to take you?'

'She's providing all the curtain fabric,' Gemma countered. 'And I don't mind doing it, so . . . '

'Don't avoid the question, Gemma Bailey. You're worth more than that, and Helen Bradley knows full well you are. She's taking advantage of you, that's what she's doing.' He swigged his beer and eyed her thoughtfully. 'Anything else lined up? Have you seen any jobs advertised in the paper that you want to go for?'

She shook her head glumly and turned the electricity bill over so that its red letters would stop shouting at her. 'I'm actually kind of scared, Harry,' she confessed. 'Spencer's so . . . not himself. I feel like we're falling apart. If I could just get something – anything – to pay off some of our debts, it would be a start, but . . . '

'There's a job going at The Partridge,' he said. 'Lunchtime cover, and a couple of evenings behind the bar. I know it's not the best job in the world – it's not the best pay, either, I'm afraid – but I'm sure Dad would give it to you, if you were interested.'

Gemma was silent for a moment as she mulled over the offer. Pulling pints and washing glasses for Bernie Sykes was a far cry from her old job at Pop, designing outfits and managing a production line. But beggars most certainly could not be choosers. Will had no trainers, the electricity bill was overdue along with all the others, and now that Melvilles, the developer, had left them high and dry, they didn't have a prayer of making next month's mortgage payment. Of course, being idiots, they had chosen not to take out insurance against future loss of earnings. 'We won't need that,' Spencer had assured the bank manager at the time. 'I've never had a day off sick in my life.'

That was back then, of course, when they still had optimism on their side.

'I'll take the job,' she said.

Chapter Seventeen

On the day of her scan Saffron must have checked her phone for new texts or emails at least nine hundred times, or so it seemed. No word had come from Max in reply to her suggestion about meeting her there, though. No reply to her letter whatsoever in fact. She was taking that as a big fat *No, thanks* both to her and the baby. So there you had it.

However hard she tried to be Zen and cool about the whole thing — so what, anyway? plenty of women went it alone, and they and their children were perfectly happy — it was difficult to ignore the hope that lit up inside her like a flame as she reached the hospital and began following signs to the maternity wing. Max might be there in the ultrasound waiting area, she thought, increasing her pace with a new urgency. She'd walk through the door to find him rising to his feet expectantly, his eyes searching out her face. *Is this okay?* his expression would ask. *Are we okay?*

It could happen, couldn't it? It really could!

She held her breath as she entered the waiting area, but he

wasn't there. Of course he wasn't. Why had she even kidded herself it was a possibility? He was probably planning a snowboarding weekend with that foxy Mia right now. Maybe they were already out on the slopes: France, Italy, or somewhere further afield, like Colorado. Snow dazzling in the winter sunshine. A gorgeous wooden chalet, no expense spared. Schnapps and a hot tub for the après-ski . . .

Don't think about that. What's the point? You were only with him for a few weeks; you shouldn't have expected anything else.

She sat down, feeling very alone as she noticed that all the other people in the waiting room were either couples or fully-fledged families. Two toddlers were racing around, one on a mini fire-engine, kicking his heels enthusiastically against the sides, the other with a fairy wand and a runny nose. Saffron flinched as the fire engine narrowly missed her toes, and she tried to smile in a 'How cute!' way, but didn't feel remotely prepared for this scary new world of wobbly-headed babies and small wild people. Plastic toys and nappies and random, unpredictable crying fits . . . She didn't have a clue about any of it. How would she manage when she was solely responsible for her own child?

Don't think about that. Plenty of time to learn the ropes. Everyone else seems to manage all right, don't they?

She lowered herself into a seat and tore into a bag of Skips, trying not to look at the way the couple opposite her were holding hands. The man was looking at the woman with such tenderness it made her want to cry. She wished someone was with her to look at her in that way. She wished someone was with her, full stop. But who? Zoe – her first choice after Max – was on the other side of the world and couldn't exactly pop round. Her friend Kate was up to her eyes in work for her new start-up business. And her mum had been so flustered about not wanting to upset Eloise, and yet do the right thing for Saffron, that Saffron couldn't bring herself to mention the scan. As for Eloise . . . she'd heard nothing more from her sister since that awful Sunday dinner. 'She's taken it badly,' her mum said down the phone, 'but I'm sure she'll come round.'

'Do you think?' Saffron replied doubtfully. Eloise had always been a sulker. Saffron and Zoe were the hot-headed sisters, who'd flare up in a row, shout and rage, then get over it five minutes later, but Eloise had the stamina to prolong a grievance for hours – days, sometimes – by dint of glowering and cold silences. And these were teenage arguments over the most trivial of things: stolen tights, borrowed hairbrushes, who was better at remembering the words to 'Rapper's Delight'. How long would the cloud of sulk last, when it came to Saffron's accidental pregnancy? A month? A year? The baby could be grown up and starting driving lessons before Eloise deigned to 'come round', as their mum optimistically put it.

'Course she will. Give her a bit of time. She's so

disappointed with her own news, she's just struggling to be glad for anyone else, that's all. But *we're* glad for you – if this is what you want to do.'

Saffron wished her mum didn't have to sound so uncertain, but never mind. They were where they were. She'd made her bed, she was lying on it and she would manage perfectly well on her own, without a bloke, and without her sisters too, if need be.

Back in the waiting area, the clinic seemed to be running late. It was already twenty minutes after Saffron's appointment and, although three other women had been called in by sonographers, she was still there, crossing her legs and trying not to feel impatient. How much longer would she have to wait? She'd told Kayla, the office receptionist, that she was out meeting a client; she didn't want to draw any extra attention to herself by being away from her desk for hours on end. Besides, she was bursting for the loo. The letter she'd received had instructed her to arrive with a full bladder, as this gave the best scan results, but all she could think about was how desperate she was to empty it.

'Saffron Flint?'

She got up in relief. 'Yes, that's me.'

She followed the stocky, fifty-something woman down a corridor and into a small consulting room with a bed. 'I'm Marie, I'm your sonographer today. Now, then, if you could lie down there for me, please, and undo the top of your trousers — that's it, just push them down a bit. Thanks, lovey.' Marie had a soft Welsh accent and a kind, mumsy face. 'Is this your first?'

'First baby? Yes.' Her fingers were all thumbs as she positioned herself on the bed, shoving down her stretchy black trousers and pulling up her pistachio-green shirt. There was a certain vulnerability about having your bare belly exposed, especially when it was newly plump and rounded, but Saffron was looking forward to seeing her baby again, being given another glimpse of that strange, watery black-and-white world.

'And you're . . . let's see. Twelve weeks and six days along, according to these dates. Does that sound right?'

'Yes.'

'Okay, good. So I'm going to do the nuchal-fold scan today, as you probably know. This is where we measure the thickness of the nuchal translucency, which is a little pocket of fluid at the back of the baby's neck.'

Ridiculously, Saffron felt tearful at the mere mention of her baby's neck. How she would kiss that soft little neck!

'And then I'll use this measurement, along with your age, to calculate the likelihood of your baby having genetic abnormalities, such as Down's syndrome. Is that all right?'

The words felt like a bucket of cold water tipped over her. 'Oh. Yes. Sure,' she stammered. *Genetic abnormalities. Down's syndrome.* Somehow she had overlooked the fact that this was why she was here at all. She had been so focused on eating healthily, taking folic acid, avoiding falling down Tube-station steps again, not receiving a reply from Max and, more recently, how on earth she was going to patch things up with Eloise that it hadn't occurred to her to worry about anything else.

'Just to confirm: you're thirty-eight,' the sonographer said, clicking something on the computer.

'Yes.' Old, in other words, to be having a first baby. Her midwife had actually written 'Elderly primigravida' on her notes. ('Elderly?' Saffron had yelped when she saw it. Elderly was a word she associated with wrinkled grannies in bath-chairs. Apparently you were considered 'elderly' if you had your first baby at thirty-five, though. Great.)

'Let's get started then. I'm just going to smear some of this gel on your tummy. It might be a bit on the chilly side, I'm afraid.'

Saffron held her breath as Marie picked up a transducer and pressed it quite hard at the base of her belly. By now, all sorts of terrible thoughts had rushed into her head. What if the baby's heart had stopped beating? It happened, didn't it? A sudden, unexplained death. She didn't think she could bear it if the baby was motionless on the ultrasound screen.

'Let's see . . . here we are.'

There was movement. A waving anemone of baby limbs. Alive and kicking. Saffron allowed herself to smile for a moment. *Hello, you.*

'Okay, so let's just get a good clear view . . . There. Now I can take a few measurements.' The sonographer clicked her mouse from point to point on screen and pressed various buttons.

'Is the baby all right?' Saffron asked, unable to bear the silence.

'Give me a minute and I'll go through everything with you, as soon as I'm done.'

Click. Click. Click. Saffron was starting to feel twitchy. Why wasn't Marie saying anything?

She's just doing her job — be patient. Stop worrying.

I can't help it. I wish Max was here. Why didn't he come? Why didn't he even reply?

'Right, we're done,' Marie said, pulling sheets of blue paper towel off a roll and handing them to Saffron. 'Do you want to clean yourself up with this first, while I just crunch the numbers?'

Marie looked shifty, thought Saffron in alarm, wiping off the goo from her belly and doing up her trousers. Was it her imagination or was the sonographer avoiding meeting her eye? Was it bad news? Was she putting off telling her something?

'So, Saffron.' Marie sat forward in her chair. A tiny gold cross rested on her plump, freckled cleavage. 'Taking measurements of the nuchal fold — the fluid at the back of the baby's neck — and combining that in a calculation with your age gives us a risk factor.'

Yes, yes, you said that already. Get on with it.

'It's important to remember that it's only a percentage of risk, and not a diagnosis, okay?'

'Okay.' She had a bad feeling about this. A really bad feeling, right in the marrow of her bones. *Please let the baby be all right. Please, Marie, don't tell me anything terrible.*

'When we measure the nuchal fold, if we get a thickness of three millimetres or more, then that can indicate an increased risk of Down's syndrome.'

Saffron swallowed, her throat horribly dry. 'Right.'

'Now your baby is measuring exactly three millimetres – so that does put you into this category of risk, but only just, okay? And remember this is simply a screening process, it's not a certainty.'

Oh no. Please no.

'Given your age and this thickness, I've calculated that there's a one in thirty-six chance of your baby having Down's syndrome. That being the case, I think it's wise for you to have an amniocentesis, which is a secondary test, to give us a clearer idea of what's happening.'

Saffron felt numbed. All colours seemed to have been leached from the room. A one in thirty-six chance was not exactly brilliant odds, especially when it came to gambling on your baby's future. She nodded shakily, trying to absorb the news. Five minutes ago she'd been worried about her full bladder and her ex-boyfriend whizzing down the slopes at

Courchevel. Now she felt as if the ground had fallen away in front of her, revealing a whole new chasm of worry. 'Where . . . ' She took a deep breath. 'Where should I go for this other test? Or can you do that here?'

The sonographer looked surprised at the question. 'Oh. Sorry – I should have made that clear. You'll have the amnio at sixteen weeks, we'll send you a letter to book you in.'

Saffron stared at her. 'You mean . . . I've got to wait four weeks before I know anything?' She must have misunderstood. Only the worst kind of sadist would keep you dangling that long, surely? 'Can't I have the test now? Or tomorrow?'

'I'm sorry, love, no. It has to be done at a certain time in the pregnancy – when you're sixteen weeks along. The doctor will . . . Well, they'll explain everything in the letter. In fact I've got some leaflets here for you. Oh, darling, don't cry. Come on, have a tissue. Can I phone someone to come and get you?'

Saffron couldn't remember how she made it home afterwards. Somehow her legs must have walked her out of that awful room, onto a bus and all the way back to her flat, but none of the details about the journey registered in her brain. It was only when she was back in the safety of her living room, weeping into her own sofa, that she realized it was three-thirty in the afternoon and she had completely forgotten to go back to work. She turned her phone on and stared in horror at the twenty-seven missed calls and sixty-three new emails. It hadn't even occurred to her that the rest of the world might be carrying on around her regardless.

The weekly team meeting would be under way by now and she'd completely failed to show up for it, let alone give any word of excuse or explanation. 'She just said she was meeting a client,' she imagined Kayla shrugging in that dippy, who-me? kind of way. Charlotte was no doubt livid and calling her all the names under the sun, but Saffron struggled to even care. There was no room in her brain right now for thoughts about meetings or clients or conference calls. All she could think about was Marie's sympathetic face as she broke the news to her. *A one in thirty-six chance.' Genetic abnormalities. You're going to have to wait another four weeks to be sure, though.*

Saffron couldn't remember ever feeling so confused and alone. She had read through the leaflet from the stenographer several times now and it made for very difficult reading. First of all, the amniocentesis itself sounded absolutely horrible – a long needle inserted into the womb to take a sample of amniotic fluid from around the baby. Her arm curled around her belly protectively at the thought. She didn't want anyone sticking needles anywhere near her baby, thank you very much. Worse, there was a small risk of miscarriage, caused by the test itself. In other words, by having the amnio she could actually be putting her baby's life at risk. How could she live with herself if that happened, if she made the wrong choice?

The worst bit of all in the leaflet – and, quite frankly, there were several to choose from – was the section headed 'What If My Test Is Positive?' Reading it just made her cry all over again. *Children born with Down's syndrome can lead very happy lives,* it assured her:

However, parents should be aware that they do risk potential health issues, such as heart problems, reduced hearing and poor vision. Other complications may include digestive problems, cervical-spine dislocation and blood disorders.

Poor little babies, she thought in anguish. As if life wasn't hard enough anyway. Then the leaflet got even harder to read:

You might choose to:
- Continue with the pregnancy and use the information from the test results in order to prepare for the birth and care of your baby
- Continue with the pregnancy and consider adoption; or
- End the pregnancy (have a termination).

Not a decision that anyone would find easy. She gnawed on her fingernails, pushing the leaflet aside, wishing she'd never gone for the scan at all. Then her phone rang and she let out a deep groan of despair as she saw the caller ID on screen. Oh, go away, Bunty. Really not the time, mate.

Sending the call to voicemail, she lay on her bed, wiped out. She should really ring the office and apologize for not being at the team meeting, lie about some terrible illness that had come upon her all of a sudden. Otherwise Charlotte would be calling for her head on a block and there would be a P45 in the post. But how could she even string a sentence together, when her head was swirling with so many fears and questions?

The only person who could comfort her now was Zoe, and she was halfway round the world, fast asleep on a warm Perth night, one tanned arm flung across Alexa, no doubt, without a care in the world. She couldn't speak to her parents about this — no way. How they would fuss and flap; her mum would be on Google in a nanoflash, scouring forums for stories, suggesting a second opinion, crowding Saffron's head with unhelpful information she'd discovered, articles she'd read in the *Telegraph*. All stemming from kindness and concern, undoubtedly, but with so much hand-wringing and sadness — 'Our poor little grandchild' — it would only make Saffron feel worse.

As for Max . . . Tears filled her eyes. Maybe it was just as well he hadn't come with her to the scan. He already had two healthy children, hadn't he? If he'd been at the scan today and heard the news, he'd probably blame her for her crap DNA or aged ovaries, even if he didn't say it out loud. He might even have backed away, hands up in surrender. *Sorry, but do you know what? I can't actually go through with this.*

Ugggh. She couldn't even drown her sorrows with a bucket of wine.

She wiped her eyes, blew her nose and took a deep breath, just as her phone started ringing again. Bunty. She let out a howl of frustration, sent the call to voicemail once more, then glared suspiciously at her phone as yet another new email pinged in. *Get away from it all for the weekend!* the subject line said enticingly.

Yes please, Saffron thought. Getting away from it all sounded exactly what she needed. She thought longingly of her solitary New Year break in Suffolk – the long walks and open skies, the freedom to do whatever she pleased without anyone hassling her, a little bolthole away from London, clients and Max.

She glanced back at her phone and realized that the email was a newsletter from the Cottage Holidays website, through which she'd booked her New Year retreat. *Get away from it all for the weekend*, she read again, clicking open the message. *20 per cent off deals for last-minute bookings. Give us a call and we'll find you the perfect place for your mini-break!*

God, it was tempting. She could do it right now, she told herself – book a cottage somewhere, pack a few things and jump in the car. Maybe the world was giving her a little nudge, showing her what she needed to do.

She thought about it for at least three seconds, then made her decision. If she stayed in the flat much longer, the walls would start closing in. She'd send a grovelling email to Charlotte saying she was on her sickbed with gastroenteritis and violent diarrhoea (embarrassment and Britishness should put a stop to any awkward questions), then she'd escape from London, just until she'd pulled herself together.

Why not? What was stopping her?

Nothing was stopping her. She pressed Dial on her phone and got her credit card ready. 'Hello,' she said, when a friendly-sounding man answered. 'I was wondering what availability you've got for a cottage this week. Anywhere in the South-East, to be honest, although Suffolk would be lovely . . . How long? Er . . . Four nights? It's just for me.' She paused to listen, then smiled. 'That would be absolutely perfect. I'll take it.'

Chapter Eighteen

'So, what seems to be the problem?'

She must stop thinking about dodgy old porn films, where the tradesman came to the door, all buff and hunky, and the lonely housewife let slip her sheer dressing gown and bent over the kitchen table. Oi, enough. Stop it, Caitlin!

'Um . . . The cooker's not working properly. It never gets very hot.'

Talking of hot, Harry Sykes was looking particularly fine today: white T-shirt and battered jeans, toolbox in hand, just a fuzz of sandy stubble along his jaw. Mmm. Hello, sailor. 'How about the kettle?' he asked, raising an eyebrow.

She was so busy trying to keep her composure – had she placed too much emphasis on the word 'hot'? – that she didn't get his hint immediately. 'The kettle? Yeah, it's fine. Oh,' she said, the penny dropping. 'Do you want a coffee? Tea?'

'Thought you'd never ask,' he said with a grin. 'Coffee, please. Milk and two sugars.'

She had her laptop open on the kitchen table, with the

baby-food website to be getting on with – *Don't mind me, I always work in here, honest* – but once she'd made them both coffees, she found herself distracted by the sight of him heaving the cooker out from its place against the wall so as to fiddle with the electrics. All the muscles in his back stood out as he did so, and his biceps bulged under the fabric of his top. Corrr.

'Hey, by the way,' he said, turning round unexpectedly and catching her perving. Embarrassing – she was totally acting like a dirty old housewife. 'I told my sister I was coming here today, and she said that your mum delivered Clemmy, my niece. Small world.'

'The One Direction fan?' Caitlin asked, remembering the stickers all over Harry's van.

'The very same. Probably came into the world singing and dancing, that one. But yeah, my sister Sam said your mum was amazing. The most wonderful midwife ever.'

Caitlin felt warmth rush into her face. First Gemma and now Harry gifting her these lovely shared memories of Jane. 'That's so nice to hear,' she said after a moment. 'She was a pretty great mum, too.'

'I bet. Sam said she absolutely doted on Clemmy whenever she came round. Bet you've got tons of baby photos piled up here, haven't you?'

Caitlin smiled. 'Probably, yeah.' She hadn't actually got

round to sorting through the photo albums yet. Another job she'd been putting off.

Harry cleared his throat rather self-consciously. 'Shame she's not around any more,' he said, bending to fiddle with a complicated tangle of wires. 'Could have done with her help this summer.'

Once again Caitlin was too distracted by the way his shirt strained over his broad back to register what he was saying straight away. 'This summer? Oh!' *What?* Did he mean what she thought he meant? 'You're having a *baby?*' she asked in a too-high pitch. 'I mean, not you, obviously. But . . . you're going to be a dad?'

He shrugged. 'Looks that way.'

The erotic home movie of electrician-meets-lonely-designer (*Sparks Will Fly!*) abruptly stopped playing in her head, as if the movie reel had spun off its axle. Oh shit! Damn it. Was it the stiletto-stamper who was up the duff? Bollocks.

'Congratulations,' she said after a too-long pause, remembering that this was what you were supposed to say in such situations. 'Does this mean you're going to break your New Year's resolution about not marrying anyone?'

He shrugged again. For a father-to-be, he didn't exactly look over the moon about this development, it had to be said. 'Dunno,' he mumbled, selecting a screwdriver from his tool-box. 'Me and Jade had split up before she found out, which kind of dumps on the whole romance-vibe. But anyway, it is what it is. She's happy. I'm . . . happy.'

He so *wasn't* happy. It was the first time she'd seen him without any kind of smile. 'Right. Good. Excellent,' she said, busying herself with a tricky piece of code. Inside, her mind roiled as it tried to digest this major piece of news. Now was definitely not the time to start trotting out the flirty lines of banter she'd planned. By announcing his imminent parent status he'd politely drawn a line in the sand, over which she was forbidden to tread. Maybe the whole spiel he'd given about her mum was a load of cobblers, and merely a means of getting round to the subject of babies.

She glanced at her laptop screen where she'd typed a string of utter gibberish. *Take a chance*, the fortune-cookie had said, but she was barking up the wrong tree here. A tree that was already taken.

You stupid bitch, you are MENTAL, Flynn gloated in her head, the words from his letter leaping out at her again. *Do you think anyone else is going to want you? You're not even attractive. You're a fucking JOKE.*

'Ah,' said Harry just then, leaning forward and twiddling his screwdriver. 'Gotcha.'

He gave her a triumphant grin and she forced herself to smile back at him. Idiot, she thought, feeling dejected. Look at him, will you? He's bloody scrumptious. Way out of your league. Don't kid yourself he'd ever be interested in the likes of you, Lanky-legs.

Still, if nothing else, at least she'd get a working cooker out of today. She'd go crazy and celebrate with another can of beans, piping hot this time. 'Woooo,' she muttered under her breath. Living on the edge.

Once Harry had gone, she abandoned her pretence at doing any website work – she couldn't concentrate – and went on with her mission to sort out the cottage. With Gemma's help, she had sorted through her mum's wardrobe earlier in the week and cleared out all of the clothes and bags stuffed in there. Gemma, who was always on the lookout for interesting material, had taken lots of the clothes with her, and the house felt lighter without them, as if a heavy emotional layer had been lifted away.

The living room was her next port of call, and boy, did it need help. The wallpaper – cream vinyl, with a repeating pattern of roses – was scuffed in places and peeling away above the window. The three-piece suite was in dusty plum-coloured velour, worn on the armrests, with cushions so flattened they looked as if they'd been lounged on by a family of elephants. The carpet was cheap and manky – brown-and-white swirls – and had been there for as long as Caitlin could remember. She had perfected headstands on this carpet, her feet against the wall, and could still remember the giddy feeling of delight as the room swung upside down. But now it all had to go.

She heaved and hauled the furniture into the dining room, where she crammed it in, higgledy-piggledy. The faded, dusty curtains were fit only for the dump, and came down, and then she ripped the carpet from its spiky grippers and began rolling it up, revealing lovely wide floorboards beneath.

While she was doing this, the disappointing conversation with Harry replayed endlessly in her head. Thank goodness he'd said it, really, before she'd done something rash, like throw her bra at him. (*Take a chance!*) Imagine the humiliation if she'd actually come out with a cheesy pick-up line and he'd knocked her back. *Er . . . wow, I'm really flattered, but, like — you know, NO. You weirdo.*

Yeesh. She should be grateful she'd spared herself *that* little moment at least.

It wasn't until she was halfway across the living room, with the carpet and underlay in an enormous bulky Swiss roll, a thick cloud of dust swirling in her wake, that her mind snagged on something Harry had said. *Bet you've got tons of baby photos piled up here, haven't you?*

A perfectly innocuous comment, at face value. He'd probably not even been conscious of saying it, preoccupied with making his bombshell baby-father announcement. The weird thing was that, now that he'd said it, she couldn't remember seeing a single picture of herself as a baby. Her mind had gone completely blank. What did she even look like?

She stood in the middle of the room, hands on her hips, sieving uselessly through her brain. For goodness' sake. This was ridiculous. She was having a senile moment at the grand old age of thirty-two. What *did* she look like as a baby?

Abandoning the carpet, she wiped her hands on her jeans and went to remind herself. As soon as she opened the photo albums she'd surely remember, and then she'd feel like a total spanner for forgetting in the first place. Her mum and dad had documented everything else so thoroughly in her childhood – finger-painting at playgroup!, The infants' sports day!, Sitting on a donkey at Great Yarmouth, absolutely rigid with fear!, In Brownie uniform proudly doing a three-finger salute! – that there had to be hundreds of tedious small-baby-in-hat photos. She'd probably blanked them out through sheer boredom.

The photo albums had all been on the bookshelves in the living room, but due to her recent clear-out were now in a box on the dining-room floor. Right. Let's see you then, baby Caitlin, in all your embarrassing naked-in-a-bath glory. She lifted out the first few and leafed through. A very early collection, with Jane and Steve in cool Seventies gear, back when they were first married and still living in Scotland. Bless.

A much later album with Caitlin as a teenager, all white panstick make-up, curled lip and bovver boots. Like that was ever a good look.

A book of photos of Caitlin as a toddler, most of which

featured her with food all over her face and a naughty grin. Some things never changed.

On and on Caitlin went through the lovingly assembled collections, feeling increasingly confused. There were no baby photos. Not one. Why would that be? She didn't understand. Her mum loved babies. Given her time again, Jane Fraser would have been one of those annoying mums on Facebook documenting every last fart her precious child produced. *Like!*

She reached the final photo album, but it was a fairly recent one, of Mum and some friends on a cruise, all in big sunhats, brandishing lurid cocktails. Harry was wrong. There weren't tons of baby photos at all. She couldn't find a single one. 'What's going on?' she asked aloud, trying to ignore the sick, strange feeling churning up inside her. 'I don't understand, Mum. Where are all the pictures? I wasn't that ugly a baby, was I?'

She must have missed something. There must be a whole box of them somewhere. There just had to be.

Rocking back on her heels, she checked through all of the albums again, more painstakingly this time. The earliest photo she could find was when she was about two, at a guess, dressed in a corduroy pinafore dress with her dark hair falling in a shining bowl-cut. Jane was holding her, a dazzling smile on her face as she looked down at little Caitlin, real love in her eyes. Meanwhile Caitlin had the same expression she'd had on the seafront donkey: shell-shocked and kind of nervous, her body held rigid.

Very, very faintly a bell was ringing in her head as if this picture had great resonance. But what?

Caitlin stared at this page in the album for a long time. Then, her fingers clammy, she peeled back the protective cellophane and took the picture from its sticky backing. Turning it over, she saw in her mum's careful cursive handwriting: *A special day. June 1st, 1983. Caitlin!*

She dropped the photo as if it were red-hot. June 1st? That was Family Day, the day they'd always celebrated with Victoria sponge, fresh strawberries and champagne. *Just because,* Jane had said, shrugging, as if the date were a purely random selection. *Sometimes it's good to celebrate your family and think about how lucky you are.* Champagne, though. On her parents' meagre salaries! They weren't the sort of people to splash out on champagne unless it was a special occasion.

A *really* special occasion.

She glanced at the photo again. She looked so uncomfortable in Jane's arms. Frightened, almost. Jane was gazing at her with adoration, but Caitlin looked as if she didn't know what the hell was going on. *A special day. June 1st, 1983. Caitlin!*

It was that exclamation mark that kept nagging at her. That wasn't normal, was it? As if it was the first time she'd appeared in their lives. As if they'd only just met.

No. Just no. Shut up, Caitlin. She was definitely losing the plot.

I'm sorry, hen, she remembered her mum saying as she lay dying. *I should have told you. I never knew how to say it.*

I'm sorry, hen.

I'm sorry, hen.

Nausea rose inside her, hot and sour, and she ran from the room, her heart booming.

Chapter Nineteen

'That's nine pounds fifty-eight, please. Thanks very much.' Gemma took the ten-pound note offered to her and opened the till.

'Thank you, darling. Earning a bit of extra pocket money, are we?'

Gemma's smile tightened on her face as she put the forty-two pence change into Bill Perkins's outstretched hand. 'Something like that,' she said and walked away down the bar. 'Ladies. What can I get you?'

She'd been working in The Partridge for three days now and was slowly getting to grips with having a job for the first time in twelve years. She had learned to pour a pint of Adnams without topping it with two inches of yellow froth, how to work the glass-washer and navigate the temperamental electronic till, and she was getting to know the regulars and their particular quirks. For instance, she now knew that Brian Butters kept his own silver tankard behind the bar and refused to drink from anything else. Tight old John McNaught would always wait for his single penny change, rather than wave an airy hand and say, 'Don't worry about it', like every other normal person did. And Louise Brierley, who was supposedly on a health kick, would lean over the bar and whisper huskily for a sneaky vodka to be added to her orange juice, 'But don't tell my hubby, love, all right?'

Like Bill Perkins, a few other people had raised an eyebrow when they saw Gemma behind the bar. 'Don't you live in that lovely big farmhouse?' one lady asked in surprise when Gemma served her, as if people in lovely big farmhouses couldn't possibly need to earn a couple of extra quid.

'Yes, that's me,' she replied briskly, hurrying through the order before the next question, starting 'So why . . . ?', could be asked.

It was fun enough work, though, sociable and varied, particularly in the evenings when they had a bigger crowd. She enjoyed chatting to people she wouldn't normally mix with – some of the old men, for example, were just adorable; and Bernie, the landlord, was brilliant. What she was most looking forward to, though, was the Friday pay packet: the little brown envelope with cash and a payslip, every penny of it earned by her. It might be 'pocket money' to the likes of Bill Perkins, but it would make a big difference to Gemma. Hard cash in her purse again, money actually coming *in* to the family, rather than pouring out. Admittedly the sum she was earning was a pittance, as Harry had said so apologetically, but a pittance could at least contribute in its own small way.

She'd telephoned the utility companies and told them she was now working and was very much going to pay the bills, but please could she have a bit of leeway for the time being? Most of them agreed that she could pay off a small amount of what she owed every few weeks, provided such payments remained regular and consistent. So that had bought them a tiny gasp of breathing space at least. As for the mounting credit-card bills . . . well, she'd have to cross that bridge when she came to it. Until she could scrape together some more money, she had simply decided to stop looking at them, stuffing the envelopes unopened in a drawer. There were only so many sleepless nights of worry that a woman could cope with, before she had a nervous breakdown.

The next mortgage payment was due at the end of the month. She was trying not to think about that, either, although the panic often seized her as she lay in bed at night, with images of bailiffs at the door leaving her unable to doze off. There was still no sign of any compensation payment for Spencer, even though she had made the application herself now and gone round to the scaffolding firm in person, only to beg despairingly in their office. (How to make a tit of yourself, part 937.) But anyway, she was doing her best.

Unfortunately, news of her job hadn't gone down too well at home. Darcey had been positively dismayed. 'But I will miss you,' she said, her lower lip sticking out. 'What about my bedtime story?'

Will, too, was unimpressed. 'Oh, great. How intellectual! My mum's a barmaid? You'd better not tell any of my friends.'

As for Spencer . . . he wasn't exactly thrilled, either. 'I don't want all those blokes leering at you,' he grumbled, although she suspected it was more the fact that she had replaced him as Family Breadwinner that he didn't like. It obviously offended his macho ideas of how a husband and wife should operate. *Yeah, well, that's been really successful lately, hasn't it?* she felt like saying. It took all of her patience not to fling the red bills in his face and point out that this outdated mindset would see them ending up on the streets with a begging bowl, if they weren't careful.

'I'm just being practical,' she said through gritted teeth. 'I thought this was a good solution.' When he said nothing, she couldn't resist adding, 'Otherwise, maybe we should seriously consider what Will suggested the other evening and sell some of our things to raise a bit of capital. While you're not driving, we could sell the M—'

'I'm not selling my Mazda,' he said furiously. 'I'm not a fucking cripple. I'll be able to drive again in a few months, the doctor said.'

'All right, I just thought I'd mention it.'

'I'm not selling, Gem. No way.'

'All right! In which case, I need to work. We've got no choice.'

To make a point about how disgruntled he felt, he went and sat in his wretched car, all alone, in the gloom of the garage, like a big sulky baby. Gemma ignored him. She had a job to go to and didn't have the energy for yet another argument. Besides, Spencer was due to have the cast off his ankle soon, and she was clinging to the hope that this would lift his mood again. Something had to.

'He's been quite low,' she had blurted out to the doctor, when they went back to the hospital for a check-up the week before. 'I've been wondering if maybe he's depressed. I've been reading up about Post-Concussion Syndrome and . . . '

The look Spencer gave her was so ferocious she could have sworn the ground quaked. 'Wouldn't anyone be depressed?' he spat. 'I'm not exactly going to be cheerful about this, am I? Who would?'

The consultant – a woman in her fifties, with watchful brown eyes and a calm, measured manner – said to Spencer, 'This sort of thing tests everyone's patience and good humour. But if you're finding it too much, then we can certainly talk about—'

'No,' Spencer said, visibly annoyed. 'I'm not finding it too much. And I don't want to be drugged up on any happy pills, either. Got that?'

They hadn't spoken the entire way home. He didn't even

moan about her driving, as he usually did. At last, as she was pulling into the driveway, he rounded on her. 'Don't ever do that again.'

'What?'

'Talk about me as if I'm not there. Tell a doctor your opinion of me and how best to fix me, like I'm some kind of child who can't speak for himself. Let me handle it, all right?'

He clambered awkwardly out of the car, with a painfully slow shuffle and swing of his crutches, silently daring her to offer help. She knew better by now. Instead, she sat there in the driver's seat, watching as he leaned shakily against the porch, fumbled for his door keys, then let himself in. The front door gave an imperious slam behind him.

She let out a long shuddering sigh, her breath steaming in the cold air. When Spencer behaved like this — so pig-headed, so bloody self-centred, as if he was the only person who mattered in the entire world — she sometimes fantasized about driving away and leaving him behind. And good bloody riddance!

But in the next moment she thought of her mum, doing exactly that with the waiter from Ibiza, and a thousand childhood hurts reared up and stung her all over again. For years she had lain in bed every night listening for the sound of her mum's footsteps tottering up the front path — footsteps that never came. She had wished on every blown-out birthday candle, and every stir of the Christmas pudding with Grandma, that Karen would come home. On every significant occasion growing up – Christmas concerts, wobbly teeth, her first period – she'd wanted her mum there. Her dad had been Superman, nobody could have been a better father, but despite his best attempts there was still a gap in the house, an empty, ghostly presence. And now here she was, wishing herself away, to leave her own empty space.

More like your mother than you thought, after all, whispered a mean voice in her head.

No. She wasn't like her mum. There was no way she would ever walk out on Will and Darcey. But Spencer? It had crossed her mind a few times lately.

She twisted the wedding ring on her finger and steamed up the windows with another sigh. *In sickness and in health, remember?*

Yep. She remembered. For richer, for poorer, too. If ever there was a test of her marriage vows, then this was it.

As well as working in the pub, Gemma had a couple of sewing jobs on the go – the bridesmaid dresses and the curtains – and had taken to working up in the tiny box room at the front of the house, away from the blasting telly and Spencer's complaints. Sewing had always been her thing, right from the summer when she was about Darcey's age and staying with her grandparents for a fortnight while her dad worked. Grandma Pepper had the most wonderful bag of scrap material – all colours, all fabrics – as well as a button tin and a bulging sewing box. While Grandad took the boys out fishing and kite-flying, Gemma had a crash-course in sewing with Grandma, threading her first needle and making her first clumsy, wobbling stitches. By the end of the fortnight she had stitched an entire wardrobe of outfits for her dolls and teddies and was hooked.

These days Will wouldn't be seen dead wearing anything his mum made for him, but Gemma still made skirts and dresses for Darcey, and for herself too of course. She had set up her sewing table by the window of the box room so that she could gaze out at the street below while she sewed, and enjoyed seeing the comings and goings of her neighbours: Mrs Belafonte walking her Labradoodles; and Jan, the harassed-looking mum from number twenty-six, hurrying to playgroup with her three-year-old toddler twins. And you could set your watch by Mr Ranger, the elderly gent who lived in the rundown corner house, setting off for his midday pint of ale.

One afternoon she was surprised to see a different person walking up the lane. A young woman with a carrier bag of groceries from the Spar, who was familiar, yet not instantly recognizable. Long red hair that streamed like ribbons in the wind, a black trench coat, a short flared skirt over leggings and boots. Then she realized it was the woman who'd stayed next door over New Year. Sophia, was it? An unusual name, beginning with S. Sapphire? Suzanne?

Gemma frowned, the name on the tip of her tongue.

Saffron, that was it! She had been really funny and nice, teaching everyone the 'Single Ladies' routine after the clock struck midnight. They'd had a right laugh that night.

She watched, her sewing forgotten, as Saffron reached the cottage next door, put down her bag of shopping and rummaged in her coat pocket for the door key. Then, as if she could feel the weight of Gemma's gaze, she turned and looked in the direction of The Granary. Busted, Gemma thought guiltily, feeling herself blush. Caught noseying. She held her hand up in a little wave and tried to look surprised, as if she'd only just seen her.

Saffron smiled and waved back, then pointed at her door, holding up her hands in a T symbol. Then she mimed drinking something, which might have been a cup of tea or possibly a pint of wine. Gemma wasn't about to say no to either. She put two thumbs up, switched off her sewing machine and hurried downstairs. 'Just popping next door,' she yelled.

'You came back!' she cried as Saffron opened the door and let her in. Then the smile slipped from Gemma's face as she saw how terrible Saffron looked close-up. Puffy bloodshot eyes with enormous bags underneath, spots around her mouth, a general look of despair. Oh my goodness, she must be ill, thought Gemma, her heart squeezing in worry. Ill or recently dumped — maybe both. 'Is everything okay?' she asked tentatively, hoping her alarm wasn't too visible.

'Well, I've been better,' Saffron replied breezily with a brave, trying-her-hardest sort of smile, but her shoulders sagged, a dead giveaway. *No, she was not okay.* 'Come in. It's good to see you again.'

'You too. When did you get here? And how long are you staying this time?'

'I arrived a few days ago. Kind of a spur-of-the-moment decision really, just upped and left. I'm not sure how long I'll stay.' She hesitated as if she was about to say more, but then plastered on that terrible fake smile again instead. Who was she trying to kid? Gemma had been staring despair full in the face herself recently and she recognized a fellow sufferer from twenty paces.

'Come in, anyway. My drink options are limited to tea or coffee, but I've just bought some chocolate Hobnobs, which you're welcome to share.'

In the small kitchen Saffron filled the kettle and took two clean mugs out of the cupboard while Gemma sat at the table. 'How are things then? Last time I saw you, we were dancing under that glitterball in your living room and making our New Year's resolutions.'

'That's right.' Gemma snorted. 'And planning world domination after reading our fortune-cookies. Not that I've made my fortune yet, sadly. Quite the opposite, to be honest.'

She must have been sounding more despondent than she intended, because Saffron quirked an eyebrow. 'That doesn't sound good.'

'No.' There was a waiting sort of silence. Cards-on-the-table time. 'It's my husband,' she said heavily after a few moments. 'Gone and broken his back, hasn't he? Well, a couple of vertebrae anyway, and an ankle for good measure, too. So he's stuck at home, out of work, and it's all been pretty . . . ' Her throat felt tight all of a sudden. 'Pretty shit, frankly.'

Saffron slid into the chair opposite her, abandoning the tea-making. 'Oh no. So sorry to hear that. He is going to be all right, isn't he?'

'Yeah, eventually. But in the meantime things are a bit tight, money-wise. I'm working in the pub and taking on some dressmaking jobs, but we're kind of hand-to-mouth right now.' Now it was Gemma's turn to slap on an artificial smile. Enough already. 'But we'll be okay. We'll manage. How about you?'

Saffron knotted her fingers together in her lap. 'Well, the short version is that I'm pregnant and the father doesn't want to know, which is absolutely fine by the way – I mean, I can totally cope on my own.'

Whoa. So that was why she looked so strained and tired. 'Of course you can,' Gemma told her bracingly; the only possible response.

'But then the other day I went along for a scan and . . .' Her face crumpled. 'And they said there might be complications – because I'm so bloody ancient and decrepit, basically. But I've got to wait f . . . f . . . four weeks for another test to f . . . f . . . find out!' She put her head in her hands and burst into sobs.

'Oh, love,' cried Gemma, rushing round the table to put an arm around her. Every pregnant woman's worst fear. 'Oh God, what a nightmare. How awful.' She stroked Saffron's hair, feeling desperately sorry for her. 'And the father . . . He doesn't know this yet?'

Saffron shook her head, red-eyed. 'He wouldn't care anyway. I tried to tell him about the baby, but he . . . he's got another girlfriend now.'

Gemma's jaw dropped in indignation. 'Already? That's bloody charming, isn't it? Sounds like you're better off without him.'

'Well, that's the thing,' Saffron said, her voice laced with misery. 'It was an accident. We'd only been together a few weeks.'

'Oh no.' Gutted. 'That must have come as a surprise.'

'Tell me about it. And at first I was so freaked out and shocked I wasn't sure if I even wanted to keep the baby. That's why I came here at New Year, to try and get my head around everything.' She wiped her eyes with the back of her hand. 'Then I decided I really *did* want the baby, so I wrote him a letter to tell him about it.'

'And what did he say?'

'Nothing.' You could see the pain in Saffron's face. 'Absolutely nothing. In the letter I mentioned the scan, in case he wanted to come along, but no. Didn't show.'

Gemma shook her head. 'The bastard. Honestly, *men*. What would it have taken for him to make one phone call? To meet you and talk about it, like a grown-up? Some people have no sense of decency.' She squeezed Saffron's shoulder and straightened up. 'Let me make you that tea. No, sit there, I'll do it. Where are these Hobnobs, then? You need to keep your strength up, remember.'

'Thanks,' Saffron said, as Gemma made the tea and tipped half the packet of biscuits onto a plate. 'I don't know how I'm going to manage. I'm terrified of having to do everything on my own. I haven't got a clue about babies.'

'Most people feel like that at first,' Gemma assured her. 'I know I did. As for the test — an amnio, is it? It's the hospital taking precautions, that's all, taking extra care of you. Look, if you give me a bit of notice, I'll come with you if you want. I will!' The words were out before she remembered her new job in the pub, not to mention how expensive it was to get into London on the train these days.

Saffron looked as if she was about to cry again. 'That is so sweet of you. Thank you.' She rubbed her eyes. 'My sister said the same when I Skyped her last night, but it's not exactly practical because . . . ' She broke off, sniffing, and stood up. 'Sorry, let me just grab a tissue and blow my nose. Back in a minute.'

She left the room and Gemma heard her thudding upstairs to the bathroom. Just then Saffron's mobile started ringing on the table. *Caller unknown*, it said on the display.

Gemma hesitated. 'Your phone's ringing!' she called, but there was no answer. The walls in these stone cottages were so thick, the sound didn't travel much at all. After three more rings, Gemma picked up the phone and answered it. 'Hello, Saffron's phone?' she said politely.

'At last!' came a flustered voice. 'I tried the office and they said you were ill, but I was so desperate to talk to you, I had to try. You won't *believe* what Troy's done now, the despicable little shit . . . '

'Oh. Excuse me? This isn't actually Saffron,' Gemma said over the garbled torrent. 'Sorry, I just picked up her phone. She's upstairs.'

'In the flat? But I just tried ringing there. Where are you?'

'I'm . . . ' Gemma hesitated. 'Well, in Suffolk. I live next door to the cottage where—'

'Suffolk? She didn't tell me she was going to Suffolk!' The voice was familiar for some reason, shrill and indignant as it was. 'So where are you? I'll drive over.'

'Um . . . ' Gemma wished Saffron would hurry up and

take over this call herself, but now she could hear the loo flushing and water running upstairs. 'I . . . Look, who is this?'

'It's B—' For a moment Gemma thought the line had gone dead, but then the woman said, 'It's her sister.'

'Oh! Shall I get her to call you back?'

'Tell you what, just give me the address and I'll drive over. Chat about it with her in person. I could do with getting out of London.'

There was something odd about this conversation, but Gemma didn't want to be rude or start quibbling, especially when Saffron had just said herself how nice her sister had been about offering to come to the amnio with her. Besides, judging by the state Saffron was in, a visit from her sister was probably exactly what she needed right now. 'Okay,' she said haltingly, then proceeded to give her directions to Larkmead and the cottage.

'Splendid. Thank you! I'll head off immediately. Tell her to put some wine in the fridge, for goodness' sake!'

Gemma put the phone down, frowning. She hadn't expected Saffron's sister to sound quite so bossy. And why would she think Saffron had any wine, when she knew she was pregnant?

'Sorry about that,' Saffron said, coming back into the room a minute later. 'My bladder — honestly, it thinks it's a tap these days.'

Gemma smiled faintly. 'I remember that, from being

pregnant with my two.' She nodded down at the phone. 'I just took a call for you while you were upstairs, I hope that's okay. I did try shouting to you, but I don't think you heard.'

'Who was it?'

'Your sister. She said she's going to get in her car and come straight over. I gave her the address.' She paused. 'It was a bit weird, really.'

Saffron's pale-blue eyes had opened very wide. 'Eloise? What does she want? How did she sound?'

'Well . . . Kind of manic, really. She was saying something about Troy. Being a despicable little shit?'

'*Troy?* But he's . . . ' Saffron's jaw dropped and a few seconds ticked by while she stared in disbelief. 'Oh no. She wouldn't.'

'What? I don't understand. Have I done something wrong?'

'I've got two sisters – one's in Australia, and the other's not speaking to me right now. I think the woman you just spoke to is . . . ' She groaned. 'I can't believe this.'

'What? Who?' Gemma felt absolutely mortified. She should never have answered that phone. Meanwhile Saffron looked as if she might be sick.

'Bunty fucking Halsom, that's who. My client from hell. The woman I'd love never to see again.' She made a growl of frustration. 'It must be her – she's been seeing someone called Troy and is completely obsessed with him. Oh Christ!'

Gemma clapped a hand to her mouth. Bunty Halsom from

the telly? 'That's why her voice was familiar,' she said weakly. 'I'm so sorry. She told me she was your sister, and I just thought . . .'

'That bloody woman. Of all the nerve. Honestly, I could throttle her, I really could. No idea about boundaries. No idea whatsoever!' She grabbed her phone and began dialling. Gemma heard it ring a few times and then a voicemail kick in. 'Bunty? This is Saffron Flint. Please do not come to Suffolk. I do not want to see you right now. I am on holiday and will not answer the door. Do you understand? I will not answer the door!'

Chapter Twenty

Saffron could not believe the brass neck of Bunty. To lie like that, so outrageously, pretending to be her sister in order to weasel out her whereabouts . . . It was an atrocious way to behave. What was this woman *on*? And of all the times for her to turn up unwanted, this was definitely the worst. Saffron could hardly cope with living inside her own head right now, let alone gear up to deal with Bunty in any kind of professional manner. In the space of two minutes her place of refuge had become a trap, with the clock now ticking down to the arrival of her uninvited and decidedly unwelcome guest. Incandescent with fury, it was only Gemma's utterly stricken expression that prevented Saffron from going nuclear.

'I did think there was something strange about the conversation,' Gemma gulped, wringing her hands. 'But I thought: I can't start arguing with your sister and refusing to tell her anything. I'm so sorry, though. I'm really, really sorry. You can hide at my house if you want. I'll deal with her and send her packing when she gets here.'

Saffron's rage cooled a fraction at the sincerity in Gemma's brown eyes. She had only acted as any other normal person would, in assuming that the 'sister' on the other end of the phone was kosher. It wasn't Gemma's fault that Bunty was a complete bloody lunatic. 'It's all right,' she said. 'If I had an ounce more energy, I'd just drive back to London right now, but I'll stay and face the music.' She pulled a face. 'I'll probably turn the air around Pear Tree Lane blue by the time I finish with her, though.'

'I'd drive you back myself, but I've got a ton of sewing to do, and then I'm working in the pub,' Gemma said, still with that anxious look. 'I could juggle things around, though, if you really want to go.'

Saffron heaved a sigh. It had taken her an hour and a half to get here; she couldn't ask Gemma to do such a thing. 'No. You're all right. Tell me about this sewing then: what are you making?'

She drank her tea and listened as Gemma described the pale-pink organza dresses she had designed, and her anger subsided a little more. Privately she couldn't get over how different Gemma looked, since she'd been the hostess-with-the-mostest back at the New Year party, with that divine blue dress, her hair coiffed, lashings of lippy. She hadn't stopped laughing and teasing everyone the whole evening. Now her face was sunken and her eyes had lost all their humour and sparkle.

'Talking of which, I'd better go,' Gemma said eventually, glancing up at the clock. 'I meant it, by the way, about that awful Bunty woman. If you can't face dealing with her, I'll put a flea in her ear and send her packing. Or I'll threaten her with one of Spencer's crutches. Okay?'

'Okay. And thanks for earlier – listening to me going on, I mean. I swear I didn't invite you over just to burst into tears on you.'

Gemma patted her arm comfortingly. 'Any time. Seriously. And hey, thanks for listening to me, too. Cheaper than therapy, right? I feel much better for having a bit of a moan.' She paused at the front door, then surprised Saffron with a hug. 'Take care of yourself,' she said. 'Pop round if you want some company, all right?'

'Thanks. I will do. Bye, Gemma.'

After she'd gone, Saffron sank onto the sofa feeling wearied by the prospect of Bunty's imminent arrival and wishing she knew what to do. Her friend Kate would probably tell her to see Bunty off the premises with a shotgun, which was tempting, but perhaps not advisable. In the past, her boss Charlotte had assured her she could take any gripes about Bunty straight to her desk, but Saffron had always preferred to tough it out, rather than admit defeat. Anyway she could hardly phone the office for advice now, because as far as Charlotte was concerned, Saffron was at home, puking over the toilet bowl, rather than in a holiday cottage in Suffolk.

She shut her eyes and put her feet up, too tired to think any more. She would keep her cool, she vowed, and be polite, yet firm. Whatever happened, though, she would not let Bunty Halsom step one foot over the threshold, and that was that.

'Cooee! Anyone home?'

Saffron jolted awake at the sound of the voice. The room was dark. How long had she been asleep? She rubbed her eyes and wiped what felt suspiciously like dribble from her mouth, then sat up straighter as she heard footsteps.

'Saffron? Are you in here?' came the voice again. A voice that sounded suspiciously like . . . oh no. Already? So much for warding Bunty off at the threshold.

Saffron scrambled to her feet as the living-room door opened and Bunty came in and switched the light on. 'Ah! There you are. The door was on the latch, so I let myself in. Lovely place! Shall I pour us an aperitif, or do you have wine? Did you get my message about Troy, by the way? He has been unspeakably vile, you know. You'll never guess——'

It was like being in a nightmare. Saffron immediately forgot all her plans to be calm and professional. 'What the hell do you think you're playing at?' she snapped.

Her curt unfriendliness stopped Bunty mid-sentence. 'I . . . Sorry, what?'

'Lying that you were my sister so as to get my address. I

have come here to *convalesce*,' she said angrily – not strictly true, but Bunty didn't need to know that – 'and you have the nerve to invite yourself over to tell me about Troy sodding Blake? Have you lost the plot? How dare you? And how, in any way, do you think this is a good idea?'

Bunty's froggy blue eyes looked even moister and more bulging than usual. 'Well . . . ' she stammered, floundering for words in a most un-Bunty-like way. 'Well, because you're my adviser on these things.'

Her adviser on crap tabloid-stunt boyfriends? Er, no. Actually not. Honestly, for a well-educated, middle-aged woman with a good career record and pots of money in the bank, Bunty was like a child sometimes. A helpless, needy child who couldn't do a single bloody thing for herself. Saffron took a deep breath. 'With the greatest respect' – ha! – 'I am not at your beck and call, especially when I've taken time off work to . . . to recover. Besides, listening to you banging on about your airhead boyfriend is *not* part of my job description. Okay? You can save all that shit for your friends, not me, because I don't want to hear it!'

Bunty's pastel-pink mouth quivered and she seemed to shrink in height. 'I . . . I . . . ' she began, blinking a few times. 'I thought *you* were my friend.'

What? Since when? And how on earth was Saffron supposed to respond to that, without mortally offending her client?

'Well . . . ' *Deep breaths, Saffron. Grit your teeth.* 'Ours is first and foremost a business relationship, isn't it?' she replied; a polite way of saying No. 'And of course it's great that we get on so well' – she'd be struck down with lightning, telling such porkies – 'but it's important we both respect our positions here. My job is to help boost your career, to tell the world about your talents, Bunty.' *Come and zap me, lightning, I deserve the full frazzling for that.* 'It's not my job to . . . '

Then she broke off, noticing that her client had tears streaming down her face, glistening tracks through her make-up.

'I thought he loved me,' Bunty sobbed, choking on each word.

Saffron opened and closed her mouth wordlessly. Oh, help. She wasn't used to seeing Bunty as anything other than brash and bombastic. Now she seemed an absolute wreck.

'He said he loved me,' Bunty wept, shoulders shaking. 'And now he's gone to the *Daily M-M-Mail.* Some nasty little K-K-Kiss and T-T-Tell story!'

She buried her face in her hands and Saffron suppressed a groan. No. Not now, Bunty. Why, oh why, was she even listening to this? Why was Bunty still on the premises at all? She pressed her lips together, resisting the urge to put her hands around her client's fat neck. Much as she wanted to, she could not push Bunty away when she was in this state, though.

'Go on then,' she said resignedly. 'You might as well sit down and tell me the worst. Let's hear it.' Ten minutes, she thought. Ten minutes and then she would politely but firmly show her client the door.

Bunty lowered herself onto the far end of the sofa and clasped her hands in her lap. 'There's a sex tape,' she said shakily, not meeting Saffron's gaze.

Saffron's mouth fell open, and she closed it with a snap. Oh, great. And now her brain had gone on strike at the terrible images this announcement prompted. 'Right,' she said, her heart sinking. It was already obvious this would take a lot longer than ten little minutes to sort out. 'And is he enough of a bastard to go public with it?'

'Probably.' That parping nose-blow again. 'I've had a journalist from the *Mail* ringing up, wanting to know if it's true about my love-eggs. If *he* didn't tell them that, then who did?'

Saffron did not want to think about Bunty in relation to love-eggs or any other kind of sex toys. 'I see,' she said. Working in PR did throw up these nasty little surprises now and then. Last year the agency had had to put a gloss on a story about one of their footballer clients being caught with his pants down during a brothel raid. Then there had been Charlotte's famous actress client with the squeaky-clean, wholesome reputation, who'd been done for possession of some truly filthy pornography; and the restaurateur beloved of the gossip mags for his fiery relationship with his wife, who'd been stitched up by not one but two mistresses, both of whom were expecting his babies. They were all at it.

She gazed blankly around the dingy room, wondering if she could possibly shape this predicament into something positive. Should she advise Bunty to maintain a dignified silence until the storm blew over, or use the opportunity to gather support instead, cast Bunty as the betrayed victim and maybe sell an exclusive story to a journalist from another paper? Her mind leapt from one option to another. This could even be a new avenue of work for Bunty, she realized: a consultant on magazine sex-columns, or articles about sexual experimentation for the over-fifties . . .

Her brain ached. How she wished this hadn't come to her door today. She wasn't in any fit state to start assembling a press strategy. 'Bunty, perhaps we should pass you on to Charlotte,' she said weakly. 'I'm not sure I'm up to this at the moment, whereas she's had a lot of experience with this kind of thing.'

Bunty's mouth turned down at the corners. 'But I don't like Charlotte,' she confessed. 'She looks down her nose at me, like I'm not good enough for her. Lady Muck.' She rummaged in her handbag for a monogrammed hip flask and brandished it in the air. 'Shag it all, darling, let's just get sloshed. Maybe I'll send some heavies round to kneecap Troy instead. That'll shut him up.' She unscrewed the lid and took a hefty slug. 'Can I tempt you?' she asked, holding it out towards Saffron.

Saffron's stomach curdled at the smell and she recoiled, shaking her head. 'I can't,' she said when Bunty raised a questioning eyebrow. 'I mean . . . I'm not drinking. Because I'm ill, remember. Ill, and on the wagon. Allergic.'

A look of perplexity crossed Bunty's face at this torrent of rambling, one lie after another. Then her eyes narrowed. 'What's going on?' she asked.

Shit. She must have guessed about the pregnancy. 'What do you mean?'

'You said you were ill. Is it contagious?' Bunty was up on her feet again and backing away. 'Because my immune system is already in tatters with all this stress. I'm taking extra vitamins and wheatgrass supplements, but I can't cope with any more strain. I'm supposed to be auditioning for *Wanna Be A Dancer?* next week, darling. I've got to be at the top of my game, health-wise.'

Saffron's sympathy evaporated in a flash, swiftly followed by the last dregs of her patience. That would teach her to be a sucker for a sob story. 'Oh right, because it's all about *you*, isn't it?' she said, breathing hard as she stood up to face this dreadful, horrible, shallow person who'd invaded her space without a second thought. 'Well, I've had enough. I quit. Do you hear me? I'm through with trying to help you and look after you. So you can just bugger off back to London and leave me alone. Find some other sap to put up with you, because I can't bear it a minute longer!'

Bunty stared at her open-mouthed, eyes boggling. 'You can't *quit*, just like that,' she said, taken aback. 'What about Troy, and the tape?'

'I couldn't care less about Troy and your mucky little tape,' Saffron said, her voice rising in pitch. Sod it, she might as well go for broke. 'You have absolutely no idea, do you? You turn up here, uninvited, and expect me to drop everything for you. Then, when I tell you I'm ill, you immediately think of yourself. You don't even bother to ask how I am, or why I'm here. Well, I'll tell you, shall I? I'm waiting for a test to see if my baby's okay. Is that good enough for you? Will that do? Now get out!'

Bunty looked stunned. A full five seconds passed before she spoke. 'I'm . . . I don't know what to say.'

'Don't say anything, because I don't want to hear it.' Saffron pointed magisterially at the door. 'Please just go. I'll ask Charlotte to find someone else to represent you.'

Bunty didn't take any notice of the pointing. In fact she sat right back down again. 'I'm sorry,' she said quietly. 'I didn't know you were pregnant.'

'Yes, well,' Saffron said, already wishing she had kept her mouth buttoned. She lowered her arm, feeling spent.

'And you're right, I shouldn't have turned up like this, expecting you to drop everything for me. Bad habit of mine.'

She pulled out a plastic cigarette and sucked hard on it. 'Do you want to talk about the baby?' she asked hesitantly.

'Not really.'

'That's fine. I understand. I'm sorry. You're not really going to quit, are you? Please don't.'

Saffron's fury was ebbing away as quickly as it had flared up. She couldn't exactly afford to quit right now, however badly her client behaved. 'No, I'm not going to quit,' she mumbled, looking at the floor. She gritted her teeth. 'And I'm sorry I shouted at you. I'm a bit hormonal.'

'Of course you are. Anyway, I asked for it. I've been too wrapped up in myself lately. Wasn't thinking straight.' Bunty took another slug of the gin, or whatever it was in her hip flask, wincing as she swallowed. 'Now, look. It's getting on for seven o'clock, and I don't know about you, but I'm famished. How about I take you out for dinner somewhere lovely? My treat. You do look a bit pale, you know. You could probably do with some good hot food. What do you say?'

It was on the tip of Saffron's tongue to say a polite *No, thank you, and can you go now, please*, but then she thought about the dull ingredients she'd bought from the shop earlier — some pasta, packets of rubbery-looking cheese and shiny pink ham, plus a slightly flabby lettuce. Given the choice, 'dinner somewhere lovely' was winning, hands down. 'Okay. Thanks,' she said eventually. 'There's a pub along the road — we could go there.'

'Marvellous! And then I promise I'll be on my way and I'll leave you in peace. Right, then. Shall we?'

The Partridge didn't have any of the fancy-dress and glitter of New Year's Eve, but it did have a real fire, an excellent list of food chalked up on a blackboard, and Gemma behind the bar. She raised her eyebrows in surprise to see Saffron walking in with Bunty, but Saffron gave her a little nod to say, *It's okay*.

As soon as they stepped foot in the pub, Bunty put on her mingling-with-the-public face. She walked taller, tossed her hair and declared, 'What a charming place' in such a loud voice that everyone stopped to look. Just as she'd intended, no doubt. Saffron rolled her eyes surreptitiously at Gemma. Ever the professional, Bunty knew when to switch it up a gear.

Gemma looked better than she had done earlier that afternoon at least. She was wearing a glorious scarlet dress, which gave her a dramatic cleavage, and her hair was pinned up, revealing dangly gold earrings. 'Evening, ladies, what can I get you?' she asked. 'Would you like to see our menu?'

'Yes, please,' Bunty said, taking charge. She bestowed a toothy smile on Gemma. 'What a splendid dress that is, if I may say so.'

Gemma looked rather star-struck. 'Oh! Gosh. Thank you very much,' she said, blushing. 'It was my Valentine's dress. Not that I ever got to . . . ' She stopped herself. 'Anyway. What would you like to drink?'

A mischievous thought struck Saffron. 'Is that one of your own creations?' she asked, then turned back to Bunty. 'Gemma here is an up-and-coming fashion designer. You know that gorgeous black dress Nigella wore in her last show? Well . . . ' She tilted her head meaningfully at Gemma.

Bunty's eyes lit up. 'No! You dress Nigella?'

Gemma shot Saffron an agonized look. 'Um . . . '

'Sorry, I shouldn't have mentioned that. Pretend I didn't, okay? Gemma's rightfully very discreet about her clients,' Saffron said quickly. 'I'm just proud of her, that's all. She's done really well.'

'Thank you,' Gemma said in rather a strangled voice.

'Well, good for you, darling, good for you. I could tell, as soon as I looked at it, that your dress was quality. Very flattering.'

'Thanks very much.' Gemma smoothed her hands down the fabric, looking chuffed. 'I've made my own clothes for years,' she went on, 'because I got so sick of nothing fitting me on the high street. When you've got a figure like mine — all hips and boobs — it's not that easy to buy clothes that actually fit properly, let alone flatter your shape.' She was warming to her theme now. 'The way I see it, every woman can look a million dollars in the right clothes. And it's the best thing ever when someone puts on one of my dresses and I can see they feel really gorgeous in it.'

'How wonderful!' Bunty cried, clapping her hands. 'And I

241

know exactly what you mean. All woman, that's me, but most designers seem to think we're built like stick insects. Well, all power to you, darling. And do you know, I think that particular style of dress would suit me, too.' She gave a tinkling laugh. 'I came in for a glass of wine and some dinner – I had no idea I was going to find myself tempted into a new frock while I was at it!'

Gemma flushed pink. 'Oh! I wasn't trying to give you the hard sell,' she said, embarrassed.

Saffron couldn't resist egging on her client. 'It *would* be nice to have something special for the TV awards next week, though, Bunty,' she said. Hell, Bunty owed her, she figured, and Gemma could do with a lucky break. 'And this is an extremely flattering style, as you say.' She paused delicately. 'Are you *very* busy right now, Gemma?'

Bunty, however, was frowning as if something had struck her as odd. 'So wait . . . You're a full-time dress designer . . . but working here, as well?' she asked, gesturing around the pub.

Ah. Bollocks. That was where fibbing got you. Luckily Gemma had her wits about her and let out a peal of laughter. 'Goodness, no! Bernie, the landlord, is an old friend of the family. I said I'd help out, you know, just as a favour tonight. I don't actually *work* here. What a thought!'

Bunty laughed too, thankfully. 'I was going to say! You don't see the likes of Stella McCartney working behind a *bar*, do you?'

They all chuckled at the very idea of Gemma being employed somewhere so lowly. 'Anyway,' Saffron went on, keen to steer away from the subject, 'I say: go for it, Bunty. As a friend and colleague' – here came that lightning again – 'my advice is to jolly well treat yourself to a new dress. At times like these you need a pick-me-up. Am I right, or am I right?'

'You are right,' Bunty said immediately. She glanced quickly down at the menu, then beamed up at Gemma. 'I'll have a glass of red wine, the beef stew, and a frock just like yours in a size sixteen, please.' She clapped her hands with glee. 'How exciting! Do you think I can get away with that colour, or will it be a bit mutton on me? And how much do you charge, if you don't mind me asking? Will I need to take out a second mortgage to afford you?'

'God, no,' Gemma replied, seemingly forgetting that she was supposedly a designer to the stars. 'I could do you one like this for . . . fifty?'

Saffron had an emergency coughing fit to drown out this pathetically low price. Her client was the sort of person who would go off an outfit if she thought for a second that it was too cheap for the likes of her.

'I'm sorry, what was that?' Bunty asked, ferreting around in her bag for her e-cigarette.

'Three hundred and fifty,' Saffron said swiftly. 'Sounds like a bargain to me. Cheaper than Stella, by a mile.'

Gemma let out a gasp, but recovered herself valiantly. 'And

obviously I'd do a personal fitting with you, in my . . . studio,' she said, her eyes flashing a mix of panic and excitement to Saffron. 'Every dress is made-to-measure, you see. Here, let me write down my number. Why don't you give me a call tomorrow and I can book you in?'

Bunty looked up, e-cigarette retrieved, and reached across the bar. 'Marvellous,' she said, shaking Gemma by the hand. 'Marvellous! You've got yourself a deal.'

Chapter Twenty-One

After the alarming experience of searching through her parents' photos and finding the one that had freaked her out so badly, a whole week went by when Caitlin worked savagely, day after day, painting and decorating like a woman possessed. *Just don't think about it,* she kept telling herself. *Forget you ever saw that stupid photo.* What photo? *Exactly.*

While she was not thinking about the photo she stripped all the wallpaper from the living room and painted it a soft, pearlescent dove-grey, with white gloss around the skirting boards and cornicing. She cleaned up the floorboards and slapped on two coats of golden varnish. She polished the windows with vinegar, until light poured into the house and her muscles ached.

She did not go back in the dining room, or anywhere near the photo albums, in all this time. The whole thing was a silly misunderstanding, she told herself. She'd got it wrong as usual, leapt to ridiculous conclusions – there was absolutely nothing sinister about that photograph of her and her mum.

A special day! Jane had written on the back. No, it wasn't. It was just an ordinary day in their lives. It *was*.

At the end of the week the living room looked completely different: spacious, minimalist and serene, more art gallery than lounge. It was hard to imagine her and her parents ever sitting companionably in there together, playing Scrabble or watching *Doctor Who*. *Good*, she thought blackly, before she could stop herself. If only it was as easy to paint over your worries.

Later, after a hot bath and a large glass of wine, she gave herself a brisk talking-to. She was stir crazy, that was all, from being cooped up in the house for so long. Switching on her laptop, she reconnected with the rest of the world for the first time in days and saw that an email from Saffron had arrived more than a week ago:

From: Saffron@PhoenixPR
To: CaitlinF@fridaymail
Subject: Another website request

Hi Caitlin,
We all LOVE the Yummy Mummy site – the clients are absolutely thrilled. They are happy to green-light your idea of the
animated fruit and vegetables, and I'm attaching details of the
artist they've used for their labelling etc. herewith. Would you
be able to commission/direct him on this work? They have

included details of a pretty generous budget and more information on their brief/spec. THANK YOU!

The other thing to mention is that another client of mine, Bunty Halsom, is keen to have some work done on her website, if we could schedule that in, too. We could talk about perhaps sorting out a monthly retainer for, say, the next six months, so that the site can be kept fresh and up-to-date on a regular basis. Is this something that would interest you?

It's really great to work with you – you are my new secret weapon! So glad we met at the New Year. Talking of which . . . any news on the tall, dark stranger you were hoping for? Don't suppose this has anything to do with the 'taking action' that you hinted so cryptically about last time??

Otherwise, I'm still on for the girl band . . . I reckon an arena tour would be a laugh?!
Love Saff xx

Caitlin felt instantly cheered to be somebody's secret weapon. And more work, too! Proper, paid, interesting work with . . . whoa, yes, another stonking budget, she saw, opening the client's brief. She'd enjoyed the design jobs she'd had previously in her career – bits and bobs for the university and small businesses back in Cambridge – but this felt like the jackpot, the big time.

From: CaitlinF@fridaymail
To: Saffron@PhoenixPR
Subject: Another website request

Dear Saffron,

Apologies for the radio silence, I have been awash with paint and varnish all week, trying to get Mum's house in order before I sell it. Back in action now, albeit smelling slightly of Eau de Turps.

That's no problem re the Yummy Mummy animation; I'll get on the case immediately. And I'm happy to work on Bunty Halsom's site, too – a monthly retainer sounds great. Thank YOU. I'm glad we met as well.

Sadly, I have failed on the 'taking action' front – because the dude in question announced, out of the blue, that he's about to become a father. D'oh! I am convinced that the Fortune-Cookie Guru is actually the Wizard of Oz, a nobody behind a curtain, who doesn't have a clue what he is on about . . .

She hesitated, reliving that awkward moment in her kitchen as Harry broke the news. Oh, right. A baby. Instant recalibration of expectations to ZERO. She should have known: he was far too sexy and handsome for an oddbod like her.

Speak to you soon, and thanks again.
Caitlin xx

She sent the email and rubbed her eyes, feeling wrung out. She'd spent too much time on her own recently; it wasn't good for anyone. It was all very well receiving and sending friendly emails, but she needed to get out of the house and speak to another human being for a change, before full-blown cabin fever set in. The thought perked her up. Yes, she would like that. Maybe she could catch up with Gemma again soon, for a chat.

On impulse she picked up her phone, snapped a photo of the empty, revamped living room and texted it to her new friend. *Look what I've been doing!* she typed. *How are things with you guys? Hope all well, let's meet up soon.*

Message sent, she put down the phone, shut her eyes and breathed deeply. Tomorrow, she decided. Tomorrow she'd dredge up the courage to start delving into her mum's paperwork, in the hope that she'd find the answers that lay behind that strange, unsettling photograph.

Right now she was going to get completely trolleyed on this bottle of wine, though. So there.

She was woken from a deep sleep the next morning by the phone ringing. The curtains were edged with pink-gold daylight and she was surprised to see it was almost nine o'clock. Her head pulsed with a beating hangover and her mouth felt as dry as a Gobi sandstorm. Urgh. Go away, daylight. Go away, phone.

'Cait, it's me, Gem,' came her friend's voice when she answered. 'Oh my God. You won't *believe* what happened to me last night.'

'What? Are you okay?' Caitlin opened one eye a crack and then shut it again. Blaaarggh. She was never drinking again. Seriously: never.

Gemma giggled, a glorious, gleeful sound. 'Get this: I've just sold a dress to Bunty bloody Halsom — you know, that awful old bag off the telly. Three hundred and fifty quid she's going to pay me, Cait. Three hundred and fifty big ones!'

Caitlin wondered for a second if her friend was on drugs. What was she on about? 'Bunty Halsom? I might be doing her website,' she said, befuddled. 'I don't understand what you mean, though. What dress?'

'She was in The Partridge last night with that Saffron, who was here for New Year, remember? Anyway. She liked my dress and I said I'd made it, and then Saffron started blagging that I had all these celebrity clients, like Nigella — can you believe? I didn't know what to say, but before I knew what was happening, she'd talked Bunty into buying one herself!'

'Oh my God.' It took Caitlin a moment to digest all of this, then she laughed, forgetting her hangover for a moment. 'That's hilarious. Brilliant!'

'I know. It's the best news I've had all year. Anyway, the only thing is, then I started blagging it a bit, too. God knows what got into me, but I only went and told her I had my own studio! But I can't let her come here and see where I really work – I mean, if she steps a single foot in our dumpy old house, I'll be rumbled in a second. She was already kind of suspicious about me working in the pub, but I just about got away with that one. So I'm ringing because I saw that photo you texted me – of your shamazing new living room – and had a little light-bulb moment . . .'

'Bring her here,' Caitlin said, reading her friend's mind. She suddenly felt wide awake; Gemma's excitement was contagious. 'Yes – do it. We could totally make this look like Fashion Empire HQ, if you bring along your sewing machine and a rail of clothes.'

You could almost hear the smile on Gemma's face as she replied. 'Are you sure? That would be fantastic. Thank you! I can't let an opportunity like this slip through my fingers, I just can't.'

'Absolutely not.' Caitlin was perking up by the second, her mind already busily transforming the space downstairs into Gemma's design studio. Good – a distraction. Just what she needed. 'Come over whenever you want,' she said, swinging her legs out of bed. 'This is going to be fun.'

Thankfully her hangover wasn't the sort to stick around doggedly, and after a hot shower and a kick-ass mug of coffee, Caitlin felt almost human. It was just as well, because two minutes later Gemma was there ringing the doorbell.

Somehow or other she'd crammed all manner of equipment into the back of the family car – a folding trestle table, her sewing machine, a huge sketch pad and easel, a laptop, a tailor's dummy and a rail of beautiful clothes she'd made.

Gemma had so much nervous energy crackling from her, she didn't seem to know what to do with herself. She hugged Caitlin, exclaimed over how gorgeous the living room looked, then actually bounced up and down on the floorboards, clapping her hands. 'This is perfect!' she cried.

Caitlin took the lead, suggesting that they create an office 'area' at one end of the room, with the laptop and phone perched on an old card table. They also set up a 'design area', with the tailor's dummy wearing a teal-coloured satin cocktail dress, alongside a rail of other outfits, and Caitlin ran up to her mum's bedroom to unhook Jane's full-length mirror and bring it downstairs. They unfolded the trestle table and positioned the sewing machine on top of it, then Gemma hunted through her pile of fabrics for a Liberty-print square that she draped over the card table, just to add some prettiness. The final touch consisted of the jars of buttons, cotton reels, zips and beads that she arranged artfully along the mantelpiece.

'It looks like a shop,' she said afterwards, standing back and gazing around. 'A really beautiful shop. The kind of shop I could actually live in.'

'It looks gorgeous,' Caitlin agreed, putting a wooden chair at each of the tables. 'So now what do we do?'

'We wait for her to call,' said Gemma. 'And hope that she hasn't already rumbled me.' Her face fell at the thought. 'All it will take is a few clicks online for her to discover that I'm a complete fraud . . . '

'*Courage, mon amie*,' Caitlin told her, sitting down at the laptop. 'Tell you what: if you make some more coffee, I'll get cracking on a temporary website. What shall we call you?'

'What do you mean? Oh – my company?'

'Yes, Gemma: your highly successful, celebrity-dressing company. I can do a quick holding page for a site, just in case she decides to check you out. Any ideas for a brand name?'

Gemma looked blank. 'Um . . . '

'Imagine this really was a shop. What would go up above the door? We need a good strong name. Something punchy or witty – something that completely nails what you're all about.'

'Er . . . ' Gemma glanced down at what she was wearing that day: a simple black dress with clever tailoring that flattered her generous hips. She'd teamed it with a sparkly black bolero cardigan and had knotted a red silk scarf around her neck. 'I can't think of anything punchy or witty,' she said doubtfully. 'Er . . . Fuller Figure Fashion?'

Caitlin pulled a face. 'That is awful, Gem. I'm not putting that anywhere near a website with your name on. You might as well call it Fashion For Fat Birds.'

'My mind's gone blank! Um . . . Voluptuous. No, that's too much. Silhouette? Pear-shaped? God, no.'

'Cleavage and Hips?' Caitlin suggested, then shook her head in the next second. 'No, we'll attract the flasher-mac brigade.'

'Hourglass?' said Gemma. 'Er . . . '

'I like Hourglass,' Caitlin said. 'Hourglass Designs. How about that?'

They looked at each other, both testing the name in their heads. 'I like it, too,' Gemma pronounced and smiled. 'Hourglass Designs. Yes!'

Caitlin began typing and Gemma had just turned to go and make the coffee when her phone rang.

'Gemma speaking,' she said politely. 'Oh, hello again, Bunty.' She looked excited and terrified at the same time as she spun round to make the thumbs-up sign at Caitlin, eyes wide. 'Today? Let me just check with my assistant.' Lips trembling as if she were dying to burst out laughing, she called to Caitlin, 'Do we have space for a fitting this afternoon?'

'Let me see . . . ' Caitlin paused as if consulting a real appointments book, then winked. 'You're free at one-thirty for an hour or so.'

'Lovely, thank you,' Gemma said, then returned to Bunty. 'How does one-thirty sound? I can take your measurements and we can discuss designs . . . Excellent. I'm at the studio, so do come straight here. It's White Gables Cottage on River Street. Look forward to seeing you then.'

She ended the call, put her hands up to her face and

screamed with excitement. 'Oh my God!' she cried. 'I can't believe this is happening. I just can't believe it!' She paused then, and an anxious look crossed her face. 'This is all right, isn't it, me inviting her over here? I'm not keeping you from doing anything urgent, am I?'

'Me, no,' Caitlin said, brushing off the question. 'I didn't have anything on today anyway.' *Apart from investigating skeletons in the closet*, a small voice piped up in her head, but she quickly pushed that thought aside. 'So,' she said. 'What's the plan?'

Chapter Twenty-Two

When the doorbell rang at precisely one twenty-nine Gemma thought she might very well faint with nerves.

'Here we go,' Caitlin said. 'No, let me answer it. I'm the lackey, remember; you're the glamorous designer. Deep breaths!'

Ever since the night before, when the astonishing conversation with Bunty took place in The Partridge, Gemma had felt as if she was living in a strange and rather thrilling dream. The sort of wonderful dream that usually only ever happened to other people. A famous person wanted to commission *her* to create a gorgeous new dress for a large sum of money. Opportunities like that didn't come knocking every day, especially on Gemma's front door.

Of course Spencer had scoffed when she'd arrived home from the pub that night, breathless with this news. 'Three hundred and fifty quid, my arse,' he said disbelievingly over the sound of the television. 'She was pissed, I bet. Off her nut on coke. That's what all those telly people are like – full of shit.'

It was like taking a bright, fizzing sparkler into a cold shower. All Gemma's confidence was snuffed out in an instant. 'Well . . . I don't think she *was* pissed,' she said after a moment. 'Spence, I think it could really happen. She seemed genuinely keen.'

He snorted, not even looking at her. 'Course she was.'

Lying in bed that night, his words kept coming back to her, until she convinced herself that he would be proved right. Things like this didn't happen to her, did they? Surely it was too good to be true. But the next morning Caitlin showed that she believed in Gemma sufficiently to help create this whole studio facade; Bernie had shown faith in allowing her to swap her shifts so that she could be here; and her friend Eliza just squealed with sheer excitement when Gemma phoned, and said that of course she'd pick up Darcey from school — no problem, just as long as Gemma told her *all* the details later.

So you were wrong, Spencer Bailey, she thought now, with a quiet, nervous triumph as Caitlin vanished into the hall. Not everyone off the telly *is* full of shit, thank you very much. And now this telly person has just rung Caitlin's doorbell because she's here to see me. Got that?

Gemma took a last glance around. Everything was in order. There were pastries in the kitchen that she'd picked up from the bakery, tinkling piano music playing from Caitlin's retro DAB radio, and even the sun was obliging her by sending long rays of honeyed light onto the polished floorboards. The room looked so pretty and colourful with all her equipment and fabrics, she could almost believe this was her actual studio. How Grandma Pepper would have loved to see it!

'Hello, come in,' she heard Caitlin say from the hall, and a flurry of butterflies swirled up inside Gemma's tummy. Oh my goodness. Now it was showtime. Could she really pull this off?

More voices, and then Caitlin was asking if she could take their coats, in a polite, subservient tone that made Gemma want to splutter with laughter. 'Thank you. Would you like to follow me? Gemma's in the studio.'

Heart thumping, Gemma went over to the rail of clothes and pretended to be hanging up a silk dress. Her fingers trembled on the material and she tried to breathe deeply. Do not blow this, she ordered herself with sudden fierceness. Three hundred and fifty pounds would be extremely welcome in the bank right now. She could not afford to muck this up.

The footsteps and voices drew nearer and she turned as Caitlin showed Bunty and Saffron into the room. Saffron was wearing a long grey cardigan and dark trousers, with just a hint of a bump showing under her pale-grey T-shirt, whereas Bunty was dressed in the same tight pink suit she'd had on the day before, now somewhat more creased.

'Hello again,' Gemma said, trying to channel the image of

a confident, self-assured fashion designer, well accustomed to celebrities popping round for a fitting. 'Thanks for coming today.'

There was nowhere for them to sit, she realized in a panic the next moment. How could they have forgotten something so basic? If only she could magic up a purple velvet chaise longue, or some other lovely seat to offer them. As it was, she'd have Bunty Halsom standing up with her coffee and croissant, which would not be relaxing for anyone. 'Um . . .' she faltered, her mind going blank. Shit – now they were all looking expectantly at her, and she'd completely forgotten what she'd planned to say.

Saffron rescued her. 'What a fantastic space,' she said, gazing around. 'It's so light and airy in here.'

'It's divine,' Bunty agreed. 'Such simplicity – perfect for creativity, I always think. I can't bear these places where there's too much going on. Enough to give you a headache.'

'Absolutely,' Gemma said, recovering herself. 'I find it best to work without too many distractions.' Inspiration struck her. 'In fact, I deliberately don't have any creature comforts in here, otherwise I might be tempted to curl up in the nearest armchair and take an afternoon snooze.' Phew, they were smiling. 'Now then, before we start talking about designs and fabrics, would either of you like a coffee or tea?'

'We have tea, coffee, sparkling water, orange juice . . . and I believe there are some pastries, too,' Caitlin said politely.

You had to hand it to her, Gemma thought, hiding a grin. She was playing the part of dutiful assistant brilliantly.

'Jolly good,' Bunty said. 'A coffee would hit the spot. I think I had one too many in the pub last night.' Her eyes were rather bloodshot and baggy-looking, Gemma noticed. 'That Bernie's a card, isn't he? Kept plying me with alcohol, glass after glass. What's a girl to do, though, eh?'

Saffron pulled a funny face, unseen by Bunty, and Gemma had to force herself not to giggle. Bernie was a terrible flirt, it was true, but from where she'd been standing last night, the flirting had definitely not been a one-way street. 'He's a devil,' she agreed, trying to keep a straight face. 'But lovely, too. Single these days as well, I should mention . . . ' She winked. 'And, on that bombshell, let's make you a coffee and get started.'

Once she had recovered from her initial rush of nerves, Gemma soon began to relax and enjoy herself. Bunty was much more charming than she'd anticipated – naturally warm and chatty, and not at all up-herself. She also had an excellent stock of gossipy showbiz stories that always began 'Between you and me . . . ' and ended with them all shrieking with laughter.

Over mugs of milky coffee and the pastries, they discussed what Bunty was looking for in her dress: namely something gorgeous and jaw-dropping that she could wear to the upcoming TV awards ceremony, and that would, with a bit of luck, make Troy — her horrible ex — drop dead with regret for his vileness, right there and then on the red carpet. 'Actually, no, on second thoughts, not there on the red carpet,' Bunty amended hastily. 'He can jolly well stay out of my limelight and drop dead alone in the gents' toilets instead. Face-first into the urinal preferably. Ha!'

Beneath all the bluster, Gemma realized there was something rather vulnerable about Bunty. 'Then I shall make you the most splendidly I-Am-Fabulous frock you've ever worn,' she promised. 'That's what brings me satisfaction, at the end of the day — creating outfits in which women feel invincible. Everyone needs a dress that makes them feel beautiful.'

'Hear, hear,' Saffron said, breaking a corner off her second almond croissant and chewing it. She looked much more chipper than she had done the day before, Gemma thought to herself, and seemed to be getting on quite well with her client, which was a relief.

Caitlin was playing a blinder. She must have been sneakily calling the landline number from her mobile, because it kept ringing every ten minutes or so, and she'd hop up from the table, excusing herself. 'Hourglass Designs?' she'd say, her voice carrying as she walked through to the living room-cum-studio. 'Oh, *hi*, Olivia. How are you? Congratulations on the BAFTA nomination!' 'Jennifer, hello — great to hear from you again! Gemma's with a client right now, but I can . . . Oh, okay, when does your plane land? We could see you on Friday, I should think, let me see . . . four o'clock in the afternoon?'

Each time you could see Bunty eavesdropping, obviously tremendously impressed by how in demand Gemma must be, and trying to work out who the callers were.

'So all we need to do now is decide on fabric and colour, and I'll take some measurements,' Gemma said, once she'd sketched out a design to Bunty's satisfaction. 'Let's go back into the studio and you can have a browse.'

Just as Bunty was deliberating between dark-purple satin and emerald-green crêpe de Chine, her phone rang and she glanced at the screen. 'Ah. It's Callum,' she said to Saffron, rather grim-faced. 'My lawyer,' she added for the benefit of the other two. 'I'd better take this call. Excuse me a moment.'

'We'll give you some privacy,' Gemma said, sensing it was important. Besides, she was dying to chat to Saffron and Caitlin alone. 'Take your time.'

In the safety of the kitchen she did a silent scream of excitement, hands clapped on either side of her face. 'This is amazing,' she hissed to Saffron. 'I can't believe it's happening.'

'Why shouldn't it? You obviously know your stuff. And when "Olivia" and "Jennifer" are calling round the clock, wanting new outfits, well . . . '

They all giggled like naughty schoolgirls. 'I couldn't resist,' said Caitlin.

'You're a bloody genius,' Gemma told her.

Saffron gave Caitlin a hug. 'Lovely to see you again,' she said. 'And sorry for being so formal at the door. I thought it would confuse things if I introduced you as my hot new website designer – I didn't want to arouse any suspicion.'

'No worries,' Caitlin said. 'I emailed you last night by the way, I don't know if you've seen it yet?'

'I did. Sorry to hear about the handsome-stranger situation.'

Gemma felt confused, not following the conversation. Emails? Handsome stranger?

'Caitlin's been doing some work for me,' Saffron explained, and grinned. 'Don't you just love that we all met completely randomly on New Year's Eve, and now we're all working together? How cool is that?'

'It is awesome,' said Gemma. 'A million, gazillion times better than my doomed cocktail-mixing career, or whatever I was on about at the time.' Then she addressed Saffron, lowering her voice. 'So it's going all right, with you and Bunty, is it? She's not driving you completely potty?'

'Surprisingly, no,' Saffron said. 'She's actually been really sweet and phoned Charlotte – my boss – saying she's had to commandeer me for the next week or so, to help manage her press, after Troy the wanker did the dirty on her. I don't think Charlotte was very impressed, as I've got other clients who need me, but Bunty offered to pay double apparently, which swung the balance, *and* she's putting the cottage rental on her expenses. Oh yes, and she was straight back down to The Partridge the minute it opened this morning to see Bernie – any excuse, if you ask me – and proceeded to flirt outrageously in order to get some discount on an extra week here.'

'Cool,' Caitlin said. 'I rather like her, you know. She's a smart lady. Smarter than she seems on telly, if that isn't too rude.'

'She's very smart. Went to Cambridge, and is incredibly well read and opinionated.' Saffron lowered her voice discreetly. 'Bloody annoying half the time, yes, but she's not a dumb bimbo, despite how the press try to paint her. I just wish she wouldn't keep going for these awful men who screw her over for a handful of cash. She makes it too easy for them.'

They fell silent for a moment, as Bunty's voice rose from the other room. 'Well, pull as many strings as you can; make a few threats, take out an injunction if you have to, but I'm not being held to ransom by that little cockhead and his hamster-penis. That's all there is to it, Callum.'

They smothered their giggles at this. 'What's really good,' Saffron went on quietly, 'is that she's actually dealing with the situation herself for a change. In the past she's been like a kid – always turned to her manager, or agent, or me, or any other sucker, and got them to sort out her problems. But yesterday . . . ' Her mouth twisted. 'Well, basically, I had a go at her and told her to get a grip, and that I quit. Spoke a few home truths that I probably shouldn't have, to be honest.'

'Yikes,' said Caitlin.

'Yeah, that's what I thought, too. Goodbye, job; hello, unemployment. But it must actually have struck a chord with her, because for the first time ever she's taken a bit of control over her own life. She's instructed her legal team to handle cockhead-Troy, rather than have someone else organize that for her, and now she's calling all the shots. I'm glad for her.' She grinned. 'And I'm glad for you, too, Gemma, because what you said to her – about creating dresses to make women feel beautiful – that's exactly what Bunty needs right now. Play your cards right, and you might just have a customer for life.'

Gemma felt herself turning red. 'Oh! Well, great,' she said. 'I meant it, though, it wasn't just flannel.'

'I know, you were totally sincere. But nobody else in her world is, you see. She's usually surrounded by flatterers and bullshitters. You wait, you'll be in her little black book faster than you can say "hamster-penis".'

'I hadn't even thought about future dresses,' Gemma said dazedly.

'Well, you should,' Caitlin said. 'Twenty or so women like Bunty, each buying a few new dresses every year . . . You'll be laughing all the way to your new Swiss bank account, dude.'

'Definitely,' Saffron agreed. 'And make sure you give me a

few business cards to pass around my other clients. I'll even write you a press release!'

'We can get your website up and running in no time,' Caitlin said. 'Design a logo for the brand . . .'

Gemma held up her hands, feeling shell-shocked. 'Whoa, whoa,' she said. 'Hang on. I don't really think . . . I mean . . . I'm not a *brand*! This is just one dress for one lady, remember. The sort of lucky strike that only happens once in a blue moon. I'm not sure I need press releases and websites and business cards, when it's just little me sewing a dress for another person. Do I?'

'Remember the fortune-cookies,' Saffron said. 'What was it again? Something about following your bliss, and doors opening . . .'

'Purses opening, too,' Caitlin said, elbowing her. 'Go for it, Gem. This is your chance. It could change everything.'

Bunty clip-clopped back into the kitchen just then and they fell silent. 'Sorry about that, girls,' she said. 'All sorted, Callum's on the case. Troy Blake will be grovelling at my feet by the end of the week, you wait.' Then she held up the purple and green swatches of fabric. 'Do you know what, I simply can't decide which colour I love the most,' she said, beaming. 'So I'll take one of each. Will that be all right?'

Caitlin kicked her under the table and Gemma had to swallow hard to stop herself from letting out a very unprofessional screech of excitement. 'Of . . . of course it will,' she managed to stammer. 'No problem at all.'

'Good news!' Gemma exclaimed later that afternoon, as she burst into the house with Darcey in tow. 'Spencer, where are you? I have great news!'

Amazingly he was not in his usual spot on the sofa. He was in the kitchen, hobbling to the table with a can of lager, looking thoroughly fed up. 'I thought you said you'd be back at lunchtime?' he grumbled. 'What have you been *doing* all day?'

Gemma tried to ignore the bubble of guilt that popped up inside her. 'Sorry, it just took longer than I expected,' she said. 'But guess what? Something really incredible happened. She's commissioned me to make two dresses. Two dresses, Spen!'

'God,' he said. 'Sure you've got enough material to get round that arse of hers twice?'

Darcey giggled at the rude word and looked sideways at Gemma, who flushed. Bunty wasn't that much bigger than she was, at the end of the day. 'She's actually all right,' she said, taking no notice. 'I quite liked her. Not least because she's paying seven hundred quid for them.'

'Seven hundred *pounds*?' Darcey echoed. 'WOW! In real life?'

'In real life,' Gemma replied with a laugh, but then noticed how Spencer's face tightened at the mention of money. She'd been so proud of herself that she hadn't stopped to think about *his* pride and how badly it had been dented recently, with him being out of action so long. 'Spence?' she prompted, wishing he would say something.

'Brilliant,' he said, his tone expressionless. 'Great. Fan-dabby-dozy. Gemma to the rescue!'

Was he joking, or just being snide? Whichever, her mood had soured like milk on a hot day. 'I thought you'd be pleased,' she said, crestfallen.

'Oh yeah, delighted,' he said, his voice dripping with sarcasm. 'Makes me feel a real man, when my wife is having to put food on the table because I still can't bloody work.'

'What *is* for tea?' Darcey asked, seemingly ignorant of the sudden change in atmosphere.

Coming home, Gemma had envisaged treating everyone to a celebratory takeaway – even she was starting to tire of her cheap and hearty stews – but she realized now that such a suggestion would only rub her husband's nose in it. She sighed, feeling tired and unappreciated, wishing the buzz of her good mood could have lasted a bit longer. 'I don't know,' she replied heavily. 'Pasta probably. Whatever's left in the fridge.'

Back to the real world, Cinderella, she thought, as she washed her hands and started chopping an onion. Back to cooking tea and wondering why Will was late home again – she must talk to him about what was going on at school – and tiptoeing around Spencer's volatile mood swings. Already the afternoon felt like a daydream.

She let herself float back to the camaraderie and loveliness she'd experienced at Caitlin's house – her studio. She'd really enjoyed playing the part of sought-after designer, having her own beautiful space in which to sew, discussing her client's ideas, sketching out possible designs and finding one they both liked. It had been a wrench to start packing that lifestyle away, along with all the equipment at the end of the day: game over.

Her thoughts must have been obvious as she began taking down her Kilner jars from the mantelpiece, because Caitlin cleared her throat and said, 'You can always carry on working here, if you want. For real, I mean. I've got some new work to do for Saffron, too; we could be colleagues for a while longer. What do you think?'

Gemma's eyes lit up at once. She had loved being there and pretending, just for a few hours, that this was her actual life. It had felt like the good old office days that she missed; as if she had a purpose again, other than as cook, nurse and taxi-driver. 'Seriously?' she asked. 'I would really like that. I could bring biscuits . . . '

'You've got yourself a deal.' Caitlin gestured at the rail of clothes. 'And leave those here, too: I can photograph them all later and start putting them up on the site. Stick a few hefty price-tags on them, and then you can tell me about fabrics and sizes and whatnot. Does that sound okay?'

Gemma could feel herself getting emotional. Did it sound *okay*? It sounded better than okay; it was wonderful, she loved it — and she loved her friend too, for taking this whole venture so seriously. A website, a cool brand name, an initial order for two dresses in her book . . . *This is your chance*, Caitlin had said to her. It was a chance Gemma wanted to take. If you listened to Caitlin — and Saffron, come to that — anyone would think that she was in danger of becoming a proper businesswoman.

Apart from her husband, that was, she thought now, nearly chopping into her thumb as she reached the end of the onion. Was it too much to ask for him to feel as proud of her as she did of herself? Too much for him to say 'Well done' or 'How exciting' or ask for more details of her triumph today? Obviously it was.

She tipped the onion slices into the frying pan, relieved as she heard the front door open and the thud of Will's sports bag as he chucked it down in the hall. That was one less thing to worry about at least. And if Spencer wanted to sulk, then let him. She could do this with or without him. Just watch her.

Chapter Twenty-Three

'So,' Gemma blew on her coffee and raised her eyebrows. 'You didn't tell me about this handsome stranger yesterday. What's all that about then?'

It was the following morning, and Caitlin and Gemma were both at their new workstations. The radio was playing, Gemma was drawing out a paper pattern for Bunty's first dress on the trestle tables, and Caitlin had started work on the Hourglass Designs website, playing with a home-page design that featured a twisting tape-measure running around the screen as a frame.

Deep in thought, trying to choose the perfect font for the tape-measure numerals, Caitlin only caught the end of Gemma's question. 'Sorry, what?' she asked, raising her head.

'Saffron said something about you and a handsome stranger. Why do I not know about this? What have you been getting up to behind my back?'

Oh. That. She was regretting being so forthcoming in her emails now. 'Nothing,' she said, feeling a total plum. 'Really.

Nothing,' she repeated, as Gemma gave her what could only be described as a hard Paddington Bear stare. 'Oh, all right — it was Harry, okay? I was getting vibes from him, but nothing happened, because he's got some woman pregnant and is sticking by her. So that's the end of that.'

'Harry Sykes? Wait, I didn't know about this. Who's the woman: is it Jade? And she's up the duff?'

'Yeah, I think so. They had split up before she realized, apparently, but he wants to do the decent thing, he said. Didn't look wildly joyful about it, though. More a man resigned to his fate.' Harry's glum face appeared in her mind along with a screaming infant and a pile of smelly nappies.

'Bummer.' Gemma bent over her paper as she drew out another shape. 'That's a shame. I reckon you two would be pretty good together.'

Caitlin affected nonchalance. 'It's cool. Sounds like he's a bit of a Romeo, anyway. Probably best to steer clear of someone like that.'

'Ye-e-e-es. I don't know. Harry's a really great guy, I just think he's a bit crap with relationships. He falls head over heels in love at the drop of a hat — this is it, this is the one — but it's always with the most tragically unsuitable women, ones he's got absolutely nothing in common with. Jade Perry, for instance, she's a total airhead. Zero to say for herself, beneath the big hair and perky tits.'

Caitlin twiddled a lock of her own fine, wispy, definitely

not-big hair and tried not to think about her own fried-egg, blink-and-you'll-miss-them, in-no-way-perky chest area. Flynn had actually asked her if she'd ever thought about implants, the tosser. Was Harry really as shallow as that? No wonder his own sister had resorted to giving him a 'Ten-Date Rule'. 'How depressing,' she said.

'It is. Mind you, when I said to Spencer that I didn't know what Harry saw in Jade, do you know what he said? "I can think of two reasons." They're all as bad.'

Caitlin laughed. 'How is he? I bet he's dead proud of you doing all this, isn't he?'

'Who, Spencer?' Gemma stood back and looked critically at the shapes she'd drawn on the pattern paper. 'I hope so. I'm not sure, to be honest. He's still kind of resentful. Of everything. Of the whole world.' She pulled a face. 'Let's not talk about him, though. Quick, change the subject.'

There had only been one topic on Caitlin's mind for the last week and it surfaced in her consciousness for the thousandth time. 'Um . . . ' she began, altering the background colour on the web page from a mint-green to a beautiful sky-blue. 'Did your parents take lots of baby photos of you?' she asked, before she could stop herself.

Gemma looked surprised at the question. 'Not loads, no, but then I was the fourth baby in the family,' she replied. 'Plus my mum is like the most unmaternal woman in the whole world. There are a few pictures, though, mostly of me looking fat, cross and egg-headed. Maybe that's why they didn't take many.' She cocked her head. 'Why? Not thinking of putting some on the website, are you? From the cradle to the . . . er . . . treadle?'

'No, just . . . ' Caitlin changed the sky-blue to rose-pink and then back to the original mint-green. Then she took her hands off the keyboard and gave the question her full attention. 'There aren't any of me, that's all. Not one.'

'Maybe your parents didn't have a camera,' Gemma said. She heaved a roll of calico onto the table and started spreading it out. 'They were much more expensive back then, weren't they? Not like us now, snapping away at everything with our phones.'

Caitlin thought of the faded holiday pictures of Jane and Steve, their dated bathing costumes and bug-eye sunglasses, posing in front of crumbling Welsh castles and on the beach at Cardigan Bay. 'They definitely had a camera,' she said. Her voice wobbled. 'Maybe I'm reading too much into it, but . . . '

'What?'

'Well, I found this picture, and . . . ' She went on to explain about the apparent awkwardness between her and Jane in the photo, and how the writing on the back had led her to new suspicions about the relevance of June 1st. 'There are other things, too. Like . . . Well, I don't look anything like either of them. I was just thinking a minute ago about how wispy my hair is, and Mum had really thick, lovely hair. I'm so much taller than she was. I've got this big old beak of a nose – God knows where that came from, and . . . ' She spread her hands out. 'It all adds up.'

'What are you saying; that you think you were *adopted* or something?' Gemma gaped. 'Whoa. It's a bit of a leap, isn't it, from one photo to all of this?'

'But it makes sense. I've been trying not to think about it, but I can't help formulating a theory. Otherwise, why didn't they have loads of kids? Everyone keeps telling me how much Mum loved babies. Why didn't she have loads of them herself?'

A childhood memory flashed into her head, of her asking why she couldn't have a brother or a sister like all her friends. 'We think our family is perfect just the way it is,' Jane had said, ruffling her hair.

Was that the only reason? she wondered now.

'Is there anyone you could ask? An aunty or grandparent?' Gemma suggested.

'No. Nobody. I had an Aunty Nancy, my dad's big sister, but she's in South Africa somewhere; we lost touch with her after he died.'

'Well, what about your birth certificate then? That has the names of your parents on it. What does yours say?'

Caitlin had already thought about that. 'I've only ever seen the short version of mine. Mum said she'd lost the other one.'

They looked at each other, pattern-drawing and websites forgotten. 'Shit, Cait. This is sounding a bit weird. Have you looked through her paperwork? I mean, this could all be a complete misunderstanding, right? You might come across a massive stack of baby photos and your lost birth certificate and . . . I don't know, magic hair-thickener that your mum always used in secret, and a follow-up appointment from the nose-job clinic . . . '

Caitlin gave a weak smile. 'Yeah. I guess. I need to bite the bullet and start looking, but I can't help feeling scared. I mean, if I really *was* adopted, it would change everything. My whole life would be a complete lie.'

Gemma said nothing for a moment. 'It would be a shock, yes, but she did love you,' she replied eventually. 'And your dad did too, going by what you've said. You were loved and cherished; your childhood sounds as if it was a really happy one. Don't underestimate that, okay?'

Caitlin thought about the way Gemma had described her own mum with no small degree of contempt. The most unmaternal woman in the world, she'd called her. Jane had been the opposite. Jane had been so maternal she'd devoted her whole life to bringing babies safely into the world. She was a heroine among mothers, a life-saver. *The most wonderful midwife ever*, Harry's sister had called her, she remembered. *An angel*, Gemma had said.

An angel wouldn't lie to her own daughter, though. Would she?

'Sure,' she mumbled, returning to her keyboard. Mint-green looked crap, she decided, changing the background colour to a soft grey. A picture formed in her head of a wispy-haired woman with a conk of a nose who'd taken one look at mewling baby Caitlin and thought, *Nah. Don't want her.* 'Probably jumping to conclusions anyway,' she said, wincing as she remembered TV footage of babies abandoned in Romanian orphanages, left alone to cry all day. Had her first weeks been similarly desolate? It might explain why she was such a fuck-up when it came to relationships.

'Yeah, I reckon,' Gemma said, in a voice that was more hearty reassurance than actual sincerity. 'Now, stop worrying and let me make you a coffee, okay? I think we've both earned a few biscuits as well.'

Gemma headed off around three to pick up Darcey from school, having cut and stitched the toile, a copy of the dress in calico, so that she could check all the measurements fitted Bunty properly.

Unfortunately Caitlin hadn't been quite so productive. Her conversation with Gemma had buzzed around her head all afternoon, despite the bakery lunch, the five cups of coffee and half a packet of Jaffa Cakes. Images of possible birth mothers grew and coloured in her mind, like photographs in developing liquid. A cruel-eyed witch from a scary fairy-tale, Miss Hannigan from *Annie*, Cruella de Vil . . .

As soon as Gemma left, Caitlin switched off the laptop and abandoned their bright, hopeful workspace. She couldn't wait any longer. She wanted to know.

She marched into the dining room and went straight to the small grey filing cabinet. Right, then. Let's see what was stashed away in here.

I'm sorry, hen, Jane said again, weak and tremulous, and Caitlin felt her heart harden.

Yeah, well, she thought, pulling open the top drawer and dumping everything onto the carpet. Too late to start saying sorry now, Mum. I need answers, not apologies. The truth.

'So did you find anything out about your mum? Have you taken the plunge and had a hunt through?'

It was the third day that Gemma and Caitlin had been working together in the gleaming white space of Caitlin's living room and they'd quickly settled into an enjoyable routine of chat, sugar-dusted almond croissants and background music. Oh, and work too, obviously. Bunty had been back for her first fitting in the toile, and now Gemma was carefully cutting the glossy emerald-green crêpe de Chine in order to begin the finished dress.

Caitlin meanwhile had finished setting up the basics on Gemma's Hourglass Designs website, and was now storyboarding an animation for the Yummy Mummy baby-food campaign. From high fashion to singing and dancing vegetables, this week had definitely been one of extremes.

She felt her chest tighten at Gemma's question. 'My mum? No, nothing. I searched through a whole bunch of papers in her filing cabinet, but I haven't found my full birth certificate yet, or anything to say that . . . you know, Mum and Dad weren't legit.' Instead there were bank statements from the 1990s, guarantees for ancient white goods that had long been and gone, the 100-metre swimming certificate she'd got aged eight and even some hilarious school reports. Jane had kept *everything*, by the look of it, all jumbled in one messy collection – the detritus of life. No adoption papers, though. Nothing that had shocked or surprised Caitlin.

The relief was enormous. She'd let her crazy brain run away with her for a mad moment, that was all. *Sorry, Mum. Must have got the wrong end of the stick, after all.*

'I was probably reading too much into it,' she said lightly. 'Imagination getting the better of me.'

'Yeah,' Gemma agreed. 'And these things do get lost. I couldn't tell you where Will and Darcey's birth certificates are right now; probably still in a box, waiting to be unpacked somewhere.' She smoothed the fabric carefully, before pinning another piece of the paper pattern to it. 'You can always order a replacement anyway.'

'Mmm,' Caitlin said, turning back to her keyboard and

typing. *No*, she thought. There would be no ordering of a replacement, no more digging around. She would let sleeping dogs lie and try to forget she'd ever had any doubts.

Chapter Twenty-Four

'This has been the strangest few days,' Bunty mused, waggling her still-wet, shiny red nails as if playing an invisible piano. 'Strange, but actually rather good in the end, don't you think? I don't know about you, but I feel like a new woman.'

It was a week later, and their last evening together in Baker's Cottage, and Saffron and Bunty were still up, even though it was past midnight and the boiler had long since clicked off. Wrapped in dressing gowns, with creamy green facepacks and freshly painted nails, and an almost empty New York cheesecake box nearby, there was a relaxed, companionable atmosphere, with neither of them in any hurry to end the night. They'd already polished off fish and chips, courtesy of Bunty, who'd driven out to Longwood, the nearest town, to pick them up, as well as the cheesecake and several enormous packets of Kettle Chips, which she claimed had fallen into her basket in the shop.

'It's been great,' Saffron said, glad of her extra-stretchy pyjama bottoms. She wasn't quite sure how much of her small bump was baby and how much was chips right now. 'I could stay here forever, you know.'

She was only half-joking. She'd come to Suffolk in search of a refuge, a bolthole in which to tuck herself away, far from her ordinary day-to-day life. Despite it not turning out to be the solitary, hermit-like few days she'd anticipated, she'd ended up laughing and enjoying herself more than she'd ever thought possible. Hanging out with Gemma and Caitlin had been great; she and Bunty had managed to get along without killing one another; and for the last few days Bunty had been spending a lot of time in The Partridge, flirting outrageously with Bernie, while Saffron had laced up her hiking boots and set off into the unknown, walking for miles on her own in blissful peace, not thinking about anything other than taking one step after another. In short, it had been the break both of them needed.

'I agree. Glorious countryside,' Bunty agreed, even though Saffron knew damn well she preferred her 'countryside' viewed through the window of a pub or car. 'Lovely people, too. And there's something about being out of London and away from all those grabby little show-offs and mucky, snooping journalists . . . Well, it really clears the brain.'

'Yes. There's space to think.' Saffron had done a lot of that over the last few days, tramping up hills and through woodland, filling her lungs with the cool, fresh air. Yesterday she'd even driven out to the coast and walked along the beach at

Southwold, her hair flying up in the air, her ears ringing with the sound of the gulls. While she wouldn't exactly say she'd come to terms with the prospect of an amnio, or really thought beyond getting the results of it, she'd made a temporary peace with the situation at least, accepting there was nothing she could do right now but wait.

'Plus, I've had a hoot this week with Bernie, and you and the girls,' Bunty went on. 'And isn't my dress glorious? I can't wait to go out somewhere fabulous in it.'

Gemma had dropped round the first of Bunty's dresses that afternoon, and tears had actually glistened in Bunty's eyes when she put it on and saw her reflection. The vibrant emerald-green fabric looked classy and expensive, and the garment was tailored so skilfully that it clung to all the right places, while skimming over the others.

A hush fell while Bunty turned sideways to examine her bum in the mirror; her bum, let it be said, that now looked deliciously rounded and pinchable, thanks to the seemingly magic contours of the dress. 'Wow, Bunty,' Saffron couldn't help blurting out. 'It's gorgeous. *You're* gorgeous.'

For once Bunty was lost for words, as if the dress had worked an enchantment on her. 'I *feel* gorgeous,' she said eventually, then hugged Gemma and gave her an enormous smacking kiss on the cheek. 'Thank God I met you,' she said, only half-joking. 'I've never felt so womanly and . . . well, desirable, frankly, in my life!'

Gemma looked as if she wanted to cry, too, and seeing them embrace gave Saffron a genuine glow of contentment. She had made that happen, she thought proudly.

'If Bernie sees you in the dress, he'll probably propose to you on the spot,' she teased now, stretching a slippered foot along the sofa to nudge Bunty. Troy already seemed like last year's story, after Bunty and her lawyer had successfully seen off his attempts to smear her. The legal team must have pulled out all the stops, because the sex tape had apparently been destroyed as a result of their proceedings.

'Bernie has asked me if we can . . . you know. See each other again, once I'm back in London,' Bunty said, an unusually coy look on her face.

'Really? And what did you say? Do you feel ready for a new relationship yet?' Saffron hoped this wouldn't be yet another case of her headstrong client leaping recklessly out of the frying pan and straight into the fire. Been there, done that too many times already.

'Not really,' Bunty admitted honestly. 'But a fling would definitely put a spring in my step, if you know what I mean. I bet he scrubs up a treat in a suit, too, don't you think?'

Saffron laughed. 'I'm sure he does.' She chose her words carefully. 'Just promise me you'll be more careful this time, all right? I know he seems a nice guy and a bit of fun. But . . . ' She broke off, unsure how much to say. The client/PR exec boundaries had become blurred over the week.

'But no more sex tapes — yep, got it.' Bunty pulled a naughty-girl-at-the-head-teacher's-office face and then reached forward to clink her empty wine glass against Saffron's cocoa mug. 'The new, demure Bunty Halsom starts right here, right now. I promise.'

Returning to her flat in London the next day, Saffron couldn't help feeling as if she was crash-landing back down to earth. There was nowhere to park near her flat, so she had to cruise around all the side-streets, trying to find a space big enough to wedge her car (how she loathed parallel parking). Then on her way up the High Street she was asked three times for spare change by different men slumped in doorways on pieces of old cardboard. When she finally reached her flat, she was greeted by a pile of junk mail, a dead plant in the kitchen and a gargantuan spider in the bath.

It was a tip, as well. She'd left in such a hurry that everything was all over the place — several self-help books her mum had lent her after that fateful Sunday lunch still dumped on the side-table unread; piles of old newspapers waiting to be bagged up for the recycling box; two mugs growing beards of blue mould in the kitchen sink. The washing basket was stuffed with dirty clothes and the bed was unmade and rumpled.

She sorted through the mail in case there was any word from Max, but of course there was nothing. A Jiffy bag with her mum's handwriting on caught her eye, though, and she opened it to find a tiny white Babygro, with a little hedgehog embroidered on the chest. *Saw this and couldn't resist it,* her mum had written on a little card. *Hope you're both keeping well. Lots of love, Mum and Dad xxx*

A lump rose in Saffron's throat at the word 'both'. *Oh Mum,* she thought helplessly. *There's so much I haven't told you.* But where could she begin?

She laid the soft clean Babygro out on her lap, unfolding the teeny sleeves and legs. It hardly seemed possible that her own baby, small and wriggly, might eventually be tucked into this doll-sized garment. If she had the baby, that was. If they got that far.

She opened the next letter to see that it was from the hospital, with an appointment for her amniocentesis test in two and a half weeks' time. *Here we go.* It was real. It was happening.

Maybe she should try contacting Max again. She should probably just ring him, pin him down once and for all. *Well? What do you think? What have you got to say about this?*

Soon, she told herself. She'd do that really soon.

She picked up the Babygro and pressed it against her cheek. 'We'll get through this,' she said aloud, clutching the tiny garment close as if a real baby was inside, needing comfort. 'Don't worry. We'll be okay.'

*

And so real life swallowed her up again as if she'd never been away. Back to work: writing press releases for Yummy Mummy baby foods (why was there no baby food called Yummy Daddy? she wondered churlishly, although she managed to refrain from emailing Head Office to enquire); trying to stir up the sludge in her brain to make creative contributions in team strategy meetings; deflecting flack about one of the more stupid footballers she represented (arrested for taking all of his clothes off and 'frolicking', as the *Daily Mirror* put it, with three semi-clad teenagers in the fountain in Trafalgar Square).

Bunty, meanwhile, seemed a reformed character. Gone were the hourly phone calls and needy, attention-seeking emails. She had come out of the Troy saga with her dignity intact for once, and had gained much sympathy on social media and in the press, as far as Saffron could tell. Someone had started a #TeamBunty hashtag on Twitter, and apparently Troy had been roundly booed by the other customers when he walked into a Soho bar, if you believed the tabloid gossip columns anyway. She wished she could care more about any of it.

Then, a few days later, Saffron was on the Tube, flicking through that morning's *Metro*, when she turned the page to a fashion round-up from a glamorous black-tie party following a TV magazine's annual awards. And there, right in the centre, was a large colour picture of Bunty looking sensational in Gemma's emerald green dress. *BUNTY-LICIOUS* read the caption underneath.

Oh, my goodness. Did Gemma know about this yet? She fired off a quick text, the minute she had a signal:

Have you seen *Metro* this morning? Your dress is on page 5 – amazing photo!!!

A text came back a few minutes later.

What?! No way!

Gemma didn't know? Her phone wasn't already ringing off the hook? This was no good, thought Saffron to herself. This was no good at all. Major press coverage should automatically equal major public interest – end of story.

I'm going to put out a press release, she texted back.

That okay? Give me an hour and then stand by your phone. Prepare to receive a few more orders! xxx

Once in the office, Saffron got straight to work, bypassing her philandering soap actor who needed help with a cover story, and ignoring her whinging celebrity chef, Mario Fratelli, who'd been stitched up with an incriminating drugs photo.

Oh, get over yourself, love, she thought briskly, opening up a new document and flexing her fingers. I've got more important people to help right now. Then she began typing:

HOURGLASS DESIGNS
PRESS RELEASE

It's the question on everyone's lips: who dressed Bunty Halsom for the TV Quick Awards? We've all seen the stunning photos, the flattering dress of emerald-green crêpe de Chine that dazzled the crowds and viewers at home. We're proud to announce that the designer behind this outfit is none other than rising star **Gemma Bailey***, the creative genius behind* **Hourglass Designs***.*

She paused, trying to remember what Gemma had said when talking about her work, then went on:

Bailey's philosophy is simple: 'Everyone needs a dress that makes them feel beautiful,' she says. 'I make gorgeous clothes for real women, not stick-insect models.'

Saffron frowned and back-spaced through the last sentence. No, Gemma wouldn't have said anything rude. Better to stay positive in a press release anyway, rather than taking potshots. She tried again:

We've all endured the misery of high-street clothes shopping: communal changing rooms, bad lighting and clothes that are meant for a slim build, rather than anything curvier. Gemma Bailey knows that only too well. 'I started making clothes for myself when I couldn't find anything in the shops that flattered my shape. When clothes fit properly, they look a million times better — and make YOU feel better, too. It gives me real satisfaction to create an outfit that makes a woman feel she's invincible. We all need an I-Am-Fabulous dress for a special occasion, don't we?'

Saffron read through what she'd written so far. Good, she thought. This is something that a lot of women will really respond to.

Tucked away in an idyllic Suffolk village, Gemma Bailey's Hourglass Designs label has so far been a well-kept secret in the little black books of many TV and film stars. With her personal service, sharp eye for detail and vivid sense of styling, however, it's only a matter of time before all the very best-dressed people have her number on permanent speed-dial.

'I've never felt so gorgeous in my life as when I'm in a Gemma Bailey dress' — Bunty Halsom.

For more details, or to arrange an interview/feature, please contact Saffron Flint on the number below.

The Hourglass Designs website is——

She broke off to check the state of the website, but there was still only a holding page. She'd have to get Caitlin to update that, and fast.

The Hourglass Designs website is due to go live very shortly. You can register your interest here [she added her personal email address] *and we will sign you up to an exclusive mailing list, with 10 per cent discount on your first order.*

Then she added her mobile number, rather than the company one. There was only so much blagging she could get away with before Charlotte noticed. She read through the whole thing again, emailed it to Gemma and Caitlin, marked 'URGENT!', and sat back with a smile to await their approval.

That was when she noticed Charlotte eyeballing her across the office. 'Everything all right?' she asked.

Saffron flushed. How did her boss always seem to know when she was skiving off? She wheeled her chair closer into her desk, so as to hide her burgeoning bump, and quickly opened a new document on her screen. 'Great, thanks,' she said. 'About to arrange a meeting with Jonah to discuss the fountain episode. Lovely coverage of Bunty in *Metro* today, by the way — and not even a mention of Troy, so that's all behind us now. Then I'm onto Ashley P—'

'There's no need for the full rundown, thank you.'

Charlotte's face looked pinched. She walked over and perched on Saffron's desk, smelling strongly of Dior, mingled with a leathery whiff from her ox-blood knee-high boots. 'Saffron . . . this little escapade which you took with Bunty Halsom . . . ' Her mouth twitched. 'It's all very irregular. I know she's a bull in a china shop at times, but you must not let her dominate your entire working schedule. We were left picking up the pieces from your absence for the whole of last week.'

Saffron bowed her head. 'Yes. I'm sorry about that. I didn't feel I . . . '

'I mean, one minute you're phoning in ill, the next you're off in Sussex or wherever, and you're shacked up in some bolthole with a client?' The potted Christmas cactus on Saffron's desk would start withering any second, in the heat of Charlotte's criticism.

'I can see that it must have looked . . . '

'That's not how we do things at Phoenix. Bunty is a long-standing client, but she does not automatically take priority. You have other commitments here.'

'Yes.' Saffron's mobile chose that moment to start ringing, thank goodness. Both she and Charlotte glanced at the screen. *Gemma*, it said.

Charlotte didn't seem in any hurry to leave. 'Is this a work call?'

'Yes. New client, I hope,' Saffron said. Well, it was sort of true. She slid her finger across her phone's screen to take the call. 'Gemma. Hi! Oh, good,' she said. 'Brilliant. And you're happy with the copy? Great. Is it all right for me to put that discount offer in, by the way? I just thought it would add an extra . . . Excellent. So what's the latest on the website?'

Charlotte, to her relief, slid off the desk and moved away, although she remained in earshot, Saffron noticed.

'Caitlin's on the case right now,' Gemma said, her words bubbling down the line. 'She's going to pretty up the holding page, she said, and will put a sign-up box on it, so that people can register their interest. She's going to try and finish some more pages today.' Her voice was getting higher and higher with excitement. 'I can't quite believe this, you know. Thank you so much. It's just . . . amazing. Beyond my wildest dreams!'

'Just you wait,' Saffron said. 'We've barely started, mate. Get that website up and running properly as fast as you can, and I'll circulate the press release. And brace yourself — we're in for a busy time.'

She ended the call, feeling energized. Doing this favour for Gemma would be far more satisfying than trying to pick up the pieces of a spoiled-brat celebrity's tarnished career, that was for sure. Humming to herself, she returned to her press release and began compiling an appropriate contacts list: the gossip magazines, fashion editors at newspapers and glossies, feature editors who might want to interview Gemma as a

'New Businesswoman Success' story, local Suffolk press who'd probably want to big her up . . .

'New client, did you say?' Charlotte must have crept up on her, because the sound of her voice made Saffron jump.

She faltered. She had not exactly intended to take on Gemma as a 'real' client, which would involve getting her to sign a contract with the agency and billing her for any work undertaken. This was more a case of giving a break to a nice person who deserved it, rather than an abject money-making exercise. 'Hopefully, yes,' she said blandly.

Charlotte nodded, lips pursed, then walked away. She said nothing, but she didn't need to. Her message of *I've got my eye on you* was received loud and clear.

Sometimes you could send out a press release and it was like throwing glitter up at the stars – a brief sparkle of hope, only to be swallowed up by the darkness. At other times you lucked in with a combination of a good story, a strong visual and a news lull, which saw every journalist's interest piqued. Today just happened to be one of those golden days. By the time she was leaving the office, Saffron had taken well over twenty phone calls, passed on at least the same number of prospective customers to Gemma and had even taken details of a couple of people who wanted to order dresses right now – and did Gemma take commissions?

Her heart sang as she imagined the orders pouring in to

her friend's laptop, with the promise of large sums of money to follow. Her only worry was that Gemma would be overwhelmed by the demand. *Make sure you start a waiting list*, she texted her as she waited for her bus, her phone still warm after constant use all day. *And maybe rope in an assistant! Get that husband of yours on the case, all right?!*

It was nearly seven o'clock by the time she reached her flat, and her mobile was *still* ringing. She'd have to start sending enquiries to voicemail soon, she decided wearily, taking the call without looking at the screen and tucking it under her ear, so that she could rummage for her door keys at the same time. 'Hello, Saffron Flint?' she said. Lipstick, gloves, purse, more lipstick, notebook, pen, more lipstick — where were her bloody keys?

'Saffron, it's me. It's Eloise.'

She hardly recognized her sister, she sounded so timid and ground down. Forgetting about her keys momentarily, Saffron leaned against the door, braced for an unpleasant confrontation. They still hadn't spoken since the Sunday dinner of doom. 'Hi,' she said warily. 'How are you?'

'I'm . . . I'm okay. Listen, I was wondering. Can we talk?'

'Yes, of course.'

'I just . . . ' Eloise sighed. 'Oh, I can't do this over the phone. Can I come over sometime?'

'Here? To the flat?' Whenever Eloise had visited in the past, she'd spent almost the entire time checking out the window that her car wasn't being stolen or vandalized. 'I mean – sure, yeah. Of course. When were you thinking?'

'Saturday would be good for me, if you're not too busy.'

'Saturday it is then. Do you want to come for lunch?'

'Great. Thank you. I'll see you then.'

Saffron said goodbye and put the phone in her bag, an odd sense of foreboding stealing over her. Then she shook herself and began searching for her door keys again. She was being fanciful, that was all. Tired, fanciful and silly. The sooner she and her sister were back on proper speaking terms, the better.

Letting herself into the dark hallway, she took a deep, weary breath, then climbed the stairs up to her flat.

Chapter Twenty-Five

Working with Caitlin at White Gables was so companionable and fun that Gemma felt a pang of loss when she had finished both the dresses Bunty had commissioned. The hefty wallop of money going into the joint account was amazing – right off the satisfaction scale – but all the same, Gemma couldn't help wishing the experience had lasted a little longer.

But then Bunty appeared in *Metro* wearing the gorgeous green dress that Gemma had made her, and life suddenly accelerated up a whole new gear. When Saffron's call came, she was hurrying through the drizzle to get Darcey into school on time, but as she heard the magic words cascading down the line, she could have sworn that the sun came out and a choir of angels began to sing 'Hallelujah'.

Fizzing with such unbelievable news, Gemma kissed all the breath out of her daughter ('Euurggh! Mum, stop it, you weirdo') and pelted straight round to Caitlin's house.

Caitlin answered the door with a half-eaten piece of toast

in her hand. 'I was just having my b— What's going on?' she asked, as Gemma bustled past and hung up her coat.

'You'll never guess what,' she burst out breathlessly. 'Something amazing has happened. And I'm begging you like I've never begged anyone before: will you help me? Please?'

'Of course,' Caitlin said, startled. 'Are you all right?'

'I'm better than all right,' Gemma told her, and the story bubbled out of her: the newspaper, the phone call, how she just couldn't *believe* it (several times) and wasn't it just the most amazing thing *ever*? (ditto). Caitlin wasted no time in switching on her laptop, pulling up the *Metro* website and finding the article about the TV awards. Then they both squealed at top volume as they saw the glorious picture of Bunty in her full splendour.

'No way,' Gemma cried, clapping her hands. 'I bloody love that woman. Look at her working the dress. Look! At! Her!'

'She actually looks . . . stunning. She really does,' Caitlin said, open-mouthed. She high-fived Gemma and pulled her in for a hug. 'Bloody hell. And you *made* that. Hourglass Designs goes national, dude!'

'I know, that's what Saffron reckons. She said if we could finish the website, put up some way to register email addresses of potential clients . . . '

'I'm on it,' Caitlin said at once. 'No problem at all. I can easily add a registration widget and all the prices; plus we could even put up a little video interview with you . . . '

Gemma threw her arms around her. 'Thank you,' she said. 'You're the business. Did I mention that I'm actually a bit in love with you?'

Caitlin laughed and clicked open another screen. 'Let me show you what I've done so far . . .'

The Hourglass Designs website wasn't yet fully live, but there was already a decent number of pages ready to go. Caitlin had gone with her original idea to have the home page framed by a twisting pink tape-measure design, and she'd used the silhouette of a curvy woman as the logo. She'd added three of Gemma's designs to a 'Dresses' page – Valentine: the cap-sleeved, cleavage-enhancing scarlet dress she'd made for Valentine's Day (but ended up wearing to work in the pub); Midnight, the dark, shimmering blue, off-the-shoulder velour dress she'd worn on New Year's Eve, which had three-quarter-length sleeves and a panelled bodice; and Olivia, a shorter, vampier cocktail dress in jet-black sateen that she'd made to wear for her sister-in-law's fortieth birthday party. 'I've been matching up colour and fabric samples to each page, so that prospective customers could order direct,' she explained. 'Is that okay?'

'Absolutely,' Gemma said. 'Good idea.'

'We'll need a page about you and your vision,' Caitlin went on. 'Hey, and I'll tell you what would be really cool: some kind of gizmo that would let customers upload a webcam image of themselves, type in their measurements and see what they'd look like in each dress. What do you reckon?'

'That would be awesome,' Gemma said excitedly, leaning over her shoulder. 'Can you really do that? Oh God, and you must tell me how much I need to pay you for all this, by the way.'

'Leave it to me,' Caitlin said, and started typing. 'Team Hourglass — let's do this!'

They could tell, almost to the minute, when Saffron's press release went out to the journalists. Gemma's phone immediately started pinging dementedly with forwarded email enquiries, the laptop chirruped like a flock of hysterical birds as people signed up, one after another, for news alerts from the website, and there were even requests for bookings and fittings. 'Already? This is insane,' Gemma marvelled, trying to keep track. 'They don't even know how much I'm going to charge yet, and they still want to buy my dresses. Who are all these mad people?'

'Ah, you're the new hot ticket,' Caitlin said with a grin. 'I'd better get my order in quick, before you get so rich and famous you don't want to know me any more.'

Gemma gave her a look. 'As if,' she said, then gaped at her computer screen, which was positively rippling with new emails. 'Help,' she cried, suddenly feeling overwhelmed. 'What have we started? I'm not sure I can do this.'

'Of course you can,' Caitlin told her. 'You totally can. Buy yourself a big business diary and book in your first few fittings. And get some champagne on ice, while you're at it. You're in business, lady. The empire starts here.'

'*We're* in business, you mean,' Gemma said, clicking open the first email. It was from a fashion blogger who wanted to interview her. Her! She pulled herself together and took a deep breath. 'You, me and Saffron – this is all of us. I couldn't have got this far without either of you. Oh God, I'm going to cry in a minute.'

'No crying allowed,' Caitlin ordered. 'We're too busy to cry. Smile!'

Many, many emails later, with six people booked in for fittings and another thirty or so requesting fabric swatches, it came as something of a wrench to leave White Gables that afternoon for the school run. They had been so busy with the sudden crazy wave of media and customer interest that Gemma hadn't once thought about Spencer or the rest of her family, she realized with a pang of guilt. Boy, was he going to be grumpy about that. Still on crutches and finding it difficult to get around on his own, he hated being left alone for hours on end, like a dog abandoned to howl and pine. Bad wife. Negligent wife. But also wife who felt as if she'd scored a glorious hat-trick in the game of life, and was now running round the pitch high-fiving all her mates.

She somehow managed to restrain herself from dancing and singing all the way home like the heroine from a musical, although she did cave in instantly to Darcey's requests for chocolate brownies from the bakery as they passed. Hell, yes. It was definitely a chocolate-brownie sort of day.

But then they arrived home to find Spencer sitting in his sports car, parked in the dingy garage, and the vibrancy of her wonderful mood immediately dimmed like a low-watt bulb. 'Are you all right, love?' she asked anxiously, peering into the window. He was sitting there motionless, his hands on the steering wheel. 'Sorry I've been out so long. Do you want a cup of tea?'

He blinked, as if only just registering their presence. 'Please,' he said quietly, making no movement to get out.

'What's he *doing*?' Darcey asked in a too-loud whisper as they trooped back into the kitchen, with Spencer still in the car.

Gemma sighed. 'I think he just feels sad,' she replied.

She made him a tea and got in the car next to him, but he made no effort to speak. All you could hear was the slow, sliding tick of the electricity meter on the wall as it notched up the watts. 'Spence,' she said after a few moments. 'Come on. It'll be all right.'

'I'm just trying to remember what it felt like to drive her,' he said, staring straight ahead. 'What it felt like to rev the engine and go. Remember that weekend in Walberswick?'

Did she ever. His parents had agreed to look after the children while she and Spencer zipped off in the Mazda to

302

Walberswick for a surprise treat. It had been a cloudless blue-sky June day, and they'd put the roof down and let rip. Stretched out around them were the green-and-yellow fields of Suffolk, the old flint churches and brick barns, hedgerows bustling with birds and butterflies. The world had never seemed more beautiful. 'Course I do,' she said, reaching over to squeeze his hand. 'And just as soon as you're better, we'll go back there.'

He sighed. 'I can't imagine it, though. I feel as if that's never going to happen.'

'It will. I promise it will. Your ankle's nearly better, you'll be able to start physio soon . . . You'll get there. And . . . ' She hesitated over her news. Could he handle it? *Not now*, she decided. *Not when he was so vulnerable.* 'We're a team, remember. Let me pick up the slack for a while, just until you're better.' She reached out and took his hand. 'Don't worry.'

'Oh,' Gemma said at teatime that evening, as if it had just occurred to her, 'by the way, I'm giving up the job at the pub.'

Will muttered something that might have been 'Thank God for that', although Darcey at least was more enthusiastic.

'YAY!' she cried. 'So you'll be here at bedtime again?'

'Every night,' Gemma smiled. 'And we can start a new story together now, can't we?'

'How come?' Spencer asked.

'I've got some other work,' Gemma said. And then she

couldn't hold back any longer. 'One of my dresses was in the newspaper today. Wait, I'll show you.'

Abandoning her food, she got up and switched on the iPad and opened the *Metro* website. 'Look,' she said, showing them the image of Bunty. She'd never get tired of seeing that picture, she thought to herself proudly. 'And basically everything's gone a bit mad. Lots of people want me to make dresses for them and . . . Well, I've kind of started a little business.'

Darcey's eyes were big and round. 'Whoa. Are you, like, *famous*, Mum?'

She ruffled her daughter's hair. Darcey's ambition was to be famous, although the finer details changed on a weekly basis. Last week she wanted to be a famous vet ('a telly vet with nice hair'), but the week before, when she'd started an Instagram account for Waffle – the cat over the road that was always finding his way into their house (sample posting: 'Sleeping on Darcey's bed, yo!') – she'd announced that she now planned to be a wildlife photographer (an extremely famous one).

'I'm not quite *famous*,' Gemma said now. 'But I think you'll be able to start pony lessons again soon. And, Will, if it's not too late, we can see about getting you back on the school trip for France. And we'll be able to pay off our bills a bit quicker now. Best of all . . . ' She grinned. 'I can stop making horrible soup, for a change.'

'No more soup! No more soup!' Darcey cheered, punching the air.

'Great,' said Will, which was pretty much the teenage equivalent of *him* whooping and punching the air. 'Thanks, Mum.'

She turned warily to Spencer, not quite sure what to expect. He wouldn't object to her moment of glory, would he? 'Spence?' she said, trying to read his expression. 'I mean . . . It's too good an opportunity to turn down. Don't you think?'

There was a long agonizing moment, then he forked up another mouthful of food. 'It's brilliant, love,' he said gruffly. 'Well done, Gem.'

That would do. That was enough for her. 'Thanks, guys,' she said, trying not to show just how relieved and exhilarated she felt. Her heart was beating a tattoo inside. 'I'm really pleased. Anyway, enough about that. How was everyone else's day? How did you get on in football, Will?'

After tea, Gemma texted her dad, her brothers and everyone else she could think of about the image from *Metro*, then went along to the pub to explain the situation to Bernie. His face sagged in dismay when she said she was going to have to leave her job, but she was able to cheer him up pretty quickly by getting out her phone and showing him a photo of Bunty in all her glory. 'Fine figure of a woman there,' he said appreciatively. 'Bloody marvellous lady she is, too.'

'Better get your skates on then, Bern,' Gemma said with a wink. 'I reckon she'll have all sorts of new admirers after her now, you know.'

Walking back through the dark village, her mind whirled with dresses and designs. What to do first? Well, she needed to clear the decks of all her outstanding work before she could even think about her new customers, that was a definite. There wasn't too much to do, thankfully: Helen Bradley's curtains just needed the webbing attaching and a final press, and one of the bridesmaid dresses needed altering where the bridesmaid in question, ten-year-old Lottie Mayes, had had a sudden growth-spurt.

Once she'd done all of that, she could go through her first orders and work out how much fabric she'd need, then make a dash tomorrow to the wholesaler to pick everything up. She had someone coming for a fitting next Monday, another lady the Thursday after and . . . Her head swam. She was never going to manage this. It was too much for one person to cope with alone.

Her phone buzzed with another text from Saffron. It was as if her new friend could read her mind, all the way from London. *And maybe rope in an assistant! Get that husband of yours on the case, all right?!*

She snorted to herself. Yeah, that would be the day. But he'd taken the news well, at least. He'd actually congratulated her, hadn't he?

Maybe, just maybe, things were taking a turn for the better at last.

Chapter Twenty-Six

Of all the hiding places in the world, surely only Jane Fraser would pick a shoebox with a picture of stiletto heels as the safest spot to stash her secrets. She must have guessed it was the last place her clod-hopping, trainer-wearing daughter would be interested in noseying around while she was alive.

And how right she'd been. Caitlin had never fathomed why some people – her mother included – became so shrieky and excitable about something as silly as a pair of *shoes*, especially when they looked about as comfortable as torture implements. When it came to clearing Jane's wardrobe, Caitlin had painstakingly sorted through all the clothes, belts and handbags, but had left the shoe collection still boxed in piles on the bedroom floor, meaning to take the lot to the charity shop just as soon as she had an hour to spare. She hadn't so much as lifted any of the lids to peep in at them. She could so easily never have known.

But then, on a quiet Sunday afternoon, she rushed in there, having decided to bring her mum's antique dressing-screen down to the living room. Over the next few weeks there was a whole rash of new customers booked in for appointments with Gemma, all of whom would be disrobing and having the cold tape-measure held expertly around various parts of their bodies. It would be far nicer for them to have a proper space in one corner to undress, instead of being sent up to the bathroom, as they'd done with Bunty. Maybe she should buy a pretty silk dressing gown too, she thought, hurrying across the bedroom, so that—

'Ow! Bollocks!'

All long limbs and awkwardness, Caitlin had been born clumsy and, in her haste, she'd skidded on the polished floorboards and stumbled right into the shoeboxes. Down they toppled like dominoes, lids bouncing off and disgorging sequinned slingbacks, black patent courts, silver sandals . . .

She rubbed her knee where she'd banged it on the floor and began stuffing the shoes back in their boxes with a huff of impatience. The sooner she got rid of this lot, the better. But then she noticed that a box near the back had tipped on its side, revealing a heap of folded papers inside. Stupidly her eye went to the description on the cardboard box – *Jacquetta, size 6* – and then back to the papers. Uh-oh. What were these, then?

Her hand closed around the documents and her heart bucked violently as she saw the logo on the top letter: *Aberdeenshire Council Children's Services: Adoption and Fostering Unit*, it said.

Her breathing was rapid and shallow. 'Adoption and Fostering Unit', right there in black-and-white. Oh no. *Oh no.*

So it was true, she thought dully. I guessed right.

But it was little consolation when her world was falling apart.

Five minutes was all it took to recalibrate her entire ancestry. Five short minutes to realize that everything had been a lie. According to the certificate she'd just discovered, she'd been born Josephine Wendell, to Alison Mary Wendell, no mention of any father. So she wasn't even called Caitlin Fraser. She was Josephine frigging Wendell, who sounded like a repressed Victorian aunt straight out of a black-and-white photograph.

She put a hand to her mouth, trembling, unsure whether she dared read any more. Josephine. That was her. She didn't feel like a Josephine, though. Not even slightly. As for Alison Wendell . . . that was her mother. Her real mother. Oh, *Alison*, she thought, with a stab of sadness. Didn't you want me? Why did you give me away?

Tears trickled down her face as a terrible catalogue of possibilities turned like a carousel in her mind. Maybe Alison had been mentally ill. Maybe she was an alcoholic or drug addict. Maybe she was a frightened teenager. Maybe she'd been raped.

The papers slithered from her fingers as Caitlin put her

head in her hands, haunted by so many dreadful thoughts. She could hardly take it in. How long had they spent together, she and Alison? Had Alison held her, cuddled her, stroked her warm baby-head and wished things could be otherwise? Had they even been together a single night? What had happened next?

Maybe Alison was terminally ill. Maybe she'd passed on some genetic catastrophe that was lying dormant in Caitlin's cells right now, waiting for the right moment to explode and wreak havoc.

She squeezed her eyes shut, wrapping her arms around herself. Maybe she should stop bloody well terrifying herself with all these 'maybe's, she thought.

A little while later, she blew her nose and stiffened her resolve. Well, Pandora's box was open now, she might as well know it all. Heart pounding, she began leafing tentatively through the other documents saved and hidden for so many years by her mother. (Could she still even call her that? Was it allowed? Oh, why hadn't Jane told her about this before? Why hadn't she explained? Why had she blurted out an apology as she lay dying, then left Caitlin to piece together the awful, life-changing pieces by herself? Talk about selfish. Talk about lame!)

There was the case file: details of her birth and the particulars of the foster home where she'd spent almost two years. (Why so long? Didn't anybody want her?)

There was the Deed Poll certificate, confirming that Josephine Wendell was now Caitlin Rose Fraser. One piece of paper, and she was a different person. How could that even be allowed?

There was the adoption certificate, dated June 1st, of course. *A special day.* And last but definitely not least, there was her birth certificate, with Alison's name on it. Not lost, after all. Right here, tucked away the whole time.

Josephine Wendell, born in Inverdowie, Aberdeenshire. Just down the road from where her parents had grown up, which was handy. Very handy, if you wanted to pop along and adopt someone else's baby.

Bloody hell. This was seismic. This changed everything. How she wished she could have remained in blissful ignorance a while longer; that she'd walked, not run, into the bedroom and kicked open the box of secrets. Five minutes earlier she had been Caitlin Fraser, head busy with thoughts of a screen and a dressing gown. Now she was no longer sure who she was, or what she should even call herself.

She stared blindly around at the room where her parents had slept for so many years. As a child, she'd been allowed to come in here after eight o'clock on weekend mornings and scramble into the double bed with them, lying snuggled between their warm bodies, safe and secure. She could still remember the joy she'd felt, turning the handle of their door and clambering up onto the bed.

When she was a bit older she'd tottered in here on Mother's Day and Father's Day mornings, carefully clutching a home-made card decorated with felt-tip drawings, as well as a slopping lukewarm cup of tea and, as she grew older still, a congealing fried breakfast for the lucky parent. Mother's Day and Father's Day. That was a laugh now, wasn't it?

They'd lied to her the entire time. A veil of deceit had been carefully constructed, wrapped tight around her whole life. Secret social-services meetings, folders of paperwork up in Aberdeenshire, the stupid June 1st celebration cake and champagne – *Oh, just because!*

Nobody had bothered to tell her, to explain a single thing.

A sharp pain pierced her as her gaze fell on Jane's favourite framed photo: Caitlin aged about four in a blue nylon nurse's costume, a plastic baby doll cradled in her arms. You could almost hear the far-away childish voice echoing through the years: *I want to be like YOU, Mummy.*

Well, not any more. She did not want to be like Jane – a liar, a deceiver. Fuck that.

A cry escaped her throat and she snatched up the picture, drew her arm back and hurled it right into the centre of Jane's huge gilt mirror. The mirror that had reflected the face of those liars for too long. Glass smashed everywhere in long, jagged shards and the room was left distorted, kaleidoscoped in mirrored fragments.

Caitlin didn't care. She just didn't care. She whirled out of the room and out of the house, slamming the door on the whole toxic place. And good riddance.

Chapter Twenty-Seven

It had taken well over two and a half hours of headless-chickenesque frenzied activity, but at last Saffron felt ready for Eloise's lunchtime arrival. The carpet was hoovered, the bathroom pristine, and she'd even got down on her hands and knees and scrubbed some of the more mysterious and lingering stains from the kitchen lino. She had bought fresh bread, ham, tomatoes, houmous and cheese from the deli two streets away, as well as a salted caramel torte for afters. A bunch of white tulips in a striped ceramic vase completed the 'Single and Pregnant but Coping Magnificently, Thank You Very Much' effect she was aiming for. Mind you, she did scoop up all the pregnancy books and magazines she'd acquired and stuffed them at the bottom of her wardrobe, along with the beautiful baby outfit from her mum. There was such a thing as rubbing salt in a wound, after all.

Still, she was not about to apologize for being pregnant. Absolutely not. She hadn't done this to spite Eloise in any way. It had just happened. She hoped, more than anything, that she could make her sister understand this.

The doorbell rang and she took three deep yogic breaths — *cool, calm, collected*, she reminded herself — before going to answer it.

'Eloise, hi. Come on in. No Simon today?'

'No, he's at home. It's just the two of us.'

'Lovely,' said Saffron, although she felt apprehensive without the steadying presence of Simon there. Eloise could be fairly intense at the best of times, and Saffron's walls were not the thickest. She made a note in advance to apologize to her neighbours for what could potentially end up a shrill-voiced, door-slamming encounter. 'Come on up. Lunch is ready.'

The two sisters sat opposite each other at the small dining table under the window and Saffron couldn't help seeing the flat through Eloise's eyes: cluttered, small and not remotely baby-proof. Unlike Eloise and Simon's large detached house in the countryside, in other words, which already boasted teddy-bear wallpaper and a mobile in one of the bedrooms. ('We like to be prepared,' Eloise had smiled five years ago, when they decorated.) How that room must torment them now, Saffron thought with a twist of sympathy.

'So,' Eloise said, buttering her bread with exaggerated care. 'I wanted to say sorry, for the way I behaved at Mum's the other week. It was unfair. I completely overreacted.' She raised her eyes and fixed them earnestly on Saffron. 'I'm sorry.'

Wow. That had come a lot easier than Saffron had expected. 'I'm sorry, too,' she found herself saying, despite her earlier vow not to apologize. 'I know how hard it must have been for you to hear my news. I should have found a way to tell you more sensitively, before you guessed.'

'The thing is,' Eloise went on, as if she hadn't spoken, and Saffron stiffened at the determined look on her sister's face. Ah. Okay. Maybe it wasn't going to be as straightforward as all that. 'Simon and I, we've been wondering if . . . well . . . ' She faltered as if she'd forgotten the lines of her script. 'Well, we're all set up for a baby, you see,' she said in a rush. 'We've got the house and the security, plus we really, really desperately want a child. Whereas . . . ' She broke off again, dedicating her attention to the butter knife.

Saffron felt her skin prickle. *Danger, danger. Proceed with caution.* '"Whereas" . . . ?' she prompted, narrowing her eyes.

Eloise leaned forward and Saffron caught the faint waft of violets. 'Whereas . . . Well, don't get me wrong, this is a lovely flat, but have you seriously thought about having a baby here?'

'Yes. Quite frequently.' Saffron could feel her gaze becoming steely. Where exactly was Eloise going with this?

'Only . . . Well, we'd be happy to help. Look after the baby, I mean. It could . . . ' At last she lifted her gaze, the naked desperation vivid in her wide blue eyes. 'It could stay with us some of the time. If you want.'

Saffron had not been expecting that. 'What do you mean?'

Her hands rose instinctively to rest on the soft swell of her belly, as if guarding the contents. 'Stay with you? Why?'

'We could look after it sometimes. Maybe during the week, while you were working . . . ' A pleading note had entered her sister's voice.

Had she actually gone mad? Saffron stared at her in astonishment. 'No, thanks,' she said. 'The baby will be here with me.'

'But we just thought maybe . . . '

'No. Thank you. I can look after my own child.'

Eloise's eyelid twitched. 'It's just that you'll be on your own.'

'I know. I don't need reminding. But I'll manage.'

'But we've got a nice garden. And the baby could have its own bedroom.' Full-force pleading shone from Eloise's face.

'You're asking me if you can have my baby.' Saffron could hardly believe what she was hearing.

'Of course I'm not! Not exactly.'

'Well, the answer is no, Eloise. No way. Whether you've got the fanciest garden and biggest bedroom in the world. What the hell is this? You can't just come round and ask someone for their baby! Have you lost the fucking plot?'

'No! It was only an idea, Saff . . . '

'A bloody awful idea. How dare you? Coming round suggesting I can't look after my own child. What a nerve! Who do you think you are?'

The butter knife slipped from Eloise's fingers, chinking against the plate. 'Simon said I shouldn't,' she mumbled, chin trembling. 'He told me not to ask you. But I had to try. The last I heard, you didn't even want children, so I just thought . . .'

'Well, you just thought wrong.' Astonishment gave way to rage, and she felt the same lioness instinct she'd experienced during her first ultrasound. *Back off, Eloise.* My *baby.*

'I'm sorry. I just . . .'

Saffron didn't want to hear any more. 'You haven't even asked me how I am,' she snapped, over her sister's wheedling. 'Let alone about the pregnancy. Would you still want the baby so much if I told you he or she might have Down's syndrome?'

Eloise's head jerked nervously at the question. She licked her lips and said nothing for a moment. 'Does it?' she whispered.

Saffron banged a fist on the table, making the tulips quake. '*It?* Can you stop calling my baby "it", please?'

'Sorry.' Eloise hung her head and there was a pause while the room seemed to be holding its breath, waiting for the answer to her question.

'I don't know yet,' Saffron muttered eventually. 'There's a one in thirty-six chance. I've got to have an amniocentesis the week after next, which will tell me. That's if it doesn't terminate the pregnancy, that is.' Her pulse ticked faster, too. So much for cool, calm and collected. 'Hadn't factored that into your calculations, had you?' She stared her sister down. 'I guess that means you've changed your mind.'

'Oh, Saffron.' Eloise seemed to shrink in her chair. 'I had no idea.'

'No, you didn't, because you didn't even bother to ask. You just jumped right in with your stupid, selfish suggestions. You might as well leave, if that's all you've got to say.'

Eloise's voice was barely a whisper. 'You must think I'm awful.'

'I do, right now. Yes. I do.'

'I *am* awful. I'm a complete bloody psycho. What's wrong with me? What is *wrong* with me?' She wiped her eyes. 'Sorry. I'm really, really sorry. Can we just rewind, and delete all of that?' Her lip trembled. 'I know it's not your problem, but I've turned into one of those obsessive madwomen. All I can think about is babies. I've even started eyeing them up in other people's prams. I feel my hands twitch, as if I'm going to snatch one away.'

Angry as she had been, Saffron's rage began to cool. She had never seen competent, success-story Eloise so anguished.

'I could do it, you know,' she went on. 'Steal one, I mean. I can totally see myself stealing a baby.' She made a sound that was somewhere between a laugh and a sob. 'And I couldn't even pretend it's because I'm hormonal, because I'm not. Lose-lose!'

They were both silent for a moment. Eloise crumbled some cheese over her bread while Saffron dolloped a lump of garlicky houmous onto her plate. Her appetite had deserted her, though. 'Eloise . . . I'm sorry, okay? I really am. I wish more than anything that you could be pregnant too. But this is my child and I can deal with it, whatever the consequences.'

Eloise blew her nose, eyes bright and wet. 'I know,' she said, looking away. 'And you'll be a lovely mum. You'll cope brilliantly, just like you always do.' She sniffed. 'Tell me what happens with this amnio test then. What did the doctors say?'

And so, even though Saffron was pretty sure Eloise already had an encyclopaedic knowledge of amniocentesis procedures, due to her vast collection of pregnancy and baby reading material, she dully repeated the few facts she knew about what would happen and why.

'I'll come with you, if you want,' Eloise said, after a deep breath – an incredibly magnanimous offer, given the circumstances. 'Will the father be there? I'd love to meet him. Max, did you say his name was?'

'Yeah. But he won't be there. He's not interested. Couldn't even be bothered to reply to the letter I sent telling him I was pregnant.'

Eloise twisted her wedding ring on her slim, pale finger; an unconscious 'thank-goodness-I'm-married' reaction. 'What a sod,' she said. 'Shall I send Simon round to punch his lights out?'

It took a leap of imagination to visualize Simon, the human guinea pig, punching anyone's lights out, let alone squaring up to Max, but the notion did make Saffron laugh for the first time since her sister had arrived. 'I might just take you up on that,' she said.

The rest of the afternoon ran on smoother tracks, thank goodness. Conversation turned to safer subjects: work and holidays, and Simon's promotion hopes. When Eloise looked at her watch and said she really must be getting back, Saffron was able to hug her with genuine fondness, assuring her that their earlier conversation could be put firmly behind them and never referred to again.

A moment of madness, Eloise said, and then a wistfulness stole across her face as they parted from the hug. Her hand hovered above Saffron's belly. 'May I?'

'You may,' Saffron said.

A whole array of emotions was visible in Eloise's eyes as she gently put a hand to Saffron's bump, fingers outspread. 'Wow,' she said.

The sisters shared a proper smile. 'Wow,' Saffron agreed.

Chapter Twenty-Eight

Gemma might have become Businesswoman in Demand overnight, but you'd never think it from her family's reaction. It was still Gemma who had to make breakfast and load the washing machine and drop Darcey at a friend's party. It was still Gemma who had to run Will into town, and push the Hoover around, and load up with groceries and supplies for the week ahead. That was on top of visiting the wholesaler to buy the silks and satins in the bright jewel colours she had chosen to offer as swatches to interested customers, as well as the thread, zips and buttons she would need. She'd now had ten orders for dresses through the website – two Midnights, three Valentines and five Olivias – on top of the private appointments booked in her diary. She hoped she hadn't bitten off more than she could chew.

By Sunday she felt positively frazzled and wished heartily that she hadn't invited her dad round, today of all days. With Judy, too! It was meant to be a 'Meet the Family' sort of thing, suggested in a charitable moment, but now she felt churlish to the point of unwelcoming instead. *And* the house was still so shabby and neglected. She must whip round with a paintbrush soon. She must!

The night before she'd stayed up late, cutting swatches with her pinking shears and sending them with a polite typed note – she really should order some proper stationery – to everyone who'd requested one. That left just the whole house to clean, a mountain of potatoes to peel for lunch, the children to remind about their homework, Will's muddy rugby kit to wash . . .

'Why is your face like that, Mum?' Darcey asked, coming into the room just then.

'Like what?'

'All sort of fierce and frowny. Like you're cross about something.'

Gemma laughed. 'I'm not cross, love. Just . . . ' She shrugged, searching around for the right word. 'Just determined, I guess.'

Darcey bent down to fuss over the cat from over the road, which had got in again and fancied his chances with the chicken. 'Determined to do what?'

'Keep all the plates spinning, Darce, without letting any fall. That's all I'm trying to do. That's all any woman can do.'

While Gemma was doing her impression of a bluebottle on speed, Spencer was, as usual, on the sofa, playing *Halo* with

Will on the Xbox. His ankle had now fully healed and he was meant to be doing more gentle exercise, but he had barely left the house in days, complaining that the spring sunshine made his headache worse.

Hearing them mucking about together while she was charging about doing everything single-handedly was starting to irritate her. Had it not occurred to them that she might appreciate a hand? Clearly not. Eventually she put down the peeler and marched through to the living room. 'Will, come and make yourself useful, won't you?' she said. 'I'll teach you how to peel vegetables – a very important life-skill.'

'Oh, leave him,' Spencer said, not moving his eyes from the screen. 'It's not that important a skill. Any idiot can do it – even me.'

Gemma resisted mentioning that she had never seen him with a kitchen utensil in his hand, let alone peeling a single potato. 'It'll take you five minutes to learn,' she said. 'And, Spence, maybe you could mow the lawn? It's a lovely day out there.'

'Aw, Gems, come on, it's Sunday. Give us a break.'

'Will?'

Will glanced over his shoulder at her, then across at his dad, clearly torn. 'Can't Darcey do it?'

Gemma was damned if she was about to teach her daughter to peel spuds before her much older son learned to do so. 'I'd really like a bit of help,' she said steadfastly.

He sighed and paused his character onscreen. 'Oh, all right then,' he muttered, getting up with exaggerated reluctance.

'I'm sorry, love, but we all need to muck in now,' she said.

Spencer rolled his eyes. 'Yeah, yeah, we know. Now that you're the power-mad businesswoman, you don't need to remind us.'

'I'm not power-mad,' she replied, taken aback by the bitterness in his voice. 'I'm only asking our son to peel the carrots for Sunday dinner. It's hardly the end of the world.'

'Yeah, and me to mow the frigging lawn, even though it doesn't need doing . . . Just because you're busy, Gemma, don't start bossing everyone else around.'

'I'm not,' she protested, but he was already getting to his feet, one hand to his back, to show her how painful his injury still was, just to rub in how unreasonable she was being, forcing an invalid to move.

'Course you're not. And now I'll go and mow the lawn with my bloody front teeth, shall I? Because you told me to. Fat old nag.'

Gemma's jaw dropped. She actually felt as if she'd been slapped. 'Wh-what did you call me?'

His eyes were hooded and sullen. 'You heard.'

Yeah. She'd heard, all right. And it was pretty much the worst thing he could have called her. He knew full well the angst she'd suffered over her size in the past, how she'd lived on thin air and black coffee when she was young and self-conscious, how she'd made herself sick if she ever weakened and gave in to a doughnut or a bag of chips. She had battled so hard to overcome those feelings of low self-worth, and he had helped her through, by telling her she was beautiful, that he couldn't keep his hands off her.

Until now, that was. Until he'd just thrown that word at her as if it had all been a lie.

'Well, if that's how you feel, maybe you should find someone else to try and look after you,' she said, her voice cracking with hurt. 'If that's how you feel, maybe you should get lost!'

Back in the kitchen, Gemma's hands shook as she put the potatoes on to parboil, Will sulkily hacking away at the carrots and parsnips beside her as if he was enduring some kind of Guantanamo torture. She couldn't believe Spencer had called her that. Her very least-favourite word. And he knew it was, too. He had said it deliberately, as if he couldn't care less. It was the worst thing he'd ever done in the fifteen years they'd been together.

Will clumped out again, vegetables done, but Gemma's unhappy mood continued as she set the potatoes roasting, mixed the bread sauce, basted the chicken and chopped broccoli florets. Of course there was no whirring of the lawnmower to be heard outside. What a surprise, she thought bitterly. Spencer was definitely spoiling for a fight.

She slammed the plates into the warming drawer of the

oven with unnecessary force, and crashed the cutlery around as she laid the table, unable to help banging out her frustration. Well, she thought, if he was going to start name-calling, she was not about to take it lying down. She would not be made to feel bad in her own home – she wouldn't!

Just as she was crossly wiping a splatter of gravy from her left boob, the doorbell rang and her eyes swung up to the clock in horror. What? It was only ten past twelve and they had definitely agreed on half-past. Surely her dad hadn't broken the habit of a lifetime and turned up somewhere *early* for once, had he?

Gemma let out a groan. She was still in her oldest jeans and a horribly unflattering sweatshirt, smelling strongly of roast potatoes and now splotched with gravy. The plan had been to change into something more attractive as soon as the chicken was out and resting under its foil blanket, and the Yorkshire puddings were gently fluffing up in their tray (the childrens' favourite – they had Yorkshire pudding with every kind of roast). If her dad had been on time, she could have answered the door to him looking composed and sane; as it was, she had no make-up on, and instead appeared red-faced and scruffy. This was not the Superwoman image she'd intended.

'Hello, love, sorry we're a bit early. We were going to pop into the garden centre, but there was such a queue to get in the car park, we couldn't be bothered.' Her dad enveloped her in one of his mammoth, crushing hugs. 'Judy's been telling me off, saying that nobody wants early guests, but I said you wouldn't mind. You don't, do you?'

'Of course not!' Gemma laughed a bit too heartily. 'Not at all. Excuse the state of me. I was just going to change, but . . .' She shrugged, feeling uncomfortable. 'Hi, Judy.'

'Hello! What a lovely big house! My goodness, it's like something from *Footballers' Wives*.' Judy pressed a bunch of gladioli into Gemma's arms.

'Well, not exactly . . .' Gemma said weakly. She doubted any of the footballers' wives these days had Artex ceilings and peeling wallpaper, but whatever. 'Thank you.'

Judy's charm-offensive had already moved on. 'And you must be Darcey, what a pretty face! It's lovely to meet you. I'm Grandad's . . . friend,' she said coyly, batting her eyelashes. 'Now I've got a present for you somewhere.' She dug a hand into her bag. 'Where are they? Ah. Sweeties!' She produced a large bag of Percy Pig sweets and Darcey's eyes lit up.

'Thank you!'

'Not before lunch,' Gemma found herself saying, although Darcey was already skipping away, apparently struck by selective deafness, judging by the way her hands were tugging eagerly at the opening of the bag. 'Darcey! Did you hear me? Don't spoil your lunch!'

'And where's William? And Spencer? I've been so looking forward to meeting the fellas,' Judy gushed, with that annoying, toothy smile.

Gemma could guess exactly where they were: locked in battle once again on the Xbox, the lawn pointedly left untouched. It could be three feet tall by the time Spencer deigned to give it a mow. Sod it, she would have to do it herself, she thought crossly. Like everything else around this bloody place. 'Spence! Will! Come and show your ugly mugs,' she yelled, annoyed that they hadn't the manners to end the game at the sound of the doorbell. 'Let me take your jacket, Judy,' she said after a moment, as neither of them appeared. Brilliant. Thanks, guys. 'Come on through.'

She left the flowers on the worktop as she filled the kettle. 'Spencer! Will!' she shouted again in exasperation. Where *were* they? 'Sorry,' she muttered as she clattered down four mugs and the box of teabags. 'I'll go and track them down in a minute.'

'Oh, don't worry! No rush at all. Can I help with anything?' Judy asked, hovering expectantly. 'Everything smells absolutely wonderful. Barry's been saying what a great cook you are.'

'It's just a roast,' Gemma said. *Dad's favourite, thank you very much.* 'And I think it's pretty much under control. The chicken's due out in a few minutes and then . . . '

'Mum.' It was Will, looking wired and twitchy.

'Oh, there you are. Will, this is Judy, and . . . '

Judy was already coming over, her hand outstretched. 'Lovely to meet you! What a handsome lad you are!'

'Mum, it's Dad,' Will said urgently, side-stepping Judy.

'What do you mean? Is he all right?'

'He's gone.'

Gemma stared at him. 'What do you mean, he's gone? Gone where?'

'I . . . I don't know. He just said he was fed up and went out.'

Barry cleared his throat. 'I thought I noticed the garage door was open.'

Gemma's head was jangling from all this strange and unwanted information. 'What, he's gone out in the car? He's not meant to be driving yet!' She ran a hand through her hair. 'What's he playing at?'

'Was the thought of having us for lunch really that bad?' Judy joked, but nobody laughed.

'I don't understand.' Gemma turned dazedly to her dad. 'I don't know what he's thinking.'

'Don't worry, love. He'll be back in a minute.'

'I mean, he's been in a strange mood for weeks. We had a bit of a row this morning, but . . . ' She stopped, not wanting to air any dirty laundry in front of Judy. 'What exactly did he say?' she asked her son. Maybe Will had got it wrong, misunderstood somehow.

'He said . . . ' Will cleared his throat, looking agonized. 'Er, he said . . . '

'What? For goodness' sake, spit it out. What did he say?'

Will squirmed miserably in the limelight. 'He said, er, "Eff this for a life. I'm off. See you around."' He hung his head. 'That was about it.'

Gemma's mouth fell open, then shut. Fuck this for a life? 'Oh God,' she said weakly.

'Where will he have gone?' asked Barry. 'Do you want me to drive around, see if I can find him?'

'I don't know,' Gemma replied. She didn't seem to know anything any more. Her marriage, so rocky since the accident, appeared to have cracked wide open in the space of a few minutes. *If that's how you feel, maybe you should get lost!* she heard her own voice shrieking, and a cold sensation trickled down her back. 'I just don't know.'

Spencer didn't come home at all that day. Gemma phoned and texted him numerous times, until she discovered he'd left his phone at home. She called Harry and his other mates, but nobody had seen or heard from him. He'd taken the Mazda and vanished. She could hardly bear to think about what could have happened.

'Has he shown any suicidal tendencies?' Judy had asked unhelpfully, eyes wide, as the kitchen filled with the smell of burning roast dinner.

Gemma had felt like slapping her at the time – *I'll give you suicidal tendencies in a minute, Judy* – but the words refused to dissolve and disappear, hours later. *Was* he suicidal? He'd certainly been depressed for a long time, there was no doubt about that, but she hadn't thought things were that bad. What if he felt so desperate, though, that he'd gone out in the car and deliberately crashed, ending it all?

'Where *is* Daddy?' Darcey asked at bedtime, her little face screwing up in confusion. 'Where has he gone?'

That was the question Gemma couldn't answer. 'I'm sure he'll back soon,' she told her daughter, hugging her close and kissing the top of her head.

She wished she could believe her own reassuring words. Lying in bed that night, she couldn't sleep for terrifying visions of Spencer, wild-eyed, ramming his sports car at top speed into a brick wall and collapsing over the wheel. The knock at the front door, police officers with their caps removed, eyes sorrowful. 'Mrs Bailey? I'm afraid we've got some bad news for you.'

Has he shown any suicidal tendencies?

Where is *Daddy?*

If that's how you feel, maybe you should get lost!

Tears leaked from Gemma's eyes as she grabbed Spencer's pillow and breathed in his scent. She bitterly regretted losing her temper, but the words had burst out before she could hold them in. She hadn't meant it, though! She didn't really want him to get lost! She just wanted him to love her again, to look at her and smile as he used to do.

'Oh, Spencer,' she wept, wrapping her arms around the pillow and wishing it was him in her embrace instead. 'Please come home. I'm sorry. Please just come home.'

Chapter Twenty-Nine

'Bloody Nora, Gemma, you look terrible. Are you all right?'

Caitlin herself had had a sleepless night following the discovery of the adoption papers in Jane's bedroom, but Gemma looked like the walking dead; her eyes bruised-looking, her skin pale and puffy.

She steadied herself against the hall radiator as she took off her coat. 'Spencer's gone,' she said, her voice wobbling.

'He's gone? What do you mean, he's gone?'

'He's left us. Walked out. Just disappeared yesterday: no note, no phone call, nothing. He hasn't taken his medication or his phone, he hasn't even taken his toothbrush.'

'Shit. Have you phoned around? Has anyone seen him? He might be with Harry.' She blushed as she said his name, like a stupid teenager.

'I've phoned everyone. I've even phoned the hospitals around here. Nobody's seen him.' Tears broke free of Gemma's lashes and spilled down her cheeks. 'He's taken his car, the stupid idiot. When he's not even meant to be driving again yet.'

'Oh God. How come? Did you have an argument or something?'

'Kind of. I lost my temper with him when he . . . ' She looked at her feet, her rosebud mouth turning down. 'Well, he called me fat, and it was the last straw. I did shout at him a bit.'

'Oh, Gemma.' Caitlin put her arms round her, feeling Gemma's tears wet through the jumper she was wearing. This was horrible news. Gemma and Spencer had once seemed the golden couple of the village. He wasn't supposed to say things like that to her! 'I'm not surprised you lost your temper. You've had the patience of a saint, you really have. And you're not fat anyway, you're absolutely bloody scrumptious.'

Gemma sagged and Caitlin could tell she wasn't convinced. Gemma was the bubbliest, most cheerful and lovely person she'd ever met, but today it was as if there was a dark cloud hanging over her. Head-injuries or no head-injuries, right now Caitlin felt very much like giving Spencer a good old slap.

'Anyway,' she said, squeezing her friend before letting go, 'let me remind you of one of the perks of being your own boss. In times of crisis it is perfectly feasible – in fact, I'd say, essential – to eat cake at nine o'clock in the morning and not even *think* about rushing on with work.'

Gemma's lips quivered, then turned upwards at last in a

little smile. 'Yeah, stuff it, I'll get even fatter just to spite him,' she said. 'I'll be the fattest woman who ever lived. Then he'll be sorry.'

'Quite right,' said Caitlin bracingly. 'That'll show him.'

They discussed the Spencer issue over the first cup of coffee and then Caitlin talked about her own trauma over a second, her hands shaking on the mug as she relived the moment when she discovered that she wasn't the person she'd always thought. Now it was Gemma's turn to look concerned and dish out a comforting hug.

'Oh, love. I know you were wondering, but all the same, what a shocker.'

'Yeah. It's really thrown me. I feel like my whole childhood was a lie. I mean, none of it was what I thought.' She gazed out at the garden where the cherry tree was in full pink bloom now, bright and beautiful. Jane had loved that tree, she remembered with a pang. *Spring's on the way!*, she would say every year when it flowered.

'It wasn't a lie. They *did* love you and, from what you've said, they were great parents. And yes, they probably should have told you – they *definitely* should have told you – but . . . ' Gemma spread her hands. 'People do make stupid mistakes. I bet they thought they were protecting you by not saying anything.'

'I kind of know that. But oh . . . ' She clutched at her heart. 'It feels so raw, you know. So painful. I don't know if I'll ever be able to forgive them.'

They were silent for a moment. 'Are you going to try and trace your birth mother? Is she still alive, do you know?'

'No idea.' Caitlin got to her feet and changed the subject. 'We'd better get on with some work. Isn't What's-Her-Name coming round later, that actress?'

'God, yes, I'd completely forgotten. Look at the state of me! And I've got my new orders to be getting on with before then. Right. Come on, Gemma. Come on, Caitlin. Let's find some happy music on the radio and get stuck in. We'll get through this, you know. We will.'

'We damn well will. To work!'

The afternoon fitting turned out to be great fun. The actress was in her twenties, beautiful and exuberant. Somehow or other her niceness hadn't been knocked out of her, and she arrived with a box of colourful macarons and lots of excellent *EastEnders* gossip. Like Bunty, she ordered not one but two evening dresses, one in a rich plum-coloured shot silk, another in black velvet, and both Gemma and Caitlin ended their working day feeling more cheerful.

After Gemma left to pick up her daughter, the house fell silent, but Caitlin refused to allow the demons back in. Instead she kept herself busy clearing away all the shattered glass she'd left on Jane's bedroom floor, and wrapped the broken mirror in sheets of newspaper and parcel tape so that the bin men wouldn't slice their fingers on it. She tidied the pile of secret papers and put them in a big envelope on the chest of drawers, to be looked at when she felt strong enough.

Gemma's question kept playing on her mind, though. *Are you going to try and trace your birth mother? Is she still alive?*

Caitlin was curious, there was no denying it. Would they have anything in common, she and Alison Wendell? Did Alison ever think about Caitlin and wonder what had happened to her daughter?

She poured herself a gin and tonic and turned on her laptop again.

I just found out I was adopted she typed into Google and a long list of forum posts immediately appeared.

I am still in shock.

I am devastated.

Help!

Why didn't they tell me?

I found out on Facebook.

My aunt told me.

Everybody knew except me.

Oh Lord. This was awful. There was a whole world of bewilderment and betrayal out there, so many thoughtless parents making bad decisions. She felt like reaching an arm into the Internet and scooping up all the people who'd been let down, like her, for the most enormous group hug. *Me too. I understand. It's shite, isn't it? I just don't know who I am any more.*

There were stories of people tracking down their birth

mothers and, to a lesser degree, their birth fathers. There were also stories of lost siblings, half-brothers and sisters, even *twins* who'd been adopted by different families. Who had thought *that* was a good idea? They should be strung up for it!

It made her think, though. Siblings. Had Alison Wendell had any babies after her? Or before? There might be a whole clan of Caitlin-alikes up in Scotland, tall and clumsy, with big noses and fine hair. She couldn't help a tiny smile at the thought. They could hang out together and have a good old bitch about the crap genes they'd inherited, and then be best big-beaked friends forever and ever.

The thought tore at her. She'd always wanted a brother or sister. Hadn't she always longed for one?

Two gins into the evening and the situation felt decidedly unreal. Should she? Dare she? Her fingers hovered. Her heart boomed.

What the hell, she thought, clicking back to the Adoption Search Reunion website that she'd looked at previously. She would just register her name and see if it linked to anybody else. It didn't mean she had to go and meet them, if she bottled out later down the line. It wouldn't commit her to doing anything she didn't want to.

Taking a deep breath and a last swig of Dutch courage, she began to type.

Chapter Thirty

'Can I have a word please, Saffron? In my office.' Charlotte's voice was so icy it practically etched a pattern of frost across the agency windowpanes.

'Sure,' Saffron replied, sweat beading between her shoulder blades. She put an arm self-consciously across her stomach as she walked across the room. This didn't bode well. Had Charlotte guessed her secret? It was a distinct possibility. Now fifteen weeks pregnant, Saffron was bulging in a way that even the loosest, swingiest tunic tops and blouses couldn't hide. But until she had the amnio next week and knew what the future held, she didn't want to start discussing her condition with her unsympathetic boss. It was hard enough to get through each day while the test was hanging over her, let alone have to confide in someone who had all the bedside manner of a viper.

Legally, she cannot sack you for being pregnant, she reminded herself, taking a deep breath. *Don't let her push you around.*

Charlotte's office was like a boutique hotel in miniature,

with soft lighting, dark textured walls, a huge vase of fragrant white lilies, a leather sofa and a wall of inspirational quotes in different fonts:

We are all made of stardust.
Let yourself shine!

TOGETHER WE ARE STRONGER.

FEEL THE ENERGY.

Let's Go Team!

Whenever she saw this wall, Saffron always had the urge to add in some of her own favourite quotes in marker pen, but so far hadn't quite dared. *IF AT FIRST YOU DON'T SUC-CEED, GIN AND CHOCOLATE'S WHAT YOU NEED.*

Maybe not.

'Have a seat.' Charlotte waved a hand at the leather sofa and Saffron sat, assuming her boss would join her at the other end. Instead, Charlotte walked around behind her desk so that however high Saffron tried to pull herself up, her boss was still a good foot higher. No doubt this was intentional. 'So.' Charlotte steepled her fingers together and gave Saffron an inscrutable look. 'You've been working hard lately.'

'Yes,' Saffron replied guardedly. 'Yes, I have.'

'Your phone's been ringing a lot. I've seen you typing frenziedly over at your desk.'

Saffron had the uneasy feeling she was walking into a trap. 'Yes,' she said again.

'Yet when I took the liberty of checking through the system, I couldn't find any evidence of what you've been doing.' Her voice was silky smooth. 'Very few emails sent from the company account. Very little saved to the hard drive, in terms of press releases or strategy plans.' Her pastel-pink lips twitched as if she was dying to smirk at her own cleverness. 'Perhaps you can tell me exactly what you *have* been doing lately?'

Saffron quailed. What she'd been doing, of course, was running around trying to help Gemma with her PR, but she couldn't fess up as much to Charlotte. 'Well . . . '

'You mentioned something about a new client. Have we signed this person up to our books?'

'Not exactly.'

'But I trust you are in the process of drawing up a contract and agreeing terms?'

Saffron faltered, lowering her gaze. 'N-not yet.'

Triumph flickered across Charlotte's face and her smile became steely. Time seemed to elongate as she held Saffron's gaze, a fox eyeing a rabbit. 'Make sure you get a contract out to this client today then, and start billing them at once. I'll expect to see the paperwork very soon. Yes?'

'Yes,' mumbled Saffron. The fox had pounced, jaws open.

✻

Coming home that night from work, Saffron felt utterly fed up. Of the slow-moving crush of people dawdling through Soho and getting underfoot. Of the black cab that veered towards the pavement, sending a spray of muddy water fountaining over her from a kerbside puddle. Of the man eating a smelly burger and chips next to her on the Tube, the random nutter yelling expletives in the opposite seat, the teenage girls sassing the guy on the ticket barriers who was old enough to be their grandad. She was tired of worrying incessantly about the baby and how she would cope, of what would be revealed at the amnio and how it would make her feel.

Most of all she was ground down by Charlotte, peering over her shoulder and checking up on her work as if she were a two-year-old who needed constant supervision. Yes, okay, so she *had* been spending quite a lot of time recently on matters that were not strictly company business – but give her a break! After all the shite she'd put up with from Bunty and all the Z-list celebrity clients on her books, any other boss would have cut her a large length of slack and turned a blind eye when she wanted to do a favour for a friend.

Not Charlotte, though. As if. And they both knew she'd be as good as her word when it came to following up on her coded ultimatum: show me the contract, or face the music. What should Saffron do?

The answer came to her as she was slotting the key into her front door: *Leave. Quit. Get out before she chucks you out.*

Saffron was not by nature a quitter. She had always been a grafter, slogging through revision for exams, taking her driving test three times rather than admitting defeat, doggedly sticking out awful temp jobs in the hope of being noticed by the powers-that-be in HR; and, since working at Phoenix, sucking it up when it came to self-obsessed clients, all in the name of being professional. She'd even hung on to her marriage until it was obvious, even to a complete stranger, that the relationship was in its death-throes. She had never quit anything in her life. But this time . . .

She wandered up the stairs to her flat, undeniably tempted by the prospect of sticking up two fingers at Charlotte. Just imagine the glee, the sheer up-yours joy. She'd have dignity and freedom again, a new source of self-respect. Unfortunately, dignity and freedom didn't pay the rent, did they? Nor did they cover a maternity leave.

Tipping half a carton of tomato soup into a pan, Saffron lit the gas ring, still thinking. Her job had been a millstone rather than a joy for some time now. When had she last leapt out of bed, eager to get to her desk and start work? She couldn't remember the last project for which she'd felt genuine enthusiasm, the last client for whom she'd really rooted. Well, apart from Gemma, of course, who wasn't a real client at all.

She cut two thick wedges of granary bread and put them

under the grill to toast, still mulling it over. Her whim about quitting was becoming more appealing by the minute. Why not? She could do it. She had some rainy-day money stashed away in an account, enough to keep her going for a while if she was careful.

But . . . hold on. She wasn't thinking clearly. The baby wouldn't be here for months yet. She couldn't blow all her money before she'd even given birth. Anyway, what was she going to do with herself all day long? The thought of her phone going silent, her diary becoming a wasteland with no meetings or client lunches or product launches to juggle . . . It felt alien and frightening, scarily empty. And there were actually some clients she would miss if she never saw them again. Well, one anyway. In a surprising kind of a way.

She buttered the toast, wondering what would become of Bunty if she left the agency. Then she remembered how Bunty had shaken her head at the prospect of dealing with Charlotte. 'But I don't like Charlotte,' she had said in alarm. 'She looks down her nose at me, like I'm not good enough for her.'

On impulse Saffron picked up her phone, forgetting all about her soup and toast as she dialled. Sometimes you just had to take a chance in life, roll the dice and have a bit of faith. 'Bunty?' she said when her client answered. 'It's me. Listen, I've had an idea . . . '

*

The next morning as Saffron walked from the bus stop to the office she felt herself noticing everything about the journey and mentally wishing it goodbye. Tourists clustered around an A–Z, blocking the pavement . . . farewell, you inconsiderate sods. The X-rated 'private bookshop' from whose doors you occasionally saw red-faced men stumbling . . . good riddance, dirty old bastards. The lift that took forever to arrive and whose doors sometimes jammed unnervingly for a few seconds . . . thank God I'm leaving you behind. Kayla on reception, slurping coffee out of her Benedict Cumberbatch mug . . . Fifty-something David, with his wife and three children, who was known as 'Shagger' for his bad behaviour with female clients . . . Mel, who always stank of fags and had the hardest face of anyone Saffron had ever met . . . Goodbye, all of you. This is me, signing out, right here, right now.

In her office Charlotte was reading the *Daily Mail* online, dipping a hand absent-mindedly into the bag of watercress that was a permanent fixture on her desk. (She was fooling no one with her saintly display of health; they all knew she'd be tucking into a blood-oozing steak and chips later, washed down with red wine.)

'You're doing *what*?' she yelped, when Saffron coolly delivered her news. Charlotte swung round abruptly on her chair, nostrils flaring like a spooked horse.

'I'm leaving,' Saffron repeated, a wild dancing feeling starting up inside. She stood there – higher than Charlotte now, having decided not to sit on the leather sofa this time – and felt a thrill of satisfaction as she looked down on her boss. How she'd dreamed about this, never once imagining she'd actually have the guts to go through with it. 'I've decided to go freelance and move out of London.'

One life-change after another. It made sense for practical reasons, though. Eloise had been right – the flat was too small for an extra person, however tiny they might be for the first year. And renting any place outside London would be about a million times cheaper. But the decision wasn't purely a sensible one – it had come from her heart, too. She had been yearning for wide skies and fresh air for months now. London had long since lost its lustre.

'But . . .' Charlotte's eyes suddenly became slit-like. 'You're not taking any clients with you. I absolutely forbid it.'

Saffron smiled. Most of the agency clients she'd be more than happy never to see again. 'I wouldn't dream of it,' she replied politely. 'But obviously if they decide to come with me, that's their choice.'

She decided not to let on just yet that she'd already spoken to Bunty, and Bunty had immediately agreed to become her first client. Why pour petrol on the fire?

Charlotte glared at her with genuine dislike. 'You'd better clear your desk and go,' she said. 'We'll pay you until the end of the month, and you're lucky to be getting that much. Just remember that your contacts book is the property of this agency. I want it left on your desk, along with your smart-phone and key-card. No funny business.'

Well, Charlotte was certainly showing her true colours – mistrustful and paranoid until the last. Saffron bestowed a dazzling smile on her, determined to teach her a lesson in professionalism. 'Of course. And all the best,' she said, hold-ing crossed fingers behind her back. 'It's been fun.'

Then she turned and left Charlotte's office for the very last time, and didn't look back.

Saffron took the executive decision to give herself the rest of the day off. After depositing the meagre contents of her desk back at home – her Violet and Mushy Pea Pantone mugs, her stash of pistachio nuts and peppermint teabags, hand-cream tubes and all the personal thank-you cards she'd kept pinned up on her noticeboard – she packed a swimming bag and went along to her local baths. There she spent a most relaxing hour tanking up and down the pool while a group of elderly ladies in flowered bathing hats splashed about in the shallow end, waving their arms around to the strains of 1980s pop hits in the name of Pensioner Aquaro-bics. *This is my new life*, she thought to herself, walking home with wet hair and the faint whiff of chlorine emanating from her bag. *So far, so good.*

She phoned Gemma later on to warn her against calling the office line, for fear of having a belated invoice fired off to her by an irate Charlotte. 'Whoa! You've quit? Good for you!' Gemma exclaimed. 'So what's the plan now?'

'The plan . . . Well, I don't know exactly yet, but I'm taking Bunty on as my first client and I'm going to move house, find somewhere in the sticks before the baby comes along.' She pulled a face, trying not to dwell on just how woolly and vague that all sounded. 'But I was really ringing to say that I'll have a bit more time on my hands for the next few weeks. Technically I'm not supposed to work with Bunty until she's seen out her contract with the agency – a whole month away. So if you want me to help you at all, I'm a free agent.'

'Oh, really?' Gemma's voice rose in pitch. 'God, I need all the help I can get right now, Saff, especially since Spencer—' She broke off. 'Yes, *please*. That would be totally bloody amazing.'

'Great. You're on. Just let me know what you need me to do.'

'You superstar. Thank you. I could do with some good news. Will it freak you out if I tell you I actually seriously love you? I mean it!'

Saffron laughed. 'You're welcome.' Was Gemma all right? she wondered. She sounded kind of manic.

'Oh, and hey, this is just a totally random thought, but you could always come and stay here, if you want? We've got plenty of room, if you don't mind undecorated granny-chic, that is. We've set up a bit of an office, me and Caitlin, you'd be welcome to join us.'

Saffron paused for thought. Stay in Larkmead? She had made the offer assuming that she would tackle any work remotely, from her laptop in the flat, but the prospect of a return to the Suffolk village was tempting. Larkmead had become something of a haven for her this year. She could immerse herself in Gemma's business, pop over to her mum's for Sunday dinner, indulge in Rightmove fantasies about where to live next . . .

'Sounds perfect,' she said without needing to think about it any more. 'Are you sure? It won't be until next week anyway, but I can always ring Bernie and—'

'Don't be daft. We've got room here, and it's the least I can do after all your help. Listen, I'd better go, I've got someone coming for a fitting in ten minutes – a TV newsreader, can you believe? You know where I am anyway, so just turn up whenever. See you soon!'

'See you soon.'

In for a penny, in for a pound, Saffron decided. Without pausing to weigh it up, she rang the estate agent through which she rented her flat and briskly gave a month's notice, just like that. Putting the phone down afterwards, she felt exhilarated by her own recklessness, as if she'd just crossed a rope bridge and cut it loose behind her. No turning back now. She was doing this.

Besides, she'd never truly loved this flat, had she? It was the place she'd come to, broken-hearted after the end of her marriage, the 'this'll-do, handy-for-the-Tube' flat that she had never bothered to decorate. The very walls were papered with unhappy memories, the bedroom echoed with sighs. She would find somewhere better and move out, she vowed. She'd like a garden, after living up in an apartment block with only one window that opened. Fresh air and friendly neighbours. A spare room that could be either a cheerfully painted nursery or a crash-pad for visiting friends.

Carried along on a wave of energy, she began packing up. She filled a suitcase with all the work clothes she could no longer squeeze into and wouldn't be wearing again for a while, then started filling a box with books. Her eye was caught by the pile of self-help manuals that her mum had lent her when she was last there for that fraught Sunday dinner. She still hadn't opened any of them, having just dumped them on a side-table when she returned. Maybe she should use her newly acquired free time to read up on mindfulness and inner calm, she thought, lifting them up and scanning their blurbs with a new sense of zeal and self-improvement. Besides, if she . . .

Her train of thought faltered and promptly crashed into a siding, as she glimpsed what lay under the books. Hold on a minute. What the hell was *that*?

As if in a dream, she reached out and picked up the letter that must have been hidden there all along – several weeks now. The letter she'd written to Max, telling him about the pregnancy. The letter that, as it turned out, she had never actually posted.

Her knees buckled, her mouth gaped open and she sank onto the sofa, stunned at this new discovery. This changed everything. There she'd been, assuming that Max hadn't turned up to the twelve-week scan because he wasn't interested, when in actual fact he had no idea whatsoever that she was even pregnant.

'Oh my God,' she said aloud, her voice hoarse, her breath juddering. All the anger and hurt she'd felt, and he didn't even *know*. Because she'd been so bloody airheaded that she'd never managed to get the letter in the post! How could she have been so thick?

She was holding the letter so tightly it was already crumpled in her grasp, and she began smoothing out the creases, before checking herself. No. It was too late to send this letter. Way too late. She wouldn't write another one, either, and risk it becoming lost in the post or undelivered, or falling from a postman's sack into a muddy puddle and ending up in the nearest dustbin.

The time had passed for leaving things to chance. She couldn't risk it any longer. It was half-past three in the afternoon; it would take her about forty minutes to reach Max's office in Covent Garden.

Sod it. Needs must. She would go there and tell him in person, so there could no longer be doubt in anyone's mind. She owed him that much at least.

Chapter Thirty-One

Spencer didn't come back on Monday. There was still no word from him on Tuesday. It was as if he'd been swallowed up by the earth. Gemma even went and checked the garage, and then all the rooms of the house, just to make sure she hadn't gone completely mad, but his sports car was definitely missing, and so was he.

It was affecting them all, as if a dark cloud had permeated the brick walls of the house and blocked out the light. Darcey had had nightmares for two nights on the trot. Will had retreated into new depths of sullenness, playing awful music at top volume and scowling when Gemma told him off. And when she woke up every morning, alone in the double bed, it hit her all over again. Where was he? Why hadn't he come home?

On Wednesday morning she couldn't bear it any more. Voice shaking, she phoned the police to report him missing.

The policeman who took down her details sounded rather unsympathetic. 'So you haven't seen him since Sunday,' he said.

'No, or heard from him. He's got his wallet, but not his phone, or even a change of clothes. He just upped and left. He's in a back-brace, driving a black soft-top Mazda. I mean, he's pretty visible. People will have noticed him. If you could notify the other police forces . . . '

He gave a polite cough. 'I'm afraid that, as he's over the age of eighteen and the circumstances aren't suspicious, I can't do that, madam,' he said.

That took the wind out of Gemma's sails. 'You can't . . . What? Why not?'

'We see this kind of thing quite often, unfortunately. A domestic, a row – one person takes off to cool down.'

'Yes, but . . . ' She couldn't believe how lightly he seemed to be taking this, how little he appeared to care. 'But he's been injured. He's depressed. I'm worried he's going to do something silly.'

His tone softened a fraction. 'I'm sorry, madam. The best advice I can give you is to contact the Missing Persons Bureau. They can put your husband's details on file and will get in touch if they have any news. But hopefully he'll come back under his own steam anyway. They usually do.'

'I hope so.' Gemma gazed out of the window unhappily. If only she hadn't nagged him about the lawn; if only she hadn't torn a strip off him for the 'fat' remark; if only she'd bitten back all that anger and frustration . . . 'Thank you,' she remembered to say, before hanging up.

Any news, lovey? You must be worried sick. Do shout if I can
help with anything around the house, or looking after the kid-
dies. I know it can't be easy. Love Judy xxx

What would help most, Judy — Gemma thought meanly,
glancing at her phone as she pushed cubes of braising steak
around the frying pan — is if you could stop texting me every
five minutes, acting like you're my new bezzy mate. You're not
part of the family yet, you know. Butt out!

Just as she was thinking this (totally unfairly, yes, but she
couldn't help herself) her mobile jangled with Number
Unknown, and her heart skipped a beat, as it did every time.
Please let it be Spencer. Please let it be him. From a phone-
box or a B&B or a police station, she didn't care where. Let it
be him and she'd go straight out and bring him home.

'Gem?' said a deep, unfamiliar voice. 'It's Jonny.'

Jonny? She was so frazzled that it took her a moment to
remember who Jonny was. Then it hit her. Spencer's cousin,
who'd moved up to Newcastle. 'Hi,' she said tremulously.
'Hello. Is he . . . ? Have you . . . ?'

'He's here. He's safe, love. He's hitched up here — just
arrived this afternoon.'

'Oh, thank God for that.' She let the spatula fall into the
frying pan and sank to her knees on the kitchen tiles, half-
laughing, half-crying. 'Is he all right? What's going on?' The
words processed through her mind. He'd only just *got* there?

He'd left three days ago. And where was the car? 'What do you mean, he hitched?'

'Stuck his thumb out and got a lift, I should think. He's a bit knackered and quiet, but all in one piece.'

Gemma could hardly speak for a moment, she was so overcome with relief. She'd take knackered and quiet in Newcastle over dead in a ditch any day. 'Can I talk to him? Is he with you now?'

Jonny paused. 'He . . . ah . . . I'm sorry, love, but he doesn't want to chat, he said. Wants to sort his head out.' He sounded awkward. 'It was all I could do to give you a call, to be honest.'

It was like being slapped around the face. Why was Spencer punishing her like this? Had she really been so awful?

'Gemma? You still there?'

'I'm here.' She ran a hand through her hair. 'Tell him . . . Tell him not to worry. Tell him I love him and just hope he's okay. If he wants to speak to me later, I'm right here. I'm not going anywhere, okay?'

'All right, doll. I'll tell him that. You take care of yourself, all right?' Jonny lowered his voice and it crackled into her ear. 'I'll get on his case about ringing you, okay? I'll sort him out.'

'Thanks, Jonny. Thank you so much.'

She sat on the floor for a full two minutes, trying to take this in. So Spencer had made it up to Newcastle, but didn't want to speak to her. And what did Jonny mean about him hitching there, when he'd driven off in the car? What on earth was going on?

Slowly, dazedly, she got to her feet and fished the gently melting spatula out of the frying pan, anguish slowly giving way to anger. Selfish, that's what it was. Why did everything have to always be about him? If there was any justice in the world, this should have been a gloriously happy period for her as she made great strides of progress, racked up new career achievements, and smashed her way magnificently through every tiny ambition she'd ever dared dream about. There were women queuing up to buy her dresses. Rave write-ups in the press. Her order book filling faster than she could keep up. It was like the best rollercoaster ride ever . . . except for one thing: Spencer wasn't beside her, holding her hand and sharing her delight.

No, he was up north, sulking and refusing to speak to her. 'Well, up yours then,' she said, giving the frying pan a shake. 'Be like that!'

A few days passed without any word from Newcastle. She telephoned Jonny several times for updates, but each call brought the same response: Spencer didn't want to talk right now, but yes, he was fine, a bit tender where he'd knocked his ankle playing golf, but in increasingly good spirits. They'd picked up some new medication from Jonny's doctor. It was no bother at all.

Jonny's words didn't exactly go a long way towards comforting Gemma. Golf-playing? Good spirits? she thought in disbelief. Was this the same man they were talking about? He'd barely left the house, let alone cracked a smile for his own wife and children since January, yet all of a sudden he was living the life of Riley with his cousin? *Not cool, Spencer*, she thought, bundling warm sheets out of the tumble drier and snapping them into sharp folds. *Not cool at all.*

Still, somebody had to keep the home fires burning, and the home laundry ironed, and the home fridge full: muggins, of course. Mind you, the children had been admirable under the circumstances: unloading the dishwasher, unasked, and helping her set up an online supermarket account, to save her dragging round there every week. Of course then they'd promptly added all sorts of Creme Egg bags, Pom Bear superpacks and several gallons of Ben & Jerry's ice-cream to the initial order, but she let it pass. She was earning some decent money at last, and they all deserved a few niceties, after so much soup. The newsreader had commissioned an evening gown, as had the professional violinist who'd been in the other day. Saffron was coming to stay next week and Gemma would have the full Dream Team back at Hourglass Designs. Win-win-win. It was all win, frankly, apart from on the marriage front.

On Saturday, Gemma took the children shopping in Bury St Edmunds as a treat and shelled out for new shoes and jeans all round, a jacket for Will and a party dress for Darcey, then some DVDs and a game each for the Wii. It felt like Christmas. They had hot chocolate and gooey cakes in Harriet's Tearooms, and then she picked up the ingredients for their favourite dinner of lasagne. Let Spencer play golf and keep up the silent treatment, if he wanted to. She and the children would have a lovely time if it damn well killed her.

Later that afternoon she was just sliding the lasagne into the oven when the doorbell rang and her hard-heartedness vanished in a heartbeat. Was it him? Was he back? Oh, please let it be him, she thought, dumping the oven gloves on the side and hurrying to find out.

Pulling open the door, she gave a start. It wasn't Spencer standing there with a bunch of flowers and an apology. Not an early appearance from Saffron, either, with her suitcase and PR brilliance. Instead she saw a tanned woman in a tropical-printed jersey dress, incongruously teamed with an enormous fur coat and moonboots, arms spread wide in greeting. 'Darling. Surprise!'

'Mum,' said Gemma, inadvertently taking a step back. Karen's hair was an unnatural shade of auburn these days, which clashed horribly with her fuchsia-pink lipstick. 'God. I . . . I wasn't expecting you.'

'I know. Which is why I said "Surprise!"' Karen waggled her pencilled eyebrows. 'Are you going to let me in then, or what? Where's that divine husband of yours? And my adorable grandchildren? Aha! There's my little Billy. Goodness, haven't you grown? Not so little any more! You remember Grandma, don't you? Except I'd rather you called me Karen, to be honest. Nobody can believe I'm old enough to be a grandmother, least of all me, ha-ha!'

Gemma turned to see Will behind her in the hall, looking as if he'd quite like to shrink into the floor with discomfort, while his rarely seen grandmother cackled with laughter.

'Come in, Mum,' Gemma said, trying to recover herself. Was she planning on staying? She must be – and yet now wasn't exactly the best time. The spare room had been set up in readiness for Saffron's arrival and, besides, the family atmosphere had been kind of leaden recently, despite her best attempts. 'Er . . . you'll have to take us as you find us, I'm afraid, we're a bit all over the place.' She tried to relax as her mum hugged her in a furry, perfumed embrace, but it was difficult. Every last childhood insecurity had immediately risen to the surface, like iron filings to a magnet. 'Have you eaten?' she managed to say. 'Dinner's on.'

Her mum didn't reply, strutting across to cluck over Will. 'Look at you! My word. How old are you now? Fifteen, is it? Got a girlfriend, eh? You can tell me. I won't breathe a word.'

'Mum! He's thirteen,' Gemma said. 'Give him a break.'

'Darcey! Yoo-hoo! Spencer!' She cocked her head on one side. 'I guess Spencer's not back from work yet, is he?'

Gemma wasn't sure where to begin. So much had happened,

it was impossible to condense events into a single sentence. 'Let me put the kettle on,' she said. Then, knowing her mother, and feeling slightly desperate already, she amended her own suggestion. 'Actually I think there's some wine in the fridge.'

'Now you're talking,' said Karen with a laugh. 'Follow that daughter!'

Pouring glasses of wine, Gemma did her best to have a word with herself. Forget the irritation and inconvenience, she ordered. Forget the hurts from years gone by. This is your *mum* – the woman you've missed having in your life for over twenty-five years, remember. Your mum, who's chosen to come and see you for once, with the chance to rebuild bridges and forge a new grown-up woman-to-woman relationship. With Spencer away and business booming, she needed every ally she could get. What better ally was there than your own mum?

'Cheers,' she said, placing a full glass in front of Karen, before taking a long, thirsty gulp of her own. 'How long are you planning to be around?'

Karen had lived in Ibiza since Gemma was eight, and subsequent visits had been few and far between; it was like glimpsing a phoenix or a unicorn or some other mythical, read-about creature, when she did actually show her face for her children's weddings or a cursory look at new grandchildren. Blink and you'd miss her, though; she was not a fan of damp, drizzly England and was always desperate to hop back on a plane to the sunshine.

It came as a surprise then – another – when Karen replied in a rather subdued voice, 'I'm not sure, love. Maybe I'm back for good this time.'

'Really?' Hope flared inside Gemma like a shooting star through the darkness. 'How come? What about Carlos?'

Karen pulled a face. 'Carlos who?' she muttered. 'We've split up. Men, honestly. Why do they have to be such bloody . . . children?'

Gemma winced at the way her mum said 'children' as if they were the most tiresome creatures ever to exist. *Er, hello? Daughter sitting right opposite you, Mum. Yeah, me. Your child?*

Mind you, she thought in the next moment, look at the way Spencer had behaved – flouncing off without so much as a goodbye, taking umbrage the one time Gemma had lost her patience with him – for insulting her, no less. Maybe Karen had a point. 'Tell me about it.'

'Well, I'd been getting sick of him for a while, ever since he—' Karen broke off, frowning. 'Wait – did you mean for me to actually *tell* you about it, or are you having man-problems of your own?' Her nose twitched, as if expertly sniffing out marital strife right there at the kitchen table.

'Oh, Mum,' Gemma said, unable to keep up appearances

any longer. She took another long swig of her wine. 'I've got a lot to tell you.'

Karen flicked her a quick, understanding glance, patted her arm and rummaged in her bag for a box of Marlboros. Lighting up, she puffed two quick smoke-rings, then fastened her gaze on Gemma. 'Now then. Mummy's here. Tell me everything.'

Gemma did. In between mixing the salad dressing, opening the window to let in some freezing fresh air, laying the table and slicing tomatoes and cucumber, she told Karen the whole sorry saga.

'My goodness, darling! You've been through so much!' Karen's hand flew to her crêpey décolletage. 'You poor thing. Makes my little troubles look like nothing.'

'What troubles?'

Karen took a dramatic, shuddering breath and tossed her long hair. 'Oh, you know. Going bankrupt. Carlos cheating on me. Being mugged in the Old Town . . .'

Gemma was bending down at the oven, sliding the hot lasagne out, but jerked round sharply at this list of woes, burning her wrist on the oven door. 'Mum! God, why didn't you say? You shouldn't have let me go on for so long.'

Karen waved a hand as Gemma went to run her scorched skin under the cold tap. 'No matter. It's not a competition, is it: who can have the shittiest life? Anyway we're here for each other now, right? We'll both get through this. I'll help you however I can.'

'And vice versa.' It would be different this time, Gemma vowed. *Here for each other* — just like a mother and daughter should be. And of all the times for Karen to have appeared offering support, this was the best time she could have picked. Gemma went over and hugged her suddenly. 'I'm glad you're here.'

It quickly became apparent, however, that Karen and Gemma had quite different opinions on how Karen's 'help' would best be effected. Gemma, for example, had envisaged assistance in the kitchen for mealtimes, so that she could squeeze in an extra hour's work; Karen picking up some of the school runs, which would afford her greater flexibility with client visits, or the chance to run slightly over time at Caitlin's place, if she was immersed in a particular piece. She'd even imagined Karen mucking in about the house, too — a push-around with the Hoover here, a laundry load put on there, maybe even a few school shirts ironed . . .

Karen had other ideas, though. Her version of 'supporting Gemma' seemed to consist largely of the two of them sinking endless bottles of wine together, slagging off Carlos and Spencer for their general bastardliness, and offering reiki head massages, her fingers digging too hard into Gemma's scalp.

After a few days of this Gemma was starting to despair.

Her mum seemed to do very little in the daytime, apart from stay in the spare bed smoking and then move down to the living room and lie there, smoking even more and watching daytime TV. She had already made it impossible for Gemma to keep any fabric in the house, because the smell of cigarette smoke clung to everything with horrible persistence. She hadn't cooked a single meal or offered to wash up once. When she grew tired of bitching about Carlos, she slagged off Barry – Gemma's dad – instead, leaving Gemma with an impossible conflict of loyalties.

'Maybe getting out of the house will give you a lift,' Gemma suggested that night, when the four of them were eating dinner. 'Why don't you go for a walk tomorrow, or drive out to the coast?'

Karen raised a skinny eyebrow. 'Are you serious?' she asked. 'The North Sea's not exactly the Mediterranean, is it? I might end up hurling myself off a cliff.'

'You could come and see my school,' Darcey piped up. Gemma got the feeling that Darcey was rather impressed by her glamorous, young-looking grandmother, who swore and smoked, two things she knew Gemma disapproved of. 'Some of the other grannies come in and listen to us read.'

Karen scowled at being likened to 'the other grannies'. 'No offence, sweetie, but I bet those grannies are boring old biddies who have nothing else to do with their lives,' she said cuttingly.

Darcey's face fell. 'Perhaps you could pick Darcey up one afternoon,' Gemma suggested, feeling a pang of sympathy for her. 'I'm sure she'd love to show you her school, and her teacher.'

'Oh yes! Yes, I would, Grandma. I mean Karen. Would you?'

Karen twirled spaghetti around her fork, not answering immediately, and Gemma's heart ached to see the imploring expression on her daughter's face. *Come on, Mum. Think about someone else for a change.*

'Maybe next week. If I'm still here,' she said vaguely. 'I've got a few plans to sort out first.'

Darcey looked crushed, but Karen didn't notice. 'What sort of plans?' Gemma asked.

Karen tapped her nose and winked a turquoise-lidded eye. 'I need to think ahead,' she said. 'I've got my next big adventure to work out, haven't I?'

This was the first Gemma had heard of it. 'What's that then?'

'Maybe a bar,' Karen said with an airy shrug. 'I'm thinking Corfu. Love a bit of Greece. Feta and olives, and all those white-sand beaches.' She winked at Darcey – a sluttish, knowing sort of wink; highly inappropriate for a grandmother. 'As for the Greek men . . . don't get me started, darling.'

'But I thought . . . ' Gemma began, then shut her mouth,

hearing the accusatory tinge in her own voice. *Already?* she felt like shouting. *You're going already?*

'I'm not one to hang about,' Karen said, and picked up the wine bottle. 'Who wants another?' she asked. 'Just me? You bunch of lightweights!'

Darcey giggled. 'Grandma,' she said. 'I'm only nine, you know.'

'*Are* you? You look at least seventeen to me.'

'Probably because you're pissed again,' Will muttered under his breath and Gemma shot him a look.

She got to her feet, wondering why everything had to be so complicated. At times like these, there was only one thing for it. 'Who wants pudding?' she asked.

Chapter Thirty-Two

'Max Walters, please,' Saffron said, her heart giving a thump of anticipation. Determination had marched her all the way to the brightly lit reception area of the swishy sports company where Max worked in Covent Garden, and she wasn't about to leave again until she'd done what she'd set out to.

'Do you have an appointment?'

'No, I don't.' She gave the receptionist a quick, businesslike smile. *Pregnant woman here on a mission, love. Don't mess, if you know what's good for you.*

The receptionist had scraped-back hair and flawless make-up. 'Can I take your name? I'll see if he's available.'

'It's Saffron Flint.'

'Thank you. Would you like to take a seat?'

Saffron did want to take a seat. Her ankles had taken to puffing up whenever she stood up too long in high heels. She lowered herself cautiously into one of the bright-orange bowl-shaped designer chairs, hoping she'd be able to haul herself up and out again. Then she clasped her hands in her lap and prepared to wait. This was it. Cards on the table. Bump on display. News told, however badly it might be received.

The receptionist was murmuring into the phone. 'No, she didn't say . . . Well, she's sitting here in reception, so . . . Okay, great, thanks. I'll tell her.' She caught Saffron's eye as she hung up again. 'He's on his way down.'

'Thank you.' Saffron's mouth immediately went dry. Her armpits felt wet. She wished she'd blow-dried her hair properly after swimming, rather than pulling a comb through it and tying it back in a ponytail. Still, she had chucked on her nicest wrap-dress at least, a red jersey number that was forgiving on the bump, teamed with some black opaque tights, although during the adrenalin-pumped walk from the bus stop here, these had ridden lower and lower. Right now, they were balanced perilously low under her belly, prone to rolling down her hips at any given moment. A pair of tights around the ankles was an ice-breaker, she supposed.

There was a soft chiming sound and then the lift doors to her left opened, and out he stepped. Handsome Max, shirt sleeves rolled up, his hair standing slightly on end as if he'd just raked a hand through it. Bloody hell, he'd only gone and grown a little silvery goatee beard on his chin. It looked absolutely ludicrous. 'Hi,' he said. 'This is—'

With a bit of effort, she pushed herself up and out of the chair, her black wool coat falling to the sides to reveal her belly. He stopped mid-sentence as he noticed the new shape of her, and then his face blanched.

'Hi,' she said after a moment. You could practically feel the atmosphere electrify, crackling with the static of myriad unspoken messages.

Is that really what I think it is?

Yes. It is.

She cleared her throat, aware of the receptionist in the background, who was unashamedly goggling at the unfolding drama. 'Is there somewhere we can talk in private?'

'Uh . . . sure.' His eyes flicked between her belly and her face and then to her belly again. He looked dazed and panicky. 'Yes. Right. Let's go and grab a coffee.'

The receptionist belatedly remembered her job just then and glanced down at a diary in front of her. 'Max, just to remind you, you have Anil Bhatia coming in at four-thirty?'

He waved a hand. 'Just . . . sort it out. Get Nicky to cover for me or something. Thanks.' Then he turned back to Saffron. 'Shall we?'

She nodded. 'Let's.'

Outside on the street Max said, 'I suppose alcohol's out of the question then? Christ, sorry. I don't know what to say. I'm kind of in shock.'

'I'm sorry, too,' she said. 'Sorry to spring the news on you like this, I mean. I thought you knew; I wrote you a letter about a month ago, but I've been such a flake recently. I only just found it, unposted, this afternoon.'

'So it's mine?' he said. 'The baby's mine?'

'Yes,' she said. 'The baby's yours.' They were on St Martin's Lane, with black cabs honking, a couple pausing in front of them to snog each other's faces off, and tourists crowding round a silver-painted street entertainer pretending to be a statue. Saffron would have preferred not to be having this conversation right there in the street, but it seemed too late to press Pause. 'I tried to tell you in person too, that night we went out, but we got interrupted.'

'We did.' He passed a hand over his eyes. 'Oh God, Saff. How do you feel about all of this?'

How did she *feel*? It was hard to know where to begin. Frightened, excited, joyful, alone? 'Up and down,' she said, after a moment. A woman in a red mac talking loudly into her phone barged between them just then, almost knocking Saffron off the pavement. 'Look, this is ridiculous. We can't do this here.' She gestured to a pub across the road. 'Let me buy you a brandy or a coffee, or both. Whatever you want. It's the least I can do.'

He seemed to be working something out as they entered the dingy pub and went to the bar. 'I wondered what had happened, to make you go quiet on me like that,' he said slowly, not taking any notice of the barman, who glanced up from where he was stacking the glass-washer and came over, drying his hands on a tea-towel. 'Is that why you blew me out on the phone?'

Saffron felt self-conscious with the barman standing opposite them, waiting for their order. First the receptionist, then the hordes out on the street, and now him . . . Was it too much to ask, to have this conversation in private? 'I'll have a lime and soda, please,' she said. 'Max, what do you want to drink?'

'I knew something weird was going on,' he said, not listening. 'I knew it. It seemed completely out of character. We'd got on so well before that moment, and then for you to turn so offhand overnight . . . Oh, pint of Doom Bar, please, mate. Cheers.' He drifted into a reverie. 'Shit.'

'Yeah.' She waited until their drinks were poured and paid for, then they found a small corner table and sat facing each other on uncomfortable bar stools. He still looked stunned, as if the news hadn't yet sunk in. She stirred her drink, ice cubes cracking together, and tried to find the right words. 'Listen, I know this is a shock. I know you've moved on since me, and that's fine.' She thought of the way he'd been with his foxy female colleague in the Pillars of Hercules pub, how she'd felt like Gooseberry of the Year. 'I know you already have children, and this might be the last thing you want. And that's fine.'

'So you're having the baby.'

'Yes. But I can manage on my own, if you don't want to be

involved.' How tough and determined she sounded. She wondered if he had any idea how scared she felt inside.

'You're having our baby.'

'Yes.' Her foot jiggled under the table, a sudden attack of nerves. 'I can't work out if you think that's a good thing or a bad thing. Please will you just tell me?'

He frowned at his pint. 'The times we went out together at the end of last year – they were the most fun I've had for ages. I felt like we really clicked.'

She allowed herself a brief smile, but still couldn't tell where he was going. *Answer the bloody question, Max.* 'Me, too,' she said. It seemed so long ago now, that carefree whirl of excitement. Now she had a bump and he had a beard; they were like completely different people.

'Yet, realistically, we barely know each other. All this has been happening to you, and I had absolutely no idea.'

'I know. I'm sorry. I didn't know what to do.'

His eyes softened a fraction and he looked at her. 'A baby, Saff. Fuck! Talk about a . . . a . . . grenade through the window.'

Saffron didn't really like the image of her baby as an explosive device, but she got where he was coming from. 'Yeah. I realize it's not ideal. And it's fine if you don't want to—' she began again, but he held up a hand, jaw clenching.

'Stop saying that – about me not having to get involved. I'm not a total bastard, you know.'

'Sorry.'

'And you don't have to keep saying sorry, either. I was the one who failed us on the contraceptive front.'

A moment passed where she remembered the last time they'd had sex: on the stairs at his place, frenzied and horny, devouring each other with lust. The joyful kind of sex where you just couldn't keep your hands off each other, where you were confident there'd be plenty more where that came from, where you were just too damn passionate to think about sensible things like condoms. She wondered if he was remembering it, too.

'Well.' She shrugged. 'These things happen, don't they?' She sipped her drink, aware that she was holding back a vital piece of information. 'Max, before you say anything else, there's something I need to tell you.' Haltingly, her heart thumping, she explained the situation – the scan, the risks, the amnio lurking on the horizon like a dark cloud.

He listened intently, and she rushed to the end of what she had to say, fearful that he was going to shake his head and tell her: sorry, but do you know what? He'd never signed up for any of this, it was too much; he'd bung her a few quid in the name of child maintenance, but that would be his lot.

'So now you know,' she finished lamely, terrified of his response. She looked down at the table. 'Sorry to tell you everything at once like this. Your head must be spinning. I wish things were different, that I didn't even have to have this stupid test, but . . .'

He didn't say anything immediately, then reached over the table and took her hand. 'Don't then. Why don't we just . . . not go?'

She glanced at him, fearful that he hadn't fully understood what she was saying. 'Well . . . don't you want to know?'

He looked deep into her eyes. 'It's not that I don't care. I do. But sometimes these things can put such a strain on you, it's almost not worth doing.' His brow creased. 'When Jenna was pregnant with Leo, our son, they said at the second scan that he had very short legs, and made this enormous fuss about it. We spent the rest of the pregnancy having lots of tests and extra scans and worrying ourselves sick.'

'And was he okay? What happened?'

'He was absolutely fine. He was perfect. But Jenna had been so stressed, it made her ill and she couldn't enjoy the pregnancy at all.' His expression was far away for a moment. 'I don't want that for you – or me. Especially if there's a risk that the amnio might actually harm the baby.'

They were silent for a moment. *Why don't we just . . . not go?* Saffron kept hearing in her head. It hadn't occurred to her that she could opt out altogether, and the thought of not turning up for the dreaded test made her feel light-headed and giddy. It wouldn't be a case of hiding her head in the sand. It would be taking a stand, saying, *I've weighed everything up and I want this baby, full stop. I don't care what the amnio says, thanks all the same.*

Max looked worried, as if he might have said too much. 'Of course, if you really want to have the test, then I'll go with you,' he assured her. 'And we'll cross any bridges when we come to them, right?'

'Seriously? You mean it?'

'I mean it. We made this happen together. We'll see it through together as well. Okay?'

Don't cry. Do not cry. You are forbidden to start blubbing. She swallowed hard and tried her best to control herself. 'Okay,' she said with a watery smile. 'Thanks. Let's both have a think about it and decide in a few days. I realize this is a lot for you to take on board.' She blew her nose, feeling better than she had done in weeks. After all her worrying, this meeting had been so easy. If only she had plucked up the courage earlier! Then a smile quirked her mouth. 'By the way,' she said. 'What's with the beard?'

He looked startled at the question, then stroked it defensively. 'What do you mean? Don't you like it?'

'I . . . I didn't say that.'

His eyes twinkled and suddenly he was Max again, the man she'd fallen head over heels in love with back in the autumn. 'You hate the beard, don't you? Admit it. You hate the beard.'

She giggled. 'I don't *hate* it, but . . . '

'Tell you what.' He took her hand in his. Oh, he had lovely

hands, she thought, suddenly feeling as swoony and fluttery as a teenage girl. Strong and manly, with long, shapely fingers. 'I'll do you a deal. I'll shave my beard off if we can go out together again. Just lunch, nothing heavy. Just . . . getting to know each other again. What do you think?'

She looked at him, so handsome and lovely in his shirt-sleeves, even with that ridiculous tuft of hair on his chin. Her lips were just forming the shape to reply, 'Hell, yes' when she remembered the last time they'd met, the female colleague on his lap, twining her arms around his neck. Not so fast, she told herself. 'I thought you were seeing someone else?' she asked.

He looked taken aback for a moment, then shook his head. 'What, Mia? No. That was a bad rebound decision. A two-week fling. She's moved on to the finance director now.'

Saffron breathed out the last bit of tension that had been coiled up inside her. 'In that case, lunch would be lovely,' she said. 'I'd really like that, Max.'

Chapter Thirty-Three

From: CaitlinF@fridaymail
To: Saffron@SaffronFlintPR
Subject: Hello

Hey Saff,

How are things? Gemma said you have your test at the hospital this week – I hope it goes well; fingers crossed here for you.

Gem also said that you were planning another trip to Larkmead – excellent news! Her mum has turned up out of the blue, so we were wondering if you would like to stay at mine instead? I have a spare room and you'd be welcome to camp out here as long as you like. Just let me know when you want to come.

Love Cait x

From: Saffron@SaffronFlintPR
To: CaitlinF@fridaymail
Subject: Hello

Hi Cait,

Thank you, that's so kind of you. I'd love to stay. I'll probably set off tomorrow, if that's all right?

I decided not to have the amnio after all. Some people – i.e. my sister – think I've lost the plot, but I know it's the right decision for me. For us. I feel so much happier now, as if a weight has been lifted from my shoulders.

Really looking forward to seeing you and Gem tomorrow . . . I have a LOT to tell you!

Saff xxx

The imminent arrival of her guest prompted Caitlin to contact a charity that collected unwanted furniture, and two men rolled up that afternoon to load their van with Jane's old mahogany table and chairs, one of the armchairs and the huge Welsh dresser, which had all been gathering dust in the dining room for weeks. With the living room still in use as their workplace, she could now rearrange the dining room as somewhere for her and Saffron to sit in the evening. It would make a change from perching on her bed with the laptop and a glass of red wine on her own every night.

Up in Jane's bedroom, she put a jug of creamy narcissi on

the mantelpiece, clean towels neatly folded on the bed and opened the windows wide to let in the chilly spring breeze. Then she decided to empty the chest of drawers, so that Saffron would have somewhere to put her clothes, filling yet another charity bag with Jane's tops and trousers, unused packets of tights and bedsocks. The bottom drawer was a mish-mash of ancient swimming costumes, pyjamas, a box full of old jewellery and . . . Caitlin's hand paused in mid-air as she saw the stack of small leather-bound books at the back of the drawer. Diaries?

She hesitated for a moment before taking them out – even glancing over her shoulder, as if Jane might walk in and catch her snooping. Jane had been a private sort of person after all. Perhaps Caitlin should honour that privacy and put the diaries straight in the bin, unread.

Yeah, right, she thought in the next second. Like anyone had that kind of willpower.

She picked up the first one – 2004, more than ten years old – and flicked through the pages, feeling a twist of sadness at the sight of her mum's familiar spidery handwriting. What secrets did these pages hold? From the sentences that caught her eye, though, it was fairly pedestrian stuff:

January 22nd: Delivered Anna Simms's baby this morning – the sweetest wee girl, lots of red hair already. Breech, too, the little monkey!

April 6th: *Glorious weather, the tulips are out — stunning this year! NB 'Ronaldo' and 'Negrita' v. good, must plant more next autumn.*

May 19th: *Caitlin's birthday! Have been thinking about her all day. Jeremy's taking her to a fancy restaurant, she said. She sounded really happy on the phone. Can't wait to see her at the weekend.*

October 15th: *Poor Gwen — Robert's been so poorly. The doctors want him to go in for tests; he's been coughing up blood, apparently. Only sixty-one, too.*

Caitlin came to the end of the diary, to find Christmas shopping lists scribbled on the back cover and various jottings, including a diagram of Jane's spring-planting plans. She was just about to close the book when something occurred to her and she flicked back to the entry for New Year's Eve. Her mum had always loved her New Year's resolutions, hadn't she? What had she promised to do this time?

The last entry was a full one:

December 31st: *The year's almost out, just a few hours left, and then it'll have been another twelve months without Steve. How I miss him still. I went to the church today, just to have a chat with him. He always loved this time of year: feet up with the tin of Quality Street, a glass of port and the Bond film on TV. But anyway, I'm trying not to get too down-in-the-dumps. Next year will be better, won't it? Next year it won't hurt so much; I'll stop feeling sad whenever I hear the football scores, I won't cry when a Bruce Springsteen song comes on the radio, I'll get the vegetable patch going again in a way he would have approved of!!*

Also – here's the big one. I'm going to tell Caitlin the truth. I'm really going to do it this time. I can't keep putting it off; she has the right to know about her birth mother, etc. I am ashamed of myself for being such a coward all these years. Steve always said we should have told her, right from the start. It was the only thing we ever really argued about. I just wanted her to love me, though. I didn't want to hurt her or make her feel rejected. I know it was selfish. I wish I had been braver before now.

A sob burst from Caitlin's throat and she had to look away from the pages, the words almost unbearable to read. *Oh, Mum,* she thought, the room blurring as tears filled her eyes. It was like discovering a secret message, an apology – as if Jane had guided her to the diaries right when she needed to read this page most.

But this year I'll pluck up the courage. I'll do it for Caitlin, AND for Steve, the two people I've loved the most in my life. I'll make things right, I promise.

That's it for 2004 . . . going to get my glad rags on now and meet Maggie and the girls for drinks in The Partridge. Here's to a smashing 2005. x

Caitlin closed the diary and sat back on her heels, a wry smile on her face. So much for New Year's resolutions. Her mum had never stopped becoming choked up at Bruce Springsteen songs (Steve's favourite), and the vegetable patch had long since turned into a flower-filled border. As for her main resolution . . . well, clearly she hadn't managed that, either. But she'd wanted to. She'd had the best intentions about doing so. And she'd loved Caitlin so much that it was love, not thoughtlessness, that had held her back.

Caitlin pressed the diary against her chest and took a long, raggedy breath. 'Thanks, Mum,' she whispered.

Saffron arrived the next day, just in time for lunch, and over slices of flaky spanakopita and salad – Caitlin was fast becoming the Larkmead Deli's most loyal customer – she, Gemma and Caitlin shared their news: the continuing success of Hourglass Designs, Saffron's delight at having left her job and then, best of all, the gossip about Max.

'So – you're dating? You're back together?' Caitlin asked hopefully.

Saffron looked as if she was fizzing inside. 'We're not exactly *dating*,' she replied. 'It's all very tentative so far, a few chaste kisses and that's been it.' She giggled. 'It's a bit weird really, we've done everything the wrong way round. Now it's as if we've started completely over – first dates and getting to know each other; even though: hello, I already happen to be pregnant with his baby.' She rolled her eyes. 'My mum doesn't know whether to be disapproving or thrilled.'

Gemma frowned. 'Hang on a minute, though. I thought he was dating someone else?'

'That was just a fling, apparently. They're not together any more.' Saffron could not have looked happier to be divulging this information. Her smile could hardly have been broader.

'So it's full steam ahead for you guys then?' Caitlin asked, pouring glasses of elderflower pressé. 'He's in it for the long haul?'

'I've no idea,' Saffron replied. 'I don't think he knows yet, either. But we're going to muddle along for the time being and see how it goes.' She shrugged bashfully. 'I really like him, you know. I liked him from the start. And for him to say, "Let's not have the amnio" – this might sound weird, but it actually felt really romantic. And brave. And strong. I mean . . . Who knows what's going to happen? It's all still completely up in the air. But right now I feel positive about the future. We're having a baby, we're in it together and he's a good person. I don't think he's going to bail out on me.'

Gemma hugged her. 'That all sounds pretty bloody great,' she said. 'I'm pleased for you.'

'Me, too,' Caitlin said. 'Good for you both. And it's fab to have you back here with us, too. Maybe we should go out tonight? Toast the Dream Team being together again?'

Saffron smiled. 'That would be lovely,' she said. 'Hey, and

I can pass on Bunty's regards to Bernie, too. She still talks about him a *lot*.'

'Sounds good,' said Gemma, 'although I'll need to make sure my mum can babysit the kids.' She speared a cherry tomato and popped it into her mouth. 'I know, why don't you two come over to mine for dinner tonight? That way we get to hang out for some of the evening, and hopefully Mum won't mind holding the fort afterwards, so we can go on for a drink.'

Dinner! Whoops. In all her bedroom-clearing kerfuffle, Caitlin hadn't even thought about actually feeding her new guest – let alone a pregnant guest, who would need super-healthy nutritious food, and plenty of it. Left to her own devices, she was used to existing on bowls of porridge, apples and whatever the deli had in that day. The cupboards were bare, she realized with a jolt. Some hostess she was! 'Well, if you're sure . . . ' she said, with the guilty relief that she might just have got away with it. She would go out first thing and do a massive Tesco run, she promised herself.

'That would be great,' Saffron said. 'I'd love to meet your kids.'

'That's settled then,' Gemma said. 'I'm afraid the decor at our place hasn't moved on very much since you were here at New Year, but if you can ignore the Anaglypta and disgusting carpets, there's plenty of food up for grabs. Does seven o'clock sound okay?'

Seven o'clock *did* sound okay. Seven o'clock sounded great. Besides, Caitlin was curious to see what Karen was really like, after all the damning things her friend had said about her. Nobody's mother could be *that* bad, surely?

As Caitlin and Saffron rang the bell at Gemma's that evening and waited to be let in, Caitlin found herself thinking back to New Year's Eve, and how she'd envied Gemma and Spencer their perfect life. The big house, the happy couple, the photos of family holidays and children with smart school uniform and neatly brushed hair . . . all things she didn't have in her own world. Gemma was a proper grown-up, she'd thought, feeling self-conscious in her Febrezed top amidst the sea of cocktail dresses and high heels. Gemma had achieved all this, while Caitlin had nothing, except an inherited cottage and a broken heart.

Stepping over the threshold this evening, though, it quickly became apparent to Caitlin that this dream life of Gemma's had unravelled at an alarming rate. Spencer had been gone for ten days now, suffering some kind of midlife crisis, and the house was untidy and unkempt, compared to the fairy lights and disco-ball sheen of the New Year party. Added to that, there was Karen in the mix now, too: a tall, strapping woman with a husky laugh and lots of glittering eye make-up, dressed for the beach in a flowing tie-dye dress and flip-flops, even though there was a clear sky that night and the temperature had already plunged.

'Have a seat, let me get you a glass of something,' Gemma said, once she'd introduced everyone. She looked rather flustered, with her hair making a break for freedom from her ponytail and her cheeks flushed with high colour. 'Will!' she yelled. 'Come and set the table, please, it's your turn.'

'Lazy bugger,' Karen said, pulling a face at them. 'Gets it from his dad.'

Caitlin gave a quick polite smile to Karen, but felt disloyal in doing so. 'Gems, what can I do to help?' she asked, as her friend rushed around, lifting one saucepan lid and then another to check the contents, a hot cloud of steam pouring forth each time.

'And me,' Saffron volunteered.

'Um . . . ' Gemma seemed distracted. 'WILL!' she shouted again. 'TABLE!' She turned back, wiping her hands on her jeans. 'Sorry. We've had a bit of a row; he was late home again and . . . ' She rolled her eyes. 'Would you mind helping yourself to a drink, guys? Mum can show you what we've got.'

'Well, I can tell you all about the wine collection – or what's left of it, anyway,' Karen said with a wink, leaning back in her seat. 'Is there any other kind of drink?'

Caitlin smiled politely. 'Wine would be lovely, thanks.'

'Just something soft for me,' Saffron said. 'Water's fine.'

Karen snorted. 'Water? You sound like my ex-husband, PC Sensible.'

'She's pregnant, Mum,' Gemma added, opening the oven door and taking out a red casserole dish.

Karen looked at Saffron as if seeing her for the first time. 'Ah! So you are. First one, is it?' She gave a short, barking laugh. 'Good luck with that.'

Caitlin saw a muscle tighten in Saffron's jaw, but she said nothing. 'Sit down, Saff,' she instructed. 'I can sort out drinks.'

'What is that boy doing?' Gemma muttered. 'Will! WILL!'

Lanky Will shambled in just then, his hands up in surrender. 'All right, all right, keep your hair on,' he muttered. He looked like his dad, with his mop of dark hair and broad shoulders, although he was pale and glowering. Caitlin smiled brightly as he went by, but he blanked her.

Karen gave Saffron a meaningful look. 'This is what you've got to look forward to,' she said in a stage whisper from behind her hand. 'Teenagers — complete and utter nightmare. Aren't you, darling?'

Will grunted, crashing a handful of cutlery down on the table and stomping out again.

'Let me do that,' Saffron said, laying the knives and forks.

'Thanks,' Gemma mumbled. 'Don't take any notice of him. We're going through a tricky patch right now.'

Caitlin, pouring the wine, was starting to feel as if they

shouldn't be there at all. Perhaps the loneliness of a night in on your own wasn't quite as terrible as she'd thought.

Karen was hooting and slapping her thigh, though. 'Tricky patch? You wait! Darcey'll be next, and it'll be even worse. Girls!' She pulled a comical face at Caitlin and Saffron and shook her head.

Gemma turned back to the hob, but not before Caitlin caught sight of the slapped expression on her face. Karen was not exactly tactful when it came to family dynamics, moaning about girls in the presence of her own daughter. And she still hadn't got off her bum to help with anything, either. No wonder Gemma looked as if she was at the end of her tether.

'Dishing up! Wash your hands!' Gemma called to the children, plonking the casserole dish in the middle of the table and removing the lid to reveal a fragrant, still-bubbling chicken chasseur. Then, and only then, did she give Caitlin and Saffron wan smiles. 'Sorry about this madhouse.'

'No! Don't apologize – it's lovely to be invited,' Saffron said at once.

'It smells amazing, thanks so much,' Caitlin added. *Someone* had to appreciate Gemma around here, she thought with a sidelong glance at Karen, still sat doing her Lady of the Manor impression at the head of the table. Someone had to notice what a great job she was doing, keeping the family going like this. Caitlin had a feeling that appreciation and attention had been rather lacking in her friend's life for a while, and put the largest glass of wine in front of Gemma. 'Here you go,' she said pointedly. 'I reckon you've earned this.'

'This one's definitely on me. What can I get you, ladies?' asked Saffron.

By some kind of miracle, Karen had actually agreed to babysit her own grandchildren – shock! Kindness klaxon! – meaning that Gemma could join Caitlin and Saffron for a post-dinner drink in the pub. Caitlin had never been so glad to get out of a house before. Not that the food hadn't been delicious – it had. Not that she didn't appreciate being cooked for, and having a meal with friends – she really did. But oh, Karen was the most toxic woman alive. She was a monster. Everything Gemma said, she laughed at or crushed. Everything Will said, she took the mick out of, leaving him scowling and murderous-looking. She even rounded on Darcey at one point, when the little girl complained that Will had more pudding than her.

'Someone's sounding like a spoiled little madam who needs a smacked bottom,' she said, draining yet another glass of wine.

Then, and only then, did Gemma lose her cool. 'Nobody's getting a smacked bottom in this house, and that's that,' she'd said. 'And if you were any kind of a grandmother, you wouldn't be saying that, either.' She lowered her eyes, looking as if she regretted her outburst. 'Sorry,' she mumbled in the next moment. 'But I don't smack my children. Nobody does.'

Karen merely raised her eyebrows and said, 'Jeez, love, there's no need to be uptight. No wonder Spencer left you.'

Will slammed both hands down on the table. 'For fuck's sake, leave Mum alone,' he shouted and stormed out of the room.

Gemma didn't speak for a moment. 'I am so sorry about this,' she said eventually.

Caitlin couldn't bear seeing her look so vulnerable. 'Don't worry,' she began, although Karen was already chipping in again.

'No bloody manners – that's your son's problem,' she said snippily.

'And your problem is that you don't know when to butt out and be quiet,' Gemma snapped in reply. She drained her own glass of wine and put her head in her hands.

'Don't cry, Mum,' Darcey said, sounding scared and leaning over to pat Gemma's arm, as Caitlin and Saffron exchanged glances. *Poor Gemma*, the glances said. *Poor, poor Gemma.*

Anyway they had made it out now, thank goodness, and were sitting down with a round of drinks, the mortified flush gradually leaving Gemma's face. *Some people just aren't cut out to be good mothers*, Caitlin remembered her saying, back at the time of the terrible adoption discovery. Well, that was certainly true. What if Alison, her own birth mother, was a woman like Karen? The sort of woman who did a bunk and abandoned her children; a woman who didn't know how to speak to them with any kind of empathy or compassion?

At least Jane had been kind and motherly. At least she'd shown nothing but love for Caitlin. She and Steve had always been there for her, giving Caitlin the best and safest childhood possible. Thank goodness they were the ones who'd chosen her for their daughter and that she'd been able to grow up feeling wanted and adored.

'Oh my God,' Gemma said just then, elbowing Caitlin so violently she nearly fell off her chair. 'Do you see what I see?'

Was it Harry? Caitlin wondered immediately, glancing around the pub with trepidation. She hadn't seen him around, since the devastating settling-down-with-pregnant-girlfriend conversation – and thank goodness, too, because every time she thought about what a tit she might have made of herself, she wanted to crawl into the nearest cupboard and stay there for a whole month. She couldn't see him anywhere, though. There was Bernie Sykes, holding forth with a group of red-nosed cronies; a group of blokes with pints, who were staring up at the snooker match on the wall-mounted TV; a loud, pissed collection of women screeching over cocktails together; but no lovely Harry.

'What?' she asked, feeling confused.

'Don't stare, but over there in the corner is Jade Perry, completely langered. She and her mates have just lined up a row of tequila slammers and necked the lot – and now she's tucking into a margarita.'

'Who is she?' Saffron asked nosily.

The full heft of what Gemma was saying finally percolated through, and Caitlin's breath quickened. Jade Perry? Oh my God. Whoa. So did this mean . . . ? 'Last time I heard, she was pregnant with Harry's baby,' she explained to Saffron, feeling jittery. 'Only . . . well, if she's doing tequila slammers and cocktails, I'm guessing she might not be any more.' *Did Harry know? Was he single again?*

Saffron instinctively draped her arms across her firm, round belly. 'Poor woman,' she said, and Caitlin felt like the most selfish cow alive for thinking only of herself.

'That's if there was even a pregnancy at all,' Gemma said drily. 'She's got history, has Jade. This wouldn't be the first time she tried to trap a bloke into something.'

'Look at Bernie's face,' Saffron hissed, and Caitlin turned to see an unfamiliar coldness in the jovial landlord's expression, as he looked over at the cackling group of women.

Gemma raised an eyebrow. 'He's probably counting his lucky stars that he's escaped having her as his future daughter-in-law anyway.' She sipped her wine. 'Sorry, I know that sounds really bitchy, but I can't help feeling protective of Harry. He always goes for these women who are just completely wrong for him.'

Caitlin felt her face flame and didn't know where to look.

'Apart from you, of course, Cait,' Gemma said, catching her eye. 'You'd be good for him.'

'He's the one who was in the cowboy hat, wasn't he?' Saffron remembered. 'Yes, I liked him. Nice guy.' She leaned forward mischievously. 'So perhaps he's single as well these days,' she added. 'Interesting . . . '

Caitlin laughed, her cheeks turning hotter than ever. 'Oh, stop it, you two,' she said. 'I don't know why you're both looking at me like that.' But she did know, and her tummy was turning somersaults at the prospect. Harry Sykes back on the eligible-bachelor list? Well, well, well. She crossed her fingers under the table and sent up a little prayer to Cupid himself.

Chapter Thirty-Four

Lovely as it had been to escape with her friends for a night down at The Partridge, by the following day Gemma couldn't avoid the feeling that she was one small crisis away from a nervous breakdown. She had tried her hardest to cement a strong new mother–daughter relationship with Karen, but was starting to wonder if it was just too late. After twenty-five years of barely seeing each other, they had little common ground to build on, and Karen was not an easy person to get close to. It was like having a stranger in the house: an opinionated, lazy stranger, constantly passing judgement on her and her family in a passive-aggressive *I was only joking! Don't take it so seriously!* sort of way.

'I don't like Grandma Karen,' Darcey confessed in a whisper that evening at bedtime. 'Why can't she go away again, and Daddy come back?'

Out of the mouths of babes, Gemma thought, gazing unseeingly at the kitten and pony posters stuck haphazardly on the wall. 'It's nice to have Grandma here for a visit – we hardly ever see her,' she said in the end, stroking her daughter's soft hair. 'And she *is* my mummy, remember.'

'She's not a very nice mummy,' Darcey said reprovingly. 'Mummies shouldn't say mean things to people.'

Gemma sighed. *Tell me about it, Darce.* 'I know, love, but . . . ' She straightened up the row of her daughter's teddies, trying to think of a diplomatic response. She'd always told the children, *If you can't say anything nice, don't say anything at all!* – a lesson Karen could have done with learning herself. 'That's just Grandma,' she said, weakly, in the end.

'What about Daddy? Why doesn't he come home? Doesn't he love us any more?'

Ouch. Tough question after tough question tonight.

'Of course he loves us,' Gemma said, pulling the cherry-print duvet cover up to Darcey's chin and tucking it round her. 'He's just having a little holiday. He'll be home as soon as he feels better.'

She had to kiss her daughter and leave the bedroom then, as she had a lump in her throat and knew she was about to dissolve. Her feelings about Spencer had moved from shock and fear, to hurt (*Why wouldn't he speak to her?*), to anger (*Sod him, then*) and now despair. What was going through his mind that he still couldn't pick up the phone and speak to his own wife and children? What was so bad that it stopped him coming back to them? It had been almost two weeks now since he'd left, the longest they'd ever been apart. The bed was so empty without him, the house so different.

Come home, Spencer, she thought for the millionth time, padding downstairs to where Karen was cackling in front of the television. *Please come home.*

The next morning Gemma was in the kitchen with Darcey when Karen sauntered in barefoot, already lighting up her first fag of the day.

'Morning,' she said huskily, before her eyes fell on her granddaughter, who was sprinkling sugar over her hot Weetabix. 'Mercy me, Darce, how much sugar are you putting on there? You don't want to end up a chubster, do you?'

Gemma froze. That's *it*, she thought flatly. That is *it*. The last straw, a line crossed. 'Don't say things like that to her,' she snapped, rounding on Karen. 'Don't be so cruel.'

Karen put her hands in the air, her face still puffy from sleep. 'What have I done now?' she said waspishly. 'Pardon me for breathing. Pardon me for giving a shit about my granddaughter's *health*.'

Gemma had been making packed lunches at the worktop, but at this, she nearly threw Darcey's Moshi Monsters sandwich box at her mother's head. She marched over, grabbed Karen's arm and dragged her into the utility room, not wanting Darcey to hear what she was about to say. 'You? Give a shit? That would be a first,' she hissed. 'Do you remember what you used to call me when I was little? Do you? Cos I do. Chubs. *Chubs!* That's what you called me, and boy, did it stick. It stuck like glue, I couldn't shake it off, it followed me everywhere. All the way until I was a teenager and ramming my fingers down my throat to try and vomit, because I felt so hideous and *fat.*'

Karen blinked, taken aback at the savagery of Gemma's voice, but Gemma wasn't done yet.

'That was all you left me with,' she went on, still gripping her mother's pudgy forearm. 'A horrible nickname and the guilt that I might have driven you away. Can you imagine what that felt like? Feeling so unhappy, at the age of *eight*, that I thought me being chubby was what caused you to leave? Talk about a recipe for self-loathing. Talk about a good way to ruin your daughter's self-esteem.'

'I didn't realize . . . ' Karen said faintly.

'No. You didn't, did you? And you didn't care, either. But I care about my daughter. Oh yes. I love my daughter a lot more than you've ever loved me. So I'll thank you not to speak to her like that again. To never *ever* try and make her feel bad about herself or use nasty, emotive words to her face. Because she's lovely. She's done nothing wrong. And I won't let you knock her confidence, not for one second.' Her lungs felt tight, she was breathing hard. She had always been so desperate for Karen to love her that she'd never dared stand up to her with such vehemence before. There was so much anger boiling in her, she realized. So much unspoken rage. 'Do you understand me? Have I made myself clear?'

'All right, all right,' Karen said, not meeting her eye. 'Message received. Can I have my cigarette in peace now?'

Gemma gestured to the door, not caring any more. 'Go for it,' she said. *Go and smoke yourself to death*, she thought. *We won't miss you.*

That day, when Gemma and Darcey arrived home from school, they found the place was empty. All that was left to show Karen had been there at all was the ashtray of fag-butts outside the back door, a stray pink silk scarf down the side of the sofa and a black lacy G-string in the laundry basket. She'd taken off again, just like that, without a word of warning or explanation. Gone who knew where – a bar in Greece, back to Carlos, up a bloody gum tree.

If this had happened a year ago, Gemma might have dissolved into tears of disappointment, but there was a new hardness inside her now: a tough new shield that protected her. There was also Darcey flinging her little arms around her and saying, 'I'm glad *you're* my mum. I'm glad you're not like Grandma.'

Gemma hugged her back, comforted by the truth in her daughter's words. No, she wasn't like Karen. No way. She was a grafter and a sticker-outer; she was loyal to the ones she loved. She'd never do a bunk, dirty knickers and fag-ends in her wake — never. 'Well, *I'm* glad I've got *you*,' she said chokily. 'I'm so, so glad. Having you and Will definitely makes me the luckiest mummy in the whole wide world.'

Karen was never going to change, she realized, as she toasted crumpets for Darcey and listened to her excited description of the tadpoles her teacher had brought into school and what had happened at playtime. Karen couldn't magically transform into the mother Gemma had always wished for, because being a mother and grandmother simply didn't interest her. It wasn't Gemma's fault, or her brothers', or her dad's, that Karen had upped and left them all, swapping domestic life for one of sunshine and cocktails. It had just happened, and the way back was now closed. Next time, she'd know not to get her hopes up. If there ever was a next time, that was.

The doorbell rang as she put Darcey's crumpets on the table, and Gemma crossed her fingers that it wouldn't be Karen back for the last word. She couldn't cope with any further tumult today.

Instead she did a double-take when she opened the door, to see Will standing there with a black eye and a torn shirt . . . alongside Judy, of all people.

Gemma gaped. 'What's happened? Oh my God, Will. Who did this?'

Will barged past her. 'It wasn't my fault,' he muttered, slinging his school bag down in the hall with a thump.

'I was driving through town on my way back from the hospital,' Judy said, 'when I saw him wandering around the shops on his own. Been fighting, he said.'

Gemma leaned against the door jamb, wishing the universe would just give her a frigging break for five minutes. Would it never end? If it wasn't her husband, it was her mum; and if it wasn't her mum, it was her son. And now here was Judy, having witnessed yet another family failure, by the sound of things. 'Fighting,' she repeated dismally.

'I'm afraid so.' Judy hesitated. 'Oh, love, you look done in,' she said. 'Is everything all right?'

The genuine kindness of her voice caught Gemma off-guard. Before she could hoist up the barriers and brush Judy off with a polite, forced 'We're fine, thanks', she found herself bursting into tears of defeat and exhaustion, her defences well and truly down. Without a moment's hesitation, Judy stepped over the threshold and caught her firmly in an embrace.

'There, there, pet, you have a good cry,' she soothed. 'It's all right. Don't worry.'

It was not all right, not by a long shot. Family life was so far from being 'all right' that just thinking about how awful everything was made Gemma cry even harder. And what a luxury it was to simply sob and be held, even if it was by someone she'd previously considered a threat. It was only the thought of leaving snot all over Judy's fleece that finally helped her choke back her sobs.

'You've had a time of it lately, haven't you?' Judy said, opening her bum-bag and pulling out a handypack of tissues. 'Here — have a hanky.' She stood there uncertainly while Gemma blew her nose. 'Do you want me to make you a cup of tea? Don't worry if you're in the middle of something, but I'm not in any rush, if you want to talk.'

Again it was on the tip of Gemma's tongue to say no and shoo her away, to keep her at arm's length, but she could no longer remember why she'd disapproved of Judy in the first place. 'That would be great,' she said weakly. 'Thank you.'

Later that evening Gemma managed to prise the truth out of Will. It sounded as if a group of boys had been teasing him for a while, first about not having any money, and then more recently 'about Dad going mental', as he glumly put it. Things had come to a head when Will lost his cool, got into a fist-fight and walked out of school.

'Sorry, Mum,' he mumbled, once she'd dragged it all out of him. 'I just couldn't stand it any more. I hate Dad for bailing out and being so crap. And Grandma was doing my head in, too. Sorry,' he said again, glancing at her guiltily. 'I know she's your mum and all that, but . . . '

'It's okay,' she told him. 'I'm the first to admit she's not the easiest person to get along with.' She put an arm around him, unable to be cross. 'You know that she walked out on Grandad, me and your uncles, don't you? Just like your dad has done now. So I do understand how you feel — confused and angry and hurting. It took me a long time to stop blaming myself that she'd gone. I thought it all had to be my fault, when of course it absolutely wasn't.'

He said nothing.

'Just like it's nobody's fault that Dad's gone. Not yours, not mine, not Darcey's. Okay?'

He nodded, scuffing a foot along the carpet. They were up in his bedroom, both perched on the bed, and she was resisting the urge to kiss his poor battered face, and go out and throw a few punches at those boys herself. She'd given him arnica for the bruising, and pizza to cheer him up, but it would take a few days before the purple-blue swellings began to subside. Thank goodness Judy had been there to bring him home to her. *Thank you, Judy,* she thought for the hundredth time. *I owe you one.*

'I'm sorry you've had to put up with all of that on your own,' she said. 'The other boys at school, I mean, and the teasing. And I'm sorry if I've been so busy with work and everything else that you haven't come to talk to me. But I'm not going anywhere, you know. I'm staying right here with you and Darcey. And I'll always put you two first, if you need me, all right? I mean it.' God, did she ever. She remembered her dad making a similar speech back in the day, gruff and fierce, and it had made her feel safe. That was all she wanted for her children: for them to know she had their backs.

'Thanks, Mum.'

'I know things have been strange this year. We've all had a tough time. Which is why it's so important to stick together and help each other – me, you and Darcey. We're a team. And as soon as Dad comes back' – *If he ever bloody comes back,* she thought with a grimace – 'then he'll be part of the team again too. Okay?'

He nodded again.

She leaned against him for a moment: her sensitive, taller-by-the-day son, with pimples breaking out on his forehead; the son who'd stood up for her against her own mother, and who was feeling the absence of his father so deeply that he'd lashed out against his tormentors. He was hormonal, Will, but had always been the most mild-mannered, laid-back boy, never previously one to get in a scrap or an argument. 'In the meantime we've got Grandad, and your uncles, and friends . . . ' she went on. 'And we'll be fine. We'll get through it together.'

'And Judy,' he said.

'And we've got Judy,' Gemma agreed. Judy, whom she'd misjudged quite badly, by all accounts. She'd have to think of some way to apologize and start afresh. God, life was complicated sometimes.

*

As she left Will's room and trudged downstairs, she decided that enough was enough. She couldn't keep accepting the doesn't-want-to-speak-to-you calls at Jonny's. Driving up to Newcastle in person and persuading Spencer to come home was impossible right now, with the children and work to think about, but she had to reach out to him somehow. She had to act. In sickness and in health, she reminded herself. Through the hard times and the good. They had both said some pretty hurtful things to each other, but the marriage was bigger than that, wasn't it? She was not like Karen: bailing out when the going got tough. Her marriage was worth saving – and she would bloody well fight for it.

She curled up in her favourite armchair with a pad of paper and a pen, and tried to put her feelings into a letter.

Dear Spencer,

Hi. I hope you're okay. I've been thinking about you, and us, and our marriage, a lot since you left and, even though things have been pretty crappy so far this year, I've been reminding myself that this wasn't always the case. We've had so many happy times, Spence. So many shining, gorgeous moments.

Remember when we first started going out together and I made you that mix-tape, and you took the piss out of me for liking New Kids on the Block and Kylie & Jason?? Don't worry, I'm not about to make you another one. Instead I'm going to compile a Greatest Hits *selection of us so far:* Gemma and Spencer,

The Year of Taking Chances

Volume 1. *Just because I think we've got something special here. Just in case you'd forgotten.*

So, coming straight in at number five: Holiday in Majorca, pre-children.

Oh my God-d-d! . . . I have so many funny memories about this holiday. You thinking you'd forgotten your passport at the airport and getting your dad to drive over and turn your flat upside down looking for it — before finding it yourself, tucked in the 'safe place' at the bottom of your carry-on bag. Me thinking I was Madonna on the dance-floor in that nightclub, then skidding on a bloody ice-cube and going flying arse-over-tit in front of all those people. Having cocktails on the balcony of our room and thinking we were dead cosmopolitan, right until the wind blew the door shut and we got locked out there for hours! Oh, and do you remember that moment in the sea?? I know I do . . .

Moving reluctantly on to a new entry (boom-boom) at number four: Southwold Beach, Valentine's Day, fifteen years ago.

One of the happiest days of my life — just you, me, an empty beach and an engagement ring. It was perfect, Spence. So perfect. And then afterwards, when we went to the pub to celebrate, do you remember?, you burst in there and announced to everyone, 'I'm going to marry this woman!' and we got free drinks all night. And then of course we were too pissed to drive back and ended up staying in that weird B&B and both had to bunk off work the next day . . . I loved it, though. I loved how proud you were of me, that you wanted to tell the world, starting with every last punter in the Lord Nelson pub. A really special day.

On to number three: Corsica, two summers ago.

I could have picked so many family holidays, you know. They're all up there in the Greatest Hits compilation. But this one stands out to me as being the very best of all. It wasn't just the amazing weather. It wasn't just the stunning scenery (the colour of the sea, do you remember? I couldn't get over it!). But it was the first time since we'd had kids that it felt like a real holiday again. W & D were that bit older and we were able to do such fun stuff with them — snorkelling, going on that boat trip, horse-riding along the beach . . . oh, it was amazing. I wish we could do it all over again. (But we could, Spence. This is what I'm getting at. We COULD.) I can remember, quite clearly, rubbing cocoa-butter into your warm, sun-bronzed shoulders back at the villa, and thinking how utterly, utterly happy I was. How I had everything I had ever wanted right there in my family.

Number two: our wedding day, Larkmead Church.

Where do I start? I'll never forget walking up the aisle with my dad and seeing you there waiting for me. Was there ever a more handsome, funny, loving, loyal groom? I don't think so.

The sun shone, our friends and family were all there celebrating with us, and you had tears in your eyes as you made your vows, you big softy. (I loved you for that.) It was such a wonderful day. I don't think I stopped smiling once. And then after the dinner and the speeches and our dance (Whitney!!) and the disco, we were in

408

the taxi at last, off to spend our wedding night in that posh hotel, and it was just the two of us again, me in that big dress and you in your suit . . . Just thinking about the moment we drove off and looked at each other, it still gives me goosebumps even now. 'Hello, Mrs Bailey,' you said, a bit drunk and sexy. I'm telling you, I nearly exploded with lust right there and then on the back seat.

NUMBER ONE!

Okay, so I'm actually cheating here, with two glorious memories jammed into top spot, but I couldn't separate them. It is, of course, the days our babies arrived — our beautiful, solemn-eyed son, and our beaming, dancing daughter. I'm having a little tear right now, thinking about those precious, precious moments, a newborn baby snuffling in my arms, looking into your eyes and feeling awash with so much love. Do you remember what you said when Darcey was born? 'We're all here now. Our family's complete' and I was just like, YES. EXACTLY. Nothing will beat those two special days. They are cemented into my heart, locked in there like treasure in a vault. And we made them happen, Spence. How lucky we have been.

So there are five (okay, six) glorious moments in the history of Gemma and Spencer for you to smile over. I could have picked a thousand, though, because my whole life has been about you for so long now. And I don't know what's going to happen in the future — nobody can say. But I do know that we've got the most fantastic shared past together, a past that nobody can take away. I would like to make a few more happy memories together, wouldn't you? I want to put all the arguments behind us, and ride off into the sunset with you.

We're all here, Spence, when you're up to coming home again.

Love Gemma x

She had tears rolling down her cheeks by the time she'd finished the letter and was looking up Jonny's address. It was quite the most romantic thing she'd ever done. But would it be enough?

Chapter Thirty-Five

Since the night in The Partridge when they'd seen non-mother-to-be Jade getting completely sozzled with her mates, Caitlin had been wondering what, if anything, she should do about Harry Sykes. 'It's probably too soon,' she said the following Monday at work, when Gemma brought up the subject. 'If he's just lost a baby, he'll need some time to get over it.'

'True,' Gemma replied, 'but according to my sources – i.e. the playground mums – she wasn't even pregnant in the first place. She was angry at being dumped and was trying to stick it to him.'

'She sounds a delightful sort of person,' Saffron said, rolling her eyes.

'I know. Completely the wrong woman for Harry, right?'

Not this again. Caitlin squirmed on her chair. 'Look, I barely know the guy. There was this weird kind of chemistry at New Year and then he was lovely, taking me to Cambridge that day, but . . . ' She shrugged. 'That's pretty much the sum total of my dealings with him. He might be a complete twat, for all I know.'

'Spoiler-alert: he isn't,' Gemma said, stitching a black lace trim to the hem of the scarlet cocktail dress currently in progress. 'He's a good one, Cait. Take it from me.'

'It sounded as if he was keen on you, too,' Saffron pointed out. She glanced down at her bump. 'One thing I've learned this year is how important it is to make a move, sometimes – to take a chance and put your cards on the table.'

'Absolutely,' said Gemma. 'I'm all about taking chances these days. Look where it's got me!'

'Quite,' said Saffron. 'I'm not saying go and offer yourself up on a plate, Cait, but . . . '

'I am,' Gemma put in.

'But just take a deep breath and be brave. What's the worst that could happen? He says no. And, okay, that would be a dent to your ego, but at least you'd know.'

'Mmm. And it wouldn't be embarrassing at all, every time I bumped into him around the village, would it?'

'I agree with Saffron,' Gemma said. They were ganging up on her now. 'You have to try. That's all anyone can do, right?' Her mouth twitched suddenly, as if an idea had occurred to her. 'In fact,' she said, grabbing her phone and skimming through the contacts list, 'I'm going to help you out here.'

And before Caitlin could say or do anything to stop her, she'd pressed a button and had the phone to her ear. 'Harry?

Hi, it's Gemma. Yeah, good thanks . . . No, still no word. That's why I was ringing, to see if you'd heard anything from him? . . . Oh, okay. No worries. It was just on the off-chance.' She winked at Caitlin. 'Sounds quiet where you are. Not onsite today? . . . Oh, right. No, no reason, just being nosey. Anyway, I'll let you get on . . . Will do. Cheers, Harry, bye.'

She jabbed at her phone to end the call, then smirked at Caitlin.

'What? Why are you looking like that?'

'Well, that's interesting. He's at home. Not working today.'

'Very convenient,' Saffron said innocently.

They *were* ganging up on her. She couldn't help spluttering with laughter. 'Er . . . hello? I can't just go round to his house and knock on the door.'

'Oh, I think you can,' said Gemma.

'I think you can take the afternoon off,' Saffron said.

'Yes, do – we don't need you here today,' Gemma said.

'Laptop closing down in ten . . . nine . . . eight . . . ' Saffron chanted.

Were they for real? Caitlin lunged to press Save on the work she'd been doing that morning – a site update for the Yummy Mummies – as Gemma joined in the counting.

'Seven . . . six . . . five . . . '

'You two have lost the plot,' Caitlin told them, frantically pressing buttons.

'Four . . . three . . . two . . . one . . . Oh dear, we have no power,' Saffron said, leaning over to switch it off.

Caitlin's laptop made its farewell tune and the screen went blank.

'Do you want to borrow a dress to go round there in?' Gemma asked sweetly.

'No!'

'I could do your make-up?'

'No! God, you two!' She got to her feet, feeling flustered. 'Okay, I'll go. All right? Satisfied? I'll go and probably make a gigantic pillock of myself, and it'll be all your fault.'

'Okay, whatever.' Gemma looked unperturbed.

'I mean it. I'll hold you entirely responsible if this goes wrong.'

'Yep, got it.' Saffron was back to typing at her laptop, equally unruffled by Caitlin's threats.

There was absolutely nothing else for it but to get Harry's address and go. And so she did.

This is ridiculous, Caitlin thought, walking down the road five minutes later. *This is completely bonkers. Since when did Gemma and Saffron start telling me what to do about my love-life?*

It didn't take long before her own annoying brain came up with the answer. *Since you started being such a wuss about it, maybe?*

Yeah, all right, she thought crossly. *Who asked you, anyway?*

Oh, this was going to be embarrassing. Her toes were already curling at the thought of her imminent humiliation. Harry would greet her with a blank, quizzical sort of look

— a look that said *What the hell are YOU doing here?* — and she'd stammer some nonsense in reply, and then he'd probably think she was a stalker, or some kind of obsessive weirdo. Before she knew it, he'd have a restraining order on her, and she'd have to move out of Larkmead with the shame, and . . .

Slow down, Cait. You are actually sounding quite mad. Stop it. Shut up. Just get this over with.

Although . . . well, she didn't seriously have to go through with this, did she? She could sit on the village green in the spring sunshine for half an hour instead, then go home and tell them it had been a disaster and she didn't want to talk about it any more. She could even go to the pub and kill some time with one of Bernie's famous Bacon Butties. *Now you're talking*, she thought, slowing to a halt. It was nearly one o'clock after all, and she was hungry.

Her phone buzzed with a text just then. *Don't get any ideas about bottling it, Mrs*, it said. Gemma, of course, the bloody great stirrer. She was seriously going to kill her for this. *And* Saffron. A double murder.

She was two streets away now and starting to feel jittery, so of course her subconscious chose that very moment to remind her of all the nasty things Flynn had written in his last letter, the words sinking into her skin like little fish-hooks. *You stupid bitch, you are MENTAL. Seriously, you have major problems . . . You're not even attractive. You're a fucking JOKE.*

She stopped walking in the middle of the street, her mind

buzzing with the put-downs. Oh God. No. This was madness. This was insane. What was she *doing*?

Then a new voice piped up in her head. A soft, Scottish voice, rich with warmth. *You're the loveliest girl, do you know that?*

Her lower lip wobbled. Oh, Mum. Jane . . . whatever she was supposed to call her now. She remembered sitting on her mum's knee as a little girl, crying hot tears because the boys in her class kept calling her Lanky Long-Legs, and it made her feel like an ugly, spindly insect.

You really are. The most beautiful, funny, sweet girl. My goodness, I feel sorry for those other mummies sometimes. Because I know I got the best little girl in the world.

Caitlin lowered herself onto a nearby garden wall, the memory sweet and fresh in her mind. Her mum had always made her feel better. Maybe it was time to start focusing on Jane's words, rather than wasting another second beating herself up with Flynn's.

You can do anything you want to, Caitlin. Anything! Whatever makes you happy.

That was what she'd said when Caitlin had gone, cap in hand, one Sunday lunchtime and mumbled that she didn't want to be a nurse any more, she wanted to do something artistic. Jane's face had gone a little pink, and her eyes had been sad, but once she'd got over it, she'd given Caitlin her blessing, supporting her and cheering her along through her college course and her first new job.

That was love, wasn't it? A proper mother's love, regardless of biology.

The thought gave her courage. So, she wondered, what would Jane say if she could see Caitlin now, sitting on a wall, trying to decide what to do about Harry?

The answer came so quickly to mind it was as if Jane was right there beside her.

You go for it, hen. Stop shilly-shallying around and be brave! But mind you get off that wall soon, eh? You'll get piles if you don't hurry up.

Well, then. She'd better do as she was told.

Jumping down from the wall, she set off again, rounding the corner onto Bridge Street. Harry's road: a terrace of red-brick houses, each with a different-coloured front door. His was number seventeen, a bright-red door. Red for danger, she reminded herself with a sudden attack of nerves.

Okay. This was it. She would knock on the door and ask if he'd like to go for a drink sometime. Or maybe she'd pretend she needed to talk to him about another electrical job around the house? Yes. That was a much better idea. That was definitely what—

What?

The front door had opened before she'd even knocked. 'Hi,' Harry said with a grin. 'Come in.'

That was weird. That was completely weird. It was almost as if he'd been expecting her. *Had* he been expecting her? No, you idiot. How could he have known?

She followed him into a small, cosy dining room, where a square table had been laid with a white cloth. There was a cheese board and some ham from the butcher's, a jar of pickles, a dish of green salad and a crusty loaf. 'Oh – tomatoes,' he said. 'Wait there, I'll just grab them. What would you like to drink?'

She felt as if she'd wandered into a strange dream, or maybe a scene from a play. 'Er . . . are you expecting someone over for lunch?' she asked. 'Because I was only knocking to see if . . . ' She struggled to think of some other electrical appliance she could ask him to fix, but her mind went annoyingly blank.

He returned with a small bowl of halved plum tomatoes, their glossy skins sprinkled with sea salt and black pepper. 'Have a seat,' he said, before she could come up with anything.

She looked at him, and the tomatoes, and the wine glasses he was setting out and shook her head. 'I . . . I don't understand,' she confessed.

'Well, I thought I'd cut to the chase,' he said. 'Yes. Great idea – I'd love to go out with you.' He grinned at her and a dimple flashed in his left cheek. 'Now, I hope it's not outrageously presumptuous of me, but I thought I'd go ahead and sort out our first date. This is it, by the way. You're not vegetarian, are you?'

'N-no,' she stammered. 'No, I'm not vegetarian. But how

did you . . . ?' And then the answer became clear. Of course. 'This is Gemma, isn't it, sticking her oar in?' She should have guessed from the start. Had they planned this whole thing together?

He uncorked a bottle of Pinot Grigio. 'Yes and no. I was all set to declare my hand a few weeks ago – until Jade went and mucked that up, with her imaginary pregnancy.' His eyes darkened at the memory. 'Then I bumped into Gemma on Saturday morning as she was posting a letter off to Spencer. The most romantic letter ever written, she reckons. She just gave me a bit of a nudge to do something romantic about you, that's all.'

Caitlin remembered then how Gemma and Saffron had gone off to the kitchen together earlier that morning and taken a suspiciously long time to return again. She'd thought at the time they must be talking mum-stuff, but maybe not. Maybe all three of them were in on it. 'Yeah, Gemma gave me a nudge, too,' she said. 'A nudge right out of the door of my own house!'

He sploshed wine into their glasses and passed one to her. 'You're not mad, are you? That we hatched a plot? I couldn't resist giving it a go. I swear I'm not a tosser, like your ex. I don't have any huge portraits of me around the house, either.'

He had such blue eyes, Harry. But they were a steady warm blue, rather than the cool, emotionless eyes of Flynn.

'No, I'm not mad,' she said, feeling her heart give a happy

bounce. He had freckles, she noticed, a light sandy sprinkling across his nose. She felt like leaning over and kissing every single one of them all of a sudden. Then she laughed. 'The only thing I'm wondering is, does the Ten-Date Rule still apply?'

'The what? Oh, shit. I'd forgotten all about that.' He grinned at her. 'I might have to amend it to a Five-Date Rule. Don't tell my sister.'

'I wouldn't dare.'

'Or maybe even a Three-Date Rule . . .' He held her gaze and she felt as if she was melting inside. Three whole dates? She wasn't sure she'd be able to wait that long, personally.

'I couldn't possibly comment,' she said demurely. 'But thank you. This looks lovely.' She held her glass in the air. 'Here's to first dates.'

'First dates,' he echoed, clinking her glass.

First dates, interfering mates and lunchtime drinking. Put them all together and it was a pretty irresistible combination. Caitlin leaned across the table, feeling heady after a single mouthful of wine. She had a good feeling about this. A good, sweet, happy feeling. 'Do you know what? I think I'm going to have to kiss you,' she said before she could stop herself

His eyes crinkled as he smiled back at her. 'Do you know what? I think I'm going to have to let you,' he murmured.

And then her lips were on his, and his mouth was soft and sweet, and all of a sudden lunch was entirely forgotten.

Chapter Thirty-Six

Will was given detention for getting into a fight and leaving school unauthorized, and Gemma was called in to discuss the issue the following week with his head of year, Mr Shaw. Mr Shaw was tall, affable and tracksuited; a PE teacher who had always got on well with Will in the past. 'Between you and me,' he said confidentially to Gemma, perched on the edge of his desk, 'he had it coming to him. Sam West, I mean – the lad your Will punched. One of those kids who's always got it in for someone or other, can't keep his gob shut. Just so happened to be Will who was his target this year.'

'Oh,' said Gemma uncertainly.

'Obviously the school has to take a hard line on this sort of thing. We don't condone any kind of violence or fighting, self-defence or not.' He folded his arms, looking stern for a moment, then winked. 'But let's just say there were a few smiles in the staffroom when word got out that Sam West had taken a bit of a slapping.'

Gemma goggled. 'Right.'

'You didn't hear me say that, though, did you?'

'Didn't hear a thing.'

'Good.' He fiddled with the silver PE whistle around his neck on a cord. 'Otherwise, Will's been doing really well. Working hard, well liked, getting on with the job. And don't worry, Mrs Bailey, we'll come down on Sam West like a ton of bricks if there's any more trouble.' He stood up and stretched his long legs. 'Not that I think it's likely, mind. Kids like Sam are cowards at heart. Nothing like a smack in the chops to shut them up.'

Gemma was still mulling over this rather unexpected slant to the conversation as she drove back from the school. She hoped Mr Shaw was right, and that there'd be no more aggro with Sam. Poor Will. It was hard being a teenager, she remembered – but even harder to be the mother of one sometimes. It had been so much more straightforward when the children were tiny and her job was to keep them safe from sharp corners or tumbles, to feed and clean them, to lower them into their cots to sleep at night, with a soft rendition of 'Twinkle, Twinkle, Little Star'. These days they talked back and asked awkward questions, they had strong feelings and railed against perceived injustices or sank into silent, seething furies. Worst of all, they went around punching people when they couldn't control their emotions.

That said, after talking the other night, she felt as if she and Will had a new understanding now – and, more importantly, he knew she was on his side. With a bit of luck, she'd have this teenager malarkey nailed by the time it was Darcey's turn. God forbid.

Coming back into Larkmead, she had to brake behind the village bus, an endangered species around these parts and therefore to be respected. She drummed her fingers as she waited for it to disgorge its clutch of passengers, already thinking ahead to the new dress she was working on: a gorgeous evening gown of cranberry-coloured silk with a daring criss-crossing ribbon back. A million times more satisfying than making curtains or altering bridesmaid dresses, she thought with a little smile. She definitely wasn't 'just a mum' any more, either.

In the street two elderly ladies were being helped down from the bus by a dark-haired man – what a gent, she thought approvingly. Then she nearly stopped breathing in shock as she realized that the dark-haired man was actually Spencer, leaning on a stick as he took the first lady by her pastel-clad arm, and then the second. He had come back!

A million feelings tore through her as she watched him saying something to the old ladies that made them smile, then helped a young mum bump her buggy down from the bus – not a small undertaking, when you needed a stick for support yourself. Old feelings of fondness slowly unfurled inside her. He was a good person, really. Just like his son. But where would they go from here? Would anything have changed?

The bus drove away with a belch of smoke from the exhaust, and she crawled the car along after it, pulling up beside Spencer and unrolling the passenger window. She leaned over and caught his eye. 'Hey.'

A whole rush of feelings flickered across his face as he saw her – surprise, happiness, nerves. 'Hey,' he said quietly.

She swallowed, unable to tell much from his expression. 'Want a lift?'

He held her gaze and she remembered for a fleeting moment how she'd looked at him on their wedding day. *For richer, for poorer, in sickness and in health. I do. I do.*

I still do, she thought. *I want this to work. But he's got to want that too. We can't go on as we were.*

'Great,' he said. 'Thanks.'

She put the handbrake on instinctively, about to jump out and help him then stopped herself, remembering his pride. He'd made it all the way to Newcastle and back under his own steam, after all. If he wanted to stop being treated as an invalid, then that was progress at least.

He winced as he lowered himself into the seat, hauling the stick and a small rucksack in after him. There were dark shadows under his eyes, and he looked crumpled and tired after the long journey, but she thought she could detect a new determination about him, too, an energy that she hadn't seen in a long while.

'So,' she said, a lump in her throat. Now that he was here,

she wasn't sure what to say any more. She wanted to lean against him and breathe in the scent of his skin again, to hold him and be held right back. But did he feel the same? 'You came back,' she said after a moment.

'I did.' He cleared his throat, not looking at her. 'Thanks for the letter . . . ' He broke off and stared out of the window. 'It was the most beautiful thing I have ever read in my life.'

'Oh, Spencer.' She could have cried with relief. Had she actually got through to him at last?

'I'm serious. It made me realize exactly what I stood to lose.' He folded his hands in his lap. 'I'm sorry, Gem. I've been such a dick recently, I kind of lost the plot for a while. I just felt so angry all the time. So bloody useless. I couldn't bear it.'

She twisted her wedding ring around her finger, unsure how to reply.

'I know I took it out on you and the kids – the people I care about most in the world.' He shook his head. 'I don't know how you put up with me. I wouldn't have blamed you if you'd chucked me out the house.'

Karen would have chucked him out, Gemma thought to herself. She'd have shown him the door – injury or no injury. But Gemma was not her mother. Her love went deeper. She reached over and took Spencer's hand in hers. 'How's your back?' she asked. 'Have you been okay? You didn't take your painkillers with you.'

He shifted in the passenger seat and she could see his discomfort and exhaustion. 'It's all right. I went along to see Jonny's doctor, had a good chat. She gave me some painkillers and sorted me out. I'm just a bit stiff, after sitting down for so long.'

There was a time when one or both of them might have made a joke about him being 'a bit stiff', but the atmosphere was too fraught for jokes. 'Right,' she said.

Neither of them spoke for a few seconds. 'Are the kids okay?' he asked eventually.

Good question. 'They're fine,' she replied. It wasn't the right moment to start telling him about Will's fight and Darcey's tears and her mum's surprise visit. 'They're great,' she added with more conviction. 'Dying to seeing you again. Darcey's going to absolutely shriek with joy, she's missed you so much. We all have.' She took a deep breath. 'Why did you go, Spencer? Why did you just take off like that?'

He stared down at his lap. 'Everything seemed so bleak,' he said after a moment. 'I was this useless fucking cripple . . . and all of a sudden you were this businesswoman flying high. I couldn't handle it any more.'

'But . . .'

'I don't want to sound melodramatic, but I just couldn't see the point of going on. I thought: I'll get in the car, drive to the middle of nowhere and gas myself. You know, pipe on the exhaust — job done.' He shook his head, eyes far away. 'But then I thought of the kids, and you, and I couldn't bring myself to do it.'

'Oh, Spencer,' she said again helplessly, not able to bear the haunted expression on his face.

'I went a bit mad, Gem. Didn't know what to do with myself. Drove and drove, unable to think straight. Didn't know where I was going. For the first time in my life it was like I had no future, no clear road ahead.'

Gemma squeezed his hand, not trusting herself to speak.

'I was so sick of it,' he went on. 'I didn't feel like a man any more. My body wasn't working the way it used to, my head was killing me the whole time. I just . . . didn't know how to go on.'

'I wish you'd talked to me,' she said in a small voice. 'I wish you'd told me you were feeling like this.'

He nodded, his head still bowed. 'I know. And I really am sorry. I know I haven't been easy to live with. When I think of what I said to you . . .'

She could tell the memory genuinely pained him. 'It doesn't matter,' she said.

'It does matter! If anyone else dared speak to you like that, I'd bloody swing for them. I'm ashamed of myself,' he said gruffly. 'I let you down. And when I read your letter and remembered just how lovely and kind and gorgeous you are . . . ' He shook his head. 'I couldn't believe I'd nearly let you go.'

'It's fine.'

'It's not fine, Gemma. I've been an arsehole. But talking to the doctor helped. She reckoned it might be this Concussion Syndrome thing, too, and gave me some antidepressants to see if they help. I won't be like this forever.'

'Of course you won't,' she said.

'I do feel a bit better already, you know. Jonny forced me out to get some fresh air . . . '

'Yes, I heard. Playing golf, wasn't it?'

He had the grace to look sheepish. 'Yeah. Quite enjoyed it actually. So that was good. And then Jonny kept banging on at me to man up and go home to my amazing wife and children, before I blew it all.'

Gemma had to hide her smirk on hearing this. Thank you, Jonny. 'The man's got a point,' she replied.

'And then your letter just confirmed everything,' he said. 'So here I am.' He twisted awkwardly to face her. 'And I'll make it up to you, I swear. I'll go to physio and stay on the antidepressants to stop me being such a miserable bastard. I've sold the car to tide us over with money, and I'll help more around the house while you're out being Super-Business-woman. Seriously! What? Why are you doing that?'

Gemma was leaning forward, squinting through the wind-screen. 'Just searching for a pig flying through the air,' she teased, then turned and kissed him. It was one of the best and sweetest kisses of her entire life. 'Thank you,' she said, then put the car into first gear. 'Let's go home.'

Chapter Thirty-Seven

It was the first weekend of April, and Larkmead had never looked more glorious, thought Saffron as she and Max drove into the village. There was blossom on the apple trees, the magnolias were in full bloom and the sunlight shone golden on the old stone cottages. She parked the hired van outside Baker's Cottage just as the baby gave two energetic kicks in her belly. *We're home.*

'Yes,' she murmured, as Max jumped down from the passenger side. 'This is it, kiddo. Our home for the next six months. Aren't we the lucky ones?'

She was nearly twenty weeks pregnant now and feeling lots of movement from the wriggly little person inside. She put her hand on her belly, loving the ripples and jumps she could feel. 'I think the baby's dancing,' she called to Max, clambering out of the driver's seat.

'Let's hope for his or her sake that my excellent dance-floor genes have been passed on,' Max replied, moonwalking to the back of the van.

Saffron snorted with laughter. She loved having Max in her life again. To think they might have slipped past each other, lost each other because of one unposted letter. Look at him now sliding his feet backwards, arms held robotically, as if he was the long-lost brother of Michael Jackson. 'It would be a devastating blow to humanity if the moonwalking gene stopped at you, my love,' she said solemnly and fished in her jeans pocket for the door keys she'd just picked up from Bernie. *Her* door keys, as of today — well, for the next six months, anyway.

That morning she, Max and her parents had packed up her London flat and she'd waved a thankful goodbye to the neighbourhood kebab shops and litter, the yellow police signs and the traffic. She was renting the cottage until the autumn, and after that . . . Well, it was too early to say. By that time, she'd be a different person — a mother — and she would have to make some big decisions about where to live, and who she wanted to be with. Right now she was buying herself six months of breathing space in a pretty country cottage with two really good friends nearby, her parents half an hour away and miles of open countryside and fresh air on her doorstep. Everything else could be figured out further down the line.

The cottage looked different as they walked up the garden path. The frontage had been given a fresh coat of white paint, and Saffron could see through the window that someone — she could guess who — had added colourful poppy-patterned curtains. Apparently Bunty had had a word with Bernie about the state of the cottage – several words, knowing Bunty – insisting that it wasn't fit for a mother-to-be and her baby. And, bless him, he'd been convinced to redecorate throughout, even clearing out some of the ancient furniture to make way for Saffron's bits and pieces.

She smiled at Max as she slid the key into the lock. 'Shall we?'

'If I wasn't carrying this ton-weight of paperback books I'd carry you over the threshold myself,' he said and twisted his head down to kiss her. 'Both of you.'

'You so wouldn't,' she laughed, feeling deliciously swoony from the effects of his kiss. She could kiss that luscious mouth for Britain, given half a chance. Olympic Kissing Team? Yep, she'd be on that, no problem.

Light fell into the cream-painted hall as she pushed open the door, and the baby twisted and somersaulted again, her tiny watery acrobat. *Here we are. This is the first house you'll ever live in, baby.* 'Come on in,' she said. 'Home, sweet home.'

The cottage already felt a different place – pristine and bright, with pretty new cushions on the sofa (Gemma again, she bet) and a neat basket of wood stacked by the hearth. She could see through the back window that the garden was full of spring flowers, and there was a wooden bench under a trailing honeysuckle. She could already envisage sunny afternoons out there with a book and her feet up, maybe a barbecue for their new friends . . .

'Looks like a good fairy's been round,' Max said, as they went into the kitchen. There was a vase of red tulips on the table alongside a white cardboard bakery box containing lemon-drizzle cake, with further investigations revealing a slab of Cheddar and some smoked salmon, fresh orange juice, butter and milk in the fridge. A note propped against the vase said: *Family day out in Southwold! Will drop round this evening when we're back. Love from Gemma and Spencer x.*

'Is Gemma the dressmaker?' Max asked, breaking open a packet of cookies he'd spotted behind the bread. 'I like her already.'

'She's great,' Saffron replied, taking a cookie from the packet. Dressmaker, neighbour, friend, newest client . . . It was going to be fun working together for the next few months.

Hourglass Designs was going from strength to strength: a solid list of customers, with many more clamouring for appointments. Such was the demand that Gemma had now roped in Gwen, Caitlin's elderly neighbour, as an extra machinist, so that they could keep up with demand. Gwen had spent her entire working life at the knicker factory in Ipswich and was nimble-fingered and competent, by all accounts. She was also prone to bringing in home-made cake to work, which nobody was ever going to complain about.

Help had come from another unlikely source, too: Gemma's husband Spencer. Although he was still recovering from his accident and unable to return to building work just yet, he'd taken it upon himself to pitch in with the Hourglass business: negotiating better deals with fabric suppliers and the courier firm, in the way he'd always done when working with timber yards and builders' merchants in the past. He would hobble down to school to pick up Darcey, if Gemma was in the middle of something, and had even taken to cooking the occasional family dinner as well. 'He's systematically wrecking all our pans,' Gemma had grumbled down the phone to Saffron, 'and you've never seen so much washing up in your life – he seems to challenge himself to use every single utensil in the house. Not that I'm complaining, though. I wouldn't dare.'

Meanwhile, Caitlin had changed her mind about selling White Gables and moving out of Larkmead, and was now officially on board as the Hourglass Designs web and tech expert. Gemma had asked Saffron if they could formalize their working relationship too, with a contract and a proper fee structure. So, along with Bunty, this made a mighty total of two new clients on Saffron's roster at McKay-Flint PR.

McKay-Flint PR? Oh yes. Yet another excellent development. After Saffron had returned to London the week before, she had met her friend Kate – the McKay of the organization – for lunch in a King's Cross gastropub, and over plates of beer-battered haddock and triple-cooked chips, Kate had made a proposition: that the two of them form their own PR agency together. No more Charlotte bossing them around, no more clients they didn't like, no more unsociable hours and feeling guilty for dashing away to doctor's appointments or children's nativity plays. 'We'll be our own bosses, with a hand-picked selection of clients we actually care about, working from our own kitchen tables, with the occasional high-powered executive lunch like this one,' Kate said. 'I'm deadly serious about wanting to make a go of it. What do you reckon?'

'I reckon it's a bloody fantastic idea,' Saffron replied at once. 'An absolute no-brainer. Between us, we've got a ton of experience and loads of great contacts.' She grinned. 'I think this deserves a celebratory pudding, at the very least.'

Over a slab of gooey treacle sponge each, they thrashed out a few plans. Kate was already working for a couple of big-name TV stars and a friend of hers, whose first novel was being made into a film. Saffron was going to stick with Bunty and Gemma for the time being, but would be on hand to pick up small, discreet jobs when necessary and chat regularly for brainstorming and strategizing.

'So are we agreed then? Shall we do this?' Kate asked, as the waiter brought them a latte each and the bill.

Saffron held up her mug. 'Here's to us, and the best new PR agency on the block,' she said. 'In it to win it.'

'In it to win it,' Kate echoed, clinking her mug against Saffron's.

And so Baker's Cottage was to become not only Saffron's temporary new home, but also a sister-hub of McKay-Flint PR. Why not? It would be fun to work with Kate, under their own steam, and although that meant no official maternity leave as such, Saffron planned to work around the baby when he or she arrived, in a way that her job at Phoenix PR would never have allowed. Now freed from her previous contract, Bunty had already booked herself in for an inaugural client meeting the following Tuesday. 'And then Bernie's going to whisk me away for a few days at the seaside,' she said happily down the phone. 'Hashtag Bunternie – what do you think? We could be the new Brangelina.'

'Mmm, inspired,' Saffron said politely, although if Bunty noticed any doubt in her voice, she was too busy leaping ahead to a new stroke of brilliance to care very much.

'Idea alert! Maybe we could pitch for a new TV show starring me moving to the countryside, too. *Town Mouse, Country Mouse* sort of thing. It could be *hilaire!*'

'*Mouse?* Bunty, nobody's ever going to call you a mouse,' Saffron pointed out. 'Country Fox, more like. Country Vixen.'

'Country Vixen, yes, I love it!' A hoot of laughter came down the line. 'Wait, I've thought of something even better. *City Chick, Country Buntkin. Buntkin* – do you get it? Like Bumpkin, but with my name in! I think we're onto something here, Saff, I really do.'

Yes, Bunty was certainly going to keep her busy for the foreseeable future, that was for sure, although this wasn't such a bad thing any more. Ever since Saffron had let rip with a few home truths, the two of them had forged a new and better understanding, one with mutual respect. No more dogsitting Teddy, the perfumed Pomeranian. No more impromptu visitations or orders barked down the phone. Moreover Bunty had twice appeared very publicly in Gemma's dresses now, winning reams of gushing coverage. When your clients started giving each other such helpful leg-ups, you knew you were onto a winner.

'Cooee! Saff, we're here! What a sweet little place this is!'

Ah, and there was the cavalry – her mum and dad – on cue as promised, to help unload the van. 'Hello, welcome; you made it,' she said, hurrying to meet them in the hallway. 'Come in, come in! What do you think?'

While Saffron's mum was exclaiming about the prettiness of the cottage, and what a lovely garden and, goodness, wasn't it going to be heaven living here, she was green with envy, her dad hauled in her desk and set it up in the second bedroom. Then he and Max heaved in the bed and wardrobe and the suitcases of clothes . . . and gradually her new home began to take shape.

She watched Max making her mum laugh one minute, and

then patiently going along with her dad's orders about the best way to get the bed up the narrow cottage stairs the next, and felt the baby kick and twist and turn, looping somersaults inside her, almost as if agreeing.

I like him.

Me, too. He's a nice bloke.

A really nice bloke.

I'm glad we sorted everything out.

I'm glad there'll be three of us in this family.

By now, a few boxes marked KITCHEN had been brought in, so Saffron went to make a pot of tea, cutting the lemon cake into slices while the kettle boiled, then foraging through the newspaper-wrapped crockery until she found some side-plates. Who knew how this would work out, her being here and Max still in the city? He had his job to think about, and two other children he loved, plus an ex-wife who was a pain in the neck, by the sound of things. She, meanwhile, had a new life in the country to get used to, the uncertainty of freelance work, a baby on the way and the whole daunting prospect of motherhood looming ahead. It could still go either way. Nothing was guaranteed.

But they would try, that was the main thing. And at the end of the day, wasn't that all any couple could do anyway? Max hadn't welched out on her as she'd feared, he hadn't bailed and slunk away into the shadows. On the contrary, in the last few weeks they'd spent a lot of time together, meeting for lunch and dinner, taking their bikes out to Epping Forest one sunshiny Saturday afternoon, and going on a trip to Lee Valley, where he surprised her with a pre-booked rafting session together (she had never been so drenched in her entire life). He'd allowed himself to be introduced to – or rather interrogated by – Saffron's sister Zoe over Skype (who awarded him a double thumbs-up in approval) and had even braved Sunday lunch in a rural Essex pub with Eloise and Simon. Thankfully they had been unfailingly polite and normal, and hadn't tried to adopt the unborn baby once. ('He is *lovely*,' Eloise said, following Saffron into the loos after the dessert course. 'Absolutely perfect for you.')

Who could say? Who knew? And what was perfect anyway? She would be forty next year and had been around the block enough times to know full well that people changed, and could fall out of love with the same unpredictability as the weather. Max already had one marriage and two children to show for that; she had her failed first marriage, too. But you couldn't let that frighten you off. You couldn't.

Besides, she really liked him. She really, really liked him. He was kind and funny and thoughtful, and every bit as sexy and gorgeous in bed as before, even when she was stone-cold sober and twice the size of her old pre-pregnant self.

He came into the kitchen just then with a box of cookery books and caught her mashing the tea with a goofy grin on her face. 'What are you smiling about?' he asked, dumping the box on the table.

She went over and put her arms around him. 'You, of course,' she said. 'And us. And this place.' The baby booted her pointedly. 'And this squirming little baby, too,' she added with a laugh. 'All of it. The whole lot. But right now, especially you.'

Chapter Thirty-Eight

'I've decided,' said Gemma, draining her second glass of Prosecco, 'that summer is a much better time of year for making resolutions. Don't you think?'

'God, yeah,' Caitlin agreed. 'New Year's Eve is a ridiculous night to be making any kind of life-plans. For one thing, you're always too wasted to think straight.'

'Plus you're at your skintest and porkiest, right after Christmas,' Saffron put in, 'which kind of throws a depressing light on everything.'

'Exactly, and the last thing you feel like doing in horrible, cold January is venturing out into the rain or snow to go jogging, let alone denying yourself wine or chocolate,' said Gemma with a shudder. 'Whereas now . . . ' She looked at her empty glass and giggled. 'Well, all right, so I'm not denying myself anything now either, but it *is* my birthday.'

'I think that's my cue to open another bottle,' said Spencer, and everyone laughed.

'Just look at that bottom, would you?' Gemma sighed, as he

walked away barefoot through the long grass, and then blushed furiously. 'Whoops, did I just say that out loud?'

'You totally did, you dirty cow,' Caitlin said, shaking her head in reproach. 'What are you like?'

What was she like? Gemma didn't need to think hard to answer that question. Very bloody lucky, that was what she was like. And very bloody grateful, too.

It was a gorgeously hot mid-July day and they were all in her back garden for a birthday picnic lunch. There were only a few chocolate-dipped strawberries left to show for the spread that had been prepared by Spencer, with a little help from Will, Darcey, Judy and Waitrose. Bees buzzed lazily around the lavender, and the smell of cut grass mingled with the perfume of the flowers and the sharp, hot stink of Max's cigarette. She was due to meet her dad and Judy, plus all of her brothers and their other halves, for dinner that evening, and she'd already been spoiled rotten with presents and cards and the most gigantic bouquet of flowers from Bunty ('Your most loyal customer,' as it said on the card). Did life get any better?

'Go on then,' Saffron said, nudging Gemma with her bare foot. With just six weeks to go now until her due date, she was half-woman, half-belly, and wore a huge droopy sunhat to shade her face. 'Forget New Year. What resolutions would you make right now, if you were doing them over again?'

Gemma paused to think. After a rocky start to the year, the traumas of being unhappy, scared and broke were still only just beneath the surface; she often woke up in the night and had to do a mental head-count to reassure herself: Spencer, Will, Darcey, all here, all okay, go back to sleep. But the worst was definitely behind them, and their family was reunited and stronger than ever. The chances she'd taken had paid off: her career had gone into orbit and she still hadn't got used to the joy she felt when someone tried on one of her dresses and their face lit up. Thanks to Saffron and Caitlin, she had a waiting list of customers and had taken on two mums from the school to work as extra part-time machinists alongside Gwen. She'd branched out into a range of Fifties-style full skirts recently, which were flying out of the studio as fast as they could make them. Things were definitely on the up.

Her friends were all looking expectantly at her. Oh yes, resolutions.

'I guess . . . just to appreciate everything, really,' she said, tipping her head back so that the sunshine warmed her face. 'To take stock now and then, and be grateful for what I've got. My family, my friends, my home – I took them all for granted, until I was in danger of losing the lot. I won't make that mistake again.'

'Good call,' said Saffron approvingly.

'I'll drink to that,' agreed Max, holding up his champagne flute. He and Saffron had spent quite a few evenings with Gemma and Spencer since Saffron had been renting the next-door cottage, and the four of them got on brilliantly, not least because Max, like Spencer, was a rabid Arsenal fan and had wangled them both complimentary tickets for the first match of the season.

'How about you, Cait?' Gemma gave her a naughty look. 'What was your New Year's resolution again? To find a new man, wasn't it? Well, that's worked out all right, I suppose . . .'

'Better than all right, I reckon,' Harry said, pulling a funny face. 'Only the hottest, sexiest, fittest——'

'Most big-headed——'

' . . . bloke in Larkmead. Can't get luckier than that, right, Cait?'

Caitlin was making a daisy chain, slicing her thumbnail through the long green stalks. She laughed as Harry nudged her and said, 'Oh, absolutely. I knew as soon as I saw that ridiculous pink Stetson that this was my Prince Charming.' Then a more guarded expression appeared on her face. 'Although technically speaking, there are two new men in my life. And a new woman, too.'

'Eh?' asked Saffron.

'What?' cried Harry, pretending to be outraged.

She elbowed him, rolling her eyes. He knew exactly what she was talking about, having sat beside her and held her hand when she was too scared to open the first email a week earlier. 'I've been in touch with this Adoption Search Reunion website,' she told the others. 'It turns out I've got a half-brother, and he and my birth mother are both living in Vancouver.'

'Wow!' Gemma cried.

'Oh, Caitlin!' Saffron exclaimed.

'Holy cow,' said Max. 'Will you go out to meet them, do you think?'

The big question. The terrifying, weird, exciting question. 'Yeah, at some point, definitely,' she said, then giggled. 'We've swapped emails and photos so far, and they both look so like me, it's really freaky. So that's *my* next resolution: to get on a plane and meet them. Maybe in the autumn, when I've plucked up enough courage.'

Harry squeezed her hand. He knew what this meant to her. Having spent her entire life as an only child, it had been the most unexpected bonus for Caitlin to discover a real-life brother out there: Michael Wendell, an osteopath in Vancouver, who had the same big nose and fluffy dark hair as her, plus a friendly, kind face, a wife (her sister-in-law!) and a guest room with her name on it whenever she could make it out to Canada.

'Awesome,' said Saffron, wiggling her bare toes in the sunshine. 'That is great news, Cait.'

Yes, thought Caitlin. Yes, it was great news. She was still getting used to her new family arrangements, but after some deep emotional wrangling, she had finally made her peace with Jane, and let go of the anger and hurt she'd felt. One cool, cloudy day in May she and Harry had driven out to Aldeburgh, a place Jane had always loved, and scattered her ashes at last, letting them fly out to sea. 'Thank you,' she said as the ashes spiralled from her fingers and up into the air. 'For everything you ever taught me. You were a great mum.'

A few days later, when it was Caitlin's birthday, Gemma had presented her with a patchwork bag she'd made, using scraps of fabric cut from Jane's old clothes. Her favourite pink silk nightie, her red-flowered sundress, a pale-blue jacket, her tweedy gardening trousers . . . they were all there, cut and stitched together in a beautiful jigsaw. Every time she used the bag, Caitlin felt close to her mum again, remembering one incident or other where Jane had worn one of the garments. Happy days. Good times.

Now that she had got over the shocking discovery of her birth, Caitlin had also come to accept that the adoption had been carried out for the best reasons: an attempt to give her a second chance, a better, safer childhood. Alison was seventeen and had been pressurized to give Caitlin up for adoption by her strict Catholic parents. 'But I never stopped thinking about you, lovey,' she wrote in her first email. 'I always hoped that you'd try to find me one day.'

And now she had. They had found each other. Nothing would diminish what Jane and Steve had been for her – two great parents – but now there was an extra parent in the mix, another family to get to know. When she thought back to how she'd felt at the start of the year – so alone, so sad, so broken – she hardly recognized herself. Now she had an extra helping of family, lots of interesting work from Saffron and Gemma, as well as their staunch friendship, and a hot new relationship with Harry to boot. He was just as lovely as Gemma had always claimed. She knew Jane would have approved.

Finishing her daisy circlet, she draped it on Harry's blond hair, where it slipped rakishly over one ear. 'Gorgeous,' she assured him, leaning over to give him a smooch. So far, to everyone's surprise, Harry had kept to his own New Year's resolution about not making any rash marriage proposals, but that was fine by Caitlin. She wasn't in any rush. Mind you, if things carried on going so brilliantly between them, she had half a mind to pop the question herself, perhaps at midnight next New Year's Eve . . .

'Harry, what about you?' Gemma asked, as he and Caitlin disentangled themselves. 'Obviously it's impossible to improve on perfection, but are there any self-improvement resolutions you'd care to share?'

He thought about it, then nodded sagely. 'Always to knock before I walk in on my dad when he is entertaining a "lady friend",' he declared. 'My eyes, my eyes. It's going to take years of therapy for me to get over seeing Dad and Bunty doing *that*.'

Spencer returned with an ice bucket and another bottle of Prosecco just as they were all roaring with laughter, and topped everyone's glasses up.

'Cheers,' said Max, as they all toasted the birthday girl again. 'Well, my summer resolution's easy: give up smoking before the baby arrives. And make sure I'm out of the country when it comes to the birth. Joking!' He leaned back as Saffron pretended to punch him. 'Seriously, though. I want to be a really good dad. Better than I was for my first two children. I don't want to let this child down – or you, Saff.'

'You'd better not,' Saffron joked, but she knew there was real regret behind his words. He'd been an absent dad for them, he'd said, so wrapped up in his career that he'd missed all sorts of baby milestones: first steps, first words, first days at school. These days his priorities had changed; he'd already promised her he wouldn't make that mistake again.

She reached over to take his hand, noticing how tanned he was, his olive skin soaking up the sun in a way that her pale, freckly limbs never did. Who would the baby look like? she wondered for the millionth time. Whose eyes would he or she inherit, whose ears, whose nose, whose complexion? So many discoveries lay ahead of her: this brand-new little person to get to know, a whole new chapter of her life just about to start. With six weeks to go, she felt as ripe and round as a watermelon, the baby no longer quite so wriggly now that there was less room to manoeuvre, but with a good strong heartbeat and perfect measurements, according to her last antenatal check. She had stopped thinking about the one in thirty-six chance. It flashed into her mind every now and then, but she pushed it away. *Whatever happens, we'll deal with it*, she thought. *Whoever the baby turns out to be, she or he will be loved.*

'How about you, Saffron?' Caitlin asked.

Saffron blinked quickly, returning to the moment. 'Resolutions, hmm.' She thought for a moment. 'Can I say: not to poo myself on the delivery table, or is that totally lowering the tone?'

They all laughed. 'Did I mention that I'm going to be out of the country during the birth?' Max said, and she stuck her tongue out at him.

Resolutions. There had to be something. She racked her brain for anything that might be missing in her life, an area on which she could improve, but at a first sweep everything was in place. She and Max had started looking ahead to the autumn, exploring villages midway between London and here, in which they could buy a little house and live together as a family. Work was great, and made her happy. Her parents were doting on her, thrilled to bits about the prospect of the new grandchild, and her sister Zoe was due to fly in from Perth in a few weeks for an extended visit, so that she could meet the youngest member of the family when he or she arrived. Nicest of all was the fact that Eloise and Simon had announced they were going to look into adoption; a positive decision that Saffron thoroughly approved of. If anyone deserved to be a mum it was Eloise.

'Well,' she said, 'I'm a bit scared about whether or not I'll be any good at this motherhood business.' She shifted to a more comfortable position on the picnic blanket. 'But if this year has taught me anything, it's that life is full of surprises. So my resolution is to try not to stress about the unknown until it happens. That – and not poo myself on the delivery table.'

'A wise resolution,' Spencer said, with a meaningful look at Gemma.

'Don't you dare,' she warned him, laughing. 'Not now. Not on my birthday.'

He laughed as well, dodging as she kicked out at him, then rubbed his back as it twinged from the sudden movement. Out of the back-brace at last, he was getting used to a more physical life again: swimming and going for long walks; oh, and sex, of course. He was definitely enjoying that again, as was Gemma. It wasn't just his body that was healing; there had come a day back in April when he'd woken up and the tight, pinching sensation in his head had gone, as if something had lifted clean away. Concussion or depression, he still wasn't completely sure which, but he was able to think straight again for the first time all year, no longer in constant pain, no longer quite so dour about the future.

He still wasn't up to the full rigours of his old job yet, but had kept himself busy around the house decorating the living room, overhauling the bathroom and putting up a pergola in the back garden. More importantly, he was Spencer again: laughing and irreverent, Gemma's best friend and favourite person. Now that she had her husband back in soul as well as body, Gemma was fully intent on creating enough wonderful new moments and memories for them to fill *Greatest Hits: Gemma and Spencer, Volumes 2, 3* and *4*.

'My turn,' he said now. 'I can't do all the fancy words, like the rest of you. But I know damn well I was a pretty shit husband and dad at the start of the year, and I've been trying since then to put things right. As you know, I flogged the Mazda back in March and I used some of the money to contribute to the family finances while I did a bit of work around the place. The rest of the money . . . well, come and see. Time for the big unveiling.'

They all got to their feet, light-headed from the sunshine and Prosecco – even Saffron, who'd been on the sparkling water. Gemma felt skittery with trepidation, unsure what to expect. There was no hiding the fact that Spencer had demolished the old garage that had once housed his precious car, but he'd erected a marquee-sized blue plastic tent over the ground where it had once stood, and she was none the wiser as to what, exactly, he'd been up to in there – only that he'd been busy and cheerful, jumping out of bed early every morning, whistling in the shower, eager to crack on with a brand-new day, just like old times. A couple of mates had been over recently to help, and there had been intriguing drilling and sawing sounds, but whenever she tried to prise out of them what he was up to, they'd all clammed up and shaken their heads. To say she was intrigued was the understatement of the year.

They went through the house — oddly deserted — and out to the front, where her dad and brothers were all waiting for her. 'Oh!' she exclaimed, feeling flushed and tipsy and caught unawares. 'I wasn't expecting you yet!'

Then she noticed that they were each holding lengths of cable attached to the blue tent, and as Spencer counted down, 'Three, two, one, NOW!' they all pulled at the same time. The blue plastic sheeting slithered to the ground, revealing . . .

Gemma's mouth dropped open and she gave a little scream. 'Is that what I think it is?'

'Your very own studio. Yes.' Spencer looked at her anxiously. 'Do you like it?'

Did she *like* it? Did he really need to ask? At the side of the house, where the ugly 1950s garage had once stood, was a beautiful new addition: a single-storey building of mellow old brick with a solid oak frame. From the front, it looked like a child's drawing of a house, with a pale-blue door in the middle flanked by a large window on either side. 'I love it,' she whispered, not trusting herself to speak for a moment. 'Oh, Spencer. And you've done all this for me?'

He smiled. 'Go inside.'

The front door was ajar and she pushed it open, to be greeted by Darcey and Will screaming 'Surprise!' at her, with big grins on their faces, and a large strawberry-topped birthday cake on a table in the middle of the room.

'Oh!' she cried again, her breath catching in her throat. 'Oh my goodness,' she said, gazing around. 'Isn't your dad amazing? Isn't he the best?'

Her eyes swam with tears as she took in the balloons, the birthday bunting and her amazing surprise in its entirety. The whole of the studio's back wall was made up of glass bi-fold doors overlooking the garden, making the space light and airy. There was a tiny little changing area built into one corner, white painted shelves to store her fabric and accessories, and room for at least four workstations. It was, in short, going to be the perfect place to sew.

'It still needs a bit of touching up,' Spencer said, coming inside and putting an arm around her. 'I haven't quite finished painting the skirting board, and we'll need to transfer all your kit over, but . . . '

She silenced him by throwing her arms around his neck and hugging him. 'This is the nicest thing anyone's ever done for me,' she cried. 'The very nicest thing.'

'You're the nicest thing that ever happened to *me*,' he said huskily into her hair. 'And I'm not about to forget that in a hurry again.'

And then the others were crowding in and exclaiming over Spencer's cleverness, and somebody lit the candles on the cake and they all sang 'Happy Birthday', even Will, who was usually far too cool and teenagerish to do that sort of thing. Gemma couldn't stop beaming as she gazed around at her new space, planning colourful curtains for the front windows and lamps for the sewing tables, imagining the walls vibrating with chatter and laughter and the whirring of sewing machines as one beautiful new garment after another was created.

'Happy birthday, dear Gemmaaaaa . . . Happy birthday to you!'

'Make a wish!' called Saffron, as Gemma leaned in and blew out all the candles.

Make a wish? In this moment of joy, surrounded by her family and friends, she had absolutely nothing to wish for. Saffron's baby would soon be here; Caitlin had found love and a new family; and her dad and Judy were planning a winter wedding and couldn't be happier together. Closer to home, Will had just passed all his summer exams with flying colours; Darcey had three new best friends; and Spencer . . . well, he was standing right beside her, holding her hand, her truest ally, the love of her life.

She shut her eyes and wished that love and happiness would stay with them all for a very long time. That would do nicely for now.

How to make your own fortune-cookies

Genius idea! Now you can write yourself some really lovely fortunes — such as *All your dreams will come true; This will be your best year ever* — and cheer yourself up when you need a little boost. Alternatively, if you're an idiot like me, you can ask your children to write some random ones, and will end up with a fortune that says *Beware men with beards* or even *You will be kidnapped by an evil pig.*

Here's the recipe I used — it makes fifteen fortune-cookies. (My children found the cookies quite eggy-tasting, so you may want to dust them with icing sugar or even dip them in melted chocolate, for a nicer flavour.)

Ingredients

100g (4 oz) plain flour
1½ tbsp cornflour
50g (2 oz) caster sugar
½ tsp salt

3 tbsp vegetable oil
3 egg whites
1 tsp water
1½ tsp vanilla extract
½ tsp almond extract (optional)

Method

1   Preheat the oven to 170°C/325°F/Gas Mark 3. Line a
baking tray with greaseproof paper, or use a silicone mat
if you have such a thing. (We ended up using three trays
in all.)

2   Sift the flour and cornflour together in a bowl, then com-
bine with the sugar and salt. Pour in the oil, egg whites,
water, vanilla and almond extracts, then stir everything
together until well mixed. (If anyone asks 'Is it meant to
look like vomit?' at this point, just ignore them. The
answer is yes, by the way.)

3   Carefully plop tablespoonfuls of cookie mixture onto the
tray or mat (it will be quite runny), then use the back of
a metal spoon to shape them into 10cm (4 in) circles.
Make sure you space them out, as the cookies will spread
during baking.

4   Bake for 10 minutes or so.

5   While the cookies are in the oven, you can get on with
the fortune-writing. We used pieces of paper about 6 x

1cm (2½ x ½ in). (There are lots of sites online where you can download and print these, if you don't feel creative, or don't fancy being kidnapped by an evil pig.)

6 Check on the cookies. When the edges are golden brown, they are ready to come out.

7 Now for the assembly! While the cookies are still warm, they are soft and bendy, so you need to act fairly quickly. Put a fortune in the middle of each cookie, then fold the cookie in half and pinch the semicircular edges together as best you can. Now carefully fold in half again, creating a crescent shape. If you're worried about your folded cookies popping open and losing their shape, you can leave them to cool in the wells of a muffin tray.

8 Once they're cool, you're free to tuck in. And cross your fingers that you pick the cookie with the best fortune!

Best hangover cures ever

(Just in case you've overdone things at your
own New Year's Eve party . . .)

We've all been there. The thumping head. The nausea. The disgusting taste in your mouth. And the dreadful flashbacks of the night before: did you *seriously* get up and gyrate on the table? Oh dear. You did, didn't you? Never fear, though. I'm here to help. These remedies might just make you feel human again:

- Fresh air
- More sleep
- A fry-up and a cup of tea (I'd go for a fried-egg sandwich and lots of ketchup, but you'll have your own preference)
- Lots of water – preferably ½ litre (1 pint) every hour
- Lucozade or a 'sports drink'
- Some people swear by a really spicy chilli (to sweat out the toxins, apparently); or there are a few disgusting-sounding raw-egg and tabasco drink recipes online that you could try (if you are desperate; I'm afraid I failed on the research front this time)

- Lying on the sofa with a blanket, watching a funny film
- Vowing never again to be so stupid and drink so much. Ever. Seriously; you mean it this time. Talking of which . . .

New Year's resolutions and how to stick to them

If you're anything like me (and Gemma!), you'll have started the New Year with an ambitiously long list of ways to improve your life. This will be the year that you run a marathon, get a great new job, stop smoking, drop a dress size, never lose your temper, stop splurging on your credit cards and generally transform yourself into the most perfectly brilliant version of you ever.

It's great to be an optimist, but with a wish list as long as your arm, you are almost certainly setting yourself up to fail. However, these simple strategies might just save the day. Good luck!

- **Think positive.** Frame your goals in ways that don't sound as if you're denying yourself. Thus 'Don't gorge on sweets in front of the telly' becomes 'Eat healthy food'; 'Stop being grumpy with the kids' becomes 'Do fun stuff with the kids'; 'Stop drinking so much' could be 'I'll only have a drink on Saturday night'.

- **Take baby-steps.** Make sure your goals are small and achievable. Break your ambitions down into weekly targets — aim to lose a pound or two at a time, if you're on a health kick, rather than the more daunting 'Become a size 6'.
- **Step away from temptation.** When your willpower weakens, think back to why you chose this resolution in the first place, and look at the bigger picture. Are you saving for a holiday? Getting fit because of a health scare? Stopping smoking because you want to start a family? Remind yourself that your efforts are worth persevering with. If this isn't enough, remove yourself bodily from temptation. Go for a walk or out to see a friend — anywhere, as long as it's away from that biscuit tin, that bargain pair of shoes or the bottle of Sauvignon blanc loitering enticingly in the fridge.
- **Be kind to yourself.** Rome wasn't built in a day — and the new, improved you won't be, either. And if it all gets too much, don't forget, there's always next year . . .

If you enjoyed

The Year of Taking Chances,

you'll love these other books
by Lucy Diamond . . .

The Secrets of Happiness

The best things in life can be just around the corner

Rachel and Becca aren't real sisters, or so they say. They are step-sisters, living far apart, with little in common. Rachel is the successful one: happily married with three children and a big house, plus an impressive career. Artistic Becca, meanwhile, lurches from one dead-end job to another, shares a titchy flat and has given up on love.

The two of them have lost touch but when Rachel doesn't come home one night, Becca is called in to help. Once there, she quickly realizes that her step-sister's life is not so perfect after all: Rachel's handsome husband has moved out, her children are rebelling, and her glamorous career has taken a nosedive. Worst of all, nobody seems to have a clue where she might be.

As Becca begins to untangle Rachel's secrets, she is forced to confront some uncomfortable truths about her own life, and the future seems uncertain.

But sometimes happiness can be found in the most unexpected places . . .

Summer at Shell Cottage

A seaside holiday at Shell Cottage in Devon has always been the perfect escape for the Tarrant family. Beach fun, barbecues and warm summer evenings with a cocktail or two – who could ask for more?

But this year, everything has changed. Following her husband's recent death, Olivia is struggling to pick up the pieces. Then she makes a shocking discovery that turns her world upside down.

As a busy mum and GP, Freya's used to having her hands full, but a bad day at work has put her career in jeopardy and now she's really feeling the pressure.

Harriet's looking forward to a break with her lovely husband Robert and teenage daughter Molly. But unknown to Harriet, Robert is hiding a secret – and so, for that matter, is Molly . . .

'Stuffed with guilty secrets and characters you'll root for from the start, this warm and emotional novel about a family in crisis makes for delicious summer reading'

Sunday Express

'A great summer read from Lucy Diamond'   *Hello*

'Enthralling drama about family secrets'   *Heat*

One Night in Italy

How do you say 'I Love You' in Italian?

**Is Italian really the language of love?
A new class of students hopes to find out . . .**

Anna's recently been told the father she's never met is Italian. Now she's baking focaccia, whipping up tiramisu and swotting up on her vocabulary, determined to make it to Italy so she can find him in person.

Catherine's husband has walked out on her, and she's trying to pick up the pieces of her life. But she'll need courage as well as friends when she discovers his deception runs even deeper than infidelity.

Sophie is the teacher of the class, who'd much rather be back in sunny Sorrento. She can't wait to escape the tensions at home and go travelling again. But sometimes life – and love – can surprise you when you least expect it.

As the evening class gets underway, friendships form and secrets from Italy begin to emerge. With love affairs blossoming in the most unlikely places, and hard decisions to face, it's going to be a year that Anna, Catherine and Sophie will never forget.

Me and Mr Jones

Three charming brothers – which would you choose?

**Meet the women in love with
three very different brothers . . .**

Izzy's determined to escape her troubled past with a new start by the sea – but flirtatious Charlie Jones is causing complications.

Alicia's been happily married to loyal Hugh for years but secretly craves excitement. Maybe it's time to spice things up?

Emma's relationship with David was once fun and romantic but trying for a baby has taken its toll. Then temptation comes along . . .

As the future of the family's B&B becomes uncertain, Izzy, Alicia and Emma are thrown together unexpectedly. It seems that keeping up with the Joneses is harder than anyone thought . . .

'Funny, sunny and wise. An absolute treat'   Katie Fforde

'The new queen of the gripping, light-hearted page-turner'
Easy Living

Summer with my Sister

Polly has always been the high-flier of the family, with the glamorous city lifestyle to match.

Clare is a single mum with two children, struggling to make ends meet in a ramshackle cottage. The two sisters are poles apart and barely on speaking terms.

But then Polly's fortunes change unexpectedly and her world comes crashing down. Left penniless and with no-where else to go, she's forced back to the village where she and Clare grew up, and the sisters find themselves living together for the first time in years. With an old flame reappearing for Polly, a blossoming new career for Clare and a long-buried family secret in the mix, sparks are sure to fly. Unless the two women have more in common than they first thought?

'A warm and witty read for sisters of all ages'   *Candis*

'Seamless, engaging, believable, fun and heartfelt . . . a skil-fully executed and charming tale that you'll want to pass on to all your friends'   *Heat*

The Beach Café

A recipe for disaster? Or a recipe for love?

Evie Flynn has always been the black sheep of her family – a dreamer and a drifter, unlike her over-achieving elder sisters. She's tried making a name for herself as an actress, a photographer and a singer, but nothing has ever worked out. Now she's stuck in temp hell, with a sensible, pension-planning boyfriend. Somehow life seems to be passing her by.

Then her beloved aunt Jo dies suddenly in a car crash, leaving Evie an unusual legacy – her precious beach café in Cornwall. Determined to make a success of something for the first time in her life, Evie heads off to Cornwall to get the café and her life back on track – and gets more than she bargained for, both in work and in love . . .

'Romantic, dreamy and fun, this is perfect poolside reading'
Closer

'From witty to full of wisdom, sassy to sentimental . . . not to be missed'
Woman

Sweet Temptation

A story of love, friendship and cake . . .

Maddie's getting it from all sides. Her bitchy boss at the radio station humiliates her live on air about her figure, her glamour-puss mum keeps dropping not-so-subtle hints that Maddie should lose weight, and her kids are embarrassed to be seen with her after the disastrous mums' race at their school sports day. Something's got to change . . .

Maddie reluctantly joins the local weight-watching group where she finds two unlikely allies – Jess, who is desperate to fit into a size ten wedding dress for her Big Day, and Lauren, who, despite running a dating agency, has signed off romance for ever. Or so she thinks . . .

As they all count the calories, new friendships develop, and secrets are shared – but can they resist temptation?

'A healthy helping of friendship and love'   *Press Association*

'Dealing with a lack of calories, fat days and man trouble is a lot easier when you have good friends by your side. Fab!'

Closer

Hens Reunited

Katie, Georgia and Alice were at each other's hen nights but now the chickens have come home to roost: their marriages have fallen apart and their friendships have been tested to the limits.

Control-freak Katie has become a commitment-phobe – there's no way she wants to get married again. Is there?

Ambitious Georgia always puts her career first. If anyone gets hurt, it's their look-out – right?

And faithful Alice wants to make a fresh start, but can't get over her cheating ex – and Georgia's betrayal.

**Hearts have been broken, and feathers ruffled . . .
can the hens ever be reunited?**

Over You

Ever wondered how your friends see you now?

Josie, Nell and Lisa go back a long way – they were flat-mates, soulmates and best mates back in their twenties when life was one long party.

Five years later, things are different. Josie is married with kids in deepest suburbia, free-spirit Nell has travelled the world, and Lisa is on the path to career glory (and the salary Premiership). A reunion weekend in London seems a great idea to Josie . . . until she discovers something that will change the course of her life forever.

'Sassy, sexy and very funny, this is a great novel about following your fantasies and then facing up to the conse-quences'   Kate Harrison, bestselling author
of *The Secret Shopper's Revenge*

Any Way You Want Me

On paper, Sadie's got it all – the partner, the children, the house. But in real life, that doesn't feel quite enough. Sadie can't help harking back to the time when she was a career woman by day and a party animal by night. And what happened to feeling like a sex kitten, anyway? The only sleepless nights she's getting now are due to the baby. Maybe a little reinvention is the answer . . .

Sadie can't resist creating a fictitious online identity for herself as a hot TV producer. It's only a bit of harmless fun . . . until truth and fantasy become dangerously tangled. It isn't long before she's wondering if the exciting alter ego she has dreamed up really is the kind of person she wants to be after all.

Wry, funny and with a wonderful twist in the tale,
Any Way You Want Me **is an enchanting novel of
motherhood, infidelity and friends reunited.**